BEATRICE BEECHAM'S CRYPTIC CRYPT

DAVE JEFFERY

Let the world know:
#IGotMyCLPBook!

Crystal Lake Publishing
www.CrystalLakePub.com

Other Titles by Dave Jeffery

OTHER NOVELS BY CRYSTAL LAKE PUBLISHING

Blackwater Val
  by William Gorman

Where the Dead Go to Die
  by Aaron Dries and Mark Allan Gunnells

Sarah Killian: Serial Killer (For Hire!)
  by Mark Sheldon

The Final Cut
  by Jasper Bark

*Pretty Little Dead Girls: A Novel of Murder and
  Whimsy*
  by Mercedes M. Yardley

Or check out other Crystal Lake Publishing books for
more Tales from the Darkest Depths

This book is for those who have experienced, or continue to experience, any form of oppression, persecution or prejudice, and to those dedicated to making sure history never repeats its darker days.

PROLOGUE
Unlocking Evil

THE SHOP HAS been in existence for over thirty years, its huge plate glass window a lidless eye gazing out upon an ever changing street. The window has watched a country turn into something quite unrecognisable—quite *incomprehensible*. Where there had once been chaos, there is now order. Where there had once been civilisation, there is now only brutality. This is a country that has lost its soul in a quest to find a heart. This is a country in the cold, unyielding grip of Nazi doctrine: cruelty in the name of order.

This is Vienna, Austria, 1941.

Vienna is now an extension of Nazi Germany, since its annexation by the German army in 1938. A climate of oppression is symbolised all around the plaza; the quiet streets, citizens exiled by the evening curfew. Huge flags are draped from the third floor window of the *Heldenplatz*; bent, black crosses encircled in white, and languishing on a field of blood red.

Swastikas.

These flags may flap lazily in the chilly Austrian breeze, but those they represent are far from lacking fervour. Their will to inflict prejudice, oppression and inhumanity in the name of order knows nothing of laziness; a thing of incalculable evil.

Within the shop, the owner is a testament to this. He is middle aged and his body bears the scars of oppression. Some can be seen, his arms play host to wicked wheals that criss-cross his wrists like river tributaries on a map. Some scars hide beneath his shabby shirt, vicious, thick bands of tissue on his back and stomach.

But it is in his mind where the real wounds lie, held at bay by a resolve that has been his only protection over the past few years. On occasion he has stared into the face of madness and felt its lure, its potential sanctuary from what has been going on about him.

When the Nazi troops entered Vienna, they came as saviours. Now they are merely demons—soldiers of evil. The shopkeeper plays with the crude, yellow Star of David sewn on to his right breast pocket. Once it had been a sign of faith, now it is a sign of hatred and exclusion. Of the 160, 000 resident Jews, only 40,000 remain. The others have been deported to work as slave labour in the unyielding war machine that is The Third Reich.

Or worse.

The shopkeeper shivers, yet the room in which he works is not cold. He has been luckier than most. He has a trade the fascists value, making and mending locks. In these times of want and food rationing, such things are of great importance. Over the past eighteen months he has excelled at his craft. The mechanism he has created is unique and at any other time he would revel in his accomplishment.

But he is unsure what it is he has really achieved and for what purpose. Yes, these devices will ensure protection when they are applied, but what do they protect? Is it a thing that should be kept safe?

He knows that, in reality, he must only be concerned with the safety of his own kin. This is why he has adhered to schemes and kept himself ignorant.

This is why he, and his family, is still *alive*.

The man senses movement.

Silhouetted by the late spring sun, distorted shapes waver through the frosted panel in the shop doorway. As the door swings inward, the shopkeeper jolts in cold horror, the chill filling each chamber of his heart, threatening to stop it dead. The bell above the door chimes brightly—a stark contrast to the grim face that enters beneath.

The newcomer is tall and string-thin. His uniform is ditch black and peppered with silver icons stolen from more civilised cultures and made to serve desire and hate. His appearance incites crippling fear. It is what he does. It is the only reason his kind exist.

Slowly, deliberately, the man in black closes the door.

'Do you have them, *Jew*?' His voice, like his physique, is thin and emerges from a slit of a mouth, crowned with the ghost of a moustache.

'Y-yes, Herr Fleischer.' The man quakes as he speaks. 'As you commanded.'

The Nazi officer strides casually into the workshop.

As he nears, the shopkeeper can smell the sweet aroma of polish emanating from highly buffed boots. The utility belt wrapped about him bristles with bullet pouches and a huge, holstered sidearm.

The shopkeeper ducks beneath the counter for a few moments. When he bobs back up again, his face is jaundiced by the sunlight filtering through the window—his cheeks becoming deep, sunken pits, the flesh from a once full face hanging like the jowls of bloodhound.

The Nazi smiles. *These are good times. These are righteous times.*

'Here you are, Herr Fleischer.'

The locksmith places an object on the work-worn counter. It is a wrapping made from coarse sheets, which the man now pulls apart with trembling fingers. When its content is in plain view, the locksmith steps away from it as though the things he has released into the sunlight are poisonous. In reality they are three fat cylinders of glass and copper. The crooked filaments lurking inside each look like the withered outstretched arms of the starving.

'I'm sure they will not disappoint, Sir,' he whispers.

'I will be the judge of that, *schwinehund*,' the officer hisses, moving towards the counter for a better view. The locksmith stays still, his eyes cast down to the bare floorboards, his ruined skin crawling under the officers' rebuking glare. Fleisher's eyes are blue ice, but there is a fire in them; passion born from a skewed sense of righteousness.

Those cold eyes give some reprieve as they drop to the package lying open on the counter.

'Good,' Fleisher says.

4

'Thank you, Sir,' the shopkeeper mutters, relief evident in his voice.

'The compliment is not to you, dog!' Fleisher snaps. 'This will serve its purpose, just as you have.' There is a hard and dangerous edge to his voice.

'I meant no disrespect, Sir,' the man splutters. 'Forgive me. I am just anxious to please you.'

'Anxious to save your scrawny, Jewish neck is more likely.' The silver skull on the Nazi's cap shows more humour than the cold, calculating grin beneath.

There is an awkward silence and the man squirms under the officer's stare. He knows the Nazi is enjoying his torment. It is the only enjoyment these brutes allow themselves. The tormenting of Jews is now a sport to them. The locksmith considers if God has truly forsaken his kind and placed devils upon the earth to test their faith. Devils in black uniforms that march through the streets pretending they are soldiers when they are nothing more than dishonourable butchers.

The atmosphere in the shop is oppressive. Time seems to pass like treacle through a sieve. The smile that slices across Fleischer's face shows he relishes the moment.

He folds the swatch and picks it up, his mind racing. In contrast his heart beats heavily, a surge of pride threatening to swamp him. He is close to success: a plan that seemed impossible is coming to a close. It would seem to those looking from outside that there is ambiguity in his actions. Fleisher has done this in secret—without sanction from the Fuhrer. He knows the higher order will not understand, they may even call his actions "heresy". They would not understand the concept of *contingency*. It has taken several years to get to this point. Many have died in the quest to build and protect a secret. His superiors would only see his plan as a loss of faith. A sign of weakness.

But he was bigger than this—his intentions as close to honour as someone with his black heart could understand.

'Now,' Fleisher sneers, turning his attention back to the locksmith. 'What of you?'

The man shuffles uncomfortably. 'There is our bargain, Sir?' he says, his voice quivering.

'Bargain?' The Nazi smirks at the locksmith's discomfort. 'I appear to have forgotten it. Maybe you could remind me?'

'That I, and my family, would not suffer the same fate of *my kind*,' the shopkeeper mutters miserably. 'An assurance of *mercy*.'

'Ah, yes! Now I recall!'

To the shopkeeper's horror the Nazi un-holsters his pistol and aims it at him.

'B-but, Sir! Have I not kept my side of the bargain? Are you not *pleased*?'

'I am most pleased, shopkeeper,' the Nazi replies. 'But even if you had not been part of a race of conspirators, you were never going to live. Not when you have been party to my intention.'

The locksmith leans back heavily, only the shelving unit behind him preventing his body crumpling to the ground. 'But what of justice? What of mercy?'

'Those words have no meaning here,' the Nazi says coldly. 'They are the doctrine of the weak.'

A single shot ends their discussion; the shopkeeper disappears behind his counter as a stream of gun smoke rises lazily into the air.

For a pensive moment, Fleischer looks at the place where the shopkeeper had been standing. After a single nod of his head he then turns and exits the shop.

On the other side of the door stands a Nazi soldier. He snaps to attention as his commander walks past him. The black, steel helmet rammed onto his head, reflects little of the pale sunlight. Beneath the steel brim is a face heralding nothing but staunch loyalty. Blind obedience is the keystone of the *Schutzstaffel*—or the "SS" as they are more commonly known—adherence to a sworn oath of allegiance to their Commander in Chief, the Fuhrer: Adolf Hitler. An oath that has changed them from men to unfeeling robots.

'Tidy this mess, Sergeant,' Fleischer mutters before walking towards a waiting staff car.

The trooper reaches down and pulls at an object that has been wedged into his boot. He stands and inspects the grenade. It is a stubbed, metal cylinder screwed to a long wooden stave. With a fluid motion, he unscrews a cap at the base of the stave and a length of cord drops out. He yanks this and the fuse begins to hiss. His actions are unhurried as he kicks in the shop door with his heavy, shining boots and throws the grenade into the gloom.

The sergeant trots to the staff car and climbs in beside the driver.

From the back seat, Fleischer smiles and nods at his sergeant in the rear view mirror. The engine purrs as the machine pulls away.

The vehicle is turning out of the plaza when the grenade detonates, sending a ball of glass and flame out into the street. The noise is loud and devastating.

But no one will come because it is a Jewish shop, and no one here cares for such matters.

On the pavement, the window is now a myriad of sugar sprinkles that glisten like tears of mourning on the cobblestones. It is as though this eye on the world may no longer be able to see but it still weeps for what is to come.

Chapter One
Scream of the Siren

THE ELVIS BOBBED idly on the ocean. The forty-foot fishing boat was owned by skipper Blenheim 'Cockles' Cochran. At this moment Cochran paced about his weathered deck, checking lines as he sang along to the beaten-up CD player lashed to the wheelhouse with thick rope.

'You in pain again, skipper?' a squat, broad-shouldered man with a rosy- red face said, grinning. 'I can get you somethin' for it, if you'd like? You need a double dose, I reckon.'

'You're as funny as chicken pox, Jimbo,' Cochran replied with a chuckle.

'And you *still* can't sing, Skipper,' First Mate James 'Jimbo' Spirehouse said. 'You're gonna have to accept that fact some day. Why not do it now and save my sanity?'

'Because the *King* still sings, you heathen,' said Cochran, jerking his head towards the speaker as it pumped out 'Jail House Rock'. 'And you were crazy before you ever set foot on this boat.' The two men laughed heartily.

Half a mile away, the fishing village of Dorsal Finn could be seen nestling in an enclave shaped like a half moon, it's cottages appearing to hover in the air like blue, pink and white butterflies settling in the folds of the landscape.

'How come we're trawlin' this stretch of water?' Jimbo asked, his eyes fixed on the several bright red buoys marking their lobster creels. The round, fat shapes undulated on the oceans' surface like apples in a Halloween bobbing bucket. 'I thought the lobster had taken leave from this pitch some time back?'

'You been asleep this past year, Jimbo?' Cochran said. 'You know times are lean. And that means we've got to try anywhere—anyhow—these days. *The Elvis* is all I've got in this world. I don't plan to give her back to the bank without a bit of a tussle.'

'Well, just remember: you'll always have me,' Jimbo said with a chuckle.

'Is that meant to bring me good cheer?' Cochran laughed. 'Just drop anchor. Let's get these pots on board, and see if Lady Luck is wearing her best smile this mornin'.

The two men made ready.

Jimbo pulled on the ratchet brake and released the anchor, which entered the water with a splash.

Once this was done, Cochrane grabbed a long, hooked pole from its safety rack and leaned over the side of the boat. He hooked the first buoy with the kind of ease that only comes from practice, and began pulling the big plastic ball towards the boat. The buoy nudged against the hull with a series of dull, hollow thumps. The two men hauled it over the sides and onto the deck where Jimbo stowed it by tying it to a huge brass cleat riveted to *The Elvis'* decking.

Cochran pulled at the thick rope that had been attached to the buoy until he could see the wavering shape of a lobster creel just below the ocean's surface.

'Give me a hand to pull this little bugger in,' he called with delight. 'She's packin' some weight!'

'You got it.'

'We got the jackpot here,' Cochran said, pulling on the rope with all his might. 'Lady Luck's wearin' her best frock this mornin'.'

With huge effort the men yanked at the rope, but what happened next almost caused them to drop it in surprise. Just as the creel was about to leave the water, a hissing noise appeared to emanate from it and a powerful pulse of water surged away from them in one huge wave.

'What was that, Skipper?'

'Let's get this creel in then we'll chat about it,' Cochran replied grimly.

'But didn't that noise come from the creel?' Jimbo said, uncertain.

'Just yank that umbilical, Jimbo,' Cochran said firmly. 'Or I'll be goin' back to port on my lonesome.'

Reluctantly, Jimbo helped pull the creel on deck, both men ending up standing over it with some trepidation.

'What you seein', Jimbo?'

'I'm seein' only a bunch of lobsters.'

'Yeah, me too,' Cochran confirmed, nudging the creel with his foot. After a few moments he turned his grizzled face to his First Mate. 'Drama's over. Let's haul the rest of 'em in.'

With reticence they did just that, each man clutching at the ropes as though they were dragging a potential monster from the sea bed. Despite their fears, there wasn't a repeat of the phenomenon. Soon all the creels were lying on deck in a widening spread of water; laden with lobster of all sizes. Once they had seen the extent of the catch, the fishermen were soon distracted from the incident that had caused them such angst.

'Right,' Cochran said, slightly out of breath from the exertion. 'Let's get *The Elvis* back to port, and these little beauties to market!'

He made his way to the wheel-house, slapping the CD player on his way past; the air suddenly filling with bright 1950s' rock and roll music. Jimbo cast his eyes to the gull-speckled sky, his intention to make some jibe to his skipper.

But he never got the chance.

No sooner had the CD kicked into life when the music became disjointed and garbled by bursts of heavy, hissing static.

'First thing I do when we swap lobster for moolah is to trade in this lump of useless plastic in for a machine that gives me big beats,' Cochran moaned, thumping the faltering stereo with a calloused palm. The CD player began to emit a low humming noise, Cochran's heavy-handedness appearing to make matters infinitely worse.

Then the low hum began to rise in pitch.

'You hearin' that?' Jimbo asked.

'Hard not to,' Cochran replied, irritation clear in his voice.

The sound began to oscillate and suddenly the men

found its presence uncomfortable, their hands clamping over their ears in an attempt to shut it out. Without warning, the CD player discharged a terrible high pitched, sonic scream that forced Cochran and Jimbo to their knees, their faces screwed into agonised masks.

Just when Cochrane thought he would have to jump overboard to escape the terrible cacophony numbing his brain, the CD player's carcass buckled before shedding its plastic skin across the deck in a spectacular explosion of sparks and debris.

Unable to comprehend what had happened, Cochran and Jimbo remained on their knees, their breathing heavy with relief.

Jimbo looked at the ruined stereo—now nothing but a misshapen piece of plastic—and then turned to Cochran.

'I think I prefer your singin',' he muttered.

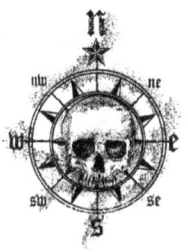

You wake up, your skin bathed in sweat. You have had the dream again, the one in which the sky burns and your body is consumed by a will that is not your own. It is as if someone—something—is wearing your skin like a suit, saying words that you would never utter and thinking thoughts that leave your mind feeling unclean and tainted.

The sheets wrapped about you are tangled and damp. Yet you drag them closer in the hope they provide some comfort—some protection—from the ill thoughts still reverberating in your mind.

It has been some time since the dream has been so vivid. You know it will leave a residue, a nasty passenger that you will carry with you throughout the day. Part of you had hoped that you would never experience the terrible images again. But the sensible part, the sensitive part, knows you cannot outrun what is real. This part knows the dream is not a dream at all but a memory of what happened one terrible night when the thing lurking in the shadows of Dorsal Finn stepped out and touched you, marking you for one of its puppets.

You lie back on the small mattress. Your breathing finally slows down, yet your mind races. It is as though you are trying to think of anything other than the obvious. The dream has returned to let you know something is reaching out to you; its minions are searching for your sensitive mind in order to use it once more.

You roll onto your side and weep, for you know time and distance is no barrier to the thing that needs to recall you back into its service.

And once its servants find you in the darkness, you will be powerless to stop them.

CHAPTER TWO
LOBSTERS AND LIBERTIES

AH, PATIENCE! Here is my little *Princess of the Nile*! How *are* you this fine morning?'

Mr Khaldun Userkaf sipped his coffee, his dark eyes studying his daughter through the mist rising from the brim of his Pharaoh-shaped coffee mug. His sharp, angular features still carried the ghost of his youth and his broad smile was infectious.

'Morning, Poppa,' Patience said as she tied her long, coal-dark hair into a ponytail. 'Just a quick status update: I'm fifteen years old, we have no connection to royalty, and the Nile is filthy brown sludge that gives anyone who falls into it raging diarrhoea. You have plans today?'

'Of course,' her father said, laughing at his daughter's diatribe. 'It's Saturday, and I *plan* to do *nothing*!'

'That'll be the day, Poppa.'

Mr Userkaf was renowned for his staunch work ethic. He had been running his travel agency from out of Dorsal Finn for over three decades, and in that time no one in the village could remember him ever taking a holiday for himself.

Patience Userkaf, purveyor of languages and fan of fashion, gave her father a big smile. Her braces had been removed only a few weeks before, and her new grin still felt as though it belonged to someone else.

'So what *are* you doing?' she asked watching as her father put his mug down on the table and hunched over last night's edition of the *Dorsal Finn Herald*.

'Planning a surprise for your Uncle Badru,' Mr Userkaf said, his concentration momentarily lost as he began to scan pages of newsprint.

Patience pulled a face, 'You mean a bigger surprise than the fact that he's *still here*?'

Patience's larger-than-life uncle had arrived in Dorsal Finn several months ago. A two week vacation had now become an extended break from his very successful Persian rug export business. He was a jolly man with a big, rotund belly that bobbed up and down each time he laughed—which was long and often. It appeared to Patience that her uncle had little intention of going back to his live-in offices in Cairo anytime soon. In fact, he'd only recently started renting a room at *Tardebigge's Bed and Breakfast*.

'Your uncle will soon be fifty years old,' Mr Userkaf said, his finger resting on a line in the paper so that he wouldn't lose his place. 'I intend to make sure we celebrate in style.'

'I'm not wearing any of that *traditional* stuff,' Patience said, shuddering at the thought of gaudy ceremonial gowns *and* the concept of being fifty years old. '*Aren't there mummies who were younger and better dressed?*' she asked herself.

'You know how your uncle feels about Dorsal Finn. He considers it to be his second home,' her father said with a smile.

'More like his first home,' Patience muttered. 'Anyway, why are you looking in the paper?'

'I'm trying to find caterers who can supply traditional food at short notice,' Mr Userkaf said, resuming his search. 'I fear that I may have left it a little late.'

'Traditional *Dorsal Finn* catering? Not *hedgehog stew*?' This made Patience shudder more than the thought of wearing traditional dress and being fifty years of age.

'No,' her father chuckled. 'You know how much Uncle Badru is taken with seafood. I think it's this that keeps him here.' Mr Userkaf tutted impatiently as he exhausted yet another page. 'But it would appear that I am rapidly running out of options. All of the local caterers are booked solid.'

'Then maybe I will have to sort it out for you?' Patience said cryptically, causing her father to look up from his paper.

'What do you mean, Princess?'

'Beatrice, of course,' she said matter-of-fact.

'The most obvious of choices,' Mr Userkaf replied sitting back in his chair as though his prayers had been answered. 'Will she do it?' he asked. 'When will you speak to her?'

The doorbell chipped in, filling the room with a bright, happy tune.

'In about ten seconds,' Patience grinned.

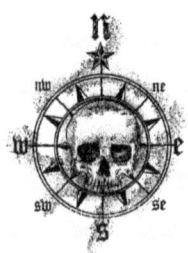

Beatrice Beecham was an inquisitive girl. It was part of her nature to know how things worked, how things went together but, most of all, *why* things went together so well. It may have been the very reason she enjoyed cooking so much. Her ability to cook was innate, a gift from some culinary god high in the gastronomic heavens. It didn't bother Beatrice that many of her peers thought cooking was about as cool as the surface of the sun. All that mattered was that it made her happy.

Beatrice was short and wiry with long hair as red as embers, which contrasted starkly with her bright blue eyes and pale skin. She had a petite nose that turned up a little at the end, and this was garnished with a crop of freckles that ran from the bridge of her nose to under her lower eyelids. As well as being inquisitive Beatrice was also incredibly patient; a trait that was at odds to the stereotypical views concerning people with red hair. She did, like most people, have her limits and it was often Thomas Beecham—her ten year old, sci-fi and fantasy movie obsessed brother—that tended to push all the right buttons and send her easily into orbit. Other than this Beatrice was a happy and well-adjusted young girl who just happened to have a penchant for attracting trouble.

She had moved to Dorsal Finn three years ago, after her father was made redundant. It had been a turbulent time. George Beecham was a proud man and struggled to accept the loss of his job at *Parkinson Paintbrush Incorporated*. He had worked there for over twenty years before he was replaced by a piece of software. For over three months he tried to find another job only to realise that every other potential employer had bought the same piece of software.

It was Maureen, Beatrice's mother, who finally came up with the novel idea of moving the family to Dorsal Finn. The premise was simple; Maureen's aunt Maud ran the *Postlethwaite News and Chocolate Emporium*. The shop was very demanding and, despite her determination, Maud had asked Maureen to help her with its upkeep on several previous occasions. In return George and Maureen would get a stake in the business. After it was clear he was not going to find work locally, George reluctantly agreed and they relocated within a few weeks.

At first Beatrice was very unhappy about the move. A new town, a new school; new friends and the emotional upheaval—the sense of isolation—was almost too much for her to bear. Then she met Patience, Lucas and Elmo—collectively known as The Newshounds—and they made her feel as though she'd always known them. They never mocked nor teased her about her interests. They just simply made her feel welcome.

In her time in Dorsal Finn, Beatrice and The Newshounds had already been involved in many adventures. To some they were heroes. To people such as Mayor Gideon Codd they were mere mischief makers; ingrates who were always undermining his authority.

Not that such a thing bothered Beatrice and her friends. Their strength was in their bond with each other. Only broken could they be beaten.

'It would be my pleasure to cook for your brother, Mr Userkaf,' she said sedately when presented with the task in the Userkaf's kitchen. 'What kind of things does he like?'

'Seafood,' Patience said pre-emptively.

'Anything specific?'

'Lobster,' Mr Userkaf said without hesitation.

'Well I do believe that I have the ideal recipe!' Beatrice grinned, amazed at the way fate was working its magic. Several months ago Beatrice had celebrated her fifteenth birthday. It had been a day made up of many surprises. First there had been the remarkable and fantastic present. Her kind and reasonable parents, had opted to buy her a twelve month, exclusive dining pass sponsored by Beatrice's all-time favourite publication, *Belchette's Encyclopaedia Gastronomica*. Her first meal occurred on the evening of her birthday in a small, almost timid place called *The Sanctuary*, a highly respected Mediterranean restaurant in the nearby town of *Ashby-on-Sea*. And in this restaurant, as well as having a great time, Beatrice also sampled the most delicious Lobster Stew she had ever experienced; enjoying it so much she had asked to speak with the chef afterwards.

Then she'd begged him for the recipe.

The chef agreed but made clear that he would only state the recipe once and she was not to write it down. This was of little issue to Beatrice. She was as likely to forget a recipe as the birds would forget to sing each morning.

'Lobster is expensive at the best of times,' Beatrice cautioned.

'Money is not an issue when it comes to family,' Mr Userkaf reassured her.

'It isn't just that, Mr Userkaf,' Beatrice said sadly. 'Lobster is getting difficult to catch in the waters around Dorsal Finn. I've heard several fishmongers saying the same thing. So even if you give me plenty of money, there's no guarantee I'll find one at market. And the dish I would like to prepare would take at least two of them.'

'Well, do what you can, dear Beatrice,' Mr Userkaf smiled disarmingly. 'If anyone will find a way to create this dish, it will be you.'

'I hope I don't let you down,' Beatrice said.

And she meant it.

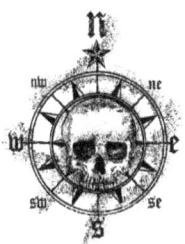

Dorsal Finn fish market was vibrant with bustle, noise and the aroma of the sea. The noise came from the many fishmongers, yelling and selling their wares in the tightly packed courtyard, a *cobblestone-throw* away from the harbour where each fishing boat disgorged its catch to the expectant traders each morning. Now these very traders stood on upturned buckets, surrounded by the *Catch of the Day*. Each prospective morsel was packed into plastic trays, filled with glittering ice.

And from the plastic trays came the smell. Every kind of sea creature you could ever imagine eating lay on their beds of ice, their skin still wet with brine. There were also plastic pails, slopping sea water onto the cobbles as shell fish pawed lazily at smooth, elliptical walls.

'This place amazes me,' Beatrice said scanning the stalls.

'Me too,' Patience said wrinkling her small nose. 'How can stuff smell this bad and still be edible?' She stopped a moment and shoved the sleeve of her cashmere sweater under Beatrice's nose. 'It doesn't smell does it?' she said with concern. 'You'd tell me if it did, wouldn't you? I mean, you wouldn't leave me *minging* all day and not let me know, right?'

'It's fine, Patience,' Beatrice laughed patting her friend's arm.

Patience had a reassuring sniff of her sleeve before allowing her arm to flop back to her side.

'Do you think we'll find what we're looking for?' she said to Beatrice as they made their way through the sizeable crowd.

'We might get lucky,' Beatrice replied, absently scanning the area before cutting left towards the harbour.

'You know something that I don't?' Patience said with a dour air.

'I know a very good fisherman,' Beatrice winked.

'Oh, God, Bea!' Patience moaned. 'You're not talking about *Crazy Colin*?'

'Don't worry, Patience, I'll do the talking.' Beatrice smiled.

'I'm warming to the idea already,' Patience said.

'I don't know why you're so against the idea.'

'Because even the other fishermen think the guy's mental?' Patience offered.

'Then they clearly don't know him very well,' said Beatrice.

"Crazy" Colin Creswell was not, of course, crazy at all. But, when the clouds above were burgeoning with rain, and waves below broiled in the wind, most fishermen remained moored in the harbour.

But not Colin.

Instead, he would be the one firing up his boat, *The Albatross*, and heading out to open water. As such Colin was branded reckless and maverick, although most of the town-folk admired his courage.

Beatrice and Patience turned a stone-slated corner and made their way to the small port where a flotilla of fishing boats was moored. Wheel housings and rigs, booms, fittings and hulls were sea-scarred and peeling. These were hardworking boats with hardworking owners; each as committed to the job of landing a huge catch as a cloud of sea birds swirled excitedly over their prows.

And it was this level of commitment, this level of passion for his work, which drew Beatrice to Creswell. She could see him, hauling trays of ice-packed fish from the hold and sliding them down the ramp linking *The Albatross* to the dock. Several market traders were below loading them onto a waiting gurney.

'Well, hello, young Beatrice!' Colin called down to them, his smile adding another line to his sea-weathered face. 'What's bringin' you youngsters out this early on a Saturday mornin'?'

'We're after lobster,' Beatrice shouted back in an

attempt to be heard over the sounds of the screaming gulls.

Colin's smile collapsed as his face scrunched up beneath his *Homer Simpson* baseball cap. Beatrice's heart sank like an anchor beneath the waves.

'Don't tell me,' she pre-empted, 'no chance, right?'

Colin paused, palette clutched to his chest and his vivid blue eyes sparkling in the bright sunlight. 'There's always a chance. But I ain't got me none,' he admitted. 'But I might be able to conjure somethin' by lunchtime. Can you wait, young 'un?'

'Can we wait?' Patience quipped. 'Do red and green clash?'

'You young 'uns are in a world of yer own,' Colin said as he shook his head in bemusement.

'That reminds me,' Beatrice sighed to Patience, 'Now we're done here, I have to go and collect Thomas from home.'

'Why?' Patience said watching the gulls.

'He's enrolling in the sea cadets,' Beatrice explained, her shoulders sagging with dejection. 'There's a small ceremony, or something. And Mum's told me to go with him.'

'Hash-tag sounds like a real drag,' Patience said bluntly.

Beatrice nodded. 'But it's part of Mum's "getting Thomas to join the rest of the human race" initiative. Seeing as everyone benefits from my brother getting a life, I guess I'll have to show some support.'

'What you mean is you can't get out of it?' Patience said.

'Tried hard—failed harder.'

'Well you get yourself back dockside at noon,

young'un, and I'll hopefully have yer lobster waitin','
Colin said alighting from the vessel, his ruddy cheeks
twin beacons as he approached.

'Can I ask where you're getting the lobster from?'
Beatrice said.

'Best not to,' Colin winked. 'Then I won't have to
tell you to mind your own, eh?'

'A secret?' Beatrice smiled.

'A big, fat one,' Colin grinned.

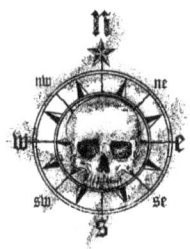

*Postlethwaite and Beecham's News and Chocolate
Emporium* was situated in Crab Mill Terrace, a row of
cottages painted in delicate pastels of pink, yellow and
blue. The store had a large frontage window with its
name painted upon it in swirling white letters. Beyond
the letters were shelves rammed with large jars of
sweets, chocolates, candy canes, and multi-coloured
jellies. A red and white awning provided shelter from
the sun and the rain to anyone stopping by to look
upon the confectionery.

There had always been the newsagents in Crab Mill
Terrace. During the war, Maud had stayed with the
previous owners—a Mrs and Mrs Jennings—who,
because they'd never had time to raise children, had
taken her in as their own. She had earned her keep
serving behind the counter, and delivering newspapers

on a battered bike with breaks that squealed like startled mice.

When Maud returned to Dorsal Finn years later, she had taken on the shop to support the Jennings' for over twenty years and was just as surprised—and eternally grateful—when they told her that they had willed the shop to her. Since that time Maud had overseen the place, and the sight of her in a bright red cardigan sitting on her stool behind the small, oak counter was as much a familiar sight to the townsfolk of Dorsal Finn as the harbour and the lighthouse.

Aunt Maud was not Maureen Beecham's real aunt at all. She was a very close friend of Beatrice's grandmother, Betty. So close, they had often been mistaken for sisters. With the exception of her two year stint in Dorsal Finn during the war, Maud and Betty had spent most of their childhood living in a small village in Worcestershire in the UK. During their teenage years, Betty had met a handsome young man called Edward Frye and gotten married. Of course, Maud was a bridesmaid. When Beatrice's mother was born Maud doted on her as an aunt would. Though she loved the idea of being with a family, Maud would never marry. She preferred being able to go off on travels around the country. Or sometimes further.

Maureen was six when Beatrice's grandfather got a promotion in London, and the Beecham's moved into a nice house in the suburbs. Aunt Maud travelled down to see them a few times but would never stay long.

By the time Maureen was seven, Aunt Maud had moved back to Dorsal Finn. With Maud busy running the store, she had only met up with Maureen during the funerals of both Betty and Edward since then. On both of those sad occasions, Maud and Maureen swore to remain in touch, and they had been in regular telephone contact prior to the Beecham's migration to Dorsal Finn.

The shop interior was compact, a mixture of free-standing carousel racks and units, as well as wall-mounted shelving, where books, newspapers, and magazines awaited the eager readers from the town. At the back of the shop counter was a small parlour that was accessed via a doorway with a curtain of vertical threaded beads. Here ancient furniture, a side board from the 19th Century and a dining table that appeared to be from a time where no one ever thought about making things with any sense of proportion, pretty much filled the entire space, but served as a place where afternoon tea could be taken whilst still keeping an eye of the shop.

Beyond the parlour was a fully fitted kitchen and it was in this kitchen, sitting at the breakfast bar, that Maud messed with the hem of her cherry red cardigan. Her deep scarlet Doc Marten's kicked out a tattoo against the leg of the kitchen table. She had shrewd yet kind grey eyes and her mouth was never far away from a warm and friendly smile. At that moment those kindly eyes were upon Maureen and Thomas, as mother did battle with son in an attempt to get him ready for his inauguration ceremony.

'Hold still, Thomas!' Maureen Beecham said as she dragged a comb through her son's hair. 'You have to make the right impression.'

'He does a pretty good *Dalek*,' Maud said from behind a copy of *Chinwag Magazine*. Her shoulders bobbed up and down as she chuckled heartily.

'Maud,' Maureen cautioned.

'Alright, me dear,' Maud said putting her magazine down on her lap and flashing a big smile. Her gold incisor flickered for a moment. 'I'll be mindin' me own this mornin'.'

'Thank you,' Mrs Beecham said gratefully and resumed grooming her squirming son.

'Will you please stop fidgeting, young man!' Maureen said in frustration.

'I can't see why I have to go and join the *Blue Thunder Foundation*,' Thomas protested. 'Or why Bea has to take me.'

'Because *The Blue Thunder Foundation* is a great place for you to meet with other kids, and give you things to do other than watching DVD's and catch up TV,' Mrs Beecham explained. 'And Beatrice is covering for me as I have some errands to run.'

Though the *Blue Thunder Foundation* first hit the headlines when the organisation announced their intention to open their first headquarters in Dorsal Finn, the charity had been in existence for ten years. The foundation believed that by keeping kids active and giving them a philosophy of looking after the local community, young people were less likely to get into trouble, and would become valued members of a future society. This notion was given further credence by the organisation's charismatic founder, Logan Frobisher. As such the representatives of *Blue Thunder Foundation* thrived in young offender centres up and down the country, helping to rehabilitate young people who had strayed. Their successes had been great. Now the plan was to set up a local pilot site ahead of a national programme.

The aim was simple enough. To embrace and influence the youth *younger;* embedding the philosophy of their motto: *Through Adversity Comes Hope.* And in the weeks leading up to the inauguration day, *Blue Thunder Foundation* advertising had pretty much dominated the TV sets in the homes of Dorsal Finn residents. And it didn't appear to show any signs of slowing down. Beatrice had stopped watching the documentaries and avoiding the advertising in between her favourite shows. If she saw another smart blue uniform she thought she'd scream.

'It's exciting to meet new people,' Mrs Beecham concluded.

'Not as exciting as The Empire Strikes Back,' Thomas grumbled.

'Especially that fight scene on Bespin,' Maud said. 'That was some ruckus Luke had with Vader. When he found out the man in black was his old man I nearly bawled me eyes into me lap!'

Maureen Beecham sighed. 'I need a little support here, Maud.'

From her armchair Maud Postlethwaite appeared pensive for a moment.

'Sorry, m'dear,' the old woman said, but her eyes glittered with a mischievous fire. 'I'm as old as Mother Earth an' me memory isn't what it was.'

'And why do I have to go with Bea?' Thomas whined. 'I mean, what have I done to deserve that?'

'What's wrong with you two spending some time together?' Maureen said.

'Bea thinks I'm weird and I think she's quite possibly a covert agent for SPECTRE.' Thomas moped over to the sofa and flopped into it. He folded his arms tightly across his chest. 'No good will come of it.'

'Comments like that only prove to me how badly the two of you need to spend more time together, Thomas Beecham.'

'It's like asking the Empire to share the galaxy with the Rebel Alliance,' Thomas said staring into space. 'Mark my words: War is coming.'

'Mark my words,' his mother said, 'you and Beatrice are to cease fire or you'll find a new villain in the galaxy.'

Thomas muttered something under his breath. Maureen Beecham presumed it wasn't complimentary and softened a little. 'There's the ceremony too, don't forget,' she coaxed. 'The new activity hut has been donated to the town by the *Blue Thunder Foundation*. Mayor Codd will be there to open it.'

'Giddy goodness, Maureen!' Maud piped up, 'I thought ye wanted the lad to go? Don't be tellin' him Gideon Codd's goin' to be slitherin' around the promenade like the fat slug he is.'

'You mean like Jabba?' Thomas asked.

'Aye,' Maud confirmed. ''cept less likeable.'

The sound of Patience chattering excitedly drifted in through the open door to the living room and caused Maud to defer a return to her magazine.

Beatrice entered the living room and Patience followed.

'I want people to answer honestly,' Patience announced before anyone could speak, 'do we smell of fish?'

'It's yer question that's fishy, young Patience,' Maud said.

'You said "fishy",' Patience said and resumed her sleeve sniffing ritual. 'That means we *do* smell, right?'

'Calm down, young 'un,' Maud giggled. 'Ye're reekin' only of youth an' I'm pretty green about it.'

'Jabba was green,' said Thomas.

'Oh, God,' Beatrice moaned. 'Mum, do I have to take Thomas? I mean, can't we just sit him in a corner with something soft to play with?'

'Don't be mean, Beatrice,' Maureen said. 'You're going and I won't hear another word said on the matter.'

Beatrice was quietly relieved by this. The only word she had left to say on the matter may have made even Gordon Ramsay blush.

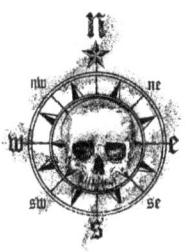

Gliding through the streets of Dorsal Finn, a grand, black car sparkled under the vivid sunlight.

On the bonnet of the Rolls Royce, an ornament of a woman with a cloak fluttering behind her was frozen in pewter. She was flanked by two matching flags bearing the Dorsal Finn Mayoral Crest, which flapped wildly in the slipstream.

The car had a regal air to it. Its purring engine and shiny, black body added to the sense of occasion such a vehicle carried with it.

In the back seat, Mayor Gideon Codd rubbed at his

neat, white goatee beard before adjusting the ruff on his ceremonial gown.

'This is quite an honour,' he said in a soft lilting voice to the man sitting next to him. 'Your donation has been widely embraced by our community, Mr Frobisher.'

'Please, Gideon,' the man called Frobisher replied. 'Call me Logan. We are colleagues, are we not?' In contrast Logan Frobisher's intonation had a deep, rich quality. It was the kind of voice that commanded and held the attention of people; the kind of voice that *liked* to be heard.

Gideon Codd smiled, but it was awkward, betraying his discomfort at shirking his shield of formality. 'Of course, *Logan*. Though I have wondered why the *Blue Thunder Foundation* chose to grace our humble town with such an auspicious occasion, the first full blown pilot site for the programme. Very exciting.'

'It is no mystery,' Frobisher said returning Codd's smile, his veneers glowing like a small sun. 'I have roots in this wonderful town. It seems poignant that I should honour them.'

'You never mentioned this in your proposal,' Codd said warming slightly.

'Are we both not men who appreciate heritage above all else, Gideon?' Frobisher said as he played with a large gold sovereign ring on his thick index finger. 'And I'm surprised at your uncertainty at such a gift from our organisation.'

'Oh, no, that's not what I meant *at all*,' Codd said, suddenly flustered.

Frobisher merely grinned at his companion's

discomfort and adjusted the hem of his neat collar. 'You're an inquisitive fellow, I'll say that for you,' he said. 'But I guess a man of prominence must always court caution. *Comes with the turf*, as we used to say.'

'Indeed,' the Mayor said relaxing a little. 'I must say that the role your organisation offers the youth of today is quite an admirable concept.'

'It has moved beyond a concept, beyond a philosophy, Gideon,' Frobisher said stoically. 'We, at the *Blue Thunder Foundation,* consider it our *duty* to uphold the values of a *civilised* society. Children are quite *feral* these days. And we, as adults, are to blame.'

'How so?' Codd asked with intrigue in his voice.

'Adults no longer demonstrate a sense of purpose to the young. It's all platitudes and easy living. Money is doled out like candy. There is little in terms of focus. The beast remains untamed, as you might say.'

'I might well say such a thing,' Codd nodded thinking of Beatrice and The Newshounds in particular. 'When I consider some of the younger elements in our town your doctrine does strike a chord.'

'Not everyone sees this, of course,' Frobisher continued. 'There are *critics*, existing organisations that have a vested interest in maintaining the status quo. But we do not balk at the opinions of naysayers; we merely embrace the challenges and, as such, grow stronger. This is why we are so *selective*.'

'Selective?'

'Why, yes, *selective*,' Frobisher confirmed, his big chest expanding to fill his blue blazer. 'Our regimen isn't to everyone's taste. Some would even call it controversial. But there is no denying the results.

Young upstarts are becoming honest citizens; the bedrock of a civilized nation. And all it takes is a sense of purpose.'

'I see,' said Codd.

'At this moment, I doubt that,' Frobisher laughed jovially. 'But you *will*. In the end you will see it all with perfect clarity. The events of the past few months are but a token of what the *Blue Thunder Foundation* has to offer the people of Dorsal Finn. The blurb our new recruits will take from the ceremony today will reveal all.'

'Really?'

'There you go again,' Frobisher laughed. 'Suspicion is the devil's pawn, Gideon. Don't worry, I shall broadcast our good intentions and attribute it all to the man who had the vision and good sense to allow it to happen.' Frobisher pierced Codd with his stare, the inference clear to all but Codd.

'Me?' Codd said with pride, though he wasn't sure why. He really had no idea what Frobisher was talking about.

'You, Gideon,' Frobisher confirmed. 'You will welcome the announcement, believe me. It's the kind of thing that makes the humblest of souls *immortal*. Would you like that Gideon? Would you like to become immortal?'

'I am intrigued,' Codd said, appearing bewildered.

'Over the coming days I will sate such intrigue, my friend,' Frobisher said with a nod. 'Soon you shall be remembered forever.'

CHAPTER THREE
THE RELUCTANT SECRET

LUCAS WALKER PEDDLED hard, the surrounding cottages zipping by, the rushing sound of the wind tousling his bleached hair and roaring in his ears. On his back, the bright orange paper-sack was now deflated, empty save for a single copy of the Dorsal Finn Herald.

There was a time when the last customer on Lucas's paper round often left him both nervous and exhilarated. In truth, when Maud Postlethwaite had originally allocated the puzzle-loving Newshound to Mr Miller, Lucas had balked at the idea.

'The guy has weird eyes, Maud,' he'd protested at the time. 'It's like he can *see* right through me.'

'There ain't nowt wrong with his eyes, young 'un,' Maud had replied. ''cept they might have seen a little too much, too young, maybe. An' he can't be blamed for that, now, can he?'

'I suppose not,' Lucas had sulked. 'But the guy's scary.'

'How he looks isn't how he *is*,' Maud assured him. 'I wouldn't be sendin' ye otherwise, would I?'

Lucas had seen enough sense in Maud's final comment to swallow his fear and go and visit Mr Miller. The mysterious hermit lived in a rundown shack; the structure was squat and shambling—tumbling out onto the beach like a gravity-defying pile of driftwood.

If the shack was ramshackle, then old man Miller was equally so. Standing at six feet six inches he was an imposing figure. His wild, white hair and tobacco stained beard made him look like a deranged Santa. And he always wore a heavy, black trench coat. Even on days when the sun beat down on the tangled landscape below.

Then, of course, there was *Wolfgang*.

Wolfgang was a big, fierce-looking Wolf Hound. An ugly scar ran along the top of his muzzle and trailed into the corner of the mouth, turning it into an endless sneer. Wolfgang spent the day growling or barking (he didn't seem to have a particular preference) and generally intimidating anyone who came near the house without Miller's sanction. Wolfgang had his own rundown dog-house in what Miller referred to as his *garden*. In reality this 'garden' was a junkyard crammed with mounds of metal and plastic and paper, capable of hiding four misshapen old cars. There were piles of tyres which appeared too big to fit any vehicle Lucas had ever seen, as well as a boat that lay on its side like a village drunk after a night on *Cinder's Cider*.

Based on these impressions, Lucas didn't beat himself up too much when it came to his initial misgivings around Miller. But over time, Lucas had come to know the man as a stoic and thoughtful person who often seemed to have much on his mind. On occasions, Miller's eyes would stare towards some imaginary horizon, pausing in mid-sentence as though a sudden thought had struck him mute. Even Wolfgang eventually overcame his suspicions, greeting Lucas with huge sloppy licks rather than guttural, threatening growls.

It was common for Lucas to stay in the junkyard once his paper-round had ended, sitting and eating cookies and listening to Miller's terrible jokes and stories of his life; stories Lucas suspected as being exaggerated for his benefit. And, as an added bonus to the visits, when Miller went to organize cookies and lemonade in his shack, Lucas was allowed to check out *Little Bertha*.

It was a coy name for something that, in its time, had been quite dangerous. Little Bertha was, in fact, a WWII anti-aircraft gun, still mounted on its turnstile plinth and facing the ocean. The gun had been decommissioned after the war, once German aircraft no longer threatened shipping lanes or radar installations along the coastline. Its 20mm cannon had been gagged for decades by a concrete bung, and its firing pin taken was stored in a military museum somewhere inland.

Mr Miller had introduced Lucas to Little Bertha on his first visit three years ago, a way of showing that the old man's bark was worse than his bite. And on that first visit a younger Lucas found himself sitting on the worn leather seat, staring through the webbed gun sight, mounted on the long, slim muzzle, and imagining the sky crammed with screaming Luftwaffe aircraft, as Little Bertha responded with her big booming voice.

These days Lucas remained awed by the pervading sense of history associated with the redundant weapon. Merely being in its presence was enough to stimulate his imagination of those terrible times.

But that morning, as Lucas navigated his way up the front path to Mr Miller's front door, the big man broke tradition, and came out of his shack to greet him.

'Hello, lad,' he said pawing at this crazy beard.

'Hello, Mr Miller,' Lucas said. 'Got your paper.'

He passed a copy of the Dorsal Finn Herald to Miller. The old man rolled it up before stuffing it into the pocket of his big trench coat.

'Any chance of checking out Little Bertha?' Lucas asked hopefully.

'Not this mornin', son,' Miller said. 'I've got things on.'

'Oh,' Lucas said without hiding his disappointment.

'How about tomorrow?' Miller said softly. 'Gives me a chance to do some cookie bakin'.'

'Okay, thanks,' Lucas said, and was about to leave when he heard a small whimper. He saw Wolfgang trot out behind Miller. The great dog appeared sullen and shaky on its feet. It sat down next to its owner, leaning against the big man's legs as though it needed support to remain upright.

'What's the matter with Wolfgang?' Lucas asked.

'Not sure,' Miller replied not looking at the dog at all. 'Might be worms.'

'Nice,' Lucas said wrinkling his nose.

'I'm goin' to take him to the vet this mornin'—see if we can't cheer the fella up.'

'Hope everything's okay,' Lucas said as he went back to the front gate and tried to close it without it falling off its bracket.

'Thanks, lad,' Miller said. 'You get yourself back here tomorrow and Little Bertha will be waitin'.'

The man watched Lucas head off the beach. Wolfgang whimpered again before lying down at Miller's booted feet.

'Don't worry, boy,' the man said to his hound. 'The pain'll pass. Just got to give it some time.'

'Must admit I wasn't expecting to see your cheery face so early,' said Elmo as Lucas skulked into his friend's bedroom, bringing with him with an air of abject misery. 'Let me guess . . . you've won the lottery but they found out you're under age?'

Sitting on his bed, Elmo adjusted the tuning keys on the stock of a very red guitar. It rested in his lap and the lead trailed from it, tumbling from the bed to the floor, where it coiled in a figure of eight before continuing its journey to a small square practice amp tucked in a quiet corner. From the grill, a small hiss emerged, broken sporadically by metallic pops as Elmo's sleeve inadvertently caught the strings.

Elmo was large and gentle. Outside of Dorsal Finn's hideous bottle green school uniform, he never wore anything other than a black T-shirt and jeans. Such was his sedate nature Elmo was usually more comfortable when people just got along with each other. He wasn't a fan of the awkward silence, and the ability for people to bear grudges was a perpetual mystery to him.

To establish such a climate where convention could flourish, Elmo exuded calm; initiating a natural gift for diplomacy and peacekeeping.

In short he was able to inject perspective into an argument, diffusing the conflict to the point where both parties could find a common ground and use it to save face. And he was able to do this effortlessly. Some said that he got this talent from his parents who, rumour had it, spent much of their youth helping charities in Africa and South America. Either way, when it came to frustration and volatile argument, Elmo provided much needed tranquillity.

Lucas adjusted the sleeve of his *Teenage FBI* tee-shirt,

'This is a song I wrote last night,' he said, dolefully holding up a wrinkled piece of paper.

'I'm right in suspecting it's another emotionally bleak piece, my bleach-blonde minstrel?' Elmo said.

'What makes you say that?' Lucas said briskly

'Well,' Elmo said. 'I'm thinking about your recent songs and the lyrics seem consistent in their *bleakness*.'

'I think that's a bit unfair,' Lucas protested, but Elmo held up a placating hand.

'Let's flash up a few recent titles from the "Lucas Walker Song Book",' Elmo said. 'You remember the toe-tappers: "MY HEART IS AS EMPTY AS A

CHEERLEADER'S HEAD"? Or "I CRIED SO HARD I SOAKED MY IRON MAIDEN TOUR SHIRT"? And, my all time, favourite: "MY LIFE SUCKS WORSE THAN A VAMPIRE WITH GINGIVITIS"? I'm definitely sensing a theme, but tell me if I'm off. I can take it. These broad shoulders ain't just to make my belly feel better.'

'I can't help it,' Lucas said after a few moments. He sat down heavily on a black bean bag, embroidered with the words, *Take the Weight off.*

'I'm guessing this goes beyond not grabbing a cookie and a date with Little Bertha?' Elmo said.

Lucas said nothing.

'You could always *talk* about it,' Elmo suggested, reaching over and placing the guitar on a stand at the foot of his bed.

'I have talked about it,' Lucas said sulkily. 'Is your memory *that* bad?'

'Not to me, *duh-brain*,' Elmo said. 'To *her*!'

'Little Bertha?' Lucas's said bemused. Then his face adopted a look of utter horror when Elmo's words finally made sense. 'You mean, talk to *Bea*? Are you joking?'

'See this face?' Elmo said dead pan. 'Observe, there is no joking parked here.'

'I can't tell her,' Lucas said, his mouth pulled out of shape at the thought of telling Beatrice how he felt about her. About how she was always on his mind and when he was with her the world seemed to go super slow-mo as his heart raced. 'How can I tell her that she makes me feel happy and sad at the same time?' Lucas asked his friend.

'It's a backward statement,' Elmo smiled, 'but Bea's

bright—she might get it. But, what do I know about such stuff? I'm still dealing with the idea that there's not gonna be a sequel to the DREDD movie. '

'It doesn't help that we've not had any mysteries to solve recently,' Lucas muttered.

'Can I remind you that this is a good thing for anyone who isn't you?'

'You need to have distractions in life.'

'Where'd that come from, the back of a packet of cheap snacks?'

'I think it did,' Lucas admitted. 'But the fact remains that I can't tell Bea. So I need to think about something else.'

'It's gonna eat you up like a giant hamster if you're not careful, bro,' Elmo cautioned. 'Besides that, we're too young to be burdened with misery. You're gonna have to do something about it sooner or later.'

'Later is good,' Lucas whispered. 'Yeah, *later* will be just fine.'

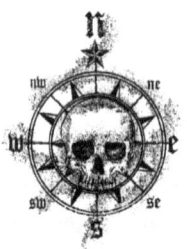

Though it no longer looked it, the hut was over forty years old. Its weathered wooden panels—buckled by the relentless assault of the elements—had been stripped away, gutted back to the frame by the *money-no-object* philosophy that signified the *Blue Thunder Foundation*. The warped, wooden slats had been replaced by weather-proofed timber and the once-boarded windows were now glazed, mirrored panes that reflected the bright sunlight overhead. Standing beside the hut was a flagpole—a thin white streak against the azure sky—with a pennant flapping fervently at the top. The material was emblazoned with the image of a white cloud—a lightning bolt punching through its base. The emblem of the *Blue Thunder Foundation* was nothing if not potent.

The mayoral Rolls Royce pulled up outside the hut, and through the tinted glass, Codd observed the front door. The double slats were painted bright blue and folded outwards as twin lines of young people trooped smartly through. As the head of each line met the kerb, they stopped and shouted 'hutt' in unison and both lines aborted their march. At another command, the rows of youths turned to face each other, forming a corridor of smart blue uniforms leading to the entrance.

'No red carpets, Gideon,' Frobisher said beside the Mayor. 'Just a welcome from the young. How much grandeur could one hope for?'

'Quite,' said Codd sounding impressed. Though, inside, he knew that this word didn't somehow cover the awe he felt.

Nor the disbelief.

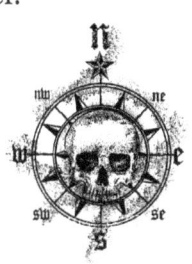

'Thomas,' Beatrice seethed at her brother, 'have you ever thought of putting one foot in front of the other, sort of rapidly? It's called *walking*. It gets you from one place to another. Sometimes on the same day!'

'It's all right for you, Bea,' Thomas whined from several yards behind. 'You don't have to enrol at this *thing*.'

'I've heard they've got smart uniforms,' Patience cajoled. 'A little too blue for my taste, but I'm sure you'll look great.'

'Uniforms?' Thomas said speeding up a little. 'Blue ones? Like in *Thunderbirds*?'

'If it makes you move any faster they're exactly like *Thunderbirds*,' Beatrice said .

'Do you get a hat as well?' Thomas asked.

'Not sure about a hat,' Patience replied causing Beatrice to nudge her in the ribs with an elbow. 'Ow! Oh, yes, of course they have a hat! Fancy forgetting that! My ribs thank your sister for the subtle reminder.'

'Come on then, Thomas,' Beatrice said with faux urgency in her voice. 'You don't want all the hats to disappear, do you?'

'You think they'll have vehicles?' her brother said hopefully.

'Vehicles?' Patience said puzzled.

'Yeah, like a big digging machine for burrowing underground or a submarine for rescuing divers from the seabed or something like that?'

'They have hats,' Patience reminded him evasively. 'That's got to be better than a dirty old digger, hasn't it?'

'I'm not sure,' Thomas frowned. 'How can a hat be better than a digging machine?'

'You get to take a hat home with you?' Patience offered.

Beatrice looked up at the gulls as though willing them to take her away from the ordeal of her brother's inauguration. But the birds proved to be noisy, unhelpful allies.

'Who's that?' Patience said. Her voice was small and warbled slightly as though she had become breathless.

'Who's who?' Beatrice said following her friend's gaze.

Across the main road dissecting the shop frontages from the promenade, Beatrice espied the figure of a boy walking towards them. He appeared to be the same age. Even over such a distance, Beatrice could tell that he was tall and slim, moving with poise and grace she'd never before noticed in a boy.

The teenager's hair was blonde, almost white, and his tanned face made his eyes a deep vivid blue which mirrored the smart two piece suit he wore. But despite his stature, Beatrice was drawn to the wheelchair the boy pushed ahead of him, and the figure slumped in it.

It was an elderly woman, easily as old as Maud and Agnes Clutterbuck, the town librarian. But this woman had succumbed to time, her frame buckled and bent as the chair housing her. Her fingers were like twisted and knotted sticks and a tartan blanket covered her legs, but not enough to hide the big Velcro slippers poking out from beneath the hem.

The girls continued to observe the two figures, both lost in thought as they crossed the road separating the promenade from the shop fronts. Their reverie was shattered by the sound of a horn and the screech of brakes. Instinctively Beatrice and her companions jumped back onto the kerb, startled and shaken as a small van sped by them, its driver shouting curses from his cab. Beatrice saw an image of a blue, horizontal horn with multitude of delicacies pouring from its open mouth and recognising it as the logo of *Cornucopia Catering*, a company based in Ashby-on-Sea. They were an establishment of repute and Beatrice held them in high esteem.

'Sorry,' Beatrice offered the retreating vehicle. Relief and embarrassment coursed through her.

'See?' Thomas said. 'I'm not meant to get there. This is a doomed mission, I keep telling you!'

'Just keep walking, hero,' Beatrice muttered grabbing hold of her brother's arm and dragging him along behind her. 'I'm embarrassed enough as it is.'

'You got some trouble there?' the boy said giving both girls a wide, friendly smile.

'Nothing I can't handle,' Beatrice said returning the amity. 'My brother isn't keen on going to the *Blue Thunder* ceremony.'

'Not keen to get run over either,' Thomas grumbled.

'I see,' the boy said. 'I guess most kids are reluctant at first. We're not tried and tested like the scouts or anything like that.'

'I don't think he'd like the scouts either,' Beatrice said. 'It's all a little too much like reality in Thomas' world.'

'I did reality once,' the youth said. 'Didn't like it that much either.'

He laughed at the puzzled frown this induced in the two girls. Thomas however appeared to relax in Beatrice's grip. She let him go.

'I'm Marcus,' he said stepping out from behind the wheelchair and offering his hand. Beatrice shook it tentatively hoping that Marcus didn't notice that her palms were sweating slightly.

The girls introduced themselves, the formality of it broken by the occasional sleepy snort or grunt from the woman in the chair.

'Nice to meet you both,' Marcus said. 'And this is my grandmother, Mabel Alice Macbeth. I can say this because she is sleeping. If she heard me mutter the name Mabel, things could get pretty ugly, pretty fast.'

'Not a fan of her name then?' Patience said, her eyes not leaving Marcus' face. Beatrice noticed that her friend's usually unblemished olive skin appeared flushed about the cheeks and neck. 'Shame,' Patience continued. 'It's a derivative of Annabel, which is from the Latin *Amabilis*, meaning lovable or dear.'

'Can't see why grandma wouldn't like something like that,' Marcus considered.

'It was also the name of one of the dogs from the *Blue Peter* TV show,' Patience added after a small pause.

'Sometimes you can have slightly too much information about something, can't you?' Beatrice said.

A small, yet firm, voice interrupted them,

'What *Mabel* means to me, dear, is a lifetime of mediocrity.'

'Ah, Grandma, you're awake,' Marcus said cordially.

'So it would seem,' Macbeth said after clearing her nose with a big, watery sniff. 'It's this infernal chair,' she explained to the children standing in front of her. 'The rocking motion on the cobblestones plays havoc with me wee tummy. It's either nod off or vomit.'

'Nodding off is good,' Patience said pulling a face.

'I would agree,' the old woman said patting her blanket. 'Vomit stains the tartan something terrible.'

'Doesn't it just?' Patience said nodding emphatically. 'I remember one time—I had this chiffon skirt, and I went baby sitting with little Nora Foster, and she was stuffing her face with a bar of chocolate the size of her head and—'

'What brings you to Dorsal Finn,' Beatrice interjected before Patience steered the conversation further into bizarreness.

'The *Blue Thunder Foundation*,' Marcus said taking up duties behind Macbeth's chair. 'Grandmother is a patron.'

'We're going to the same place,' Beatrice said. And inside she felt happy at the thought of spending more time in the company of Marcus Macbeth.

'Then we should walk together,' Marcus suggested.

'You youngsters will walk,' his grandmother said sourly. 'I shall continue to bounce along like some deranged rabbit, and try to keep down my breakfast.'

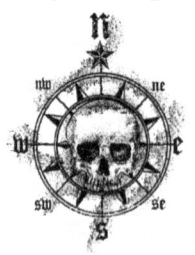

In Dorsal Finn library, Agnes Clutterbuck pushed a small trolley stacked with several neat piles of books.

As she approached the section marked *Historical Fiction*, the wily librarian hummed a happy tune in her mild Scottish accent. As she tapped a silver, thistle-shaped ring against the trolley's tubular metal frame, the leaden air was lifted by light little chimes. The quilted material of her trademark purple body warmer creaked in time with slow casual movements, and her glasses, hanging from a fine silver chain around her neck, danced in the air as she leaned forward to place a Diana Gabaldon novel on a lower shelf.

As she stood upright her hearing aids whistled, and Agnes tutted and adjusted them by poking an index finger in each ear and wiggling it around until the squeaks died down. In Dorsal Finn, Agnes' hearing aids were already things of renown. They had never been the same since she had tried to repair them with a sewing needle and a piece of fishing line. These days the apparatus had received a variety of bizarre signals ranging from weather reports from Melbourne to tactical communications between a SWAT team and their command centre in New York.

Agnes was at home in the library. Her parents had moved to Dorsal Finn over three-quarters of a century ago and Agnes had spent her very first day in the town wandering through the library's dusty halls, the heady smell of ancient paper heavy in the air. The peace the aroma brought with it as potent as any of her mother's kind words of comfort. Agnes had never felt more at home. Her parents had passed away some time ago but the library was evergreen; as much a part of her as her departed kin. In fact, the library was now her permanent place of residence. With some negotiation, she'd secured a lease on the small derelict flat situated on top of the building for as long as the library had existed. Agnes had always wanted to live there but just didn't have the motivation, or the permission for that matter, to renovate the property.

As much as she adored her home there was always a nagging doubt that came to her mind when she was in the Historical Fiction section. There was an irony in that the errant thoughts that popped into her head were indeed history, but they were as far from fiction as you could get.

Agnes paused for a moment and scratched her thin nose in an attempt to quell an itch that was threatening to build up in her nostrils. She used the time to suffocate ill thoughts of the past.

'We really must stop thinking about such things,' Agnes chided herself as she transferred a copy of *Wuthering Heights* back to its place on the bookshelf. 'You were the one who told Maud to draw a line under *that* evening. Now here you are stepping over it again. Back to work, Clutterbuck! *Less thought more haste*, to muddle an adage for my own ends.'

The librarian chuckled to herself. She was about to go back to her duties when, as so often happens in the town of Dorsal Finn, fate decided to pay a visit.

She went to the bookcase on the far wall, the bookcase that held a secret, as well as tomes on shelves. Agnes reached the unit as the massive, sonic pulse that had punched outwards from Cochran's fishing boat reached dry land.

Agnes' aids picked up the pulse. It filled her head

with a whirling, dizzying sensation that left her reeling, her hands clawing at the bookshelves for support.

Through the swirling haze, Agnes watched in horror as the bookcase shuddered violently, shrugging several tomes to the floor before teetering forward precariously. Just as she feared that the solid wooden frame would topple over and squash her flat beneath its weight, the dizziness left her and the bookcase appeared to regain its balance too. It fell back against the wall with a heavy thud, leaving the librarian staring at it as she panted.

'Oh, dear,' she said meekly. Her vision had cleared, aided by sweeping a hand up to put on her glasses. Now she could see the damage immediately. It wasn't bad enough that there were books scattered throughout the aisle, it wasn't bad enough that a huge gaping hole could be seen in the wall behind the exposed bookshelves.

To top all of this off, the whole event was made worse by the slow rhythmic voice she could now hear. It was a voice that she had not heard for quite some time. There was a reason for this, of course. She had thought the measures she had taken in the not too distant past had made things right. But Agnes had always doubted the effectiveness of these measures. Now she knew for sure just how ineffective they truly were.

With a trembling hand she delved into the pocket of her body warmer and fished out her cell phone. Then she called one of the others who knew of her reluctant secret.

Maud Postlethwaite answered on the third ring.

As Beatrice and the others approached the renovated scout hut, the maudlin sound of a bugle hung heavily on the air. Beside the flagpole, an impressive sea of blue uniformed kids stood with heads bowed; hands clasped in front of them.

'Cheerful,' Patience said in a low voice. 'What's next, *Adele*?'

'It's a dirge to those young people who have been lost to us,' Marcus explained sombrely. 'Such a waste of youth. A waste of life.'

'Amen to that,' his grandmother said dropping her chin to her chest in silent prayer.

As she watched, Beatrice was surprised to see the Marcus' deep blue eyes mist with tears. There was something so profound in this she found her heart skipping and her chest tighten. Any embarrassment turned quickly to sympathy.

'It sounds very sad,' she said.

'On the contrary,' Macbeth said. 'It's as much about life as it is death. Do not mourn those who have passed on; celebrate what they gave to life.'

'That's my grandma,' Marcus said, his mood lightening once more. 'Ever the optimist.'

Even concentrating hard, Beatrice found Marcus' statement hard to believe.

'We have to do our bit for the celebrations,' Marcus

said interrupting Beatrice's thoughts. 'I have to set up the food.'

He patted a canvas box secured to the handles of the wheelchair.

'Cool bag,' he explained.

'What do you have in there?' Patience asked.

'Something he made earlier,' Macbeth said softly. Beatrice could hear pride in the old woman's voice.

'Just a few canapés,' Marcus said with some embarrassment.

'A few *very good* canapés,' Macbeth said. 'The boy is far too modest.'

'So you cook too?' Beatrice smiled. 'I'd love to try one.'

'Then I shall save a canapé for you,' Marcus said with a bow.

'Why would you want to save her a can of peas?' Thomas asked.

'Thomas, can you just try not to be so stupid—just for today?' Beatrice chided.

'You're a curious lad who doesn't worry about asking questions,' Macbeth said to Thomas. 'The *Blue Thunder Foundation* will respect that.'

Beatrice felt her face flush in embarrassment. Her acceptance of Thomas's quirks was at an all time low and Macbeth had quietly chastised Beatrice's intolerance.

'I'd rather be watching, *Dr Who*,' Thomas said openly.

'And why not?' Marcus said nodding. 'That's a great show! But wait until you hear about *The Blue Bolt*.'

'*The Blue Bolt*?' Thomas said with immediate interest.

'Yes,' Marcus continued. 'Once the enrolment and the initiation ceremony are done, you'll get a welcome pack—complete with a *Blue Bolt* DVD and comic book. If you like superheroes then you'll love *The Blue Bolt*!'

Thomas's face morphed into a gleeful grin. He began to march on ahead, stopping only to address Patience and his sister,

'Come one you two, I don't want to be late!'

Beatrice looked after him incredulously as he continued on his way.

'Time for us to be moving too,' Marcus said. 'If you're happy for us to do it, we'll show Thomas where he needs to be for enrolment. Then we'll see you at the ceremony?'

'I'd be *ecstatic* if you'd be able to do that,' Beatrice agreed. She was really looking forward to tasting Marcus's cookery. Suddenly the event was very interesting.

'Then see you both after the ceremony,' Marcus concluded. 'The canapés will be served in the hut once the speeches are done.'

'I'm looking forward to it,' Beatrice said, feeling a little light headed.

'Me too,' Marcus conceded, his piercing blue eyes never leaving Beatrice's for one, solitary moment.

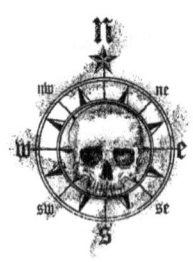

Maud Postlethwaite moved through the reception area of Dorsal Finn's Library as fast as her weary body would allow. She wasn't alone. As soon as Agnes had hung up, Maud had called the two other people who were privy to the reluctant secret nestled behind the walls of Dorsal Finn library. Behind her were two men, Dennis Hodges and Albert Smythe.

Dennis was a big framed man with a thick, black and neatly trimmed beard. He had lived in Dorsal Finn all his life, and before his job as handyman at Bramwell Hall, spent a fair few years of his adult years drunk on Cinders Cider and sleeping rough because he could never quite remember where he lived.

His home was actually a small fisherman's cottage in Gull Crescent; the place where he was raised by his mother, Jemima. His father, a trawler man, died at sea during a storm when Dennis was only twelve years old. As an only child, and the only link his mother had to his dead father, Dennis was deterred from following a life at sea. His mother insisted he was to learn a trade that would keep him land based; such was her fear of losing him.

Dennis took in basic, unskilled jobs in the town. One of them, moving barrels for The Salty Seadog Inn, led to his love of Cinders Cider. Within a month he'd lost his job for the very same reason.

As the years went by, Dennis' antics was as much a part of the ethos of Dorsal Finn as anything else; there was an acceptance of his lifestyle, especially once his mother died. When he worked, he worked hard and well. For a long time he approached play with the same ethic.

Age was catching up with him these days. At fifty

five he was starting to see changes in how quickly he could recover from his excess. So he'd reined in his drinking, limiting it to a few times a week and on the days when he wasn't working at Bramwell Hall.

In contrast, Albert Smythe was a short, rotund man with a balding crown. What hair he did have was neatly clipped. As Maud's beau, he was a man of quiet tastes and his movements were considered and delicate. He had a wide and deep knowledge of the world, having travelled it extensively in his youth when he was in the armed forces—where he was the batman for several high ranking officers. After the army he became butler to The Pontefract family, Dorsal Finn's patrons, where his skills of refined service were always respected. But his love for Maud was resolute and meant everything to him; defining his actions. And when she asked for help he responded, without question. What had happened before and what was happening now were all fuelled by his devotion to Maud and his desire to make sure she was safe. This extended to Agnes, her dearest of friends.

The *Sorry—Library Closed* sign pressing against the glass door was the first indication things were amiss. A bedraggled-looking Agnes peered through the glass when Maud rapped a knuckle against the pane and it was clear that all was not well.

'Maud,' Agnes said as she gave her friend the kind of hug reserved for someone she'd not seen for an eon. 'It's so good to see you.'

'Well, I wasn't plannin' on ye going it alone like last time, Agnes Clutterbuck,' Maud said into the librarian's shoulder. 'But if ye squeeze any harder, I'm not goin' to be much use to man nor beast.'

'Sorry,' Agnes said relinquishing her embrace and stepping back. She nodded gratefully to Albert and Dennis who stood patiently behind Maud, like two aged sentinels waiting for instruction.

'So what's goin' on?' Maud asked.

'I'll show you,' the librarian said turning and escorting her friend to the Historical Romance section.

The bookcase was now cleared of books. Beyond the frame, Maud could see a dark diagonal scar in a wall painted in magnolia.

'Well this old thing doesn't want to keep quiet no longer,' Maud said approaching the bookcase and peering into the gash in the wall. She pulled out her cell phone and punched in the numbers.

'What are you doing, Maud?' Agnes said in surprise.

'We old uns need t' be lookin' at this in a different way,' Maud said. 'An' sometimes that needs younger eyes.'

CHAPTER FOUR
TEENAGE FBI

THE ENROLMENT PHASE was a swift affair helped by the incredible efficiency demonstrated by the members of *The Blue Thunder Foundation*. Shrugging off the melancholy air prevalent at the flagpole, the boys and girls—all in their early to mid-teens—were now inside the hut, a huge space painted in blue and white with a stage and lectern at one end. A *Blue Thunder* pennant secured to the wall spanned the stage, making an imposing backdrop.

A series of small tables, numbered one to four, were manned by members of the foundation who made sure that, by the time an enrolee had worked their way to the last table, they were a member of the organisation, equipped with three sets of folded, cellophane-wrapped uniforms and a membership pack. The latter included Marcus' much lauded *Blue Bolt* DVD and comic book.

'So what do you think, Beatrice?' Patience said with a furtive grin.

'About what?'

'Marcus, of course,' she said, forcing the tone out of her voice in case anyone should hear. 'Is he a big scoop of sweetness from the honey jar, or what?'

'I can't say that I noticed,' she said without looking at her friend.

'Another lie like that and your tongue is sure to turn black, Beatrice Beecham.' Patience's accompanying giggle was infectious, knocking aside Beatrice's attempts at pretence.

'Okay,' Beatrice grinned, her cheeks now fiery red. 'How can I lie? He is nice.'

'*Nice*? The queen of understatement speaks,' Patience teased. 'And you must've seen how he was looking at you? I thought his eyes were going to bail and roll across the promenade.'

'Don't!' Beatrice laughed, covering her face with her hands. 'I'm turning crimson here!'

'Sorry, Beatrice,' Patience said. 'But let's face it, you've got the guy's attention, global. And there's no denying it's mutual. If he's cooking's up to scratch I'm demanding first dibs on Chief Bridesmaid.'

'Patience!' Beatrice laughed coming out from behind her hands. Her freckles were darkened by the rouge of her cheeks. 'We've only just met. And I'm sure you've got it all wrong. He was just being friendly.'

'Well you enjoy *being friendly* when he asks you out later,' Patience said with conviction.

'And what makes you so sure he's going to do that?' Beatrice asked in disbelief.

'Oh it's simple,' Patience said. 'It's in the eyes.'

'Oh, yes, I forgot. The ones rolling across the promenade, right?' Beatrice said. 'Well if he asks me out, I'll eat a pair of Lucas' dirty socks.'

'Okay,' Patience said swiping her cell phone from her handbag.

'What are you doing?' Beatrice asked.

'Making sure that Lucas' mum doesn't get to the wash basket in the next hour,' Patience laughed.

'If I can have your attention please?' The metallic fizz of a microphone cut the through the air. Beatrice followed the sound to its source: the portly figure of Mayor Codd standing at the lectern, fidgeting in his Mayoral ruff. A smart looking man stood beside him.

'I'd like to say a few words of welcome on behalf of Dorsal Finn,' Codd continued. 'So if you would be so kind as to be shutting your faces I shall begin.'

At this people turned to face the Mayor, Beatrice was never surprised by Codd's cold and surly arrogance. Despite her contempt for the man, she listened to his address along with the rest; a captive audience in a blue and white prison.

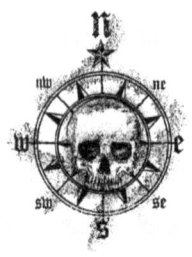

'You cannot possibly involve the Newshounds in this, Maud,' Agnes protested before Maud put the phone to her ear. 'We don't know what can of worms this involves. The danger we could be bringing upon this town.'

'I'm thinkin' that any danger's already visitin', Agnes,' Maud said quietly. 'The new door in yer library wall is proof of that.' Maud stepped up to her friend and placed a gentle hand upon her shoulder. 'If we had another choice, I'd be makin' it, ye know that,' said Maud. 'We knew this problem hadn't gone on its travels for long. Those that want the past to come visitin' aren't goin' to let this go. An' we can't tell the authorities Agnes, ye know that too. What we did wouldn't be looked on well by folk 'round here. No matter how long ago it was.'

Agnes appeared to be ready to protest further but Maud interjected softly,

'Me an' thee have rattled a fair few cages in this town, Agnes. An' the beast wants an opportunity to be out an' meetin' us in person.'

Maud felt Agnes' shoulder sag beneath her palm.

'I know,' the librarian conceded. 'But they are so *young*.'

'So were we when we committed treason in the eyes of our elders,' Maud pointed out. 'We owe The Newshounds our faith at least.'

'Those kids are resilient and smart,' Albert said quietly.

'An' discreet,' Dennis added.

'Call them,' Agnes said quietly.

In Elmo's bedroom, Lucas' mobile phone demanded

attention by blasting out the intro to Judas Priest's *You Don't Have to be Old to be Wise*. He was thus dragged from his brooding thoughts surrounding his feelings for Beatrice by a delusion that she might actually be calling him.

He snatched up the phone and was puzzled when he saw the unknown caller icon in the display window.

'Hello?' he answered cautiously.

'Good mornin' young Lucas,' Maud said unexpectedly in his ear. 'Got time to help out an old 'un?'

'Sure,' he said. 'I didn't know you had my number. Thought you were about to try and sell me insurance.'

'If ye're surprised by that, ye're goin' to be fallin' off yer perch when I tell ye what's just happened at the library,' Maud replied.

'Okay,' he said sitting up. 'I'm listening.'

'Ye need to come here,' Maud said. 'Make it easy fer us.'

'Us?'

'Ye comin'?' Maud said.

'You betcha,' he said with a smile.

Although Lucas was completely and utterly puzzled by Maud's phone call he suddenly felt at peace. For, whilst he hadn't found a way to make his confusing thoughts known to Beatrice, he had at least found a mystery to help him forget about it for a while.

'Come on, big guy,' he said to Elmo. 'We're off to see Maud and Agnes.'

'Why's that, bro?' Elmo said getting to his feet and placing the guitar back on its spindly stand.

'There's a mystery requiring our attention,' Lucas replied.

'I did mention that this is usually the start of something bad, didn't I?'

Lucas left the room. If he'd heard his friend's comment he showed no sign of it.

'This kind of thing never happened to The Beatles,' Elmo muttered as he reluctantly followed Lucas out.

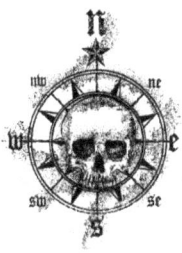

'Ladies and gentlemen, boys and girls, as Mayor of Dorsal Finn I am proud to introduce the founder of *The Blue Thunder Foundation*: Mr Logan Frobisher. Please give him a warm welcome.'

Gideon Codd stepped away from the lectern as those present gave Frobisher a round of polite applause.

The tall man stepped up to the pencil-thin microphone and delivered a brief, bright and cheery smile.

From the wings, a group of uniformed youths stepped onto the stage, each bringing with them a small chair which they deposited in two neat rows of ten before departing and standing in front of the stage, facing the audience in their own orderly line; faces impassive and staring into the far distance.

'I call to those brothers and sisters who have come here to pledge their allegiance to all that life holds dear,' Frobisher said with a resolute voice.

Suddenly the boys and girls who had enrolled that day filed silently onto the stage and took a seat.

From her place in the crowd, Beatrice could see her brother sitting in the front row, his cellophane uniforms resting in his lap. He seemed so comfortable there, as though this was meant to be.

To her amazement Beatrice felt a wave of pride sweep through her and a grin formed on her lips.

This was, she thought, turning into a day of surprises.

'Why are we here?' Frobisher's voice pounded through the hut. It was quite possible that he didn't actually require the microphone. 'It is a question that we will all ask at some point in our lives. As an idea it can be as deep as a canyon or as shallow as a trough, but ask it we will. And for many, the answer will not come readily, if at all.'

Frobisher's debonair figure surveyed the crowd for a mere moment, allowing his words to seep in—to make their presence felt.

'Be that as it may,' he continued, '*The Blue Thunder Foundation* is clear in its purpose. When we ask: "Why are we here?" there is no pause or pointed silence; there are only three words: *Faith. Loyalty. Honour.*'

Another hiatus in the rhetoric. Another stare into the crowd.

'These are small words with huge meaning—vast responsibilities. They are not easy to obtain and even harder to maintain.' He turned, this time to address the row of enrolees sitting to his right.

'It stirs my heart to see ones so young become so committed,' Frobisher said to them before turning back to the audience. 'These children are our future, ladies and gentlemen. I would go as far to say they are our *salvation* from the chaos through which our world wades. You can be sure that the foundation shall cherish them as our own. Your pride is now ours also. I thank you all for your faith.'

Frobisher stepped back from the lectern as the applause began. Beatrice turned to Patience, her friend shrugging her shoulders in a bemused fashion.

'Now what?' Beatrice asked as the audience began to thin out.

'Hope you're hungry,' Patience said spotting Marcus moving towards them with a tray of food. 'This is where we find if you've got socks as well as canapés for lunch.'

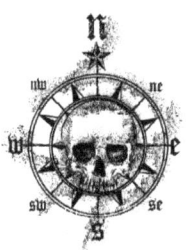

The atmosphere in the library was oppressive. Lucas and Elmo had arrived with a degree of excitement, but the sullen nature of the four adults standing in the reception area soon kerbed their enthusiastic chatter.

'What the hell happened to the Historical Fiction section?' Lucas said as he saw the bookcases pulled askew. 'You had a tornado pass through here, Agnes?'

'I thought when you tidy stuff up it's supposed to look better?' said Elmo to Lucas. 'Based on this, I guess Lucas' bedroom isn't a bombsite after all.'

'It's true that we've tried to sweep things under the carpet,' Agnes said mournfully. 'For quite some time.'

Maud and Agnes looked at each other.

Their uncertainty was reinforced by Albert and Dennis who both wore grim expressions.

'So are you guys going to tell us what's going on?' Lucas said as he sat on the reception counter. He bounced the heels of his Converse trainers against the wooden panelling.

'That's the plan, young Lucas,' Maud said. 'But give us old 'uns a few minutes to get things straight. If we're tellin' this story so it makes sense t' ye, then we have to tell it right.'

Lucas and Elmo waited patiently; the silence rolled on until both boys thought no words would come. Then Maud began to speak. Her tone was low and her voice, measured.

'Ye all know that I came to Dorsal Finn durin' the war,' Maud said wistfully. 'I was missin' me folks an' friends an' all.'

Maud reached out and patted Agnes tenderly on her arm. 'But then I met this wonderful woman. An' after only a short time it was like this had been me home forever. She certainly made me want to come back an' live here.'

Agnes smiled, and the boys could see the love between the two women. It made them think about The Newshounds, and strengthened their understanding as to how important it was to have good friends.

'In the spring of 1942 Agnes an' me, we were soap box racin' up on the bluff,' Maud continued. 'We saw an incredible sight comin' in off of the ocean. A

German bomber low in the sky, smoke an' flames spewin' everywhere.'

'So what happened?' said Elmo. He was leaning on the counter, his neck craned forwards in interest.

'The plane came down an' hit Hill Crest farm; the buildin' an' plane went up like a rocket.

'Well if that weren't enough drama for two young girls, we then saw three parachutes driftin' down over the bluff. So we trailed 'em. Two fell into the sea, an' the ocean claimed 'em. But the third, well that landed up on Monument Point, an' there we found an unconscious German airman.' Maud paused to take in a private memory. Then she pressed on, 'So we goes to him an' he's pretty bashed up; arm busted an' a big gash in his head. Yet he was alive an' that may have been a good thing in the grand scheme, but in a time of war that put him in even more danger.'

The boys were now drawn into the story, fascinated by the past and how they had potential to inform what was happening at that very moment. Such was the power and wonder of history.

'So what did you do?' It was Lucas' turn to speak. His voice was hushed and his feet had stopped bumping against the counter. They hovered in the air as if forgotten.

'We acted on impulse, that's what we did,' Maud said. 'We didn't see a German pilot. We saw a man in pain an' knew no one would help him unless we did. So we dragged him into the disused tin mines up at Monument Point an' tended to him for two months.'

'Two months?' Lucas said in disbelief. 'And no one suspected?'

'Ha!' Maud laughed. 'Most adults think kids are

invisible; it was no different back then. We came an' went; we had a Girl Guides' *First Aid Merit Badge* between us an' we did our best. An' in those two months we got to know his name was Klaus Hessel, an' we didn't see the enemy, but a man who was far from his family.'

'He spoke English?' asked Elmo.

'A little—a few broken words—but better than our German, that's for sure. He could write it better than he could say it. That's how we communicated. Chalk an' slate came in handy durin' those few months. He told about his life on his farm in Stuttgart, an' his wife Greta, an' their daughter Derika. He talked about how he missed them so.' Maud's eyes took on a distant appearance.

'So we decided to help him get back home,' Maud said eventually. 'We stole a rowboat from the bay an' moored it on the beach. On the night he left, Klaus gave us his thanks an' a hug, an' a promise that after the war was done he would come back an' introduce us to his wife an' daughter. That was the last we ever saw of him.'

A single tear tumbled down Maud's cheek, and Agnes reached out and placed her palm gently over her friend's hand.

'He never made it home,' Maud whispered. 'A motor torpedo boat shot up the scull an' Klaus was killed. We didn't know this at the time, of course. We read it in the paper later that same week. They called him a spy. But to us he was only ever a friend in need.'

'Klaus left us on Halloween, and me an' Agnes celebrate his memory with a glass or two of brandy every year. It was destined to be our secret, a secret we couldn't tell at the time. Then after the war, we kept it that way; made it special. Klaus deserved that at least.'

Lucas and Elmo were quiet for a few moments as Maud's tale sank in. The four adults all appeared as though they were at a wake. Their shoulders were hunched. Dennis fidgeted from one foot to the other.

'So, what's this all got to do with this morning's phone call, Maud?' Lucas said.

'This is where yer really need to be pinnin' back yer ears,' Maud said. 'Because this tale's just gettin' warmed up.'

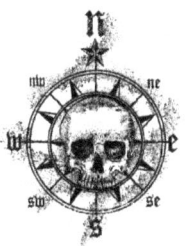

'I have to admit to being a little nervous,' Marcus said as he approached Patience and Beatrice with a wide serving tray. It was brimming with a selection of ornate, delicate parcels.

'Why's that?' Beatrice asked.

'Someone has mentioned that you are none other than Beatrice Beecham,' he explained with a voice infused with awe.' Anyone here says you are an amazing chef.'

Beatrice flushed a little. 'They're all very kind. And I think your presentation is wonderful.'

'Thank you,' he said, offering them the tray. 'Might I recommend the Canapés Berne?'

'You tell me which one it is and I'll take it on,' Patience grinned.

'The triangular one,' Marcus said, and Beatrice deftly picked up a small wedge of toast decorated with egg whites, yolks and pureed green gherkins. In the middle there was a stuffed olive, its surface glimmering under the fluorescent lights.

It had a divine smell and Beatrice took a bite. For a moment or two she merely stared into space; causing Patience to pause with the canapé hovering at her lips, and Marcus to frown.

'You hate it, don't you?' he said.

Beatrice blinked, chewed and swallowed. Then she looked at Marcus, dumbfounded.

'That was the best Berne I have ever tasted,' she said simply.

'You're just saying that to be kind,' Marcus said.

'I wouldn't ever do that,' Beatrice replied.. 'Really, this is Michelin standard. It's incredible.'

'I guess Beatrice would love to have the recipe, wouldn't you Beatrice?' Patience said nudging her friend with an elbow.

Before Beatrice could reply Marcus delivered a huge smile and his eyes sparkled.

'How about we meet up later?' he said to Beatrice. 'If you'd like to, then maybe we could have stroll along the promenade and share kitchen stories?'

So there it was. A question—a suggestion. No longer wishful thinking or supposition from Patience. And although her friend had been accurate, Beatrice was still unprepared. This was, after all, new territory for her; no one had ever asked to meet up with her for a date. If that was what this was, of course.

At one time she'd thought Lucas liked her as more than just a friend, maybe that he liked her because she was a girl who he wanted to be around. But now that seemed to have passed. Nothing had been said, nothing had really changed, and Lucas never really made any attempt to be alone with her. In fact, on occasions he even avoided the chance. When that happened, she cursed herself for thinking things were more than they appeared.

At first, Beatrice was saddened by this and hadn't spoken to anyone about it, not even Patience. Beatrice was scared that if she'd got things wrong she might destroy her friendship with The Newshounds. The thought of not being able to see Lucas at all, the thought that The Newshounds would no longer exist, were ideas she found too painful to bear. So she'd decided to wait for Lucas to show a sign that he liked her. But it never came.

As such, things remained as they were and Beatrice wasn't clear if this was right or wrong until Marcus had asked his question and the fireworks exploded in her inexperienced heart.

And because the situation was alien to her, Beatrice's mind did what it needed to do to unravel some of confusion.

Beatrice called the council together.

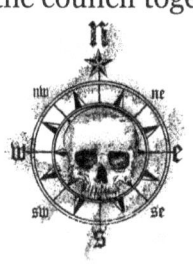

If you were to ask Beatrice just how the Culinary Council came to be she would, in all honesty, not have been able to say. What she could say was that the council seemed to drop into her head as soon as emotional confusion or major life choices presented themselves.

In reality the discussions that occurred between Beatrice and the group of esteemed chefs happened in the wink of an eye, but in that nanosecond conversations were held and conflicts addressed.

The council consisted of Gordon Ramsay, Raymond Blanc, Gary Rhodes and Mario Batali; but as austere as these chefs were, the head of the Culinary Council was Beatrice's all-time favourite, Jamie Oliver.

It was of little surprise Beatrice had made Jamie the patriarch, and in her mind's eye it was towards his wisdom she was now drawn. She may have been in the *Blue Thunder* hut, but what she saw in the moment it takes for a battery of neurons to fire across the synapses of her brain was Jamie sitting on a gingham table cloth, slicing an apple with a small Belchette's kitchen knife. About him were countless items making up a very fine picnic. The whole spread was shaded beneath the hunched branches of a Weeping Willow tree.

On a nearby river, the other members of the Culinary Council were having an argument in their boat because Gordon Ramsay had lost an oar and was trying to use Garry Rhodes' instead.

'Hi Jamie,' Beatrice said looking about her. 'I have a problem.'

'I love a good picnic, don't you?' Jamie asked.

'Yes, I do,' Beatrice said.

'Food tastes somehow better outdoors, don't you think?'

'I suppose it does,' Beatrice replied.

Jamie popped a large slice of apple into his mouth, his smile widening briefly to accommodate. He crunched slowly, in rhythm with the birdsong about them.

'That wasn't always the case,' he continued after he'd swallowed the slice. 'I once thought that without good planning things can be forgotten. Things can get left behind. And then all would be lost; the day ruined.'

'That's always a possibility,' Beatrice nodded.

'But when we're faced with the unknown, inspiration has a chance to work its magic,' Jamie said. 'Without the shackles of a recipe the true chef can work on that which separates the good from the great—'

'Are you talking about instincts?' Beatrice asked tentatively.

'Sometimes it's the only option left open to us,' Jamie admitted. 'We have to go with our gut to feed our gut. And that might mean heading into unknown territory. It might mean—'

'Taking a chance?' Beatrice suggested.

'Oh, yeah,' Jamie said.

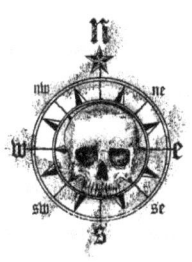

As with most of her imaginary dealings with the Culinary Council the whole process was instantaneous. So to those looking in—the expectant faces of Marcus and Patience, a prime example—her response appeared without any hint of hesitation.

'I'd like that very much,' Beatrice said.

'Then it's a date?' he said, his cheeks slightly pink.

'I guess it is,' Beatrice replied, her own cheeks several shades deeper.

'See you at the flagpole at, say, 8pm?' Marcus suggested.

'I'll be here,' Beatrice said. The light-headedness was back with a vengeance.

Marcus nodded, grinned and turned away. Had he turned back he would have seen Patience jump up and punch the air in silent triumph.

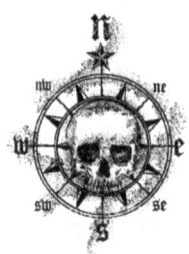

Agnes picked up the tale where Maud had left it. The librarian's voice was quiet, as though she was setting a good example regarding library etiquette. As Agnes spoke, Elmo and Lucas could see that Maud's demeanour was a mix of melancholy and wonder.

'As Maud has already said, we celebrate our memories of Klaus every Halloween,' she said. 'And the anniversary has come and gone without incident until last year's festival.'

'Really?' said Elmo. 'What happened last year?'

'I was walking through the library and suddenly I could hear Klaus. His voice came to me through in my hearing aids.'

'Wow,' Lucas said. 'It wasn't interference or something?'

'I thought that too at first, but it was Klaus,' Agnes said with conviction. 'I recognised his voice immediately. Yes, it was faint and garbled, but I knew it was definitely him. And that was before Zachery Tyrell turned up at my door.'

'Who was Zachary Tyrell?' Growing up in a village as small as Dorsal Finn meant that Lucas and Elmo knew most people. And the name *Zachery Tyrell* did not make the list.

At Lucas' question Agnes appeared uncomfortable. She shivered on the spot and wrapped her arms about herself as though trying to stave off an unexpected chill.

'He was ghost hunter,' she said after taking a deep breath.

'Oh, wow,' Lucas whispered. 'Are you saying that you were hearing Klaus' *ghost*?'

'You have to remember, young Lucas, that at the time I didn't know what to think,' Agnes said softly. Like Maud, the librarian's eyes seemed distant, as though her mind was straddling the past and the present.

'So you brought in Tyrell to rule it out?' Elmo guessed.

'Zachery Tyrell came to me,' Agnes said. There was irritation in her voice as she said the ghost hunter's name. 'He pitched up here a few days before

Halloween and claimed that he could hear voices. He called it *Clairaudience.*'

'I've heard of that,' Elmo said. 'It's when people can hear things—voices—outside the normal range. People like mediums and spiritualists. Is that what Tyrell was?'

'We ain't sure what that man was,' Maud chipped in. 'Nor his true intentions. We just saw what the bugger did when he got inside this library. An' what came after.'

'So what *did* he do?' Lucas said. His legs were swinging again with barely suppressed excitement.

'He claimed that he could hear Klaus' voice too,' Agnes continued. 'And that he was saying my name. He'd tracked me down in order to help me. But it was all a ruse of some sort—a means to get access to the library. He insisted that he must exorcise the spirit that was dwelling here.'

'And did he?' Elmo asked.

'No, young Elmo,' Agnes sighed. 'The only thing Zachery Tyrell did was make matters worse.'

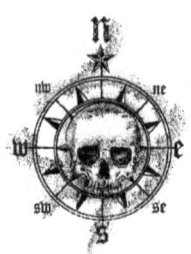

Elsewhere in the hut, Gideon Codd managed to steer Frobisher through the crowds of people who he was certain had only attended for a free meal. It was Codd's nature to feel somewhat superior to those about him.

In reality, he found the bulk of those he served a total embarrassment. There seemed to be an inability for most of the community to filter out contention before they opened their mouths. Codd was at a point where he was about to relax when he saw Dorsal Finn's finest example of tactlessness heading directly for them.

Edna Duffy was a short, thin lady. She was sixty years old and had pale skin and deep brown eyes that sank into heavy lids. Irrespective of the weather, she often wore a headscarf over her grey, bobbed hair. Today this headscarf was a sky blue to honour the event.

Edna was a woman with a sad past. A child had been lost to her. Eric had died in a boating accident when he was only five years old. She blamed Simon, her husband, as he could not pull the struggling boy out of the churning Atlantic currents, despite several attempts. It soured their marriage for some time. Edna took out her pain and misery on Simon, and then her emotions festered to the point where bitterness became her guiding principle, and the affairs of others filled the emptiness of her own life. Most townsfolk understood this, Edna was able to poke and pry without quarter; much to the irritation of Codd.

Like a heat-seeking missile streaking towards its target, Edna homed in on Codd and Frobisher, intercepting any attempt the mayor made to outmanoeuvre her.

'Ah! Mister Frobisher,' Edna said standing in front of the *Blue Thunder* leader. Frobisher towered over her but Edna was as tenacious as she was thick skinned.

'Well hello,' Frobisher beamed. 'I don't believe I've had the pleasure.'

'Quite,' said Edna coolly. 'Edna Duffy.' She offered a tiny hand. Her fingers were like pale twigs and were suddenly lost in Frobisher's huge hand.

'Yes,' Codd said quickly. 'There we go then. Now you've met our highly influential patron, perhaps you can sort of push off, Edna?'

'The whole town is very intrigued by your commitment,' Edna said.

'And why would I not wish to invest in this wonderful place, Edna?' Frobisher said.

'Many reasons come to mind,' she said. 'It's history for one.'

'As I have said to Mayor Codd, I am familiar with the heritage of this town,' Frobisher said cordially.

'Then you know Dorsal Finn was founded on tragedy?' When Edna talked her head bobbed up and down. Given that she talked a lot, her head did a lot of bobbing, making her look like a small bird foraging for worms.

'Indeed. The clipper, Charlotte Elizabeth, dashed on the rocks in 1806.' Frobisher replied. 'And the tragic death of the Pontefract heir, Julian, I believe?

'Lured to its death by a false beacon,' Edna said with a conspiratorial whisper. 'For the sake of insurance money.'

'We all know the sorry tale,' Codd huffed.

'The devil is always in the detail as they say,' Frobisher said softly. This had Edna's head bouncing up and down on her scrawny neck like a faulty Pez dispenser.

'Exactly,' Edna said. 'The Pontefract family built this town out of guilt and attrition. That is a fact plain and simple. No one here can deny it.'

'No one but you is raising it as an issue,' Codd said.

'And that is why history repeats,' Edna said firmly. 'Such things are never truly challenged. Thus, wayward Xavier Pontefract tried to stage the very same tragedy years later in order to kill his own twin brother and steal his identity. And reclaim the inheritance denied to him by his estranged family.'

'And where is this Xavier Pontefract now?' Frobisher asked. The intrigue made his eyes sparkle.

'Dead,' Edna said. 'At the hands of the Beecham girl no less. Pontefract trapped her on top of the lighthouse on The Bluff; tried to throw her to the sea after she and her friends thwarted his plans. But that youngster was resilient. He fell trying to kill her, and instead the ocean claimed him. Good riddance to bad rubbish. There, I've said it!'

'It's stopping you saying it that's the issue,' Codd muttered.

'Sorry?' said Edna.

'Shall we move on?' said Codd to Frobisher with some urgency.

'Nice to have met you, Mrs Duffy,' Frobisher said. 'And don't forget to watch the *Blue Thunder* address on TV this coming weekend.'

Codd and Frobisher disappeared into the throng, leaving Edna and her bobbing head gawping after them.

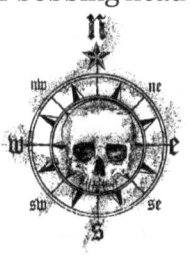

Back in the library, Agnes continued her story to a fascinated audience. Though Dennis and Albert were already party to it, the two men still appeared captivated.

'Tyrell came here on Halloween and asked that he was given privacy to perform the exorcism. Something about cluttering the astral plane or some hogwash like that,' Agnes said. 'But there was something about the man that still left me uncertain. So I called Maud and we snuck into the library and watched him conduct his ritual. Then *it* happened.'

'What?' Elmo breathed.

'The storm came,' Agnes said cryptically. 'Thunder and lightning but no rain.'

'An electrical storm?' Lucas said. 'And that's unusual because—?'

'It happened *inside* the library,' Agnes said.

'Okay,' Elmo said. 'That's going to the top of our 'pretty unusual' list.'

'There was green goo running down the walls. Then there was lightning, and it came from the ceiling and the walls at first,' Agnes said with a degree of anxiety. 'Then it all channeled through Tyrell; a lightning bolt struck his head and poured from his eyes, his mouth, and then struck the back wall of the Historical Fiction section, punching a hole in the wall.'

At this, Lucas and Elmo's eyes went towards the displaced bookcases as Agnes continued,

'Tyrell was left unconscious and taken to *Ashby on Sea General Hospital*,' she said. 'I believe he remains there to this day, still in the same sorry state.'

'And what *was* behind the wall?' Elmo said.

'That brings us to the reason why we called ye,' said Maud. 'Come an' have a look-see.'

The group approached the rear wall of the Historical Fiction section. Lucas could see that an ugly diagonal gash now scarred the magnolia paintwork, and there was enough of a gap to see a recess beyond.

'What's inside there?' Lucas said.

'A reluctant secret,' Maud said. 'An' a past that doesn't seem content with keepin' its peace.'

Dennis used his might to completely remove the bookcase and it was pretty evident that there wouldn't be any sealing the room again in a hurry.

'You sure you want to pursue this?' Albert softly asked Maud and Agnes. 'Maud? Is this what you *really* want?'

'It isn't what any of us *want*, Albert,' she sighed. 'But it's what we've been dealt. Let's see if we can play it to the end.'

'From what you've told us,' Albert said rubbing at his moustache, 'there's no putting the lid back on this once it's opened.'

'Just do it, Albert,' Agnes said sternly.

Albert nodded, pained by the hopelessness in Maud's eyes, and impressed with the resolve shown by the librarian. He turned to Dennis.

'Do it, Dennis.'

'That's if ye're happy to get involved in our mess,' Maud said solemnly.

'All I need to ask is if what we're doin' is right or wrong,' Dennis said gruffly. 'An' I'm figurin' that Maud Postlethwaite an' Agnes Clutterbuck ain't got no wrong in 'em. So I guess me choices are crystal.'

'Good on ye, Dennis,' Maud said gratefully.

'Then let me just clear some more space, young Lucas,' Dennis said bringing his bulk to bear against the damaged wall. The plaster board gave way with a crisp crunching sound, spilling dust over the big man's shoulders.

'Bit embarassin' how easy that was to bring down,' he said picking bits of plaster out of his beard and wild wiry hair.

'Can't plaster over what don't want to be hidden, Dennis,' Maud said.

'Got a flashlight?' Albert said to Agnes who produced a high powered torch from a nearby shelf almost instantly.

She powered up the bulb and aimed it into an antechamber. The group stepped through the hole where the past and the present shared company for the first time in several months.

CHAPTER FIVE
HANSEL & GRETEL

THE ROOM WAS several square feet, with walls made from red bricks dulled by tangled cobwebs. A mist of fine plaster dust was turned to glittering fire under the beam of Agnes' torch. But the bright fog didn't distract them from the bold, red and gothic lettering painted upon the back wall. The text stood out despite the gossamer veneer.

In this place
Guilt forges the script
Making way
For the Cryptic Crypt
A bird in hand
Owes much to fate
Pulling open long locked gates

'Come on up here and take a look at this, young Lucas,' Agnes said next to Dennis. The big man held the flashlight rock-steady so that the lettering on the wall was washed in creamy yellow.

Lucas came to stand with them, his face scrunched with fascination.

'Look at that symbol underneath the writing,' Elmo said quietly. But they had all already seen it; etched upon the old, dusty brickwork, a white eagle, wings frozen in flight, clutching in its talons an iconic symbol of evil:

A black Swastika.

'This is so not cool,' Lucas said as he looked upon the symbol.

'I know it's a shock,' Maud said. 'Let's just see what yer can make of it an' we'll get out of this place.'

Lucas nodded and scanned the script for a few minutes.

'I'm not seeing any anagrams,' he said, scratching his head. 'One thing that hits me is it's written in English, but there's a Nazi Swastika here.'

'What ye thinkin'?' Maud said.

'That, maybe, the person who wrote this may have been from Dorsal Finn,' Lucas said.

There was a long pause as the adults looked at each other.

'Or,' Lucas continued, 'it was written by someone to warn people already here.'

'Warn them of what?' Albert asked, his eyes never leaving the writing on the wall.

'Well let's take it at face value,' Lucas replied. 'What if someone was forced into doing something here—something they didn't want to do but felt so guilty they had no other choice? Something to do with this *Cryptic Crypt*, whatever that is.'

'Klaus?' Agnes said before she'd realised.

'Are we sayin' that this was written by Klaus Hessel?' Maud said.

'Your Luftwaffe pilot?' Albert asked. 'Is that possible? How could he do all of this without you two knowing it?'

'And what did he have to feel guilty about?' Agnes said.

'War changes what is right and wrong,' Albert said pointedly. 'The mind deals with such things in different ways.'

'I ain't sayin' what was troublin' Klaus' mind but there's only one way he could've done all this,' replied Maud pensively. 'No matter what we thought in that summer of nineteen-forty-two, me an' Agnes weren't the only ones who knew he was here.'

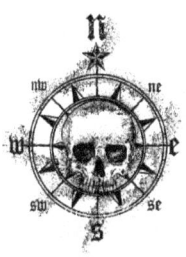

'So if Hessel is the person who wrote this message, then the rest of it may have meaning to you and Agnes,' Albert said rubbing a handkerchief across his dusty brow.

'Yeah,' Lucas concurred. 'The bit about "a bird in hand" for example. That could have reference to the Nazi eagle. Did he ever give you anything with an eagle on it?'

Maud gave Lucas a smile, her eyes brimming with surprise and pride. But there was also sadness. Maud and Agnes were at once both catapulted back to the time, on a beach at twilight with the waves lapping lazily against the shore and a purloined rowing boat anchored in the surf; the time when they said their farewells to Klaus. In that final moment, as the wind tousled their hair and sent sea spray into their faces, he'd handed a small token of his gratitude; a token that Agnes kept with her at all times.

'Ye're a canny lad, Lucas Walker,' she whispered. Maud turned to Agnes.

'Ye got yer gift handy?'

'Yes,' Agnes said, slipping her hand into the inside pocket of her purple body warmer. When she removed it she brought with it an ornate silver badge which she presented to her captivated audience.

It was palm-sized, a silver and black eagle in relief clutching a laurel with the vile image of the Nazi Swastika in its talons.

'Luftwaffe emblem,' Albert said. 'These were usually pinned on the aircrew's flight suits.'

'Not a Nazi symbol then?' Elmo asked.

'Not a true symbol,' Albert admitted. 'But when it comes down to it, what it represents is the same.'

'We can't talk in absolutes, Albert,' Agnes said defensively. 'Not every German was a Nazi. Klaus was an airman at war. He did what he was told; he did his duty.'

'You're right, Agnes,' replied Albert, 'we can't talk in absolutes. As I said, everything is tested in times of war. Duty is one of those things. Judgment is another. Since we're just starting out here I'll reserve my judgment. *For now.*'

'I think you're being a little unfair, Albert,' Agnes said. 'Kurt was our friend.'

'I'm pleased for you both,' Albert said. 'But don't forget it was a time where a lot of people *lost* friends and *family.* '

'No one's disputin' that,' Maud said gently. 'I know what you lost durin' the war. No one is goin' to forget that.'

'Least of all me, Maud,' Albert said with barely suppressed bitterness. 'Let's just get on with this.'

'You old people carry more baggage than Patience on a camping trip,' Lucas said flatly.

Maud winked at him and nodded. 'Aye, we're weird, no doubt about it,' she said wearily.

Lucas stepped up to the wall and ran his fingers across its surface, the action leaving a layer of brick dust on his finger tips. But there was little else to suggest that Agnes' brooch would be of any use here. The thought of the brooch made him reach up for its painted counterpart on the wall.

As he traced his hand over the Nazi symbol, he felt something give and the surface beneath the emblem shifted slightly backwards.

'Hey!' he called out. 'One of these bricks are loose.'

'Let's see if I can make a few more rattle, lad,' Dennis said stepping up and placing a big hand on the recessed brickwork. He shoved hard until the whole wall retracted several feet, while a curtain of dust fell from above.

'Look at the floor.' Elmo pointed.

The wall had receded to reveal a deep trench, and inside was a man sized cylinder.

'What's that?' Lucas asked as, with a series of

grunts and several swear words, Dennis stooped and manhandled the pod out of the trench.

The cylinder was mottled grey with a familiar, faded white eagle and Swastika emblazoned on its surface. At one end was a series of metal hoops and, in the middle, a locking mechanism.

'It's a drop pod,' Albert said. 'They were used to drop supplies to soldiers behind enemy lines during the war.'

'Well this bugger's bleedin' heavy,' Dennis said patting his hand on the cylinder's metal body. 'I'll bet it must have somethin' still in it.'

'Then let's take a look at what Hessel left for us,' Albert said reaching for the locking switch

As he turned it, everyone held their breath.

As Beatrice, Patience and Thomas made their way back to *Postlethwaite and Beecham's News and Chocolate Emporium* it was hard to believe that anything could dampen their good spirits.

But it only took one person to do exactly that, and, as per usual, that person was Edward Chorley.

To say Edward was mean spirited was like saying the universe was big or water was wet. He was a bully of the vilest kind, content only to make the lives of those more vulnerable a misery.

During his short life, Edward had targeted all of The Newshounds but saved the bulk of his bitterness for newcomers. Beatrice had experienced this when she'd first arrived in town. The staunch resolve of her friends had fended him off because, like all bullies, Chorley was a coward. This wasn't to say he didn't still aim the odd snide comment (or in Beatrice's case, brazenly aimed an insult) in their direction. But Chorley had learned that The Newshounds used their friendship to bat away his vitriol, reducing it to harmless pettiness.

Charles Chorley, Edward's infamous father, had once been a solicitor in Dorsal Finn. At the point where Xavier Pontefract was plotting the demise of his brother, Chorley senior was overseeing the Pontefract estate. There had been suggestions that Edward's father had been involved in the whole affair and had been exiled from the town. For some time the whole family, including Edward's mother and his older brother, Stewart, had gone with their father. Yet the Chorley's were always used to the finer life and valued their prestige above everything else. It was this that had led to Edward's mother moving back to the village where she put forward a case to Gideon Codd that she and her children should not be punished for the sake of her husband's skulduggery. The case had been won, Codd was fond of the Chorley's deep down, especially Edward's mother. They did indeed move back, but not before Stewart ended up in youth offender services for delinquent behaviour. What had happened to Charles Chorley no one, not even Mayor Codd, could say.

But at that moment, Edward was in full flight.

The girl who now stood with her back against the

wall of *Tardebigge's Bed and Breakfast*—as Edward Chorley ranted at her—knew nothing of Edward's past, but was finding out firsthand what remained of his vile character.

She was small, her hair—long and the colour of summer straw—was pulled into a ponytail. Despite her fear, the girl's dark eyes remained fixed on her tormentor.

'Are you stupid, or something?' Chorley yelled as his face flushed red with anger beneath his blonde hair. 'That's what you are, isn't it? Deaf and dumb! Stupid deaf and dumb, idiot!'

Reviled by his outburst, Beatrice and Patience ran to the girl's aid. As they approached, Beatrice could see the terror in the girl's face, but there was something else, a defiant fire blazed in her deep, brown eyes. Yes, she was scared, but she was standing her ground. Only Chorley's physical presence prevented her from moving.

'Edward!' Beatrice ran up and put herself between Chorley and the girl. 'Have you finally lost it?'

'You stay out of this, *Coppertop*,' Chorley sneered in Beatrice's face. 'This hasn't got anything to do with you.'

Given the opportunity, the girl moved away from the wall and ran off down the street, almost bowling Patience and Thomas over in the process.

Edward made to follow but Beatrice blocked his way.

'Get out of the way, *Coppertop*,' he snapped, but the venom had gone out of his tone. Beatrice wasn't scared of him and Chorley knew this all too well.

'Not going to happen,' Beatrice said. 'You leave her alone.'

'Or what?' Chorley scoffed. 'You going to set that pig-ugly face on me?'

There was hatred in his eyes but the fight had gone out of them. 'Have it your way, *Coppertop*. Emily Hannigan will keep.'

At this, he shoved past Beatrice, knocking her a few steps backwards. As he sloped past Thomas, Beatrice's brother eyed him with contempt.

'What you looking at, weirdo' Chorley said angrily.

'Evil begets evil, vile fiend,' Thomas said, his blue eyes never leaving Chorley's. To Beatrice's surprise, Edward paused for a few seconds and then hurried off. He did not look back.

'What was that all about?' Patience said to Thomas. 'Are you hexing Edward Chorley, Tom?'

Thomas thought about this for a second and then smiled.

But he kept his thoughts to himself.

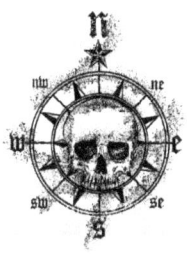

They found the girl called Emily Hannigan weeping as she sat on a bench facing the promenade. Overhead, the gulls flew in lazy circles, unaware of the human misery playing out below.

'We'd better go see if she's okay,' Beatrice said to them. No one disagreed.

Emily didn't look up at their approach; she

continued to hold her hands to her face as her shoulders bobbed in time with small, barely perceivable sobs.

'Hello there,' Beatrice said softly. 'Are you okay?'

Emily remained behind her hands. Beatrice crouched and placed a hand gently on the girl's shoulder.

Emily jolted, her hands falling away from her face, and for a moment Beatrice thought the girl was going to take off again. But as soon as Emily's eyes fell upon Beatrice, she relaxed and nodded.

'Are you okay?' Beatrice asked again.

Emily shook her head causing hair to sweep past her shoulders, yet her eyes remained blank. Then Emily held up a hand, formed a pistol shape with the index and middle finger then placed these fingers flat against her right ear.

Now it was Beatrice's turn to appear bemused. She was rescued immediately by Patience.

'Oh, *BSL*,' Patience said excitedly.

'Wash your mouth out, young lady!' Thomas said in disapproval.

'No, I mean *British Sign Language*,' Patience explained. 'Emily is deaf.'

'Oh,' Beatrice said, suddenly feeling helpless.

'Here,' Patience said. 'Let me.'

Patience waved her right arm to gain Emily's attention and then introduced herself using a series of hand gestures. It shouldn't have surprised Beatrice that Patience knew BSL. When it came to languages, her friend was a sponge. It often occurred to Beatrice to ask Patience just how many languages she could speak, but the occasion never seemed to arise.

But Beatrice wasn't the only one surprised by Patience's use of BSL. Emily was so impressed she'd asked Patience if she, too, were deaf and, if not, did she have any deaf family members. She also complimented Patience's skill and thanked her for taking the time to learn her language. At this latter comment, Patience gave Emily a big hug and told her that it was a privilege to be able to finally use BSL.

Patience introduced Beatrice and Thomas. They gleaned that Emily had moved to Dorsal Finn only a few weeks ago. To the shock of Beatrice and Patience, Emily informed them her father was the new headmaster of Dorsal Finn High school, and due to take up post in a few weeks time.

Just as Beatrice was about to ask another question she remembered the noon rendezvous with Crazy Colin.

'I have to get you back home,' she said to Thomas. 'Does Emily want to come with us to see Colin?'

Patience asked the question and Emily stood and gave Beatrice a warm smile, she followed this with an embrace.

'I guess that's a *yes*,' Beatrice thought.

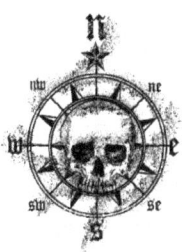

There were three items inside the drop pod. The first was a metal box that may once have been the colour of steel, but had dulled with time. Next, there were clothes—shirts and trousers and a long coat. It was mildewed and damp and almost fell apart in Maud's hands when she lifted the items from their metal coffin. The last item was actually a soggy hybrid of paper and card to which Lucas gave special attention. On closer scrutiny the papers were too damaged to make out even the most rudimentary images on their pulped surface.

'No luck with any of this stuff,' he said in a dejected tone.

'Let's see if an extra layer helped save the contents of this,' Agnes said taking the steel box from Dennis and retreating back into the library. The adults all filed out after her, but Lucas lingered, not wanting to leave the pulped sheets of paper behind. Instead he delved into his rucksack and pulled out an A4 plastic sleeve currently occupied by a piece of school work. He removed this and stuffed it back into a side pocket. Then, he carefully picked up the pulped sheets of green paper and brown card, placing them carefully in the plastic sleeve. His aim was to dry them out and see if any information remained.

Once he'd done this, he went out to the library, leaving the room to its demons.

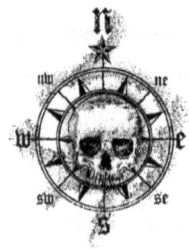

Beatrice, Patience, and Emily headed off to the harbour. They had left Thomas back at home having watched him tear into the cottage to find the nearest DVD player. Beatrice had closed the front door on The Blue Bolt's fast punchy soundtrack, knowing that Thomas would be lost in this fantastic world for many hours to come.

In the walk to seek out Crazy Colin, Beatrice learned more about being deaf and a lot more about Emily. The girl was able to speak clearly and her ability to lip read was remarkable. It was only on a few occasions where Beatrice had looked away during delivery of a sentence where Emily would stop and ask her to repeat it.

It fascinated Beatrice to learn that many deaf people didn't consider their deafness a disability at all. This was the misconception of what Emily called the *Hearing World*. Those who could hear often saw deaf people as ill and treated them that way. Deaf people had been fighting against this misconception for years.

Emily told them that deafness was a cultural matter, defined by its language. There were deaf writers, filmmakers, athletes, comedians, and poets. Deafness wasn't an illness—it was a way of life.

Emily considered herself lucky, and Beatrice did have to force herself to understand this concept.

'BSL is recognised as the UK's fourth language,' Patience explained. 'It also has its own syntax and removes all the stuff that makes the spoken word so complex.'

'Like what?' Beatrice asked.

'If you were to ask "*what is your name?*" in BSL you would sign only "*name what?*".'

'So it simplifies the way we communicate?'

'Yes.'

'The boys will be pleased,' Beatrice laughed. 'They struggle at the best of times.'

Emily appeared a lot more relaxed now that she was in friendlier company, and by the time the three of them reached the port, Beatrice knew she had made another firm friend. The day really was panning out nicely.

But as is so often the case, different people have different days. And in another part of Dorsal Finn someone was having the kind of day that was in dire need of repair.

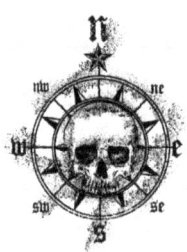

The man sitting at a table outside *The Salty Seadog Inn* stared at the harbour through a pair of expensive sunglasses. The table was on a veranda that overlooked the harbour walls, his fingers beat out a small rhythm on the gingham tablecloth that had been pinned to the round table top. The glass of beer in front of him remained untouched; the froth nothing more than thin white film. Not that this mattered. The seat at the table, the glass of flat beer, these were just a ruse; a cloak of normality behind which the man watching the boats below could hide.

The man wasn't interested in all the boats bobbing

lazily upon the water. He was gazing intently at one boat in particular—the thirty-footer known as *The Elvis*. Like all people of his age, the man had a history. But unlike most, the roots of his past were a blend of fierce secrecy and lies.

'Are these seats taken?'

For a few seconds, the man looked up at the newcomers standing over him before gesturing for them to sit down.

Two children—a boy and a girl, no more than ten years old, and both with vivid ice blue eyes and platinum blonde hair—took up their places opposite. The children had smiles that remained in place.

'Welcome, Hansel,' the man said to the young boy, who replied with a nod of his head. The man then turned to the girl, 'Welcome, Gretel.' The young girl mirrored her brother's response. 'And how are you both, this fine afternoon?' the man asked.

'Keen,' said Gretel.

'That is good to hear, my dear girl,' the man laughed. 'I have a surprise for you both.'

'That sounds nice,' said Hansel, his smile remaining as though painted in place.

'It will be,' the man assured them. 'How do you feel about a boat trip?'

'Can we play while we're on the boat?' Gretel asked.

'Of course,' the man said. 'If you are good.'

'We are *always* good,' Gretel said.

'Unless you *wish* us to be naughty,' Hansel added. 'Do you wish us to be naughty on the boat?'

'Most definitely,' the man replied, and echoed their smiles.

CHAPTER SIX
THE TRIDENT

AT **DORSAL FINN** library, the metal box retrieved from the drop pod sat innocuously on the reception counter, subjected to the curious gaze of its six liberators.

They had found out quickly that the lock on the box was unconventional: a circle with three holes, two at the top and one at the bottom, creating an inverted triangle.

'I could get an FBH from me van to open it,' Dennis offered.

'FBH?' Elmo asked. 'Sounds major.'

'To you it means *Flippin' Big Hammer*,' Dennis laughed.

'Very major,' Elmo concluded.

'Now, now, Dennis,' Maud said. 'We don't want to be man-handlin' the box an' messin' with its innards now, do we? Kid's gloves are needed if we're goin' make sure nothin' that ain't already broken stays that way.'

'I guess so,' Dennis said after some thought.

Agnes was quiet and distant.

'What are ye thinkin' Agnes?' Maud asked.

'I can hear Klaus again,' Agnes said. 'He's so faint but he's there—that voice of his, strong and wilful. But I can't understand a word of it.'

Maud sensed her friend's frustration and placed a comforting hand on Agnes' arm.

'We'll get to the bottom of it,' Maud said softly.

'Part of me doesn't want to,' Ages admitted.

'Well we're huntin' with the bottom feeders already,' Dennis pointed out. 'There ain't no goin' topside 'til we're done.'

Lucas sat on the reception counter deep in thought. He turned the brooch over and over in his hands. It seemed weird holding onto something that had evoked so many emotions in people, especially adults. And those emotions had a badness to them, like fallen apples left to rot in the sun. But there was opportunity to change that; to drag some good from a dark past.

As he considered this, Lucas found the raised studs in the eagle's belly, and all became clear to him.

'This box belonged to Klaus,' Lucas said suddenly. 'Or he could certainly gain access to it. Look closer at the locking mechanism. See the three dents? The eagle on this brooch has three studs on it. The gift Klaus gave to you is a key; a key to open this very box.'

'Then let's get the thing open,' Albert said.

Lucas reversed the brooch and inserted it into the mechanism, lining up the holes with their corresponding studs. Once he felt them engage, he turned the brooch using the pin for purchase. At first there was resistance, time eager to retain its hold on the past. But with a squeal, the old lock relented and the lid popped open like an old fashioned Jack in the Box.

And, cautiously, they all peered inside.

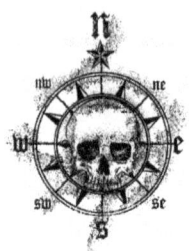

The two lobsters waved their huge claws languidly in a bucket, their green bodies writhing beneath the water.

'So what do ye think?' Colin said with a triumphant grin.

'They're beautiful,' Beatrice said. 'Perfect, in fact.'

'Yes,' agreed Patience with a sniff. 'Very green. I have a Dior silk summer dress the same colour.'

'These things would be costin' a similar price at market,' Colin said. 'Ol' Cochran did me a deal since he's just netted a charter to Rogue Rock.'

Beatrice looked at Colin as though he was speaking a foreign language.

'I'm tellin' ye that someone has just paid for a trip to check out Bishop's Cragg. And for a handsome amount, too, judgin' by the discount Cochran gave me on these critters.'

'So the money we gave was enough?' Patience said sounding relieved.

'Ample,' Colin said. He held out his hand. It was stuffed with money.

'My father wouldn't hear of it.'

'Your father isn't here to listen,' Colin said bluntly. 'I do things or I don't. Money ain't my keeper an' never has been. Nor will it become my keeper now I'm headin' fer me twilight years.'

He handed the surplus money over, Patience took it but she was still reluctant.

'Thanks for sorting that out for us, Colin,' Beatrice said.

'Thank me by makin' sommat special with them beauties, Beatrice Beecham,' he said with a wink.

'I will. I promise.'

'Then that will be me reward for today,' Colin said. 'After a nice shot of rum, that is.'

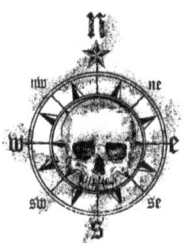

Out on the ocean, *The Elvis* cleaved a "V" in the tide as it headed towards open water.

In the wheel house, Cochran sat on a beaten leather chair, his hands firm on the throttle, jaw set tight as concentration took over. He'd spent his life on the sea and knew it deserved only the utmost respect. Riptides and weather fronts could change at a moment's notice. There was no room for error or distraction.

But despite this, he still loved his life. Days like today just reinforced this reality for him. A great catch, and now an unexpected charter out to Bishop's Cragg so that two kids could have a look at its bleak quarter of a mile landscape of sharp, slate grey rocks. Exposed to the ocean, nothing grew in that inhospitable place. Most of the time, not even the gulls stayed roosting there for long, and most of the older inhabitants considered the place cursed.

But what his kinsmen considered a curse, Cochran and Jimbo could now consider a boon—it was bringing in good money.

Even though his passengers were a little . . . odd.

The boy and girl sat astern, bright orange life jackets dwarfing their small frames and contrasting markedly with their *Blue Thunder Foundation* uniforms. They'd barely said a word since their guardian, a man with a big gold wristwatch, had secured the charter. Cochran couldn't put his finger on it, the kids were polite and well-spoken after all, but if he was forced to state his concern, he guessed it would be their eyes, and the eerie smile they both carried. He told himself to stop being silly, to stop ruining his good mood with such nonsense.

Bishop's Cragg rose from the water, its harsh shoreline hemmed with white foam. Cochran brought *The Elvis* to a full stop a hundred metres from the ragged island and called for Jimbo to weigh anchor.

'Okay, young 'uns,' he said to the boy and girl who were now standing and watching the rocks intensely. 'This is Bishop's Cragg. A more miserable excuse for an island you will not find this side of the Atlantic.'

'I think it is quite inspiring,' said the boy.

'We would like to walk on it,' said the girl.

'An' I'd like to walk on the moon,' Cochran laughed.

'But there's more chance of me doin' that than you two whelps goin' site seein' on *Rogue Rock*!'

'Yes, I would like to walk upon it very much' said the girl as though Cochran hadn't spoken at all.

And when Cochran looked at the young girl to tell her she was talking rubbish, her eyes locked upon his, and suddenly he didn't think she was talking rubbish at all. Instead he was consumed with the fact that what she said was the only thing that made sense.

'Yes, of course you should walk on it,' Cochran said, his voice monosyllabic.

'Stay here,' the girl said to the skipper. 'Wait for our return.'

Hansel came to his sister after he'd left Jimbo with the idea that he should stare at the horizon for the next half an hour in case a sea monster should emerge and sink them.

'Adults are so *suggestible*, aren't they,' he said to his sister.

'Aren't they just?' she replied. 'Now let's go and explore.'

The twins sat on the side of the boat, held hands and turned to face the glittering ocean.

Then they dropped into the writhing water.

No sooner had they bobbed to the surface, they began to swim, and their strokes were efficient and relentless; like machines powering through the water.

Within five minutes, Hansel and Gretel were pulling themselves from the waves, their breaths deep but regular. After a brief respite Gretel scanned the jagged horizon.

'Come, brother,' she said. 'It is time to find the *Trident*.'

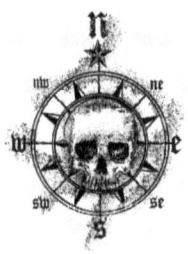

'Wow, is that a *real* dagger?' Lucas said reaching into the liberated metal box.

The knife had a black leather-bound handle and a tapered silver blade. Again there was a Swastika embossed into the handle.

'No doubt about it,' Albert said smacking Lucas' hand away. 'And you don't know how safe it is.'

'It's a knife with an accursed sign on it, Albert,' Maud said wryly. 'It isn't ever goin' to be anythin' other than dangerous.'

'Exactly,' Albert said looking at Lucas, wilfully ignoring the disappointment on the youth's face.

Albert reached in, gently lifted the knife out of the box, and placed it carefully on the counter. 'A German ceremonial dagger,' he observed. He then realised that the surface of the blade had been scored. 'These things usually had Nazi mottos on them. Any motto here has been filed off. Interesting.'

'More stuff underneath,' Elmo said. 'Looks like a bunch of papers.'

'Am I okay to touch those?' Lucas asked pointedly. No one replied. 'I'll take the collective and embarrassed silence as a "yes".'

Lucas removed two sheets of yellowed paper and laid them down separately next to the dagger. The jaundiced sheets revealed two illustrations. The first was a simple diagram:

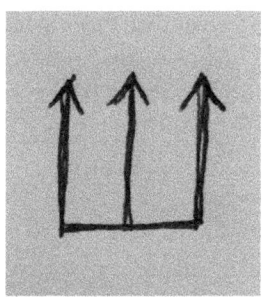

The other was a beautiful drawing in black ink of an underground chamber; rows of sculpted columns interlaced at the ceiling were supported by huge stone struts at their base. At one end there was a stone plinth and above this someone had written several sentences in German.

'I wonder what it means,' Lucas said frowning over the scrawled text.

'Hard to say,' Dennis said moving one of the sheets with a knobbly finger. 'It's all double Dutch t' me.'

'We need Patience,' Lucas said.

'We need more than that, lad,' Dennis said misunderstanding him.

'No, I mean *Patience Userkaf*. She'd be able to translate this. It has to be German right; given the odds?'

'Certainly looks like it,' Agnes agreed. 'What about the symbol? Unless I'm mistaken, I'd say that it has a runic quality to it.'

'Patience again?' Lucas offered.

'Or maybe not,' Elmo interjected. They all turned to look at him. The sudden attention made him flush a little. 'Er, guys? The group stare is giving my self-awareness issue *real* prominence right now.'

'Sorry, Elmo,' Agnes said. 'You know what we adults are like when it comes to gossip.'

'What you got in mind, big guy?' Lucas said.

'Cordelia Crust,' Elmo said.

'Who?' said Lucas.

'Viking expert,' Elmo said. 'She visited our school during history, remember?'

Lucas nodded after a few moments. 'Yeah, I remember. A right Rottweiler if I remember right.'

'She is socially challenged,' Elmo admitted. 'But we kinda hit it off after we did the Q+A session. She gave me her email address so she could send me her notes.'

'Think you can get in touch?' Agnes said.

'I can try,' Elmo said. 'Maybe set up a FaceTime meeting or something,' he added. 'If she'll agree. You okay if I share this stuff with her?'

'When ye're stuck down a hole ye're not goin' to complain about who's pullin' on the rescue rope,' said Maud. 'What say ye, Agnes?'

But Agnes wasn't listening. Or rather, Agnes was listening but not to those around her.

'Agnes?' Lucas said. 'Are you okay?'

'Klaus is in my head again,' the librarian said. 'But now he seems louder and less vague.'

'Can I suggest something?' Lucas said unexpectedly. He had a broad smile on his face.

'Go ahead,' Agnes said.

'It's pretty gross but I'm prepared to do it for the sake of a mystery,' he added.

'I can deal with mystery,' said Elmo. 'It's the suspense that kills me.'

Lucas told them his idea and they all agreed that as a concept it was really very good.

What Patience would think about it was another matter.

'There's no doubt about it.' Elmo grinned. 'This has a level of *suckishness* to it that is off the scale. Patience is going to just love you.'

'She must never know that this was my idea,' Lucas said. 'Or it's no mystery what she'll do to me!'

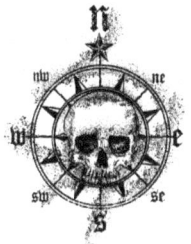

In the Intensive Care Unit of Ashby on Sea General Hospital, Zachary Tyrell was screaming. He was screaming because he was frightened and he was screaming because he was trapped.

To the nurses who cared for him, Tyrell was another patient being maintained on life support, a battery of boxes and tubes that made sure his body continued to function.

Continued to live.

The care he received was delivered with quiet respect and dignity. The nurse who currently mopped his brow with a cleansing wipe knew nothing of the war being fought inside his head. Tyrell's mind was very much alive, and the dangers he faced within this netherworld of swirling images and dark shadows were very real.

The event that had put him into a coma occurred in Dorsal Finn Library. It involved Tyrell's skills as a ghost hunter being bought as a ruse in order to evoke an event. The hapless Tyrell had been lured there under the promise of fame and fortune; final recognition that his abilities were to be recognised.

Tyrell had what his mother called *The Sight*. His mother had told him that such things were common in their bloodline. Yet it was an ability that had eluded him for many years, developing only when he'd had an accident—a head injury when he'd tripped and fallen down a flight of steps at Birmingham Grand Central Station. He lost consciousness and found *The Sight*. Days later he'd come around in a hospital bed after neurosurgery to release pressure in his bruised and inflamed brain.

Tyrell had heard voices, strange garbled murmurings that had eventually cleared until he could hear the protestations of a man repeating a Germanic phrase over and over, and names too—Agnes Clutterbuck and Maud Postlethwaite.

Then the email had come through. It was from someone known to him only as The Professor. Tyrell was asked if he'd ever experienced any extra sensory perception; or if he could hear strange voices speaking in foreign languages. Tyrell admitted that he could indeed do such things. Thus he was employed to go to Dorsal Finn and engage with the very people sent to him via *The Sight*.

But something had gone wrong. He knew this before his abilities had forged a connection with the dark thing at the heart of Dorsal Finn. Far from finding out the source of the voices in the library, Tyrell had merely opened a portal through which he was able to commune with evil. The Professor was nothing more than subterfuge, in order to begin events that were now coming to fruition.

Yes, Tyrell had known things were too good to be true and yet not acted upon his instincts. Now he was paying the price, duped and vulnerable; nothing more than a receptacle where seeds had been planted. Soon, someone was destined to come and reap the harvest, and his purpose would be served.

And he longed for that day to come. Because then the thing that held him captive within his own withering and useless carcass would allow him to die.

In the world of the Dark Heart, mercy had limited form.

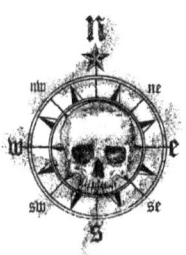

The three girls made their way to Emily's house, Beatrice carrying a pale green bucket housing two sedate lobsters. At Emily's insistence Beatrice and Patience waved her off on a street corner a hundred metres from her home. It was a polite-looking house made of red brick and interspersed with leaded windows. In many ways its structure reminded Beatrice of Dorsal Finn High school and, had she not known, it would not have been any surprise if someone had told her teachers lived there.

To their surprise Emily made them promise that they wouldn't tell anyone about Chorley's attitude towards her, making Beatrice suspect that Emily didn't intend telling her parents either.

'She's very brave,' Beatrice commented as they watched the girl walking away from them.

'Emily is like a lot of deaf people,' Patience said. 'She's proud. I guess they have had to be strong.'

'How come?' Beatrice said. 'If people think someone deaf is ill, you'd think that they'd get lots of help.'

'I remember a deaf history lesson when I took the BSL course. Deaf people have had a pretty bad deal from the hearing world. In the 19th Century, deaf people weren't allowed to marry other deaf people in case they had deaf children. Sign language was banned in European schools. Deaf kids were made to sit on their hands and learn to communicate by reading lips alone. If they were caught signing in school, teachers would cane their hands.'

'That's terrible,' Beatrice said aghast.

'That's only part of it,' Patience said. 'So I guess that's why Emily wants us to keep quiet about all of this. She wants to stand up for herself, fight her own battles.'

'I think she should be part of The Newshounds,' Beatrice said. 'What do you think?'

'We'd have to run it by Lucas and Elmo,' Patience said thoughtfully. 'And Emily would have to agree, of course.'

'Do you think she'd not want to join?'

'We can only offer.'

'Speaking of the boys, I wonder what they've been up to all day.' Beatrice said.

'Loafing around is my guess,' Patience replied. 'I'll give them a call. Hopefully they can still remember how to walk.'

The two girls headed to Crab Mill Terrace, their laughter dancing on the air.

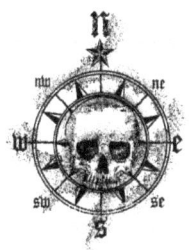

Later that afternoon, The Newshounds sat on their favourite spot in the whole world. The bluff—Monument Point to those old enough to remember—overlooked the crescent shaped enclave in which the village nestled. The wind tousled the grass, and from the top of the nearby lighthouse, the creak of a weather vane could be heard in between huge, blustery blasts.

The area had got its name from a shaft of grey granite that commemorated the loss of the clipper Charlotte Elizabeth, which had sunk when she smashed against the jagged rocks two hundred metres below. The inscription on the monument listed the names of those lost at sea. Amongst them was Julian Pontefract, the relative of Dorsal Finn's patrons who had been inadvertently killed when, according to rumour, the Pontefract's had deliberately scuttled the clipper in order to claim on insurance during financial difficulties. In their grief and guilt the Pontefracts had used the money from the insurance to build the village. All of this was a taboo subject, a tale for folk to whisper in bars and tea rooms. Unless, of course, you went by the name of Edna Duffy.

'Well you guys have been busy,' Beatrice said to Lucas and Elmo.

'You could say that since it's accurate,' Lucas said. 'We were just as surprised to get the call as anyone else. Maud and Agnes must trust us big time.'

'And why shouldn't they?' Patience interjected earnestly. 'Are we not The Newshounds, proponents of mystery and suspense?'

'Don't forget to put *modest* on our list of attributes,' Elmo said with a wink.

Beatrice remained in deep thought. So much had happened in such a short space of time. It was hard to digest it all in one sitting. No sooner had Patience contacted Lucas on his cell phone when he'd told her that The Newshounds needed to meet and discuss *developments* at the library relating to a secret room and Agnes' voices in her hearing aids.

'I can't believe Maud and Agnes were able to keep all of this hidden for so long,' said Beatrice. 'We could've helped them sooner if we'd known.'

'They weren't up for sharing before now, Bea,' Elmo said. 'You know what adults are like. They think they know everything.'

Beatrice considered the emotions both Maud and Agnes must have been feeling, and part of her grieved for them. It made her heart heavy and left a cold, watery feeling in her stomach.

'So what's the plan?' Beatrice said.

'The adults have had to go back to doing whatever it is adults do during daylight hours,' Lucas said. 'I've got the contents of the box, minus a ceremonial dagger that Albert has in safe keeping. Other than a hole in the library wall, nothing strange has happened to those outside of the loop, right?'

They all fell into a thoughtful silence as they considered Lucas' words. The strong breeze seized the moment; with a lion's roar it whirled about them and tugged at their clothes.

'So where do we go from here?' Patience finally said.

'Well, funny you should ask that, because we're reliant on your absolutely fantastic skill with languages,' Lucas said.

'You're softening me up for something bad, aren't you?'

'Well, that would be based on what you call "bad" wouldn't it?' Lucas said.

'I'll base it on whether *you* would do it,' Patience said sternly.

'I would,' Lucas said. 'If *I* were *you*.'

'Sneaky,' Patience said. 'What is it?'

'Well, the first bit is to examine the sheets of writing and the blueprints from the box,' Lucas said. 'Then I'll try and dry of the wads of paper I got from the drop pod and see if there's anything that'll help us.'

'Help us do *what*, though, bro?' Elmo enquired.

'Piece together a past,' Beatrice suggested.

'Bob-on, Bea,' Lucas smiled warmly. But Beatrice noticed that his eyes only flitted across her face as though he were avoiding her stare.

'If we can get an idea of what this is all about, then it'll help us find out what we're up against,' he said instead.

'So the first bit is translating sheets of text that may or may not be German?' Patience clarified. 'Shouldn't be too hard. Although I do better translating spoken words than text.'

'I'm glad to hear that,' Lucas said cheerily. 'Because the second bit is about translating the spoken words of one Klaus Hessel.'

'And how do I go about doing that?' Patience said. 'Do you have a recording?'

'The only way would be to use the appliances that tend to pick him up,' Lucas muttered.

'Could you say that again Professor Vague, because I could've sworn you were implying that I should wear Agnes' hearing aid, which is the most absurd—not to mention grossest—thing to ask.'

Lucas' weak smile confirmed her fears almost immediately.

'You owe me, Walker,' she scolded.

'He said you'd understand,' Elmo said. 'But I thought it was wishful thinking.'

'You really don't wish to know what I'm thinking at the moment,' Patience glared at both of the boys. 'So I've got to get Agnes' hearing aids and wear them.' Patience shuddered. 'There are some things that should never happen; friends or no friends.'

'If it's any consolation, I have Agnes' aids here,' Lucas said, humbly handing over a small velvet case. 'She told me she's cleaned them and most of the gooey stuff has—'

Patience offered her hand palm up. 'Just hand the

things over and don't say another word, otherwise I'm likely to beat you to death with my handbag.'

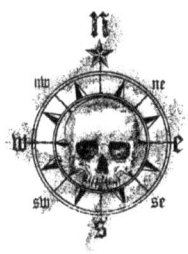

Having shared out the workload, The Newshounds made their way back down into Dorsal Finn. Once they hit the village centre, they pulled up their bikes and finalised their plans.

'I make it 5 p.m.,' Lucas said looking at his watch. 'What say you guys to meeting up at 8 p.m. this evening, to see how things are going?'

Suddenly uncomfortable, Beatrice shuffled a little. 'I can't make it tonight,' she said. Her flushed cheeks betrayed her.

'You okay, Bea?' Elmo asked.

'Yeah,' she said trying to avoid eye contact with anyone.

'You sure?' Lucas said. 'What gives? Spill, Miss Beecham.'

Beatrice squirmed under their gazes, causing Patience to come to her rescue.

'Beatrice is busy this evening, gentlemen. You will have the pleasure of *my* company,' she said adopting a haughty air. 'We can meet at Eccleston's Eaterie at 8.15 p.m. and swap notes.'

'Okay,' Elmo said.

The fact that Lucas appeared pre-occupied told Beatrice all was not well with him.

'I'll see you tomorrow then, Bea,' he said and headed for home. Elmo followed after him, giving the girls an apologetic shrug of the shoulders.

'Thanks for helping me out, Patience,' Beatrice said.

'Hey, you make sure that when the date's done I get details,' Patience smiled. 'No abridged versions either,'

'You think Lucas is okay?' Beatrice asked.

'Why shouldn't he be?'

'No reason.'

Inside, another emotion had come to party, and though Beatrice didn't recognise it straight away, it was to introduce itself soon enough, at a most inopportune time.

CHAPTER SEVEN
GUIDED BY VOICES

SHE FOUND IT quite odd, but for some reason Beatrice couldn't decide what to wear. It was only a walk along the promenade but her focus had become as fogged as kitchen windows beneath a pan of simmering pasta. Anxiety mixed with excitement, clarity clouded by unfamiliarity.

It wasn't long before she'd keyed Patience's number into her cell phone.

'What were you *thinking* of wearing?' Patience said.

Beatrice told her.

'Call the fashion police,' Patience moaned. 'We have a crime in progress.'

'Not good, eh?' Beatrice said. It was apparent she was totally rubbish at such things. No real surprise since most of her short life had been spent on dressing dishes, not herself.

'What you need is something subtle but not understated. It is your first real date after all.'

'It's my first date *ever*,' Beatrice reminded her.

'Then it's even more important to create the right impression, right?'

'I suppose,' Beatrice replied.

'You have that summer dress,' Patience suggested. 'The one with the big flowers on.'

'You said it was gaudy and looked like one of Maud's tea towels,' Beatrice reminded her.

'This is an emergency,' Patience said.

'Too late for a rescue—I spilled Bolognese sauce on it when I was cooking,' Beatrice said guiltily.

'What about that green halter-neck blouse and those white trousers?' Patience offered.

'White trousers came off second best against a tub of turmeric,' Beatrice said.

'You *have* heard of an apron, right?' Patience sounded exasperated. 'What about the blouse?'

'Got caught in a hand blender.'

'A hand blender?' Patience said bemused. 'How on earth, no—don't tell me. I don't want to know.'

'I think I'm going to have to wear my usual stuff,' Beatrice sighed in resignation.

'The green tee-shirt and jeans?' Patience asked. 'Casual and conventional?'

'I know. Just like me right?'

'I wouldn't say that.'

'You wouldn't say it because you're too polite,' Beatrice said. 'How're things going with the translation?'

'Not going on *at all*,' Patience admitted. 'Poppa has got me helping with the preparations for Uncle Badru's birthday party. It's a big deal here at the Userkaf's. Poppa's very pleased with the finding of lobster for the big night. Where are they?'

'Sitting in a salt water tank in one of Maud's stock rooms,' Beatrice said.

'I'm going to get onto the blueprints in an hour to see if I can get something for the meeting with the guys tonight,' said Patience.

'Then I'll leave you to it,' Beatrice said. 'Good luck.'

'Good luck to you, too.' Patience sighed.

'Somehow I think I may need it,' Beatrice said. And she wasn't joking.

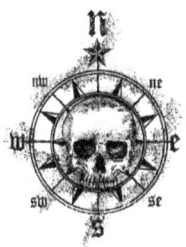

Lucas sat pensively at his PC. His bedroom was in its usual state of chaos. The blue carpet was an untidy mass of *Hardy Boys* paperbacks and *Nancy Drew Mysteries*, and the magnolia walls were adorned with icons from both music and movies. There was a huge poster of Kurt Cobain from *Nirvana* over his bed and another of Private Detective Philip Marlowe from *The Big Sleep*.

Lucas loved mysteries, but nothing was more of a mystery to him than his feelings for Beatrice. At that moment, he knew—though he couldn't say how—Beatrice was doing something later that excluded The Newshounds, especially *him*. And when he thought about it, he felt really jealous. It sounded stupid when he said it out loud but there was no helping it. And part of him wanted to know what Beatrice had planned that made Patience cover for her.

That was when Lucas decided he would see what it was Beatrice wanted to keep secret. And as unreasonable the idea of following her was, it seemed like the only thing he *could* do. In the pit of his stomach he sensed there could be only one reason why Beatrice didn't want any of The Newshounds along; why she'd put something above solving a mystery. That something had to be a *someone*.

A boy.

The horrible churning sensation in his stomach felt as though he'd eaten something several days past its sell by date. He swallowed. His mouth felt dry and his tongue alien.

He forced himself to think of something else, his eyes moving to the wads of paper that he'd rescued from the drop pod. They lay across his radiator, drying out.

Moving over to the sheets, he glanced down at them. It had been impossible to separate them to begin with. The pages were seemingly fused together with damp. For over two hours the radiator had pumped warm air into the vellum, drying it out, warping the edges to the point where the individual sheets were beginning to separate.

Lucas searched his pockets and pulled out a pair of tweezers that he'd borrowed from his mum's huge make-up bag. He used this delicate tool to carefully pry the sheets apart and lay them next to each other.

On many of the sheets the writing was too water-damaged, the ink bleeding into the paper in large blue pools. He was, however, surprised to find that some of the pages contained drawings. Again, these were too faint to make out in detail, but Lucas could see enough to tell him they were some kind of design for a cylindrical object with a clear, oval frontage. Any further intricacies were smudged and splattered, and despite Lucas' best efforts to make them out proved completely fruitless.

He placed the sheets on his bed and flopped backwards so that he stared at the ceiling.

Fruitless.

Yes, he thought. *That just about sums up the day.*

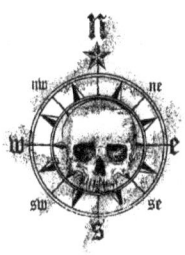

'We can only say what we saw,' Gretel said to the man at the table.

'Or, rather, what we did not see,' added Hansel. 'There was no evidence of The Trident at Bishop's Cragg.'

'Then you did not look hard *enough*,' the man hissed, slamming his hand down onto his table hard enough to make the salt and pepper pots rattle in their brackets. The occupants sitting at nearby tables ignored his antics, not keen to interrupt their high tea for someone else's mischief.

The twins watching him from across the table were as equally unflustered. They wore their smiles as though the man had just told them a funny story.

'We looked where you told us to look,' Hansel said. 'It does not bear any mark of The Trident.'

The man sighed and relaxed a little. 'I am at fault here,' he said. 'I am hasty—trying to second-guess shadows. No surprise, of course. What was once a grand design is now guesswork.' He paused for a moment, lost in his thoughts. 'This was the intention, of course. The thief intended to confound us all,' he finally said. 'Patience and observation are needed. You will be my eyes and ears, little ones. Use your guile, root out the mischief makers and report back to me. '

The twins said nothing.

'Go and join your friends,' he told them. 'No doubt you will be keen to play.'

'We have already played a great deal this afternoon,' Hansel said. 'I am very tired. '

'You two youngsters kill me.' The man chuckled.

'Is that an order, Sir?' Gretel asked raising an eyebrow.

Logan Frobisher laughed.

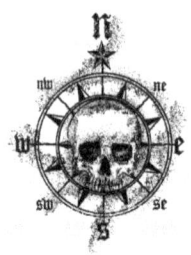

'Blimey,' George Beecham said as he laid the table for dinner. 'How come it's so quiet? I take back everything—I do believe that wishes can come true.'

At the table, Maud and Beatrice were lost in a subdued and contemplative silence. They had been this way since entering the kitchen-dining room and didn't appear to be surfacing anytime soon.

'Have you been at those new toffees again, Maud? You know how they play havoc with your dentures.'

Maud mumbled something back.

'I see you've not quite finished it. They do last a while don't they?'

Maud refused to take the bait.

'Oh this is no good,' said George Beecham, his round, ruddy face breaking into a frown. 'No point aiming decent jibes at a soft target.'

He turned his attention to Beatrice. 'Any plans for this evening, love?'

'No.' Beatrice's reply as rapid as a faulty rocket. 'No plans at all. In fact, I have never known an evening with so much *unplannedness* attached to it.'

'*Unplannedness*?' he quizzed. 'Is that even a real word?' Mr Beecham shook his head and went back to the kitchen to get wine glasses.

Beatrice felt Maud's eyes upon her and looked up.

'Are you okay, Aunt Maud?' Beatrice whispered.

'I guess the lads have filled you in?' Maud said with a watery smile.

Beatrice nodded. 'If we can help we will, you know that, right?'

'Nothin' has ever been so certain to ol' Maud, m'dear.' The old woman patted Beatrice's hand.

'So what time's yer date?' she winked.

'Oh, God,' Beatrice said horrified. 'Is it that obvious?'

'Giddy goodness, yes! But fret not, yer dad won't have a clue. Ye'll find that most blokes wear sunglasses when it comes to us girls an' our troubles.'

'That sounds a bad thing,' Beatrice whispered.

'I said *most* blokes,' Maud replied. 'The right one

will lift those shades from time to time, when it really matters.'

'Why can't they be like us?' Beatrice said with a sigh. 'It would be so much easier.'

'The good Lord can't always rectify his mistakes,' Maud chuckled. 'So I guess it's down to us girls to do some prunin' once in a while.'

Beatrice grinned, but inside she remained apprehensive.

'Ye scared?'

'A little.'

'A little is a lot in the young,' Maud said. 'Ye just take a deep breath an' go enjoy yerself. Time's an enemy to us all.'

Beatrice sensed there was more to Maud's comment; that it had poignancy for both of them. Before Beatrice could clarify it, her father returned and silence settled down to dinner once more.

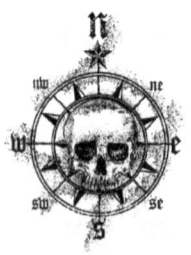

Dinner was given an unexpected lift by an effervescent Thomas Beecham, who was keen to share his day with everyone.

'Yeah, it was *great* and we got these *really* cool uniforms,' he pointed at his *really cool uniform* since he was wearing it and was currently reluctant to take it off. 'And it doesn't matter that there isn't a hat—

though Patience did *promise* there would be—but I got a great DVD and comic about the Blue Bolt.'

'Who are you and what have you done with my brother?' Beatrice chided.

Thomas looked up at her, appeared to consider a response, but then he was gone again, lost in the exploits of *The Blue Bolt*.

'That sounds great, Tom,' his dad said. 'You can't beat a good superhero. In my day it was Superman and Batman who were always putting the world to rights.'

'Oh *The Blue Bolt* is much more than just a superhero; he has *values*.'

'Listen to our boy, Maureen,' George Beecham said to his wife. 'Only one day and he's talking about values. Can you believe it?'

'You really need to check the label before you accept him as yours,' Beatrice muttered. The topic of conversation may have been different but Thomas was still great in his ability to irritate her.

Again Thomas stared at Beatrice and, for a second, she felt uncomfortable under his gaze. It was as if she was looking at something wearing a Thomas Beecham mask but the eyes were giving it away.

Then the moment moved on, leaving her perplexed and confused.

'May I be excused?' Thomas said.

George and Maureen Beecham exchanged glances and grinned.

'Why of course,' Maureen said. 'You have things to do?'

'I want to read my Blue Thunder Handbook before I go for my first meeting.'

Thomas slid off the chair and exited the room, his steps light and eager.

'I can't believe the change one day has made,' Maureen said, her grin feeling at home enough to stay a little longer.

'Neither can I,' Maud said staring at the door as it closed upon Thomas' passing.

But unlike her mother, Beatrice noticed that Maud wasn't smiling at all.

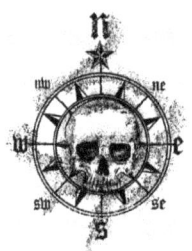

'Do keep up, young man! And I will thank you to be careful with that trunk. It has been in my family for seven generations.'

Despite her age, Viking expert Cordelia Crust marched down the central corridor of a rather large and stuffy museum. The curator—a small man in a suit that was slightly too big for him—tried keep pace with her. Lagging several yards behind was a middle-aged caretaker, who wrestled with a large leather truck, laced with belt straps, and bouncing along on rickety castors.

Crust appeared formidable. Her body was tall and square, and swathed in multilayered folds of woollen, tweed fabric. The brim of a wide, felt hat shielded her pale blue eyes from the florescent lights overhead, and the surface of her jowl-like cheeks were a web of red capillaries.

The caretaker paused to mop the beads of sweat

running from his hairline and into his bushy eyebrows with a handkerchief that may have once been white. Crust and the curator pulled up and waited.

'Goodness me,' Crust said stiffly. 'With all this huff-puff one would think the poor man was being asked to tow a small elephant.'

'That would be easier,' the caretaker complained, giving the larger woman a steely glare.

'You men,' she chirped. 'It's terrible how you let yourselves go. No shame at all.'

The curator squirmed as the caretaker muttered something unintelligible.

'It really is good of you to stay your tour and come to visit us, Miss Crust,' he said diplomatically. 'We are honoured.'

'Nonsense,' Crust said with a dismissive wave. 'It is always a pleasure to share one's passion. I consider myself an ambassador. Vikings have always had such shameful press. I blame the monks of the 8th Century, of course. Ever the axe to grind, if you pardon the pun. Bias is the historian's bane.'

'I'm sure you'll do your level best to establish equilibrium, Miss Crust,' the curator said.

'Indeed' Crust's voice echoed around the corridor. They were about to continue on their way when Crust's phone buzzed in the carpet bag slung over her shoulder. She fished inside it for a few seconds before pulling it free and seeing a FaceTime call coming in from someone she recognised.

'Must take this,' she said to her escorts. 'One must always entertain one's fan base.'

The caretaker wasn't complaining. He sat down on the trunk and started biting his fingernails.

Responding to the call, Crust smiled broadly as Elmo gave her a warm wave.

'Hi Miss C,' he said. 'Thanks for taking the call.'

'No trouble at all, Elmo,' Crust said. 'Now, tell me what you have for me, whilst my man takes my trunk and sets it up on the main stage.'

Behind her, the caretaker gave out a small whimper.

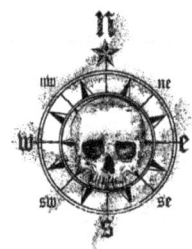

When it came to being evasive, Patience was not the best person in the world. She was the kind of girl who found it difficult to be anything other than open with people; a trait not all held in esteem.

While being open and honest is usually considered a very good thing, it isn't the best attribute when it comes to keeping a secret.

So in order to make sure that the issues with Klaus Hessel remained unknown, Patience had snuck out of the house and was now sitting on a bench facing Dorsal Finn's Museum. She had a laptop beside her and Agnes Clutterbuck's infamous earpieces in the palm of her hand.

The aids were small—the kind that fit snugly into the ear—and were only visible under close scrutiny. Carefully Patience plucked one of them from her palm and, with a grimace, popped it into her own left ear, adjusting it until the fit was secure. 'Note to self,' she said to the museum. 'Kill Lucas Walker next time I see him.'

Once satisfied, she repeated the process with the remaining ear piece

In an instant, she picked up a dizzying array of white noise, peppered with other distant sounds of voices—some intelligible, some not so. Then the strong resonant voice of a man speaking in clear German broke through the wall of fizz.

Patience pulled free a tablet from her designer handbag and started making notes. Before long she'd pretty much detailed the content since it was clear that the man, Klaus Hessel, appeared to be repeating the same phrases over and over. This was puzzling, though it meant Patience didn't have to continue with the hearing aids for any longer than was necessary.

'It's good to see a student still engaged out of school hours,' a man said from nearby. Startled, Patience almost knocked her tablet onto the mosaic floor.

Three people stood in front of her and Patience recognised Emily immediately. The man and woman with her were smiling; Patience deducing that they were Emily's parents a few seconds later.

'Sorry to startle you, Patience.' Mr Hannigan was tall and lean with neatly clipped, blonde hair and eyes of the deepest blue. He had a nose that was long with square, rimless spectacles perched on it, which made his face appear somehow stern and friendly at the same time.

'Is it all right that we call you that?' Mrs Hannigan was less austere; her face pale beneath her shoulder-length ebony hair, and her dark eyes seemed furtive as though constantly scanning what was going on about her. Despite Mrs Hannigan's disarming smile, Patience couldn't help but feel that her face looked generally sad and worn. 'After what Emily has told us, we feel we already know you so well,' she continued.

Patience was quietly assured to know that, despite her reservations, Emily had told her parents of the events of the day.

'Well, that's very kind,' Patience said and signed at the same time. 'Emily is a good friend.'

At this Emily came over and gave Patience a hug of thanks, taking everyone by surprise.

'Emily is lucky to have friends like you,' Mr Hannigan said earnestly. 'However, not everyone is so accommodating.'

'You mean hearing people?'

'Indeed,' Mrs Hannigan said. 'Children can be cruel to those who are different, don't you think?'

'Only those who don't want to understand,' Patience replied.

Mrs Hannigan nodded, her eyes resting upon Patience for a short time. 'Sadly ignorance is so easy to come by,' she said. 'That is why we discourage such friendships.'

'Mother!' Emily signed. 'What are you saying?'

'It's for your own good, Emily,' Mr Hannigan signed back. 'And seeing how Patience has made such an effort to understand the ways of deaf people, I'm sure she will *understand* too.'

'I don't think I do understand,' Patience said.

'That will be because you are a pretty, hearing girl

in a hearing world,' Mrs Hannigan said, but her tone was clipped.

'And Emily is a pretty deaf girl with the potential for hearing friends.' Patience signed the gestures fast and big to demonstrate her disgust to the Hannigan's stand point. 'That's if she's given the chance. How can that be wrong?'

'And that's very noble of you,' Mr Hannigan said. 'But Emily is *our* daughter and she has been hurt too many times before. We know what's best for her.'

'Clearly you don't.' Patience signed, making Emily laugh.

'This conversation is over,' Mr Hannigan said and his eyes bore into Patience to make it clear that she had crossed over a line. 'Thank you, once again for today, Patience. Come now, Emily, it is time for us to go.'

The Hannigan's moved away. Emily looked back at Patience and gave her a sad smile. Patience lifted her hand and waved. Then her new friend was gone, leaving Patience with nothing but the screaming gulls and her disbelief for company.

CHAPTER EIGHT
Seaside Rendezvous

THE PIER HAD been a late addition to Dorsal Finn, a gift from the Pontefract family back in the 1960's—a time when piers and ancient bands like *The Beatles* and *The Who* were popular. It was a thing of strange beauty. It's black, wrought iron struts rising from the sea and climbing into impressive archways crowned with huge wooden slats, which supported a pavilion and a few small gift shops.

Beatrice walked towards the pier, her eyes watching it grow as she drew closer, and as the elongated structure began to consume her horizon, so did the anxiety of meeting up with Marcus Macbeth. She'd tried to suppress it for most of the day, but now it was loose and hungry and baying for attention. Her heart thumped in her chest, her breathing felt shallow and useless, and when she saw his tall, regal figure—still clad in his smart *Blue Thunder* suit—standing at the railings, she faltered.

'Giddy goodness, get a grip of yourself,' she cursed under her breath, her heart instantly warmed by

Maud's favourite rebuke. And although her feet didn't stop, her mind paused for a few moments of composure. It allowed her the time to regain some perspective.

At Beatrice's approach, Marcus turned to face her. His smile broadened, revealing his perfect white teeth, and enhancing his sparkling eyes. Beatrice used her newfound strength to trample over her returning anxiety.

'Hi,' he said, surprising her by planting a kiss on her right cheek. She could feel heat crawling up her neck like ivy.

'Hi,' she said weakly.

'You look nice.' Marcus appeared awkward for the first time. 'I must admit I'm a bit nervous about this sort of thing.'

'You are?' said Beatrice. 'Well, if it's a help, you're not alone in that.'

Marcus nodded his thanks and adjusted the sleeve on his blue suit.

'You look very smart,' Beatrice said.

'Everything else was in the wash.' He grinned. 'You know how these things are, right?'

She laughed, relief forced aside the tension that had been holding her prisoner all day.

'Does the formality of a suit bother you?' he asked.

'Not at all. People are more than clothes, aren't they?'

'I guess they are,' he said. 'Shall we take a walk?'

They strolled towards the pavilion, its dome reflecting the evening sun with a myriad of tiny star bursts. Their footfalls sounded heavy upon the slats beneath them, and the sucks and slurps of the tides below filled in the gaps.

'Some people find it odd that *The Blue Thunder Foundation* encourages the wearing of uniform when its members are not on official business,' he said as they passed a small haberdashery.

'Some people?' Beatrice asked.

'Girls,' he said. 'They find it a bit *geekish*. And when I tell them that I cook as well, you can imagine where I start to sit on the *nerd-o-meter*.'

'I aim high on the nerd-o-meter,' Beatrice said. 'And there's nothing wrong with a boy being able to cook. Most of the prominent TV chefs are men.'

'Well, I guess that makes me a lucky guy,' he said.

Now it was Beatrice's turn to smile. She was feeling so comfortable, so at ease, it was like talking to someone she'd known for ages. And as they talked about cooking and recipes, it was as though the world was taking a break and leaving Beatrice and Marcus at the helm for a long, long while.

The pier was magnificent but it was finite. They soon found the yellowed boards ahead were slowly giving way to an ornate horizontal rail and the shimmering sea beyond.

'Oops,' Marcus said. 'Looks as though we're running out of pier. Are we going swimming or are we turning around?'

Beatrice looked up at him. 'We could always, just . . . '

His eyes were so blue and so beautiful, and she found herself suddenly lost for words.

'Stop?' he suggested.

'Yes,' she said. 'Stop.'

'Then what?' he asked moving closer to her. His hand was touching hers. The sensation was like electricity passing through her.

'Watch the sea?'

'Radical,' he mused as he gently took hold of her hand. Beatrice's heart paused for a few seconds. 'Any other suggestions?'

'I'm not sure I—' Beatrice began, but then Marcus dropped his head down towards hers and kissed her softly on the lips. It was so different, so wonderful and so *right*. She thought at one point she might actually pass out. Marcus pulled away and looked into her eyes.

'I like this *stopping* thing,' Beatrice said headily.

'Shall we *stop* some more?' Marcus asked.

This time Beatrice moved towards him. 'Stopping is good,' she said before kissing him back.

They were lost in the moment, lost in each other. And just as they were unaware of tide or time, they were also oblivious of the lowly figure at the other end of the pier, watching their embrace with a keen yet devastating interest.

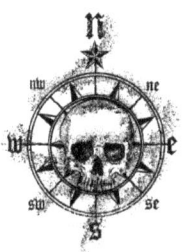

Numb. Totally and utterly numb.

It was a sensation that Lucas hadn't experienced before and hoped never to again. It was unpleasant, bringing with it the kind of detachment he felt when The Newshounds were babbling on about a great show on TV and Lucas realised he had to be the only person in the world who'd missed it.

Yes, numb was a bad place to hold out, but it was infinitely better than the heart-clutching, crushing pain that came when he'd seen Beatrice kissing the tall boy in a blue suit, their hair whipping about them in the sea breeze, and their entwined figures silhouetted in the nauseatingly romantic sunset.

So now he drifted through the cobbled streets, an emotional zombie, king of the unrequited; trying to work it all out, but not liking the answer that kept coming up. Beatrice was *on a date* and she now had a *boy friend*!

His hands were deep in his pockets, his mind in even darker places.

He found a low stone wall and perched upon it for a while. He had fifteen minutes before he needed to hook up with The Newshounds. Fifteen minutes before he was to tell them what he'd found in the dried out wads of paper currently sheathed in plastic and tucked in his rucksack.

This was an exciting time and if things were different he would be revelling in it. Instead, Lucas stared mournfully at a row of shops selling seaside whimsies but seeing nothing through a curtain of bitter tears.

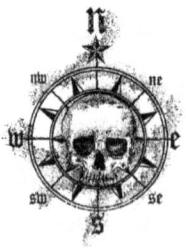

Thomas Beecham was immersed in the world of the

Blue Bolt. He sat on his bed with his laptop resting on his knees. On the 15 inch plasma screen the superhero's adventures rolled out. Thomas was astounded that the DVD case contained no less than *twenty-five action packed episodes*, each one better than the last. He was only ten episodes in and couldn't wait to see what came next. He'd never known anything quite like it; the need—the desire—to watch every single episode again and again. It was like watching *Star Wars: A New Hope* for the first time, *every* time.

So it came as a great irritation when there was a sudden knock on his bedroom door, a knock that he initially tried to ignore until it came again, louder and far more insistent. A knock that said: *I'm not going away so you may as well let me in.*

With an impatient snort, Thomas hit the pause button on the laptop.

'Come in,' he said, rubbing at his eyes to clear them.

'Ye'll be needin' window wipers if ye stare at that computer for much longer,' Maud said as she stepped into the bedroom.

'Huh?' Thomas said dropping his hands into his lap.

'Ye'll get square eyes is all I'm sayin',' Maud explained with a wry smile. 'I'm missin' our games of Top Trumps, young Thomas. When are ye comin' to play?'

'Top Trumps are boring,' Thomas said. 'Unless you've got *Blue Bolt* ones?' he added in a hopeful tone.

'I'm afraid it's only *Star Wars* or *The Hobbit* on offer, me lad.'

'Then I'll not bother.'

They sat in silence for a moment. 'So ye goin' to tell me about this Blue Bolt fella, or what?'

'You wouldn't get it,' Thomas said dismissively. 'It's for you know—?' He paused as he searched for the words.

'Youngsters?' Maud suggested.

'No,' Thomas said shaking his head and scrunching his face in one movement. 'For *members*.'

'Members?'

'Yes,' Thomas said holding up a uniformed sleeve and pointing at it expressively. 'Members.'

'Well, how about ye tell me?' Maud said. 'No one else needs to know, do they?'

'I can't tell you,' Thomas said sternly, causing Maud to take a step back in surprise. 'It's against the rules.'

'And where are these rules?' Maud said, her face impassive, but in her eyes anxiety took up residence.

Thomas pulled open the flap on a breast pocket and removed a small, buff-coloured book. 'This is the *Blue Thunder* Handbook,' he explained. 'The rules.'

'Any chance of me getting' a peek at 'em?'Maud said.

'Can't.'

'Let me guess,' Maud said expectantly, 'it's against the rules for me to see the rules?'

'Not really,' Thomas said. 'I just don't understand why you'd want to do that.'

It was a question that Maud couldn't answer with any kind of honesty. So she didn't try.

'How about we postpone that Top Trumps game for later on?' she said quietly. 'An' I'll let ye get back to yer viewin'.'

'Okay,' Thomas said. His shoulders lifted as if he'd been suddenly freed of a great burden.

'Shall I bring ye up some cocoa later this evenin'?' Maud said gently.

'Sure,' Thomas said, but his voice was distant as he switched his computer back on and *Blue Bolt* invaded the room, shutting out Maud as though she'd ceased to exist.

'I'll be back later, then,' Maud said as she left Thomas, too engrossed in his DVD to notice she had a *Blue Bolt* comic tucked under her arm.

Eccleston's Eaterie and Tea Shoppe had a voice of its own, a sonic symphony consisting of many layers. At its core was the guttural, burbling sound of the coffee machine, a bulky stainless steel thing that reflected the fervour of those serving behind the counter. The hum of the ovens melded with the drone of the microwave drifting out from the kitchens to the left of the counter. The occasional hiss of steam and the bright chime of a timer announced that an order was ready to serve to eagerly waiting customers. And sitting on top of this cacophony was the happy booming voice of Ernie Eccleston himself, chatting and shouting orders to his kitchen staff.

Sitting around their table, Patience and Elmo

listened to this din as they waited for Lucas. Patience had laid her notes out in front of her, almost obscuring the gingham table cloth. Mugs of hot chocolate topped with marshmallows and foam were placed strategically about the table, lazy tendrils of steam drifting into the air.

They looked up as Lucas entered the café and shuffled over to their table, sitting down heavily enough to ruffle the edges of Patience's notes.

'*OMG*, Lucas,' she said. 'You look awful.'

'If that's supposed to be concern you really need to work on your delivery,' Lucas said wiping a hand over his blotched face.

'You okay, fella?' Elmo asked.

'I'll be fine if you guys don't keep asking me if I'm fine,' Lucas said straightening up in his chair.

'Do you want some hot chocolate?' Elmo coaxed.

'No thanks,' Lucas said.

'Can *I* have your hot chocolate?' Elmo asked.

'Elmo,' Patience snapped. 'Don't be so insensitive. Can't you see how puffy his eyes are? Have you been crying, Lucas?'

Several people sitting about them paused to look over at their table.

'Patti, once you've nailed the concern thing I'd suggest putting in some extra work on *tact*,' Elmo mused as the diners returned to their meals.

'I've not been crying. It's an allergic reaction to—' Lucas desperately tried to find a suitable word.

'Dandruff?' Elmo offered.

'Dye,' Lucas said. 'Yes, I was adding some of Mum's dye to my hair and got some in my eyes.'

'Your hair doesn't look any different,' Patience said eyeing his scalp.

'Look, can we get on with something important? Are we going to help Maud and Agnes or not?'

'Of course we are,' Patience said. 'I just don't like the thought of you being upset, that's all.'

'Upset?' Lucas said. 'Who said anything about upset? No, I'm sure it wasn't me. In fact, I think I specifically mentioned that I was fine; which is as far from upset as you can get!'

He sat and looked at them, breathing heavily. Today wasn't going well at all. By the law of averages it had to improve soon.

'Are you okay?' Patience asked.

'Aaargh!' Lucas said putting his forehead onto the table.

'You having trouble reading your menu?' Elmo asked.

'Can we just get on with it please?' Lucas said into the tablecloth. 'What's everyone found?'

Disgruntled, Patience shrugged her shoulders and adjusted herself in her seat. 'Elmo, do you want to go first?'

'Okay.' Elmo dragged his mug of hot chocolate to him. 'I spoke with Cordelia Crust today. I couldn't believe that she got back so fast. She said that these three arrows aren't runes she's familiar with. At first she thought it was a repeat of this rune—'

He picked up one of Patience's pencils and scrawled an example upon a serviette:

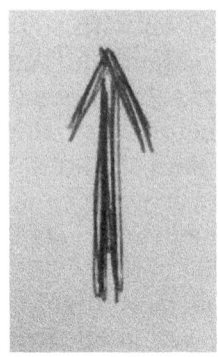

'That's the rune for Tiwaz, a Nordic god. Very big in Viking times,' Patience recalled.

'Give the girl a bun,' Elmo said having taken a sip of his drink. He wiped foam from his nose with his sleeve. 'Cordelia suggested this was something different than a repeat of the Tiwaz rune because it's joined by the horizontal line at the bottom.'

In case anyone had forgotten, Elmo added the other parts of the image until the entire image was now visible on the serviette:

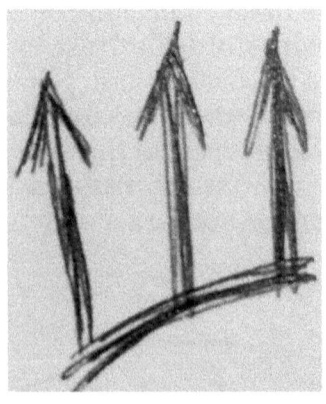

Lucas lifted his head from the table for a better look, his eyes intent on Elmo's artwork.

'Anything else?' Patience asked Elmo.

'Yeah,' he replied. 'Cordelia can get six Jaffa Cakes in her mouth at once. Now tell me you're not impressed by that. '

'I meant about the *rune*!' Patience's impatience became evident in her tone.

'Oh, sorry. Yes, there is one other thing,' Elmo said picking his mug up again, 'Cordelia did say that the rune looked like a trident.'

'A trident?' Patience reached for the serviette and turned it around for a better look. 'Yes, it does, doesn't it?'

'Pretty smart lady, our Cordelia,' Elmo said before attacking a marshmallow.

'I didn't find much in the wads of paper,' Lucas said flatly. He pulled the dried sheets from the pocket of his jacket, and tried to flatten them out on the table. Their edges remained stubbornly corrugated.

'The writing is a total wipe out,' he muttered.

'What are those cylinders?' Elmo said pulling the respective sheet of paper towards him.

'No idea,' Lucas said.

'More drop pods?' Elmo asked.

'What about the oval cover?' Lucas said tapping the shadowy image to press home his point.

'Yeah,' Elmo nodded. 'Definitely something else then. Pretty fascinating though.'

'Well, if you're impressed by *that*,' said Patience, 'wait until you see what I've brought.'

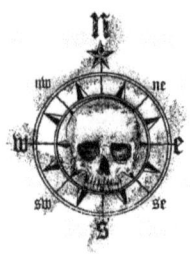

Maud adjusted her pillows—two huge feather-stuffed monstrosities—and settled back with a long sigh.

'Ah, that'll be a Godsend to yer aching bones, old girl,' she said. The room about her was a potpourri of colours and clutter. A vanity table and mirror at one end of the room, a stuffed grizzly bear at the other—paws held aloft so that coats could be draped over them. The grizzly had a *Go Bears!* Baseball cap perched upon its head, and its snarling muzzle seemed to imply that it just didn't get the joke.

Beneath the duvet, Maud drew up her knees creating a makeshift lectern, and upon this rested Thomas' Blue Bolt comic. The cover had the image of the superhero, his exaggerated muscles flexing as he lifted a terrified "villain" off of the ground. A bubble came from Blue Bolt's thin mouth: *'I shall teach you to pollute our world, vile scum!'*

Maud wasn't exactly sure what she was looking for in all of this, but something was nagging at her since Thomas had returned from his inauguration. On the surface he still seemed like the exuberant young boy she knew and loved, yet at dinner she'd seen and heard something different.

It was difficult for her to equate the idea of Thomas and anything unpleasant.

And since dinner she'd pretty much told herself she

was being old and stupid. When she'd spoken to him in his room, Maud's conviction that something wasn't right became compounded. Yet other than Thomas' newfound aloofness, she didn't really have any evidence of something being amiss.

'Now look at me,' she scoffed. 'Readin' comic books to get into the mind of a young'un. Maud, ye're an old numbskull!'

But Maud opened the comic and began to read the *Adventures of Blue Bolt*, the idea she was wrong and something terrible was not really happening quickly changed. By the time she'd finished the entire comic, Maud was so astonished, she climbed out of bed and went to her red cardigan to find her cell phone.

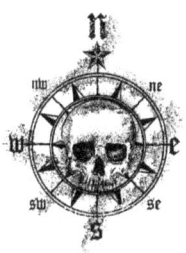

'Do you want this?' Lucas said as he waved the marshmallow in front of Elmo, who watched it the way a cobra regards its prey.

'Please don't offer me any more of those wonderful wads of sickly sweetness,' Elmo said, face paling. 'I assure you, vomiting will ensue.'

'Ahem.' Patience coughed loudly. 'Can we please get back to this?'

By "This" Patience meant the sheets of paper she'd brought with her and laid out on the table. Each leaf was covered in Patience's neat, fine script, and there were many comments in the margins followed by several question marks.

Lucas placed the marshmallow back in his mug of chocolate which looked congealed, cold, and just plain sad. 'Sorry, Patti.'

'Here we have a list of translation from the chatter in Agnes' ear piece,' Patience said.

'How was the hearing aid thing, by the way?' Lucas asked.

'Don't make me hurt you, Walker,' Patience hissed through her teeth.

'Okay.' Lucas looked at the papers to avoid her glare.

'The voice repeats all this stuff,' she said.

'Like a broadcast?' Lucas suggested. 'A radio broadcast?'

'Who knows?' Patience said. 'You want to know what he's been saying or what?'

The boys nodded.

Patience read from the first line of script, '*Atlantis wird ausgestellt* or "Atlantis is exposed" to you and me. He follows this up with: *Bücher verbergen sich mehr als gerechte kenntnisse*, which translates as: "Books hide more than just knowledge". And finally he states: *Agnes, Maud: verwandeln ein geschenk in einen schlüssel*. This means: "Agnes, Maud: turn gift into key".' Patience scanned the sheets one more time to make sure that she'd recited her findings correctly. 'Yes, that's it for the first part,' she concluded. 'Any ideas?'

'Well I recognise the word *Atlantis*,' Elmo offered.

'I think most people in this universe know that word, Elmo,' Patience piqued.

'Yes but does everyone in the universe know that, according to Plato—'

'Pluto?' Patience interjected. 'The Disney dog?'

'No.' Elmo grinned. 'Plato, the Greek philosopher, published his work *Timaeus and Critias* around 360 BC, which is considered to be the only reference specific to Atlantis. Now, Poseidon—Greek god of the sea—was said to have dominion over Atlantis and, when he fell in love with a mortal woman named Cleito, he built a hillside dwelling surrounded by rings of water and land to keep her safe. Of course, Plato's writing has courted controversy for thousands of years. The gentle and virtuous Atlantians eventually craved materialism, and Zeus, head honcho of the Greek gods, wiped the island clean by sending it to the bottom of the Atlantic Ocean. Boy was he a tough teacher.'

Elmo indicated he'd finished his report by nodding to himself.

'Maybe I will succumb to marshmallow madness after all,' he said, and retrieved the wad of sugar from Lucas' mug.

'Okay, you know plenty about Atlantis,' Patience smiled. 'But why is Klaus talking about it?'

'We need to find a link between the Nazis and Atlantis, maybe?' Lucas said. 'Seeing as you're the *Atlantismeister*, you good to follow that up, Elmo?'

'Mmumphf,' Elmo concurred behind a mouthful of marshmallow.

'So, what about the rest?' Patience queried.

'I think I have that sorted,' Lucas said.

'I think I preferred it when you were lacking smugness,' Patience said. 'Sorry, I didn't mean that.'

Lucas smiled and nodded. 'It's okay,' he said. 'But

I know about this stuff because it's telling us what we already know.'

'What do you mean?' Patience asked.

'It's Klaus telling Agnes and Maud how to find and open the box in the library,' he explained. 'The room was hidden behind the book shelf and his gift to them was the key.'

'This is what that ghost hunter, Tyrell, must've already worked out,' Patience said more to herself than them. 'That's what he was trying to do at the library, to retrieve the box.'

'But how did he *hear* Klaus Hessel?' Elmo asked.

'Who knows?' Lucas said. 'But he was able to do it *somehow*.'

'Maybe you're right about this being a radio broadcast,' Patience said to Lucas. 'But if it is, why is it starting now, after all these years?'

'Maybe something triggered it?' Elmo offered.

They all thought about that in silence.

'What about the writing, Patti?' Lucas said after a little while. 'Does it tell us about the drawing? Where it could be?'

Patience picked up her notes again. 'The writing says: *Im letzten licht des tages, lassen sie ihn die weise zeigen* or: "In the last light of day, let him point the way",' she said.

'Some sort of riddle?' Elmo said.

'A riddle for what?' Patience asked.

'Maybe it's a way of finding the place in the drawing?' Lucas guessed.

'It would help if we knew what the drawing was, or where it was.' Patience tapped the rim of her mug with a finger.

'I think it's the Cryptic Crypt that Klaus keeps talking about,' Lucas said.

'Well, let's try and be logical. If it's a crypt then we'll find it in a church, right?' Patience deduced. 'And the only church in Dorsal Finn is St. Norman's.'

'St. Norman's doesn't have a crypt,' Elmo said.

Lucas looked up at them both. When he came into the café his eyes had been red rimmed, now they were filled with excitement.

'Not one that they *know* of,' he grinned.

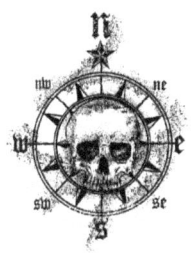

Beatrice and Marcus were walking again. They had left the pier far behind them, and ambled along the promenade, hands entwined and lost in conversation.

It was difficult for Beatrice to explain how she felt. The sensations running through her surged with unbearable and new excitement and happiness. The need to listen to everything Marcus said was like watching her favourite Jamie Oliver TV show. She was unable to pull herself away from him.

Beatrice couldn't help but laugh when he told a joke, even though it wasn't really that funny, but it was a way to vent some of the exhilaration swelling inside her. Their hour had passed by so quickly, now they were hoping to stretch it out as long as possible.

'How long have been involved with this *Blue Thunder* thingy,' Beatrice said.

'Eight years or so,' Marcus replied. 'I was a little off the rails at one point.'

'Really?' Beatrice said trying to hide her surprise.

'Yep, hard to believe isn't it? But it's true; I got into trouble a few times, my parents were,' he paused, 'pre-occupied with their own life. I sort of got *overlooked*, you know?'

Beatrice nodded though she didn't really understand. She felt lucky to have her family around her.

'But my gran got me into *The Blue Thunder Foundation*, pulled a few strings since she knew Mr Frobisher.'

'She's quite a character, your gran,' Beatrice said.

'That's one way of describing her,' Marcus laughed. 'She's as hard as nails and takes no messing from anyone. She seems to like you though.'

'Really? How do you know that?'

'Well, I'm here with you, aren't I?' he said. 'I'd have no chance of getting out the house if she had any issue.' He watched a frown spread across her face then giggled. 'I'm only kidding. She told me she liked you. In fact, she asked if you'd like to come for tea sometime.'

'I'd like that,' Beatrice said. 'Will you be there?'

'Of course,' Marcus said.

'Good,' Beatrice said, enjoying the way he squeezed her hand.

Things were just perfect at that moment.

She let out a contented sigh just as a shop door opened ahead and a group of kids came out.

In an instant Beatrice recognised the shop as Eccleston's Eaterie, and the group of kids were The Newshounds. Her instinct was to pull her hand out of Marcus' and allow her arm to drop by her side, but he held onto it and Beatrice didn't attempt to force the point. She wasn't prepared to keep lying to her friends. It just didn't sit well with her.

As soon as she'd realised, Patience came up to them. 'Oh, what about that? It's Beatrice and Marcus,' she said casually. 'How are you both?'

'I'm good,' Marcus said.

'Me too,' Beatrice agreed.

'Then that's wonderful,' Patience said brightly, but not cheerful enough to ease the tension that started to cloud the exchange.

'I don't believe we've met, guys,' Marcus said to Elmo and Lucas, who stood quietly behind Patience.

Lucas ferreted around in his rucksack, making no attempt to acknowledge either Beatrice or Marcus.

'I'm Marcus,' he said. 'Beatrice's *date*.'

'Elmo,' Elmo said with a smile. 'And I'm Beatrice's food taster. I'm pretty good at it.'

'This is Lucas,' Patience said uncomfortably when it became apparent that Lucas really wasn't planning on saying anything at all. 'He's not usually this *rude*.'

Lucas stopped messing with his bag and looked up. His face was fixed into a smile that was so artificial it made him look like a mannequin.

Beatrice couldn't believe the emptiness in his eyes.

'Sorry, I was busy,' he said with blatant effort. Beatrice watched him eye Marcus for a moment before saying, 'Nice suit. I hear *Postman Pat* has one just like it.'

'What are you guys up to?' Beatrice interjected.

'Oh, you know, the usual Newshounds' stuff,' Patience said quickly.

'Newshounds?' Marcus queried. 'Is that like a gang thing?'

'It's an *exclusive* gang,' Lucas said pointedly.

'Aren't they all?' Marcus said swiftly, looking directly at Lucas. Beatrice couldn't read the expression of Marcus' face. It remained neutral, composed. 'And what happens in this Newshounds gang of yours?'

'Important stuff. For some,' Lucas said coolly but he wasn't looking at Marcus for this. He was looking at Beatrice. And the comment, the contempt in her friend's eyes, left her feeling sick and angry all at once. She wanted to run away. She wanted to go over to Lucas and demand to know what was wrong, why he was treating her in such a way, but at the same time she wanted to ask him what was upsetting him and how she could make it all go away.

But instead she said, 'Shall I catch up with you guys tomorrow? We can talk about the important stuff then, right?'

'Good idea,' Patience said winking her left eye furiously as though there was a dead fly in it.

Beatrice watched The Newshounds turn away and head up the road. 'See you all tomorrow!' she called after them.

Only Lucas failed to acknowledge her.

CHAPTER NINE
CRUEL INTENTIONS

WHAT WAS THAT all about?' Patience said to Lucas when The Newshounds turned a corner and Beatrice and Marcus were no longer in view. 'Why were you so *mean* to Beatrice?'

'Why did you guys lie about where she'd be tonight?' Lucas snapped back. 'You *knew* didn't you?'

'About Marcus? Yeah, I knew,' Patience retorted. 'And we didn't lie about anything. We just played it down. Judging by how *stupid* you've been, I think we did the right thing. Anyone would think that you're jealous.'

No sooner had the words popped out and worked their magic, Lucas' behaviour made sense to Patience. He flinched a little as though what she'd said contained something unsavoury.

'OMG,' Patience said, hands framing her face. 'You *are* jealous! All that red-eye stuff in Eccleston's is because you *like* Beatrice, and you saw them together!'

'Yeah,' he said bitterly. 'I saw them.' Lucas turned to face the sea. Anything was better than seeing the shock on Patience's face. Elmo put a comforting hand on his friends shoulder, feeling him flinch as he did so.

'It is sweet though,' Patience said, forcing the boys to focus. 'A little weird and it may take some getting used to, but sweet all the same.'

'You're enjoying this, aren't you?' Lucas said, but his voice was lacking conviction. 'Is this because of the hearing aid thing? Should I be worried?'

'Not at all,' Patience said with a small grin. 'It's just that, well, I'm seeing you in a whole new light now, that's all.'

'I'm worried,' Lucas said despondently.

'Beatrice does seem happy though,' Elmo said.

'Yeah,' Lucas said softly. 'Yeah, she does.'

'Makes you sick, doesn't it?' Elmo said carefully.

'Obvious, huh?' Lucas said. Elmo nodded. Lucas rubbed his face with his hands in frustration. 'What's Marcus got that I haven't?'

'Beatrice?' Elmo offered.

'That's not helping.'

'You're not helping yourself,' Patience interjected. 'Being mean to Beatrice is just going to upset her. You'll make her feel that you don't like her anymore.'

Lucas hung his head. 'I can't explain it. Sometimes I like her so much I think it would be better if I didn't like her at all. I feel bad.'

'Cupid's arrow is sharp, my friend,' Elmo agreed.

'Yeah? Well his aim is off.' Lucas watched the darkening horizon. 'What am I going to do?'

'You won't have to do anything for now,' Patience said. 'I'll cover for you, but this is a once in a lifetime smoothie. You got me, Walker?'

'Yeah, thanks,' he said.

'When I've had a word then you can have yours,' Patience continued. 'It's a small word and I think you'll know what it is without me spelling it out, right?'

'Yes,' Lucas said.

'And from this point on, Lucas—no matter what happens—just remember Beatrice is your friend,' Patience warned.

'I'll *never* forget that,' he replied. 'After all, it looks like that's the only thing we'll ever be.'

Patience and Elmo exchanged glances and in their eyes the same sentiment swam: *This day needs to end, and it needs to end now.*

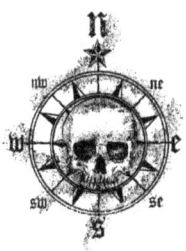

Beatrice went to bed in turmoil. Her mind was a raging torrent of images that threatened to sweep her away, tumbling and reeling and sucking her downwards until she drowned in the emotion of it all. She had found a kindred spirit in Marcus Macbeth, yet felt as though she was losing one of her dearest friends.

When she thought of Lucas, anger and sadness occupied her heart, each fighting for dominance. She tried to mediate, she tried to find some sense in it all, but she couldn't, resigning herself to the fact that she must mull things over, and calm down enough to think straight.

She drifted off to sleep, but it was far from the

reprieve she'd hoped. Instead she tossed and turned, her slumbering brain bombarded with dreams in which Lucas stared at her, aloof and angry and unresponsive to her pleas.

When she did wake, the new day brought with it no respite from her fears, and she made her way downstairs to the kitchen, eyes blurry and mind sluggish with fatigue.

Making her way to the fridge, Beatrice stopped in midstride, suddenly aware that she wasn't alone. Standing by the dishwasher, Thomas eyed her cautiously. He was still wearing his *Blue Thunder* uniform.

'What are you up to?' Beatrice said with equal suspicion.

'Keeping things tidy,' Thomas said. 'You need order in the world.'

'This is a new thing for you, isn't it?' Beatrice said pulling open the fridge door to find the carton of fruit juice.

'What is?' Thomas asked as he proceeded to empty the dishwasher.

'Being helpful,' Beatrice explained as she poured herself a drink. 'Being *normal*?'

'It's the natural order of things,' he said cryptically. 'Without order there is only chaos.'

'Whatever,' Beatrice said. 'You plan to take that uniform off at some point? It's not going to look as smart with a hoard of flies buzzing around it.'

'I have three sets,' Thomas explained. 'It means I can wear it all the time.'

'You'll be a bit warm wearing your school uniform over the top of it though, eh?'

'Haven't you heard?' he said with excitement. 'Members of the *Blue Thunder Foundation* don't have to wear the school uniform.'

'Maybe I was too quick to slap the *normal* label on you,' Beatrice said, frowning.

'I'm going to finish up here and then I'm going to make mum and dad a cup of tea in bed,' Thomas stated.

'You are now officially scaring me, little brother,' she said, but part of her had difficulty disliking the new Thomas Beecham.

She remembered Marcus' words: *'I got into trouble and The Blue Thunder Foundation bailed me out of it'* and she unexpectedly thought that maybe—just maybe—her parents were right to have encouraged Thomas to join.

'So does this mean you'll be making some breakfast later?' Beatrice said hopefully. 'Just let me know so that I can warn the fire department.'

'Always mocking,' he said flatly. 'Just like the *Psychophants.*'

'I won't ask who they are,' Beatrice said.

'They are the mortal enemies of the *Blue Bolt*, that's who,' he said as if she should know all about it.

'Well, I hope they all get along together in the end,' Beatrice said. 'Maybe have a party with fireworks and stuff. Like the end of *The Empire Strikes Back*.'

'It's *Return of the Jedi* where they have the fireworks,' Thomas said, deadpan. 'And *The Blue Bolt* would never have a party with the Psychophants, they're his sworn enemies!'

Beatrice sipped her juice and watched her brother becoming increasingly more agitated. And although she liked seeing her brother joining them in the real world from time to time, *Thomas Baiting* was a game she never found dull. Besides, it was keeping her mind off more sensitive matters, providing the reprieve sleep had forsaken.

'And what have these Psychophants done to upset ol' *Blue Bolt*?' she asked.

'Invaded his planet and taken over all the positions of power, doctors, lawyers and politicians,' Thomas said. 'And not only that. Then they undermine everything so that the world is in chaos, and this allows more Psychophants to come and possess more people. *Blue Bolt* has to take them down.'

'Sounds wonderful,' Beatrice said quickly growing bored. 'Let's hope that *Blue Bolt* boots them off his planet and they all live happily ever after.'

'It's not as simple as that,' Thomas said seriously.

'Why doesn't that surprise me?' Beatrice said getting up and rinsing her glass under the kitchen tap. She yawned loudly to give Thomas the hint that the conversation was past its interest date.

'The Psychophants suck planets dry and then move on,' Thomas said ignoring her. 'So the *Blue Bolt* has only one course of action open to him.'

'And what's that?' Beatrice said as she placed her glass on the draining board.

'*Extermination*, of course.'

'Nice,' Beatrice said turning to leave.

'Ahem.' Thomas coughed causing Beatrice to pause. He indicated the glass on the drainer with a nod of his head. 'Are you planning on putting that away?'

'Don't push it, Thomas,' Beatrice said grabbing a tea towel.

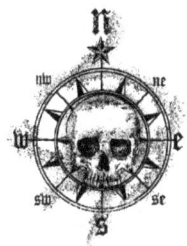

Gideon Codd approached the door of the *Blue Thunder Foundation's* hut and tapped on the door. He adjusted the lapel on his white suit and fidgeted with the brim of his white cricket hat. It was typical for him to be nervous around figures of authority. This was why he had invested so much time in carving a career where he would ultimately be the one in charge. Now he never had to be nervous, save for a few occasions. Codd was intimidated by those who tended to know more than he did, and more often than not, many people fitted this bill. But Codd was adept at steering such people away from positions of prominence, by means fair or foul (but it was more often the latter), and thus ensured his own survival. And he had honed his inherent trait of *ligging* into a fine art.

These days it was only a few people that gave him cause to fidget and faff. Dominic Pontefract, heir to the Pontefract Estate, of which Dorsal Finn belonged, was one such example.

Another was Logan Frobisher.

The problem, Codd found with Frobisher, was that he didn't know much about the enigmatic founder of the *Blue Thunder Foundation*, and when he didn't know much about people, Codd used all in his power to *find out* more about those people. He'd done the same with Logan Frobisher, only to find that his many researchers had little luck unearthing any more than was commonly known. Logan Frobisher had no secrets. This made Gideon Codd very nervous.

He tapped again on the door, irritated that it had not yet been answered. *Didn't these people realise how important he was?* The people of Dorsal Finn knew. Oh, yes. He'd made sure of that over the years.

People like the infernal Maud Postlethwaite and that young Beecham tearaway had constantly tried to undermine his authority, but most held him in esteem, coming to him when it really mattered.

One such person had come to him recently, which was the reason he now stood on the doorstep of a converted scout hut at 8am, the sea breeze smattering his hat with spray.

His thoughts were interrupted by the sound of a bolt being dragged open on the other side of the door. Codd drew himself up to his full height and sucked in his ample belly.

As the door opened he was greeted by Hansel and Gretel. He made to step through the door, but the twins didn't move. They merely stared at him with their blue, unblinking eyes.

'I have an appointment to see Mr Frobisher,' he said impatiently. 'I called this morning and he insisted that I meet him here.'

The twins regarded him for a moment and then stepped aside to allow him entry. Disgruntled, he made his way into the hall without any comment, his footfalls echoing about him.

'Gideon,' Frobisher's voice cut through the reverberations. 'How good of you to come.'

Frobisher walked towards him, having just exited a small office. The big man had dispensed with his suit and now wore a *Blue Thunder Foundation* uniform, as did the young, dour faced woman with him.

'Mr Frobisher,' the mayor acknowledged.

'Logan, remember?' Frobisher reminded him with a smile.

'Of course,' Codd said. 'Thank you for taking my call at such short notice.'

'Think nothing of it,' Frobisher said. 'I sensed urgency in it, and urgency requires decisiveness, does it not?'

'Indeed it does.'

'We shall go to my office,' Frobisher stated, indicating the small room he'd just come from. 'Would you like tea?'

'Thank you.'

'Organise some beverages, please, Mrs Caldecott,' Frobisher said to his aide.

The young woman walked away without acknowledgement, leaving Codd and Frobisher to their business.

The carpeted room was surprisingly big, and consisted of a wooden desk, garnished with office paraphernalia—a glass paperweight shaped as a mountain, a bright red stapler and three desk tidies. There were also three chairs, one leather-bound behind the desk, and two smaller ones in front of it. To Codd's surprise, Frobisher positioned the two smaller chairs so that they were facing, and sat down in one of them before gesturing for the mayor to sit in the other.

'So what's the issue?' Frobisher asked.

'To the point, as ever,' Codd said. 'I feel duty bound

to reciprocate. I have been approached by a dear friend. She has a problem.'

'Go on.'

'Her youngest son is a bright spark, but has had some issues,' Codd said. 'His father got up to mischief and had to leave town. It fragmented the family and the boy has become, how can I put it . . . ?'

'*Feral*?' Frobisher said quietly.

'I fear it may be going in that direction,' Codd replied. 'His mother is at her wits end, of course, especially with recent *happenings*.'

'Please continue,' Frobisher said leaning forward. Codd was staggered to see that the man was engrossed with the tale. It was as though he really *cared*.

'I'm afraid the lad is something of a lost lamb, so to speak. It would appear that he has taken this out upon the new schoolmaster's daughter; a young deaf girl by the name of Emily Hannigan. The master is insisting on some marked changes in the boy otherwise his schooling may suffer. I think the word *expulsion* was used.'

'Parents are funny things, aren't they?' Frobisher said nodding as though understanding completely. 'A boisterous boy, an afflicted girl, and two sets of parents; each wanting what's best. It makes one wonder who is truly at fault, doesn't it?'

'I'm not sure that I follow,' Codd said. .

'I have found that life is always about values, Gideon,' Frobisher explained. 'What is the value of one person over another? What is the value of their potential contribution to the society in which they live? We are all animals, are we not? The weak are always subjugated by the strong. Is that not the natural order of things?'

'I guess so,' Codd said slightly confused. 'Does this mean that you will help the boy?'

'Of course we shall help him,' Frobisher said. 'It is our *duty* to do so, our *obligation*. We shall make him strong again, give him direction and purpose. A sense of destiny.'

There was a knock on the door and the two men looked up to see Mrs Caldecott standing with a tray of tea. Standing beside her was Edward Chorley.

'Edward,' Gideon Codd said gently. 'Mr Frobisher has kindly agreed to help you with the situation.'

Chorley walked into the room and made for the vacant seat behind the desk, sitting back heavily into it so that it made the sound of a huge, wet fart.

'You look very comfortable behind that desk, Edward,' Frobisher said impassively. 'It was made for you.'

'Whatever.' Edward stared at the men with cold eyes. 'When do I get one of those cool uniforms?'

'It's a comic,' Agnes said to Maud as she looked down at the edition of *The Blue Bolt* on her coffee table. Agnes' lounge was cosy and welcoming; a mixture of pastel blues and yellows, with scatter cushions and vases of flowers that gave the room a sweet, floral scent.

'Ye might be as old as the sea, Agnes Clutterbuck, but there's no foolin' ye is there?'

Maud and Agnes were sipping tea from two huge yellow mugs, each one bearing the motto: *Shhhhhhhh! Librarian at Work!* Agnes had been the first person Maud had considered when she began reading the comic last night. The librarian had responded to her call by inviting her friend around for breakfast. Now, with the smell of recently cooked bacon and eggs fading in the perfumed air, the two women were settling down to some investigating.

'So, what about it?' Agnes said.

'Somethin' is botherin' me about this thing,' Maud said. 'An' I can't put me finger on it. I'm hopin' you'd help steady me hand a little.'

Humouring her friend, Agnes picked up the comic. 'I'd have thought that one of The Newshounds would be a better help, Maud. This is a young person's read, after all.'

'I got a terrible feelin', Agnes,' Maud said sincerely. 'An' it's a feelin' that doesn't belong in this day an' age. I can't explain it but I need yer thoughts.'

'So where did you get it from?' Agnes asked thumbing through the many pages.

'Young Thomas Beecham brought it back with him from his inauguration ceremony at the old scout hut,' Maud said. She told Agnes about the DVD and the *Blue Thunder Foundation Handbook*.

'An organisation like that shouldn't be encouraging children to operate in shadows,' Agnes criticised. 'Most irregular. If Thomas was so protective of his things how come you ended up with this comic, Maud?'

'Well, he was too wrapped up in his DVD to notice I had it,' Maud said.

'So you've risen from Dorsal Finn heretic to comic book thief,' Agnes chuckled. 'Congratulations on your promotion.'

'The sooner ye can read it, the sooner I can get it back to him,' Maud replied with a grin.

'Okay,' Agnes said, settling back in her arm chair. 'Give me half an hour and I'll give you my review.'

'An' I'll sit here an' drink tea.' Maud giggled. 'It's a hard life, eh?'

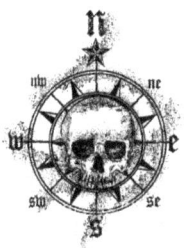

'Lucas Walker what *were* you thinking?'

In the bathroom mirror, his reflection didn't have much to say in response. Lucas splashed water onto his face from the white sink unit. The cool liquid was meant to clear his head but only succeeded in giving the terrible memories of yesterday greater definition.

'I'm sorry, Bea,' he said to the mirror and his voice cracked a little when he recalled the hurt etched onto his friend's face. 'I didn't mean to—'

'*But you did mean to, didn't you?*' said an accusatory voice in his head. '*At the time you wanted her to feel hurt, just like you felt hurt, right?*'

He was ashamed, and he was scared. Ashamed at how he had treated the person he claimed to care for, and scared that she would never be his friend again. What if Patience couldn't talk her round?

When he thought about this, Lucas felt his heart suddenly drain, as though cold water was seeping through each chamber, each ventricle. He would give anything to turn the clock back. He couldn't bear to be without Bea's friendship, even if it meant she was seeing another boy. It meant everything to him.

How could he make it up to her? How could he put things right?

Lucas was at a loss, his panic over the potential damage he'd caused slowing down rational thought. He cupped his hands and threw more cold water onto his face.

'Think, damn it,' Lucas snapped at his reflection. 'You caused it, now put it right.'

He needed to make a gesture, something that would show Bea all was well between them.

Then he had it.

'Marcus,' he said, ignoring the faint stab of pain in his chest when he uttered the name. 'I'll tell *him* I'm sorry for being a dork. Bea would like that because—' He paused, finding it difficult to say the words out loud but forced himself to do it, 'Because she cares about him. And if I say sorry then she'll know that I care about our friendship enough to put things right.'

And as he said it, Lucas knew that this would work. He knew it because he knew Beatrice Beecham always did what was right, no matter how painful it might be.

Lucas pulled the plug from the sink and with the sound of water gurgling down the drain, left the bathroom to get dressed.

Within ten minutes he was on the streets of Dorsal Finn and heading for the *Blue Thunder Foundation* HQ.

CHAPTER TEN
CLUTTERBUCK AND
POSTLETHWAITE INVESTIGATE

GEORGE BEECHAM MADE his way into the parlour whilst working his way through the post. A wad of large envelops was held securely under one arm as he rifled through several smaller ones in his hands. With the shop being busy during the week, he tended to leave Saturday's post until Sunday morning, giving him ample time to address any pressing matters.

'If bills were paycheques we'd be millionaires,' he said to Maureen as he sat down at the kitchen table.

'We're not doing too badly,' she smiled, placing a mug of tea in front of him and kissing the top of his balding head. 'Things have been worse.'

'Indeed they have,' Mr Beecham said softly and sipped his tea. He smacked his lips. 'Nice brew, love. Almost as good as the one Thomas brought us in bed earlier. Well, what I managed to salvage after I dropped it in shock.'

'It's going to take a few washes to get the tea stain out of the duvet.'

'Look on the bright side,' George Beecham said with a grin. 'If it had been hot we could have been scalded.'

They both laughed heartily.

On cue, Thomas came into the kitchen with a sprightly step. His uniform was sharp and crisp. 'Hi, Mum! Hi, Dad!'

'Hi, Tom,' his dad said. 'What have you got planned?'

'We are meeting at *Blue Thunder* HQ this afternoon. So that means I'll be watching *Blue Bolt* this morning,' he said happily. 'Have you seen my *Blue Bolt* comic anywhere?'

'Can't say I have,' his dad said. 'We'll keep an eye out for it.'

George Beecham ripped open a large, padded envelope and tipped the content out onto the table. A DVD case thudded onto the place mat.

'What's that?' Thomas said excitedly. 'Is that a *Blue Bolt DVD*?'

'It certainly is,' George Beecham said, having a closer look at the box. '*The Blue Bolt Parental Companion Guide,*' he read aloud. He scanned the back cover in silence. 'It suggests that the family all watch it together to pick up what it calls "the educational philosophy" behind the series.'

Maureen came over to take a look. 'Then I guess we'll take a look this morning, what do you think, Thomas?'

Thomas was awestruck. 'You mean all sit down and watch *Blue Bolt together*?' he gaped. 'That's *so* cool!'

'Then let's tidy away the breakfast things and get cracking,' Maureen Beecham said picking up the breakfast dishes.

Thomas leapt to her aid. 'Let me do that, Mum.'

'No arguments from me, young man,' his mother said, stepping aside to allow him to gather the plates and load the dishwasher for the second time that day.

Yes, things are certainly getting better, Mr Beecham thought, as he watched his son busy himself with the tidying up.

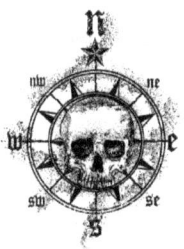

Elmo strummed his guitar and absorbed the warm, distorted fuzz this elicited from the speaker. He couldn't really explain how it worked, but the way this sound made him *feel* was explanation enough. At present he knew three chords but this didn't bother him in the slightest. Someone had once told him that A, E, G were the only chords you needed for Rock and Roll. And Elmo had practiced changing between these chords religiously for over a year, and was now pretty good at it.

As he strummed, his mind would often drift to other places, and thoughts would pop into his head— small nuggets of wisdom dropping into his mind like shining coins in a Wishing Well. But at that moment he had more thoughts than he cared to consider. A rudimentary Internet search of the links between the Nazis and the myth of Atlantis had thrown up plenty of hits. Over a million to be precise. And he'd bundled his findings into a collegiate folder in preparation for the inevitable phone call from his fellow Newshounds.

But until this time there was just Elmo, three chords and the beautiful noise from the amplifier.

It was to be some time before he found this kind of peace again.

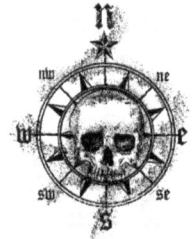

'Keep still, Beatrice Beecham,' Patience fussed. 'You'll end up looking like a Panda.'

Beatrice sat on Patience's bed allowing her friend to apply a liberal amount of eye shadow to her upper lid.

'Let's get this right,' Beatrice said carefully. 'You're saying Lucas' behaviour last night can be put down to . . . *cheese*?'

'Yes,' Patience replied firmly. 'He's *intolerant*, you see? And I don't mean that in a "*boys are intolerant of most things that girls like*" sort of way. It's something to do with its makeup, lactose or something like that. I mean, have you *ever* seen Lucas eat cheese?'

'I can't say that I have,' Beatrice replied after some thought.

'Oh, thank God,' Patience said rubbing the tiny brush against the compact case in her hand.

'I'm sorry?' Beatrice asked.

'I mean, *oh, thank God* he doesn't eat it, otherwise he'd have no friends at all,' Patience said. 'I think it was the scone he had in Eccleston's. He asked for a plain scone, but I guess it was a little cheesy critter all along. He did say that it tasted cheesy at the time, but we thought it was just, you know, past its "sell by"?'

'Well, it does explain a few things,' Beatrice said somewhat relieved. 'His behaviour bordered on weird. It was like having my brother there for a second. I thought Marcus took it all very well.'

'He's cool,' Patience said, eager to steer the conversation away from her ham-fisted attempts at platitude. 'So?'

'What?' Beatrice said opening her eyes to find Patience staring expectantly at her.

'How was it?' Patience said. 'Your date?'

'It was nice.' Beatrice blushed.

'*Nice*?' Patience repeated. 'Beatrice, a cream cake is *nice*! You're talking about a date with Dorsal Finn's newfound *Honey Bunny*. Tell me it was more than just *nice*.'

Beatrice smiled broadly. 'Well, it was great, if I'm honest.'

'So did you, like, *snog*?'

'Patience!' Beatrice turned scarlet.

'Oh, stop being so coy.' Patience placed the compact case on her dressing table. 'You're wasting good blusher.'

'We kissed if that's what you mean,' Beatrice said almost in a whisper.

'Same thing, but different *vocab*,' Patience said grinning. 'Wow! A snog, that's so radical for you, girl.'

Then she saw something in Beatrice's eyes before the blushing girl turned away from her. 'Don't tell me that you *kissed more than once*? Beatrice Beecham you're shameless.' Patience chortled, clapping her hands together.

'That was great, too,' Beatrice laughed along with her friend. 'It just felt like the right thing to do.'

'Then it *was* the right thing to do,' Patience said. 'I'm quite envious.'

'How was the meeting last night?' Beatrice asked. 'Find out anything?'

Patience explained about the translations and the Cryptic Crypt.

As she spoke Beatrice was once more amazed by how the impact of dark history was never too far away from Dorsal Finn, the way something unsightly moves underneath unblemished skin.

'We're going up to St. Norman's at sunset later to see what we can turn up,' Patience concluded. 'At the moment it's just a lead, but we're hopeful.'

'I have to familiarise myself with the recipe for Lobster Stew,' Beatrice reminded her friend. 'I don't want to leave things to chance on your uncle's big day.'

'Sometimes taking a chance is exciting as well as worthwhile, eh?' Patience winked.

'Not with a recipe like this one,' Beatrice said. 'Unless you want your uncle eating fish and chips for his 50th birthday dinner?'

'Point taken,' Patience said. 'Will Marcus be holding open the pages of your cookery book?'

'He might.' Beatrice grinned. 'I hadn't thought about it.'

'Liar!'

Both girls broke out into a fit of giggles and hugged each other tightly.

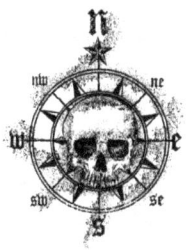

Lucas spotted the tall, wiry figure of Marcus Macbeth from some distance away, and found himself having to fend off a sudden bout of jealousy. He cursed himself. This was about resolving issues, after all, not making them worse than they already were.

The newly painted scout hut loomed, its wooden skin flickering in the sunlight, and Marcus could be seen by the flagpole. The *Blue Thunder* standard flapped in the wind, ready for the next parade.

As Lucas drew near, Marcus became aware of his presence, and surprised him with a friendly wave.

'Hi,' the handsome boy said. His smile was full of cheer.

'Er . . . hi.' Lucas shuffled from one foot to the other.

'Lucas, isn't it?'

'Yeah. Marcus, right?'

'Two for two, we *are* good, aren't we?' He grinned, offering his hand.

'The best,' Lucas said taking Marcus' hand. The bigger boy's grip was firm. Confident.

'You like Beatrice, I guess?' Marcus said unabashed.

His directness left Lucas taken aback, so much so he almost didn't feel able to give any other response but the truth. 'She's a good friend,' he managed.

'*A good friend*?' Marcus said. 'It looked more than that last night.'

'What did she—?' Lucas began but Marcus cut him off.

'Don't worry, she didn't say anything. She doesn't know how it is between you and her.'

'So how can you tell?'

'I'm a guy, right?' Marcus laughed. 'Trust me, I can tell.'

'Oh,' Lucas muttered.

'What brings you here?' Marcus asked.

'Back to last night again,' Lucas said, his mouth dry. 'The way I acted, it was wrong.'

Marcus looked at the flag over their heads for a few moments. 'I know,' he said simply. 'But you're right to say it to me. That takes guts. I like that.' He brought his attention back to Lucas. 'But it's not really me who needs your apology. You should be telling her.'

'Bea?'

'Beatrice, yes,' Marcus confirmed. 'Between you and me, she was really upset.'

'Oh,' Lucas said allowing guilt to maul him again.

Marcus put a hand on Lucas' shoulder. 'Look, Lucas, if you want me to step aside, I will. I'd hate to get in the way of you two.'

Lucas was speechless, his mouth hanging open as though he'd forgotten how it worked. But the craziest thing about all of this was that he actually thought about taking Marcus at his word; to just allow him to step down so he could ask Beatrice out on a date. It only lasted for a second but the thought had been there.

'No,' Lucas said instead. 'That's not my call to make. I would never ask that. I'll *deal*.'

Marcus nodded. 'You're a good person, Lucas. Have you ever thought about joining us here at *The Blue Thunder Foundation*?'

'Thanks for the offer,' Lucas said uncomfortably. 'But it's . . . '

'Not your bag?' Marcus concluded.

'That's about right.'

'It's not for everyone, I'll admit, but if you change your mind, you know where to find us.'

'I will,' Lucas said without conviction. He turned to leave, paused. 'Marcus?'

'Yes, Lucas?'

'Don't hurt her, okay?'

'I have no intention of hurting anyone, let alone Beatrice,' Marcus answered.

'Good,' Lucas said walking away. 'That's cool.'

Lucas followed the promenade for a few minutes then crossed the street towards the shops. He felt oddly content with his decision to make peace with Marcus now.

As he ambled along the road, he whistled a non-tune and thought about writing some new lyrics. They would be bittersweet, focusing on a love story where one person had to show their true love by letting another go. His heart fluttered in his chest, a watery sensation that made his throat hitch a little.

There was a sound that came to him on the sea breeze. It was an angelic tune, delicate and lilting, and quite beautiful. The chords almost tore at his heart and he stopped to compose himself as he recognised what the aria was: "Edelweiss" from *The Sound of Music* movie. He looked about him, searching for the source of this angelic music. He had almost given up on his search when its source made its presence known in the shape of two elongated shadows on the pavement in front of him.

By the time the newcomers had stepped from the confines of a nearby alleyway, Lucas Walker was lost in music.

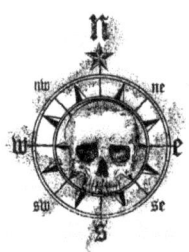

'So, what's yer thinkin'?' Maud said walking into Agnes' lounge with two fresh mugs of tea. The librarian had been reading Thomas' comic for over half an hour.

'Terrible artwork, not a patch on Bob Kane,' Agnes tutted.

'Who on God's good Earth is *Bob Kane*?' Maud said sitting down opposite her friend.

'*The Dark Knight*?' Agnes laughed at Maud's blank stare. 'Batman? Oh Maud, you've never lived.'

'I wish that were true.' Maud slurped on her tea. 'Anythin' more than bad drawin'?'

'Clumpy script; turgid plotting—'

'Giddy goodness, Agnes Clutterbuck! I'm askin' is there somethin' in that thing I should be worried about?'

Agnes closed the comic and sat with it neatly in her lap. 'Well, depending upon your perspective, and you'll have to understand this is a very loose perspective I'm talking here, there are similarities between this story and many others that describe the rise of a champion to fight off evil, and restore freedom from the oppressor.'

'That's a bigger mouthful than Edna Duffy can dole out, make no mistake,' Maud said. 'So what are ye sayin'?'

'I think what I need to know, Maud is: What are *you* saying?'

'I'm sayin' that yesterday mornin' I saw a Swastika on a wall downstairs, Agnes,' Maud replied cautiously.

Agnes held up the *Blue Bolt* comic. 'And are you saying that the Swastika, a symbol of absolute evil, is related to this?' she quizzed. 'How?'

'I don't know,' Maud said.

The two women stayed with their thoughts for a while. Through the window, a ship's horn wavered in the air. Maud continued to sip her tea as Agnes stood and went to a cabinet where she removed a small, spiral bound notebook with a stubby pen secured in its spine. She returned back to her seat and prepared to mark down her views.

'Let's look at the *Blue Bolt* backstory,' Agnes eventually said. 'A race of nomadic, parasitic creatures invades the planet of *Carbine*. These *Psychophants*, or whatever they're called, creep into the population and slowly take it over by possessing the most influential people on the planet. But not just taking it over; changing the planet to make it more attractive to their kind, and in the process undermine the will of original the inhabitants.'

'Nice bedtime readin' for yer average ten year old, eh?' Maud said. 'It's the stuff of nightmares, more like.'

Agnes continued. 'So enter this superhero, *The Blue Bolt*. He starts life as an orphan who is wandering the city streets, destitute and in need of guidance. Such is his need that the planet's gods send him a vision—a blue streak of lightning which appears to him when he's whiling away the day in the city museum. The gods tell him of the Psychophant conspiracy to gorge themselves at the detriment of the planet's people. It is his destiny to rid the planet—the universe—of these "vile creatures". And *The Blue Bolt* is born.'

Agnes paused to take a sip of tea as Maud mulled over the *Blue Bolt* synopsis.

'There's nothing here that would influence a lad to be secretive,' Maud said. 'But me gut is nigglin' somethin' horrible. Ignore yer gut, rue yer head, as me ol' mum used to say.'

'There are so many stories that tell of good overcoming adversity,' Agnes said putting the notebook down next to her mug. 'This just feels like another example of one of those tales. A remarkably bad example, but it's a fable about good and evil, pure and simple.'

'How can it be good if it makes ye feel bad?' Maud questioned.

'As I said before, what's good and bad will depend on your . . . ' Agnes' voice trailed off as she picked up her notebook again, her wrinkled eyes brimming initially with excitement and then turning slowly to dread. 'Come with me,' she said to Maud, standing up so quickly, she knocked over her mug of tea in the process.

Maud watched her friend sweep out of the room. 'Where are we goin'?'

'To get some perspective,' the librarian called back.

Maud watched the tea dripping onto the cream carpet. 'A cloth might've been a better bet,' she smiled grimly before following her friend downstairs.

'When I was your age, my mother would bake cookies that were as big as your head,' Miller said staring across the yard. Sinking into a beaten-up brown sofa on Miller's back porch Lucas felt rested and at peace. The Beatrice and Marcus issue didn't seem that big a deal to him anymore. He didn't question this new outlook.

'As big as your head? That's a big cookie,' Lucas observed behind a mouthful of biscuit. 'Did they taste this good?'

'Much better,' Miller said. 'She was a fine cook, my mother. A fine *woman*.'

'You miss her, I guess?'

Miller seemed far away. 'Yes, a boy is bound to miss his mother, I think. She had so little time on this earth. They all did.'

'Who do you mean?'

Miller realised he'd drifted off into his memories and gave an awkward laugh, shaking his head as he did so.

'Oh, ye know: family? I'm sorry, such things shouldn't concern the young. What about your mother, is she a good cook?'

'I couldn't possibly answer that on the grounds I might incriminate myself.'

Miller smiled, but still appeared distant. 'Better bad food than none at all. Ah, the cookies are gone. I've got more if you want 'em?'

'If you don't mind.'

'Of course not,' Miller said and went off to the shack.

Lucas got up and drifted over to Little Bertha. As always he had thoughts in his head of the history behind the weapon and the action it had seen. It crossed his mind if Little Bertha had been the nemesis of Klaus' doomed Henkel bomber, and such a thought left him somewhat awed. Perhaps this thought distracted him enough to not take a decent enough step as he mounted the footplate. As he climbed into the gunner's seat, the hem of his jeans snagged and caught a lever. Lucas instinctively pulled his leg away and the gear moved with a small *pinging* noise, and a hatch in Bertha's foot plate popped open.

Fascinated, Lucas peered inside the compartment and saw a leather-bound folder. But his fascination was short lived. Because there, embossed and clear in the surface of the soft and worn leather, was the unsettling image of a Nazi Swastika.

Lucas checked to see if Miller was returning with his biscuits, but all he could see in the yard was the tangled jungle of metal.

He ducked down from view and pulled the folder free, quickly flipping open the flap, the sharp smell of old leather made his nose wrinkle. Then he saw the contents: several photographs containing black and white images of stern looking men and women in uniforms. Nazi uniforms.

As Lucas flicked through the other papers, he came across three blue sheets of thick vellum with drawings in bold white lines, and accompanied by unintelligible writing. He pulled a sheet closer to his face, squinting to see if it made any difference to his ability to decipher it.

'German,' he whispered.

He also noted a swatch of cloth and risked a long moment examining what was inside—three fat cylinders made from opaque crystal and resting on a plinth of brass. They reminded him of something he had seen before. Then it came to him, the faded line drawings in the drop-pod.

The sudden sound of someone approaching made his breath catch in his throat; there was movement to his left, an elongated shadow crawling across the ground towards him.

It happened quickly, Lucas becoming aware of someone standing behind him, the owner of the shadow having arrived. Slowly, folder still in hand, his breath hot and still in his lungs, Lucas turned, just as the shadow made a lunge for him.

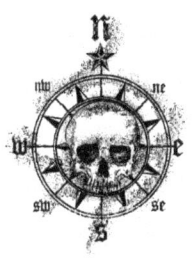

Lucas' wide eyes were momentarily blinded by a curtain of pink as Wolfgang delivered a fierce barrage of long, wet licks to his face.

'Yuck!' Lucas fended the beast off with a pat on its muzzle. 'Yes, good boy, Wolfgang. Glad to see you're feeling better. Now go and baste someone else, would ya?' The hound merely stared at him for a moment before sitting down and giving itself a huge, disinterested scratch, its tongue lolling and flopping like something trying to escape those huge jaws.

Lucas hastily returned the folder back into its compartment and pushed the metal panel shut. Then he hurried back to the sofa where he sat down and tried his hardest to suppress the excitement threatening to burst out of him.

The Newshounds made a collective decision to meet up and share their thoughts at noon that day. They mulled over the idea of going up to the Bluff but opted for the serenity of *Seer's Rock*, a knotted lump of coastline projecting out into the sea. The waves would smash into the rocks at high tide, yet Beatrice found this din restful, and the rhythm soothing.

She sat with Patience, waiting for the boys to arrive. The calls had been made and Patience had assured Beatrice that Lucas was undoubtedly in the process of planning his apology speech. Waves turned to foam at the base of *Seer's Rock* as Beatrice observed Lucas climb up onto the rocks ten metres away.

'Where's Elmo?' Patience called.

'He's on his way,' Lucas said. 'He's bringing some information on the Nazis and Atlantis. You've got to give it to him, the boy's done his homework.'

'Well, he's late handing it in.'

'Who made you teacher, Patti?' Lucas laughed.

Beatrice liked it when he laughed. It was a light and musical sound, a sound of which she never grew tired.

'Can I have a few words?' he said to Beatrice.

'I only need to hear one word,' Beatrice said.

'Told you,' Patience said.

Ignoring the comment Lucas continued, 'I really need to speak with you, Bea,' he said. 'In private?'

'Don't mind me,' Patience said. 'Just imagine I'm a hat-stand or something.'

'A hat-stand on the beach?' Beatrice giggled.

'A hat-stand that talks?' Lucas added.

'A *hat-stand* that is taking the hint and going over there of a while,' Patience said. 'Feel free to let me know when you're finished.'

Beatrice and Lucas waited until Patience was out of earshot. The waves lashing the rocks helped to quell the uncomfortable silence that followed.

'It's about last night,' Lucas said.

'Yes?'

'I'm sorry I was weird,' he said flatly.

'It's okay, Lucas,' Beatrice said relieved that they were able to start putting it all behind them. 'Patience explained everything.'

'She did?' Lucas questioned, though his face appeared preoccupied.

Vague.

'I didn't realise that you were intolerant,' Beatrice said with a knowing look.

'Intolerant?' he said bemused. 'That's one way of looking at it.'

'It does sound odd, doesn't it,' she chuckled. 'Are we friends?'

'Marcus seems like a nice guy,' Lucas said and the change in topic caught her unaware. She thought about the question and smiled at the memory of piers and kisses.

'Yes,' she said. 'Yes, he is.'

'A kind and charitable, guy,' Lucas said staring out across the bay.

'You could tell all that by just looking at him?'

'It's more about actions than appearances,' Lucas explained coming back to her.

'I'm not sure I follow . . . '

Lucas continued to look at her but ignore her all at the same time. It was as though she had become transparent and he was having trouble focusing. Maybe he wasn't completely over his cheese reaction.

'Well, let me explain,' Lucas said now blinking every few seconds. 'Marcus is an *Adonis*, right? And he's taken it upon himself to date, well, *you*.'

It took a few seconds for the words to sink in. '*And*?' Beatrice said finally. Her heart was pounding with anger and hurt.

'Not clear enough?' Lucas asked. 'Okay, I was trying to consider your feelings in all of this, but since you insist: I think the guy must be desperate for a date.'

'What's the matter with you?' Beatrice said, her eyes filling with tears. To hear words like this coming from Lucas stabbed her heart like a cold dagger. 'I thought you were my friend?'

'I *am* your friend, Bea,' Lucas said, but he stood emotionless, apparently oblivious to the hurt he was causing. 'And it's because I'm your friend that I have to tell you I think Chorley's got a point, you're one ugly-looking bitch in the daylight. '

Beatrice reeled from this, her hands going up to her face as though checking his words hadn't cursed her in some way. Her tears flowed freely now, pumping down her cheeks and through the gaps in her fingers. She tasted their salt in her mouth.

'Maybe I should be a charitable person, too,' Lucas continued. 'Maybe I should ask you out on a date. But the thought of being near you just makes me want to vomit.'

Beatrice let go huge sob and stepped up to him. She slapped Lucas hard across the face; a remarkable feat in itself given how the streaming tears blurred her vision. The slap was loud on the air, catching Patience's attention immediately.

Beatrice glared at Lucas, and at that moment she had never known such fury, such hatred. It coursed through her hot and unchallenged.

'I wouldn't go out with you if you were the last boy in the universe, Lucas Walker!' she spat.

With that she ran from the rocks, not caring if she fell, not caring that Patience called her name over and over. She just needed to be away Lucas and his monotone poison.

And that calculating, cruel smile.

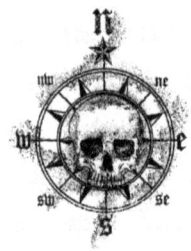

'Let me tell you something, young man,' Frobisher said to Edward Chorley. 'You remind me a little of me when I was your age.' Frobisher nodded as though saying this gave the notion even more truth. 'Yes, very much so.'

'Who are you?' Chorley asked.

'We've done our introductions,' Frobisher teased. 'Weren't you paying attention?'

'You know what I mean,' Chorley said with irritation.

'Of course,' Frobisher laughed. 'Forgive me. I, like you, was once a person who was consistently misunderstood by others. Consistently underestimated.'

'And now?'

'Now those who mocked will feel my wrath,' Frobisher said with menace.

'Cool,' Chorley grinned.

The man and the boy stood on the stage at the Cadet HQ. Edward stood resplendent in his freshly pressed uniform, his mother getting up extra early to re-polish his boots, black leather belt and silver buttons.

'I am aware that your father was once a highly respected member of this community,' Frobisher said. 'I can identify with this. My own father was—' he paused, '—let's just say that he was a man of principle; a man of *discipline*.'

Chorley regarded Frobisher, his blue eyes unfathomable.

'You are quite wise to be cautious around me,' Frobisher observed. 'But you have traits that will lead you to greatness, Edward. *If* you choose the right path.'

'And what path is that, Mr Frobisher?' Chorley replied proudly. He was surprised that his leader had used *Edward* and *Greatness* in the same sentence.

'The *principled* path,' Frobisher whispered. 'The path that allows you to follow your beliefs to the letter.'

'And where do I find such a path?'

'It is there,' Frobisher pushed a button on the lectern and a hatch in the floor slid open. 'I shall lead you down to it.'

CHAPTER ELEVEN
VEIL OF EVIL

AGNES WAS ALREADY hunched over a thick book by the time Maud had made her way down the narrow staircase leading from the librarian's flat to the main reading area.

In typical fashion, Agnes' glasses were balanced on the tip of her nose, her keen eyes fervently scanning the text.

'What ye got there, Agnes?' Maud asked standing at her shoulder. The pages under scrutiny were etched with neat text and black and white photographs.

'It's worse than we could ever imagine,' Agnes said without looking up from the pages.

'Then tell me,' Maud said, her face severe.

Agnes finally looked at her friend, and in her face Maud could see dread, pure and simple. 'Upstairs I said that this was all about perspectives, right? What if the villains in the *Blue Bolt* comic aren't villains at all?'

'Ye're goin' to have to un-muddy that for ol' Maud.'

'It's easier if I read this passage to you,' Agnes said

turning back to the book on the reading desk. '*He is no master people; he is an exploiter*,' the librarian said, her voice rhythmic and subtle. '*He has never founded any civilisation, though he has destroyed civilisations by the hundred . . . everything he has stolen. Foreign people, foreign workmen build his temples. It is foreigners who create and work for him; it is foreigners who shed their blood for him.*'

'I don't recall that from any comic book,' Maud said, puzzled.

'You didn't,' Agnes said. 'It's part of a speech delivered in 1922 at a conference in Munich, Germany.'

'Who made the speech?'

'*Adolf Hitler*!'

'Giddy goodness,' Maud gasped.

'Goodness plays no part in this, Maud,' Agnes whispered. 'This speech is about Hitler's insane views on the Jewish people.'

'Perspectives?' Maud said as she absorbed the librarian's words.

'The Nazis blamed the Jews for all things wrong in Germany at that time; selling hatred, peddling fiction as fact, accusing them of taking over all the prominent positions in society. Feeding off of the German people,' Agnes explained.

'Like parasites?' Maud asked.

'Or Psychophants,' Agnes said. 'Once you think in this way, the *Blue Bolt* story takes on a whole new meaning.'

'This is turnin' me stomach,' Maud said, her lips white with anger.

'Oh, there's more,' Agnes said sadly. 'Reading here,

Hitler was destitute as a young man, wandering the streets of Vienna as a failed artist. It's alleged that at this time he had a vision when he took refuge in the Hofburg museum, just like the *Blue Bolt*. In this vision Hitler saw his destiny unveiled, that he would lead the German people to salvation.'

'This is more than Klaus,' Maud said aghast. 'A message on a wall can be bricked up an' forgotten. But evil has come to our town, there's little doubt about that now. An' we have to stop it from taintin' those we love.'

'That's true, Maud,' Agnes replied. 'But it would take more than just comic books to peddle this garbage. And without any real evidence to change the context, *The Blue Bolt* can still be considered harmless hokum for kids.'

Maud knew Agnes was right. *The Blue Thunder Foundation* was currently untouchable. Agnes' suppositions were mere hearsay and nonsense without proof.

'We need to find out more about *The Blue Thunder Foundation*. Get past all the positive hype and advertising. Do a little digging,' suggested Agnes.

'Well, ye can't dig without dirt,' Maud said sternly. 'An' there's plenty of that on show here.'

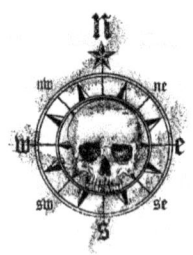

Beatrice ran.

Sobbing and her vision fogged with tears, she ran. Across the beach, stumbling upon the shale, landing on all fours then scrambling back onto her feet, trainers filling with sharp pebbles. She skittered on steps made treacherous by damp moss, and then up onto the promenade.

Seer's Rock and Lucas Walker were both behind her, but not far enough. She kept up her pace, the anguish, the fury, driving her onwards; her mind blind to everything else but the need to *get away*.

The terrifying blend of screeching tires and a blaring car horn brought her instantly back to the present as a bright red car dominated her vision, the smoke from its locked wheels were blue grey in the sunlight. It was too close to avoid and Beatrice closed her eyes and waited for the terrible impact.

Something did hit her, but it knocked her sideways and didn't feel as hard as Beatrice thought a car might. She landed heavily on the road, the wind of a vehicle passing close by, whipping her hair and clothes, before jarring her shoulder on the hard cobblestones and rolling several metres in a tangle of arms and legs.

She lay with her eyes shut for a few moments, not feeling anything at all, wondering if this was how it felt to be dead. Then her shoulder began to complain at its recent abuse, followed by someone taking hold of her hand and patting it.

Beatrice looked up, and saw the concerned face of Emily Hannigan peering down at her. The young girl had a cut across her right eye, the blood trickling down her cheek.

'Thank you,' Beatrice mumbled not quite back to

her senses. Then Beatrice was pulled to her feet, and her arm draped over Emily's shoulder as the girl bundled her back onto the pavement.

They both sat down heavily, gasping for breath as the driver of the car cursed them—his face almost as red as his vehicle. He then drove off leaving a befuddled Beatrice and Emily to watch him go.

'You saved my life,' Beatrice said to Emily. 'Thank you.'

The girl merely smiled and nodded. 'Welcome,' she said in a thick yet coherent voice. 'You upset?'

'You can *talk*?' Beatrice said trying to hide her amazement. 'But I thought you were deaf?'

'I lip read,' Emily said. 'Remember? I'm deaf but not mute.'

'You're very brave,' Beatrice said turning to see if anyone else had seen the incident. She felt Emily's hand on her arm and turned to face her saviour.

'I need to see your *lips* to read them,' Emily said. 'Can't turn away, can't stand in front of bright light, otherwise I'm gonna have to guess, right?'

Beatrice nodded. 'I'm sorry,' she said.

'Don't be sorry,' Emily said. 'Just be *aware*.'

'I will. I promise,' Beatrice said.

'So why were you running?' Emily asked.

Beatrice thought about this and said, 'I wanted to get somewhere fast?'

The other girl laughed again. 'You nearly didn't get there at all.' Then Emily noticed Beatrice's red-rimmed eyes. 'You've been crying, too.'

'Yes,' Beatrice said casting her gaze to the floor. Emily tapped her shoulder a few seconds later.

'Why?'

'Something upset me,' Beatrice said. She brushed a strand of copper hair from her fringe, noticing that it was damp with her tears.

'You mean *someone*?' Emily clarified.

Beatrice nodded.

'Can I fix it?' Emily asked earnestly. Her kindness brought fresh tears to Beatrice's eyes and she brushed them away with the back of a freckled hand. 'No, thank you. You've done more than enough already.'

'You helped me,' Emily said. 'With that stupid *hearing* boy.'

'Edward Chorley?' Beatrice said. 'I did what anyone would do.'

Emily shook her head. 'Not *anyone*.'

Beatrice smiled sadly, 'Maybe not,' she conceded. 'Will you walk me home, Emily?' Beatrice asked.

'Try stopping me,' Emily replied with conviction.

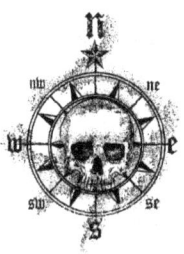

On the way back to Crab Mill Terrace, Beatrice learned a great deal about Emily Hannigan. She learned, for example, that Emily had an older, hearing brother called Harvey who was at Durham University studying to be an astrophysicist. Beatrice also found out Emily was a huge fan of football and as well as supporting Aston Villa, she also played goal for the Deaf Girl's International Football Squad; a position that had earned her many medals and trophies. Emily even suggested that she'd used her trademark half-height dive to rescue Beatrice from the oncoming car.

Emily's effervescent nature helped Beatrice to think of her near miss with the car as a thing of the past, despite her scraped knees and aching shoulder. In return, Beatrice had used her handkerchief to clean up the cut over Emily's left eye which had proven to be only a minor scratch once all of the blood had been mopped up.

The girls met Marcus Macbeth a few hundred metres from *Postlethwaite and Beecham's News and Chocolate Emporium*. He stood on the pavement talking with Thomas. Marcus' tall figure dwarfed that of her brother.

'Hi, Beatrice,' Marcus said. But as he neared, the smile slid away from his face. 'What's happened? Are you okay?'

And as soon as he'd shown concern, Beatrice's eyes topped up with new tears. 'No,' she sniffed. 'I'm not okay at all.'

Suddenly she felt Marcus' arms about her, and she put her face into his chest. Thomas watched with token interest before turning and going back into the shop.

'This is Emily,' Beatrice sniffed after a while. 'She helped me. She's deaf.'

'Thank you, Emily,' Marcus said carefully, stepping away from Beatrice for a moment so that he could slowly sign at the same time.

'Very good,' Emily signed back.

'You're full of surprises,' Beatrice said looking up at him with a weary smile.

'You don't know the half of it.' He winked. 'Let's get you inside and you can tell us all about your duff day.'

'This really isn't *necessary*, Mrs Beecham,' Marcus said, trying to juggle the plate of biscuits in his lap so they didn't slide off onto the floor.

'Please, call me *Maureen*,' Mrs Beecham said with a serene smile that Beatrice had never seen before. Her mother took the plate from him and placed it on the parlour table. 'There, that's done it.'

Beatrice had walked into the cottage to find her parents finishing up watching a DVD with Thomas. Before Beatrice could feel remotely uncomfortable with the idea that her date was in the room with her unwitting parents, it became apparent that it really didn't matter. Because Marcus, it seemed, had already met them and had a cosy chat about how wonderful Beatrice was! And to their daughter's astonishment, her mother and father didn't object to Marcus dating her at all. In fact, from the moment they'd heard about it, they had been serving him biscuits and tea.

'I still can't believe it,' George Beecham said, 'a *Blue Thunder* Group Leader sitting in our home. It's an honour, that's for sure. And asking our daughter out on a date, too. Remarkable!'

'Dad,' Beatrice said uncomfortably. 'Maybe we should allow Marcus and Emily some time to get used to us?' She tried to temper the pleading tone in her voice, but Marcus caught it and winked.

'Of course,' Mrs Beecham said. 'We'll leave you kids to it. Come on, Thomas. Let's watch the *Blue Bolt* DVD again.' With one last longing look, Beatrice's parents left the parlour. Thomas quickly followed.

At their departure, Emily began ploughing into the remaining biscuits. 'These are good,' she said in between swallows. Beatrice and Marcus laughed.

'Do you want to tell me about what happened?' Marcus asked.

Beatrice told him everything, right up to when she'd met up with him in Crab Mill Terrace.

'Boys,' Emily said. 'No brain, that's the problem.'

'I can't say I'm surprised by Lucas' behaviour,' Marcus said carefully.

'No,' Emily concurred. 'Because he's a boy and he has no brain. I just told you. And you call me deaf.'

'Well, not *all* boys are like that, Emily,' Marcus said.

Emily shrugged and went back to eating biscuits.

'This just isn't like Lucas at all,' Beatrice said, her brow creasing at the thought. 'Patience said that he has intolerance to cheese.'

'Cheese?' Marcus asked, puzzled. 'Well it takes all sorts. It might explain the behaviour, but not the spite.'

'I guess not,' Beatrice said. Her shoulders sagged in resignation. 'I can't think of anything else that would cause to him to say those terrible things.'

'He came to see me,' Marcus said. 'This morning, he came to apologise for his behaviour. I think he likes you.'

'Likes me?'

'*Likes* you,' he said again. 'That's not so hard to believe is it?'

'I don't know what to believe,' Beatrice said.

'What are you going to do?' Marcus asked.

'I'm not going to do anything.' Tears twinkled in her eyes. 'Lucas Walker has to accept he's just managed to lose a good friend.'

Marcus placed a comforting arm around her, while Emily looked away to give them some privacy. As she did so, her acute vision saw a shadow move across the carpet outside the parlour door. Getting up she peered casually around the doorframe and saw an old woman in a long, red cardigan hurrying away as fast as her pair of equally red Doc Marten boots would allow.

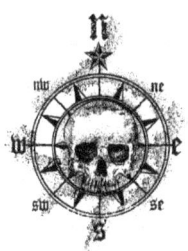

Even with the security that came with his haphazard and chaotic bedroom, even with his music and movie icons watching over him from the walls, Lucas had never felt so totally and desperately alone.

What had happened on the rocks and how he'd gotten back home was a blur. He remembered opening his mouth and saying things to Beatrice, awful things, things that simply weren't part of him. But at that moment seemed as though they were exactly who he was. Lucas also recalled the stinging pain of Beatrice's slap across his left cheek, and watching her scurry away from *Seer's Rock*. Patience had come to him, her face angry and perplexed. Over and over again she had asked him what he had done, what he had said, to their friend.

And that was it. Getting home, how he'd done it, how long it had taken, was a void in his brain, a thing to be lost forever.

His cell phone buzzed like an angry wasp on his bedside table, he'd turned the ring tone off since it kept ringing every few minutes or so. Patience and Elmo wanted answers, and he had none. He reached over and switched the phone off altogether without looking at it.

Downstairs he could hear his mother thumping and bumping around the kitchen as she prepared dinner for them. Two meals, two plates, two seats; this was the way it had always been, just him and his mum, and Gull Cottage with its wind chimes and happy atmosphere.

Sure, Lucas did think about his dad from time to time—who he was, where he was, why he wasn't around anymore—but the thoughts were fleeting. Once he had asked his mum about it, and her eyes seemed to look right through him before she changed the subject so quickly, Lucas thought he'd imagined asking the question.

As he sat on his bed, not agreeing with the old saying about *misery loving company*, Lucas felt a memory scuttle through his mind like a spider suddenly disturbed in the darkness. It was a clumsy image of a man standing over him, looming large; a Mickey Mouse mobile hovering above his head. And this man bent forward; bright silver buttons of a uniform twinkling in the lamp on the bedside table, and kissed Lucas on his forehead.

'I love you, son,' the man said and his voice was warm and rich, and the smile on his handsome face wavered a little. 'Forget,' he said softly before he stood upright and disappeared from view.

The image crumbled as a heavy knock on his bedroom door crashed into his reverie, knocking it aside, and almost making him cry out in frustration. He took a breath. He'd already done enough damage to those around him after all.

'Hello?' he said.

His mum opened the door and gave him a big smile, her bright green hair looking as though someone had placed a clod of turf on her head. 'You have a visitor, love,' she said stepping aside.

'Beatrice?' Lucas said standing up hopefully.

'Give ye another try, young'un,' Maud said from the doorway.

'I don't know what happened,' Lucas said. He sat with Maud in Gull Cottage's small-yet-busy garden, his laptop placed on a white, plastic patio table. Around them, trestles festooned with climbing, flowering plants provided a welcoming, perfumed shade from the late sunshine. Maud wore a sombre expression as

Lucas recounted what he could remember from *Seer's Rock*, nodding as though she understood everything even though she had not been present at the time.

'I opened my mouth and all this horrible stuff came out,' Lucas said miserably. 'It was as though someone else put words in my mouth, you know? And Beatrice, the look on her face . . . ' He wiped a tear from his cheek as Maud pulled a handkerchief from her sleeve and passed it to him. He nodded his thanks.

'She probably hates me right now,' he said to his hands. 'I can't say I blame her.'

'She's hatin' what was said, I'd guess,' Maud replied softly. 'When she gets thinkin' again she'll realise somethin' is amiss.'

'But is it amiss, Maud?' Lucas said hopelessly. 'What if I really meant those things? What if I said them because I'm . . . I'm . . . '

'Jealous?' Maud guessed.

'Yes. I thought, I cared about her.'

'Ye *do* care about her,' Maud said patting his arm. 'Ye do nothin' but care; all of ye do. An' when old 'uns like me and Agnes know such things, it's easy to spot skulduggery when it's workin' its mischief.'

Lucas looked up from his hands. 'What do you mean?'

Maud told Lucas about Agnes' theory surrounding the *Blue Bolt* comic. His eyes opened so wide she thought they were going to fall out of his head and roll across the table towards her.

'Things are adrift in this town of ours, lad,' Maud said sternly. 'An' people are playin' puppet master with the lives of those we care about. It's time to accept that as a fact an' do a spot of weedin'.'

'What do we do?' Lucas asked.

'Ye can do what ye do best,' Maud said tapping his laptop. She reached into her red cardigan and pulled free several sheets of paper. 'Agnes is checkin' out *The Blue Thunder Foundation* online. I've brought ye this stuff an' so ye can give us yer thoughts.'

Lucas' eyes were drawn immediately to the picture of a dagger as he unfolded the papers. 'Wow, look at that.'

'Trust ye to go spottin' that thing,' Maud said.

'A ceremonial dagger. It's just like the one in Klaus' box.' Lucas brought the photograph closer to his face. 'But look, this blade has writing on it,' he said turning to his laptop. It was a poor quality image but the lettering was distinguishable as it ran the length of the small, wicked looking blade. 'In German, of course, but we won't let that stop us.'

'We won't be needin' Patience then?' Maud asked.

'It's only a few words,' Lucas explained. '*Blut und Ehre*. A basic German to English online translator would give us an idea of what it says.'

'I'll take yer word for it,' Maud said.

She watched Lucas pull up a translation site. He typed in the inscription from the dagger and hit the *translate* key.

'Well, well,' Lucas said reading the screen. '*Blut und Ehre* means "Blood and Honour", apparently.'

'Patience would be proud of ye,' Maud chuckled.

'After today, I doubt that,' Lucas said. He clicked onto the phrase *Blood and Honour* where he copied and pasted it into the search browser.

'What ye doin' now?'

'Seeing what the term *Blood and Honour* throws

up when we put it into a search engine,' Lucas said hitting the return key. He sat back immediately, his mouth ajar. 'Oh wow!' he said. '*Blood and Honour* is a motto all right.'

'For the Nazis?'

'Oh, yes,' Lucas said. 'One group in particular: *The Hitler Youth!*'

Maud shook her head. 'Things are gettin' worse, not better. Klaus had one of those things in his box of tricks. But why file off the motto?'

'Who knows?' Lucas said distractedly.

'What's up, Lucas?'

'There's something about this inscription that's bugging me,' he said scratching his head. He pulled the photograph of the dagger towards him once more. 'Maybe it's because I've been overdosing on anagram books recently but I'm in that frame of mind, and when I look at *Blut und Ehre* I can't help thinking of . . . something . . . else . . . '

'I'm guessin' the cat's got yer tongue but ye've got yer answer?' Maud said.

'I have,' Lucas said scribbling on the picture. He passed it over to Maud. 'See for yourself.'

Lucas had crossed out each letter on the original German inscription as they emerged in the words he'd written immediately below in block capitals.

Now Maud could see that there were two words traversing the dagger, two words making all that was happening in Dorsal Finn both crystal clear and completely confusing in one huge hit.

Blue Thunder.

CHAPTER TWELVE
THE CRYPTIC CRYPT

ST. NORMAN'S CHURCH occupied a space in a small, sedate part of town, not too far away from the library. It was hidden amongst large oak trees and weeping willows, and several dense thickets peppered with bright yellow flowers. The building was made up of a high bell-tower with squared walls and a flat, featureless roof which butted up to a long narrow structure, housing the main hall, giving it the appearance of a clumsy letter "L" that had fallen over on its back.

To the left of the horizontal structure was a small cemetery with many headstones, each covered with green moss and lichen, and leaning on the undulating landscape like the misshapen molars of some giant stone ogre. And it was through these tombstones that Patience Userkaf and Elmo hastily made their way, eager to get to the church before the sun shut up shop for the day.

'Why us?' Patience muttered. 'That's all I have to say.'

'If only that was true,' Elmo said.

'Sorry?' Patience said sharply. 'Did you say something?'

'Not a consonant,' Elmo fibbed.

'Something this important needs *all* of us,' Patience pressed on.

'With Beatrice doing the *Rock Lobster* and Lucas getting crabby, the odds are stacked against us. And let's face it, the adults mean well, but it says something when I'm the most physically fit out of what's left.'

When Patience had explained to Elmo what at happened at *Seer's Rock*, he had merely sat there, pensive and reserved while calculating the possibility that his best friend had suddenly become so love struck he had gone totally mental in the process. It would have been easy for him to take things at face value but Elmo had known Lucas Walker all of his life and knew him to be nothing other than loyal to his friends.

Based on this, Elmo told Patience he would speak to Lucas first before he made any judgements. Patience had accepted this but it was a tenuous ceasefire. For now at least Patience was focused on the pending incursion into the Cryptic Crypt; a premise she looked forward to as much as old age.

'Oh, I bet there's dirt and dust and *stuff*.' Patience wrinkled her nose.

'We're looking for a crypt,' Elmo reminded her. 'So I'd say dirt: yes. Dust: yes. You'd have to be a bit more specific on the *stuff* part.'

'How do we get in?'

The building began to dominate their eye line.

'I'm gonna go out on a limb here, but how about going through the front door?'

'Elmo,' Patience said tersely. 'This is serious. Can you do serious just for a while?'

'I *was* being serious,' Elmo said. 'Reverend Darwin will have booted out the congregation an hour ago. Now he's settling down to a nice sleep after finishing off the communal wine.'

'Oh,' said Patience. 'Well done on that, then. Keep it up.'

They headed toward the large arched doorway, flanked with two smiling gargoyles. The heavy wooden doors were closed. Elmo stared up at the gargoyle nearest to him.

'At least someone's smiling.'

He pushed the door and it opened smoothly, creating enough space to allow them access.

'Nicely oiled,' Patience said.

'They maintain the hinges regularly,' Elmo replied closing the door after him.

'No,' said Patience pointing at the figure lying in one of the pews using a cushion for a pillow. 'I meant the *reverend*.'

Elmo chuckled just as the prone vicar snorted in his stupor, prompting both of them to cover their mouths before they collapsed with laughter.

'Come on,' Patience whispered. 'Let's get this done.'

Inside, the church aisles were a fusion of fading sunlight and deep shadows. Behind the alter rose a huge stained glass window depicting a Benedictine monk—St. Norman himself— etched in thick strips of lead and sitting at a table where a piece of parchment lay propped up against a small lectern. St. Norman had his pink, almost opaque, face turned towards the congregation, his smile rapturous; one hand in the air and the other with an extended finger pointing to the blank pages. His robes and the parchment were constructed of yellow glass, and in the background was a sunset of the deepest red.

'The window faces west,' Elmo observed. 'Ready to catch the evening sun.'

'But there's nothing to see,' Patience said. 'The parchment on the glass is blank.'

'Have you noticed that St. Norman's finger isn't made of glass though?' Elmo noted. 'It's a solid strip of lead. I wonder why when the rest of his hands are made of glass?'

'In the last light of day, let him point the way' Patience quoted from Klaus.

'Him? St. Norman?' Elmo suggested looking about and stopping as he faced the wall behind them. Opposite the window was a plaque with a list of names engraved onto its surface. He immediately went over to it.

'It's a war memorial,' he said casting his eyes over the names punched into the brass. 'And look what's happening now that the sun's going down.'

The large plaque was suddenly bathed in the light from the dying sun, and the ghostly image of St. Norman was superimposed over the names of those from Dorsal Finn who had given their lives for their country during times of war. But both Elmo and Patience noticed that, as the sun threw St. Norman's shape on the memorial, the leaded finger became a dark shadow pointing to a specific spot in the brass.

'That's it,' Elmo said. 'That's the way we open the Cryptic Crypt.'

'But it's too high,' Patience whispered.

'Not if you get onto my shoulders.' Elmo put his back to the wall then stooped with his fingers interlocked to offer his friend a makeshift stirrup. 'Come on, Patti, before we lose the daylight.'

'I suppose it's better than dust,' she said, reluctantly placing her foot in his hand and allowing him to hoist her up. She planted her hands on his shoulders, then her feet, and he held her steady as she reached up to the place where St. Norman's shadowy finger was indicating to the name *Robert Harold III*. Her finger probed and pressed the letters until she came to the III, and at her touch the whole numeral depressed.

'That's got it,' she said and Elmo helped her down, with a sigh of relief. She was still holding onto him when the hideous growl of shifting stone reverberated around the church, covering them both in dust.

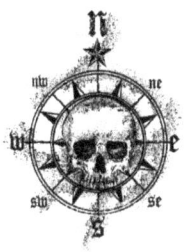

Beatrice scanned the list of instructions given to her by the head chef at *The Sanctuary*. After days of committing it to memory, she had written out the recipe for Lobster Stew to make sure that nothing was forgotten for the big night.

Perched on the kitchen counter, Emily flicked through Aunt Maud's *Chinwag* Magazine, considering the possibility that she may have to go home sometime soon.

She felt a hand gently touching her shoulder and looked up to see Beatrice standing before her.

'You okay?' Beatrice asked. 'You seem sad?'

'No,' Emily assured her new friend. 'No, I'm very happy. It's just I have to go home soon.'

'Why is that a bad thing?'

Emily explained what her parents had said to Patience.

'They mean well,' Beatrice said. 'They just want to keep you safe, I guess.'

This made Emily thoughtful for a moment.

'I know they love me,' she said finally. 'But not letting me be myself just makes me feel lonelier.'

'You'll never be alone as long as we're here, Emily,' Beatrice said. 'I promise.'

Emily gave Beatrice a long, hard hug and muttered a thank you into Beatrice's shoulder.

The two girls separated and Beatrice turned to Marcus who was busy watching the two lobsters milling about in the tank of water.

'Are you going to give me any advice?' Beatrice said.

'Not a chance,' he replied. 'Too many cooks, remember? Besides, I've never cooked lobster so I wouldn't have the first idea.'

'Well maybe I can give you a few tips?'

'I'd never turn you down, Miss Beecham,' he chuckled just as his cell phone rang. 'Marcus,' he answered swiftly. He listened to the brief burst of chatter in the headset before saying, 'I'm there now, Sir.' He tucked his phone away. 'Duty calls,' he said apologetically. 'Sorry.'

'I understand,' Beatrice said making a huge effort to hide her disappointment. She almost succeeded.

He came over and wrapped his arms about her. 'I'll see you tomorrow?'

Beatrice chewed her lip. 'Maybe not,' she said. 'I have to get my head around this meal.'

She was relieved to see him smile. 'You don't mind?' Beatrice asked anyway.

'We both have a strong sense of duty, Beatrice,' he said. 'I think that's part of why we get along so well.'

'That must be it,' she grinned and they kissed again.

'Maybe it's because you both just like snogging each other?' Emily said sliding from the counter. 'I'll leave you to each other's . . . faces!'

At this Emily left for home.

'That girl is far too observant,' Marcus laughed.

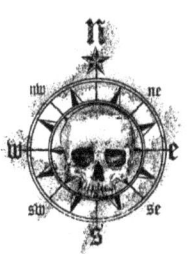

'Isn't that just bloody typical?' Patience coughed as she patted down her clothing, and clouds of dust puffed up, fogging her vision. 'This is before we go into the crypt. You recall that's the place where all the dirt was supposed to be?'

'And the *stuff*,' Elmo said. 'Don't forget that.'

'Do you want me to go any further, or not?'

'Okay, no more from me,' Elmo said.

They walking into the church as the dust began to

clear. Reverend Darwin was still lost to his stupor despite the din. As Elmo moved down the aisle, he noted something ahead.

'The Altar.'

'What about it?'

'It's gone.'

Sure enough, the large table was no longer visible. Instead there was a rectangular hole with a series of steps on the left.

'Torch time,' Elmo said pulling his flashlight from his shoulder bag.

'Great,' Patience said without enthusiasm. She pulled a slim pencil torch from the back pocket of her jeans.

Elmo pointed his torch into the chamber, the beam highlighting the stone floor several metres below. 'Want to wait here while I check it out?'

'What? And listen to Darwin's snoring?' Patience said with a huff. 'Lead the way.'

There was a short run of steps, no more than twenty, and they spiralled left before giving way to a solid floor made from uneven blocks of limestone. Elmo cast his torch about them.

The crypt was huge, extending far beyond the church perimeter above their heads. Pillars of thick stone stretched away from them in both directions, their torch beams suddenly insignificant. Each footfall echoed, hinting that the space around them was massive.

'Let's take stock here,' Elmo said. 'First of all, Patti, you're going to crush my arm if you don't let go. Secondly, that's the fourth time you've stood on my foot.'

'Sorry,' Patience said stepping away from him. 'It's pretty spooky down here.' Her voice was small, even the echo couldn't give it any real power.

'It sure is,' Elmo said. 'We'll get it done quickly and get gone.'

They turned their attention to the crypt and tried to find anything untoward. The chilled air was stale and had the smell of a dank old cellar, adding to its inhospitality. Elmo tried to forget all the Tales from the Crypt episodes he'd watched on TV.

It wasn't working very well.

They inched through the darkness, relieved when their torch beams eventually found walls. Suddenly, Patience spotted something.

'Look, Elmo, an inscription!' she said with excitement.

'Er, Patti,' Elmo said carefully. 'That's a tomb.'

'Ugh.' She pulled up and dropped her flashlight, its rubber casing sending it bouncing off, the errant beam throwing crazy shapes across the floor.

Cursing, Patience stooped to retrieve it and gasped. The torch lay on its side, resting up against one of the pillars, and caught in a river of light were sentences etched into the flagstone floor at the base of the pillar.

'What do you think?' Patience whispered.

'Terrible handwriting.'

'This doesn't make sense,' Patience said with a voice taut with frustration.

'It is meant to be a cryptic crypt, right?' Elmo said.

'No,' Patience said. 'I mean it isn't in any language I recognise. It certainly isn't German.'

'So what do we do if you can't read it?' Elmo said. 'We can't take the flagstone with us.'

'Maybe we can,' Patience replied pulling out her cell phone and activating her camera. Patience took several shots.

She retrieved her torch, and something caught her attention in the beam. Ahead, in a wall of smooth marble, was a row of tiered rectangles. The metal was smeared in green oxidised streaks. Patience pointed to one of the plates in the middle row, where the unmistakable sign of the trident from Klaus' drawings resided.

The two Newshounds made for the wall, turning their attention to the rectangle scored with the trident symbol. Elmo looked over at Patience who was staring, petrified.

'What do you think is in here?' Patience whispered.

'It's a grave, Patti,' Elmo said. 'Have a wild stab in the dark.'

Elmo reached for the plate and traced his fingers around its edges. Dust came away as a fine mist making Patience sneeze.

'Is that dead stuff?' she snuffled.

'It's just more dust,' Elmo said as his fingers probed the rim of the plate and found purchase. He placed a foot against the marble, trying to avoid the other plates. He pulled.

'Oh, I can't look,' said Patience as she continued to stare through her fingers.

Elmo braced off and hauled the plate. After a brief moment of resistance, it extended into a long tray which squealed as gears gave out their protest.

As the tray came to a juddering stop, they saw the shroud; a flowing white thing that slipped off its host, dislodged by the sudden movement.

Patience screamed when she saw the leathery face of a corpse grinning at her in the torchlight. It was a woman with white hair and a thick gold chain around her withered neck. The skin was dry and weathered, reminding Patience of parchment. The cheeks and eye sockets were dark, sunken holes and in places the dry flesh had split, and yellowed teeth could be seen through the gaps.

'Cover it up, cover it up!'

Elmo scrabbled over to the material and in panic yanked at it. With the hiss of dry skin, the desiccated corpse slowly rolled over, the sound of teeth clicking together in its loose jaws. Elmo and Patience watched in horror as gnarled and knotted arms lifted, reaching out for them.

'Oh, God!' Patience cried. 'It's alive!'

Patience stepped backwards, her feet becoming entangled in Elmo's legs and they all fell, the corpse slithered from the tray and landed with them. Elmo and Patience scrabbled away but found their exit blocked by a stone pillar.

But as the clouds of dust settled, The Newshounds gazed at the corpse a few feet away, face down, inert and lifeless.

Elmo looked at the swatch of shroud he clutched in his hand and followed the trail of material until he saw it was still wrapped around the body's waist. He laughed with relief, and Patience looked at him, her eyes haunted with fear.

'It got caught on the shroud,' Elmo explained.

Patience merely stated at him, her face streaked with dust.

'This is definitely what I'd call stuff,' he smiled weakly.

'I don't want you to talk to me right now,' Patience said breathlessly.

Elmo cut his losses and stood up. He went over to the tray, taking care not to step on the fallen body, and peered inside the tomb.

'Patti,' he whispered. 'I found something.'

'Let me guess, Dracula?

'No,' he said. 'Something way cooler.'

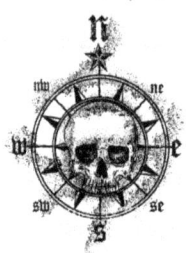

Beatrice made her way to bed, a glass of warm milk held out before her. As she passed the lounge, Maureen Beecham called out. 'Beatrice? You're not off to bed already are you?' Her mother's voice was tinged with disappointment. 'I thought we could spend some time together. As a family?'

'It's been a weird day, Mum. I'm tired.'

But Maureen Beecham had said the words 'family' in a way that made it non-negotiable. Beatrice sighed inwardly and steered her way into the lounge where Mr Beecham and Thomas were sorting out the DVD player for another episode of *Blue Bolt*.

'Are you guys planning to watch the *entire series* before bed?' Beatrice asked perching herself on the arm of her mother's chair. She sipped at her milk.

'Why not?' George Beecham said calmly. 'It's good family entertainment. There aren't many TV shows that have the whole family sitting down together anymore.'

'I guess not,' Beatrice admitted, but she was already planning several excuses in case they expected her to sit down and watch *Blue Bolt* for the rest of the evening. She couldn't think of anything worse, but that was before thoughts of Lucas and the events of *Seer's Rock* popped into her head and her heart lurched in her chest.

'Marcus really is a wonderful young man,' Maureen Beecham said unexpectedly, pulling Beatrice from her dark thoughts. 'And handsome, too.'

'Yes,' George Beecham confirmed. 'You've done very well for yourself there, love.'

'Well don't start saving for the wedding just yet,' she said, slightly embarrassed by their frankness.

'He seems like such a good boy,' Maureen Beecham said rubbing Beatrice's back affectionately. It had been a while since her mother had done such a thing. Beatrice began to relax as Mrs Beecham continued. 'The future becomes the present all too soon. You'll learn this as you get older.'

'I'm sure,' Beatrice said, not sure in the slightest.

'He's a group leader, too, Bea,' Thomas said. 'He told me that if I work hard, I could be promoted pretty quickly. So, thanks!' And with that her brother gave her a big hug almost knocking the glass of milk from her hand.

'Er, you're welcome, I think.' Beatrice stood up, completely baffled by the whole thing. 'I'm going to head off to bed. As I said, today is off the weirdness scale already and I'm scared it's showing no sign of levelling off.'

'But it's been a *good* day, too, don't you think?' George Beecham said languidly. 'The kind of day you never want to end?'

Beatrice nodded, though inside she didn't agree with either of her father's statements.

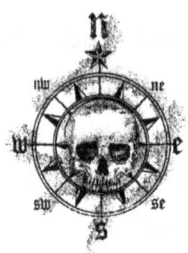

'Is that the last?' Patience gasped. 'Tell me it is before I collapse and die.'

Elmo and Patience had carefully carried three wooden crates from the crypt and into the graveyard, where they placed them behind a dense patch of gorse. The equipment was heavy, even for Elmo. The desire not to drop the pieces made their journey as painstaking as it was cumbersome.

'It's the last,' replied Elmo, leaning against a tombstone, breathing hard. 'You can die now. At least you'll be in the right place.'

'I'll call Maud and get us some transport,' Patience said as Elmo forced himself upright and made for the church.

'Hey, where are you going?' Patience called after him. 'Don't leave me here on my own.'

'To put things back the way they were,' he said without looking back. 'Otherwise Reverend Darwin might find more than a spare bottle of communal wine next time he heads for the Altar.'

'How are you going to reach the numerals?'

'I'll pull up a pew—as the saying goes.' Elmo grinned.

'What about the corpse?' she whispered.

'She's dead. Don't think she'll be able to help.'

'You know what I mean.'

'We'll make a deal,' he said, 'I'll go and put her back where she belongs and neither of us mentions it ever again?'

'Easiest deal I'll ever make.'

Patience called Maud, but it was Albert and Dennis that came for them. Fifteen minutes later, a white van with *Pontefract Estates* painted on the side bounced up the uneven path towards the church.

Without a word the two men had loaded the items from the crypt into the back of the van, and told Patience and Elmo it had been organised that they were all going to the library. Patience noted that Dennis and Albert wore a grim countenance, as though they were aware of something terrible, but didn't feel inclined or able to share it.

Within ten minutes, the van pulled up outside the library's delivery entrance, a set of double doors at the end of a small courtyard at the rear of the building. As Albert took the keys from the ignition, the double doors opened and Agnes, Maud, and Lucas stepped through to lend a helping hand.

'Hi, my spiky-haired friend,' Elmo said to Lucas, who seemed to be having trouble focusing on either of his fellow Newshounds.

'Am I?' Lucas asked.

'Spiky-haired?' Elmo replied.

'Your friend?'

'I'm glad you asked that,' Patience said, less diplomatically.

'An' I'm askin' ye to hold that thought until ye've heard a few things, Patience,' Maud interjected.

Patience nodded, but the look she gave the boys implied great reluctance before she walked on ahead.

Lucas looked on as Elmo offered him a furtive glance and the larger boy mouthed 'Always' and then followed Patience. Lucas felt cursory relief but held it in check. There was still work to do.

The double doors led to a large stockroom, lit with stark fluorescents. In the centre of the room was a wooden counter, dull with age and littered with dust jackets.

Albert and Dennis placed the boxes on the counter and the group stood around them, each person lost in thought.

'Two questions,' Patience said. 'What on Earth are these things and what's going to save Lucas from a good verbal kicking?'

'I got an answer to the first one,' Dennis said.

'That might be the case, Dennis,' Maud interrupted. 'But I'm thinkin' that savin' young Lucas from a tongue lashin' might be the first priority.'

And before Dennis could say more, Maud told

them all what she and Agnes had discovered via the *Blue Bolt* comic to how Lucas had helped her find the evidence to support their discovery.

'So what are we saying?' Patience said. 'That the *Blue Thunder Foundation* is to blame for Lucas being a total git to Beatrice?'

'I'm sayin' we know each other more than we know the boys in blue,' Maud said. 'An' Lucas is ownin' what he's guilty for, but the rest of the baggage is belongin' to someone else. We just haven't figured it out yet.'

'What's the last thing you remember before coming to *Seer's Rock*?' Elmo asked.

Lucas scrunched up his face, trying to recall. 'I remember getting dressed,' he said slowly. 'Then walking to the old scout hut.'

'To do what?' Patience asked.

'To apologise to Marcus,' he explained. 'We chatted, I said *sorry,* and left.'

'Then what?' Elmo urged.

'Nothing,' said Lucas, sighing in defeat. 'Not a single thing.'

'But you went to the BTF HQ and came away with no recall,' Agnes said. 'Given what we know about them, we have to assume skulduggery's involved.'

'Which would mean Marcus is involved.' Patience frowned.

'We have to accept anyone wearin' *that* uniform is not to be trusted,' Albert said.

'Even young Thomas?' Agnes asked.

'Aye,' Maud said sadly. 'There's a change in him, an' his parents judgin' by what I saw this evenin'.'

'But how?' Dennis said.

'Somethin' underhand, no doubt,' Maud said.

'So what do we say to Bea?' Patience said perplexed at the thought.

'We can't risk saying anything,' Agnes said.

'*Can't?* This is Beatrice we're talking about,' Patience protested. 'Our friend, remember?'

'She cares about the boy, Patience,' Agnes said simply. 'She'll be blinded by this at best. If you tell her, you might lose her as a friend for good.'

'If Beatrice found out what *Blue Thunder* stood for she wouldn't want any part of it, I'm sure,' Elmo said.

'Say that were true and she finished with Marcus,' Lucas said. 'He'd want to know why. He might find out we're onto them.'

'Lucas is right,' Maud said. 'As much as I don't like it, we have to keep this away from Beatrice. Until we know what the *Blue Thunder Foundation* is peddlin' an' back it up with proof.'

'Well whatever they are pushing is impossible to find,' Agnes said. 'I searched the internet and came up with nothing more than soft soap and accolades. It as if no one has a bad word to say about them.'

'Maybe there is nothing there to find,' Patience said.

'There's nothing there because they have found a way to make it that way,' Agnes said. 'They're a mystery, that's for certain.'

'Which brings us to these things,' Elmo said patting one of the boxes on the counter. There were three of them resting there, each had been pulled from the beaten up wooden packing crates, the remnants of which were now scattered around the floor of the storeroom. The devices were all made from dull grey metal and peppered with glass dials and thick black tumblers, their surfaces glazed with a thin layer of grease.

'What are they?' Lucas asked.

'They're transmitters,' Dennis said. 'Me old man had one on his boat many years ago. But these are old school.'

'You mean, World War II *old school*?' Lucas asked.

'Yeah, no doubt.'

'Know how to work 'em?' Maud said.

Dennis stroked his beard, his eyes staring intensely at the dials and switches imbued on the transmitter's dull, metal surface. He reached round the back of the bulky box, hunching over to peer behind it.

'No plug and lead. Where's the power source?'

'Who knows?' Albert said. 'We have to be realistic. These must be over 70 years old; the chances of getting them to work are remote.'

'They're lookin' as though they're in good nick,' Dennis said. 'Someone intended these things to *keep*.'

'If they are damaged, can they be repaired?' Lucas asked.

'The technology's from another time, lad,' Albert said. 'It's unlikely we'd get the parts.'

'Anyone noticing the marks on the top of the casing?' asked Elmo.

'What do you mean?' Patience said.

'In the bottom left hand corner, see?'

Sure enough, the group could see that there was an arrow etched into the metal casing.

'And on this one,' said Elmo tapping the middle transmitter. 'See this upside down "T" shape here?' Again the marker—an inverted T-shape finished off with an arrowhead—faded but visible. 'And finally in the bottom right hand corner of the last transmitter,' Elmo said. 'Another arrow shape.'

'Do you think these mean something?' Patience said.

'Yes,' Elmo said immediately. 'If you put all the markers together you get—'

'The symbol from Klaus' box,' Agnes cried. 'A Trident?'

'So we're saying these transmitters are *The Trident of Poseidon*?' Lucas said in awe. 'How do we use them?'

'And what does the Trident actually do?' Patience asked.

'Two very important questions, I'm thinkin',' Maud said.

'I can't say what it is these things do, but my research tells me the Nazis were fixated with trying to prove their assumed superiority was because they were related in some way to the *Atlantians*.' Elmo's fingertip traced across the markings.

'Hitler's Higher Order was nothing more than a bunch of criminal psychopaths,' Albert said. 'Their science was a contrived rationale for Hitler's obsession with exterminating the Jewish people.'

'Absolutely,' Elmo whispered. 'Heinrich Himmler, Hitler's second in command, had sent expeditions all over the world to search for the descendants of the Atlantic people in order to prove the Nazis were somehow related. But what if they found something else?'

'What do you mean?' Dennis asked.

'What if they actually found the location of Atlantis?'

The group stood in silence as Elmo's words sank in. No one spoke, the creaks and groans of the old building bled into the moment.

'That would be so cool,' Lucas muttered. 'Totally insane, but still cool.'

His words seemed to galvanise the others.

'Another layer of mystery to be ponderin',' Maud said.

'And I have another,' Agnes whispered. 'Klaus' voice has stopped repeating in my aids.'

'When did that 'appen?' Maud said.

'As soon as these devices arrived here at the library,' Agnes replied.

'Then I guess we know what he wanted us to do,' Albert said thoughtfully.

'You okay?' Maud asked a pensive Agnes.

'Yes,' she said. 'It's just strange not having him there anymore.'

Maud nodded as though she more than understood this as a concept.

'Let's take a look inside one of these things and see the damage,' Dennis said as he turned the transmitter so that its access panel faced them.

He pulled the panel off of the back of the transmitter after using a penknife to unscrew the casing.

They all peered inside and could see a series of glass cylinders and a tangle of wires that Lucas recognised.

'I'm not seein' any damage here,' Dennis said after probing the transmitter's metal innards for a while. 'No corrosion either. This thing should be workin' once we find a power source. Ah hang on, a valve is missin'.'

'Hey,' Lucas said. 'Look what's written on the panel, Dennis.'

On the inside of the metal plate was single word. Again, written in German.

Denkmal.

'Monument,' Patience translated.

'Meaning what?' Lucas said.

'Who knows? Let's see if the others have inscriptions hidden inside them,' Patience said.

It was of little surprise that the other transmitters contained a further two words.

'*Windmühle* translates as "windmill" and *bauernkof* interprets as "farm",' explained Patience.

'Places in Dorsal Finn?' Elmo suggested.

'Not the Dorsal Finn of today,' Agnes said. 'There's been no windmill in town since I was a child, and Hill Crest Farm was destroyed by Klaus' aircraft when it crashed.'

'What does it mean?' Patience tapped her foot in frustration.

'Maybe it's not the places that are important,' suggested Elmo. 'Maybe it's their *locations*. What if each box has to be placed in its corresponding location? And when they are switched on they become this Trident?'

'For what purpose?' Agnes asked again.

'That's the sticking point,' Elmo said.

'Not the only sticking point,' Albert said peering into the casings of the two remaining boxes. 'These also have a valve missing.'

'Three transmitters, all missing a valve,' Lucas said in a hush.

'Oh, wait!' Patience grabbed her cell phone from her pocket. 'We found something else in the crypt.'

224

The screen of Patience's phone played out the strange writing at the base of the stone column, and everyone stood around looking down at the images.

'Looks like yer handwritin', Albert,' Maud said.

'Doesn't look like anything I've ever seen before,' said Agnes. Everyone pretty much agreed.

All except Lucas, whose mind was very much elsewhere.

CHAPTER THIRTEEN
BIRTHDAY SURPRISE!

OVER THE NEXT few days, Beatrice focused on the birthday dinner, in an attempt to distract her from many concerns and anxieties.

Those who knew her understood cooking was the only thing that diverted her attention from the real world. As she considered the recipeshe was able to diffuse thoughts of Lucas and his hurtful words, the strange behaviour of her parents and Thomas. Even the information Patience had since told her relating to the Cryptic Crypt.

A sense of calm descended over her as the recipe—the task—consumed her. The relief that came with it was embraced like a good friend.

As the evening of Uncle Badru's birthday celebration arrived, Beatrice was in complete control—a welcomed state of mind, yet short-lived.

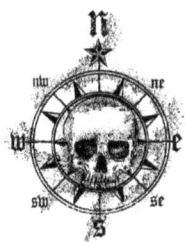

The guy standing at the door to *The Blue Thunder* HQ was large and square. The scalp of his bald head twinkled in fading sunlight. His brow shimmered with beads of sweat. One of these rivulets trickled down his temple and onto his cheek, before he dipped a big hand into a deep pocket and fished out a handkerchief. He mopped his face for a few seconds, and when he pulled the handkerchief away he was startled to see Hansel and Gretel standing sedately before him.

'Bloody hell,' he said. 'Will you quit creeping up on people?'

'We're very good at it,' Gretel said. 'Why would we want to stop?'

The big man had no answer for his inquisitors. Instead he said, 'What do you want?'

'We want to see our leader,' Gretel said.

'He's busy,' the guard growled.

'We could make you let us in,' Hansel warned. 'But we're only supposed to do that to outsiders. '

The guard shuffled uncomfortably, the sight incongruous compared to his large frame. 'Very well,' he said with a begrudging tone. 'I'll let Mr Frobisher know you're here.'

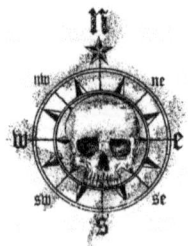

'Beatrice, dear Beatrice! Welcome.' Mrs Userkaf gave Beatrice a warm, heartfelt embrace on the doorstep. She wore a saffron-coloured dress and lots of gold jewellery. Beatrice could see so much of Patience in the woman's deep, green eyes and radiant smile.

'Thank you, Mrs Userkaf,' Beatrice said returning the woman's smile. 'Thank you for asking me to cook for you. It's an honour.'

'The honour is ours, dear Beatrice,' Mrs Userkaf said with total conviction. 'Bring your things and please do come in.'

The house was adorned with ribbons and streamers in a kaleidoscope of colours. There were balloons taped to the stairway, garlands pinned to the ceilings and walls, and as Beatrice walked down the ample hallway, she passed the living room where a huge gold banner wished Uncle Badru a *Happy 50th Birthday*.

The bright and cheerful sounds of preparation were on the air, and wonderful, joyous music pumped from huge amplifiers, adding to the sense of excitement.

Patience emerged from one of the many rooms, her face brightening as she saw her friend.

'Thank God for some sanity in this madhouse. Come on into the kitchen,' Patience greeted Beatrice.

Beatrice allowed her friend to take her elbow and

steer her towards the spacious kitchen. In her hands, the pail containing the two lobsters was suddenly not as heavy. She hoped at some point this would extend to her heart.

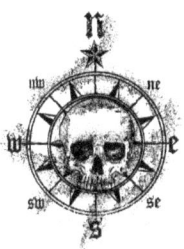

In the *Blue Thunder Foundation* cadet hut, Frobisher sat at his office desk and lazily watched tendrils of steam rising from a white, enamelled mug filled to the brim with dark brown coffee. He reached down for the beverage and lifted it to his lips before taking a tentative sip.

He savoured the bitter taste, revelled in the silence about him.

Despite the setbacks, things were looking positive; things were still on track. The loss of the trident markers on Bishop's Cragg did have him uncertain at one point, putting him at odds with his resolute nature, but he had faith. His belief in the world he was destined to create was a powerful entity. He knew this town was a strange place, it attracted the unusual, and now Dorsal Finn would soon be at the heart of events currently in motion.

He had lied to Codd, of course. He was no more part of the fabric of Dorsal Finn than the birds that migrated each winter, but he had heard the stories about the place and its mysterious heritage. Lesser men would have been struck down with fear at the knowledge of what lived here. Frobisher, however, embraced the concept. An ally was an ally, after all.

At times like these, Frobisher often questioned if he was a bad man. The thought would be fleeting but he would always take heed, pulling it back for scrutiny the way a mother would scour over an unruly child. The question had poignancy, for it reminded him of conversations he had with his grandfather many years ago.

Frobisher's parents had died in an accident when he was three years old. Their car was squashed by a huge tree blown down in a terrible storm. Frobisher was subsequently raised by his grandparents in Scotland. The house, a bothy in the Scottish highlands, was remote, and he was homeschooled. His grandmother, a quiet yet stern woman, taught him in the small kitchen as the rich smell of rabbit stew on the cast iron range pervaded the air about them.

But his education, the worldview that has steered him towards creating *The Blue Thunder Foundation*, and ultimately bring him to Dorsal Finn, was to come from his grandfather. Stories of power and glory, a world that had wronged the righteous, had fuelled his ambition.

At the thought of his grandfather, Frobisher placed his mug back on the table and laid his right hand flat on the wooden tabletop. With his left hand, he reached down and, extending the index finger, pushed at the surface of the golden sovereign ring. There was a barely perceptible *click* and the sovereign popped open. Frobisher looked fondly at the small photograph on the underside of the lid.

It was a picture of his grandparents. His grandmother was wearing a tidy summer dress, holding a small bouquet of flowers. Her smile was bright and serene.

Rather than a suit or casual shirt his grandfather wore the unmistakable black uniform of a Nazi officer.

And Fleischer was also smiling.

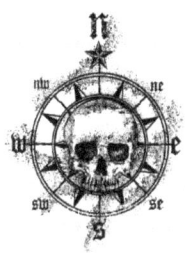

It had taken a significant period of time and resources to build a lie. The false persona that was to become Logan Frobisher and *The Blue Thunder Foundation* was as meticulous and brilliant as the Masterplan his grandfather had initiated in 1930s Germany. Just as his grandfather told him about justice and duty, so he also regaled a young Frobisher of the perils of betrayal.

He spoke of how one man had sabotaged The Masterplan at the Eleventh Hour because of misplaced loyalty, and that the road to greatness was littered with men who didn't have the gumption to do what had to be done to achieve great things.

His grandfather admitted to his own loss of faith after the war when this betrayal had undermined his plans. For a time he had been lost in the emotional wilderness that was self-reproach. Those allies who secretly sympathised with the lost cause helped the Fleischer's escape Europe and found them refuge in

Scotland where they began their exiled existence. From here Fleischer was to build his vehicle to restore order.

Frobisher's grandfather may have told him tales of duty and honour, and the promise of great destiny, but he also told him tales of the fantastic. When he was bordering on despair a vision had come to him, and in this vision memories were resurrected and hope was rekindled.

He recollected Heinrich Himmler's unfettered belief in the occult, and the creation of the *Ahnenerbe* who, under his instruction, scoured the world for objects and literature on the occult. During this time, rumour of the great and ancient power beneath this very town had come to his knowledge. Research and subsequent S.S. occult rituals were elements that allowed Frobisher's grandfather to locate and forge a token connection with minions of this terrible entity.

One night, a pact was sealed. It was intricate and reliant on an incredible level of sacrifice. But the pact gave birth to the plan currently being played out that very evening.

To the outside world Frobisher was held in esteem, a person of determination and character. It was a position that had been cultivated over many years, by people with the power and means to create such a persona, people his grandfather had courted. People with a vestige interest in the events destined for Dorsal Finn. At its heart, this was all about severing ties—connections—and Frobisher was a highly polished product of this ethic.

Yes, he had been raised in a sheltered place, with limited contact with the outside world. Yes, he only knew what he needed to know, the importance of it, nothing that would leave him vulnerable to scrutiny. But once he was in adulthood, there were alternative ways required to keep him safe if anyone ever took too much interest in his past. There were strict interview protocols for example. No reporter or academic ever saw him without stringent rules dictating the time, the place, and the venue. The latter would be a private suite in a hotel, usually surrounded by many aides, where each journalist would be screened prior to asking their questions. This would include a *credibility check*—the series of psychological tests, including a polygraph test—to establish the integrity of each journalist. It had another purpose, of course. Whilst the unknowing journalists took the test, so the electrodes gave their minds a little something in return, a subliminal *suggestion* as to the tone and content of their future article for example. It was the very same technology that allowed him to manipulate minds all over the world, blinding the masses to the obvious.

Charisma only got people so far, sometimes it needed a little help.

If journalists failed or refused to take the test then they never got to conduct an interview. Such people were rare, of course. Such was the demand in the media for any news on the Man of The Hour. The consistent media praise for his intentions should have raised some concerns, and from time to time this *did* happen, but such protestations were a small voice in an otherwise contented crowd. Besides, there were other, less *sophisticated* methods of dealing with those who became just too nosey.

Accidents did happen, after all.

Yes, there had been hiccups and yes, for the briefest of moments, The Masterplan had appeared untenable, but—based on information the twins had provided on an ongoing basis, and his grandfather's conviction that all would be well—this was in the past and a resolution in play. The children were natural spies, chameleons of incredible ability. Frobisher was always very pleased that they were on *his* side.

His cell phone buzzed in his pocket and he answered it swiftly as the screen announced a technician beneath the hut was on the line.

'Report,' he said in the handset.

'We are on schedule to launch the TV broadcast,' a small voice said. 'Do we proceed with the countdown?'

'Yes.'

'Very good, Sir.'

The line went dead.

After replacing his mobile in his jacket pocket, Frobisher sat back in his seat and took a deep breath. He exhaled—long and slow—through lips pulled into an arrogant and contented smile.

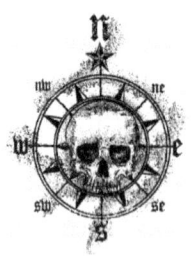

As Beatrice and Patience prepared the celebratory meal, Elmo and Lucas moved swiftly through the darkening town, their bikes visible only by the reflective strips on the wheel-arches.

When Elmo had asked his friend where they were heading, Lucas told him about the folder he'd seen at Miller's and the valves wrapped in the sack cloth.

'The *same* valves as in the transmitters?' Elmo had asked.

'That or something similar,' Lucas had replied.

'And you didn't say anything to the others because . . . '

'I've already lost one friend this week, Elmo. If I'm going to lose another then I have to be damn sure I'm right.'

'Can't believe Miller is caught up in all of this.'

'Me neither,' Lucas said.

They were heading towards Miller's shack with a simple plan. Lucas would keep Miller and Wolfgang occupied whilst Elmo went to see Little Bertha, and took photographs of the contents in the footplate compartment.

'I feel bad about duping Mr Miller,' Lucas said. 'I may have to write a song about it.'

'Let's not be *too* hasty,' Elmo said with such an unexpectedly degree of seriousness, it had Lucas laughing ambiguously. Ahead, the steps to the beach loomed and a figure suddenly emerged, causing Lucas to pull up, waving for Elmo to do the same.

'It's Miller,' Lucas whispered after the boys had snuck into a small alleyway. Lucas dismounted and propped his bike against a wall. He peered out into the street to see Miller walking away from them. 'Change of plan,' he said turning back to Elmo.

'We're going home?' Elmo said hopefully.

'Give you another guess?' Lucas grinned.

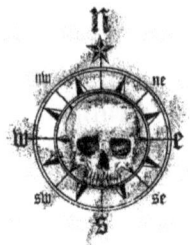

Fearing he'd be easily spotted, Elmo followed Miller on foot. He moved as fast as he could, surprised by Miller's speed.

When the shape of the *Blue Thunder Foundation* HQ came into view, Miller slowed, eventually stopping fifty metres from the building. Elmo observed the old man hunch down and move carefully to a small outbuilding adjacent to the main structure. Here Miller waited, hidden in deep shadows. Elmo edged closer, now only twenty of so metres from where Miller kept vigil over the scout hut.

There was movement outside the building.

A group of youths clad in blue uniforms approached the main doors and entered, single file. Elmo had time to count twenty kids as they disappeared inside. Once the doors closed, Miller moved again. This time, he walked directly up to the hut and listening against the doors. Seemingly satisfied, Miller edged around the walls, trying to peer in through the windows. After several minutes of doing this, he went back to the main doors. Elmo observed the big man examining the door handle and lock. No sooner had Elmo realised Miller had found a way to unlock the door, the man disappeared inside.

'Now what, Elmo?' he said to himself. 'The guy's inside. The *kids* are inside.'

Elmo knew he had choices: leave none the wiser, or follow the secretive Miller inside the hut and find out what part the old man played in all of this. When he put it in such a manner, the choice became clear, despite his urge to ignore it.

Slowly, Elmo walked towards the hut.

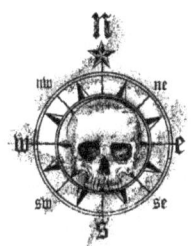

Wolfgang wasn't barking.

The slurping, sucking sound of Lucas' shoes as traversed the beach should have roused the hound, but there was no movement. Not even a growl resonated at the sound of the faulty gate as it fell noisily to one side, and not even at the din Lucas made skirting the house to access to junkyard.

He found Wolfgang as he made his way through the yard. The hound lay on a plaid blanket on the back porch, its big head on the ground, whimpering. Despite the urgency, Lucas went to the animal, but other than a token wag of its tail, Wolfgang wasn't responsive to his petting.

Frowning, Lucas made off towards Little Bertha, an intermittent shimmering silhouette under the touch of the lighthouse on the bluff.

He clicked on his torch, squatted beside Bertha,

and searched for the lever that opened the compartment. He found it quickly, and yanked on it.

Sure enough the metal plate popped open and Lucas reached inside to retrieve the folder. For some strange reason he half expected it not to be there, another thing to thwart their attempt at piecing together what was going on.

Despite his fears, the folder was where he'd previously found it. He opened it, and used his mobile phone camera to take shots of the contents. Once satisfied he placed the folder back securely.

It was as Lucas made his way back to the shack that he suddenly realised he was no longer alone.

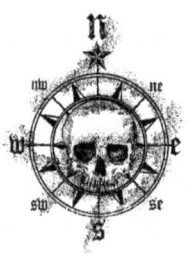

'You're going to do *what*?' Patience said incredulously.

'I have to boil the lobsters,' Beatrice replied.

'No, I think you said that you have to boil the lobsters *alive*.'

'Don't make this any worse than it is already, Patience,' Beatrice said. 'You don't have to be here when it happens.'

'But why do that?' Patience protested. 'It's so cruel.'

'It keeps the meat sweet, part of why people eat lobster. Besides, marine biologists say the lobster has no adrenal cortex so doesn't feel pain.'

'Like scientists know *everything*,' Patience said

unconvinced. This didn't help Beatrice's cause at all. She was as equally uncomfortable with this sort of practice as anyone, but she wanted the meal to be the best it could be.

'I've placed them in iced water. It's meant to sedate them. I guess you think I'm gross?'

'No,' Patience said. 'Just the procedure, that's all.'

From another part of the house, the sounds of booming voices and music drifted into the kitchen as the dinner party began in earnest. Several guests had arrived and were containing Uncle Badru in the lounge with explicit instructions to avoid the kitchen otherwise he'd be eating fish and chips from *The Tasty Plaice*.

Given uncle Badru's love of the fish and chip shop, this wasn't much of a threat at all.

Beatrice found the joviality a stark contrast to recent events. The issues with Lucas, and the mystery surrounding Klaus Hessel, seemed a million miles away. She knew it was all too easy to bring such matters back, up close and personal, with the associated heartache and pain in tow. And it seemed Aunt Maud had taken to avoiding staying at the shop for long periods, choosing instead to remain at the library with Agnes. Everything felt fragmented: The Newshounds, Maud and Agnes, her parents and Thomas. The only constant was Marcus, a beacon of stability in the changing emotional tide.

Beatrice placed a huge steel pot on the Range and began filling it with jugs of water. On the kitchen worktop, the lobsters' pincers clicked against the ice cubes in the plastic bucket and, if scientists were to be believed, remained oblivious to their fate.

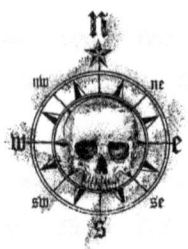

In parody of Miller not moments before, Elmo leaned up against the doors of the hut and listened for signs of movement. Considering that a large group of cadets had walked inside, the place was unnervingly silent.

Elmo held his breath and pulled the door open a fraction. He could see a small hallway leading to another set of doors, but each had a pane of glass that was illuminated by the lights beyond.

Keeping low, Elmo went into the building, each step muted by a surprisingly lush, red carpet. He straightened when he got to the double doors and peeked into the hall.

Empty.

'Where are you, guys?' he asked the dark passageway.

'You really want to see where they are?' a voice said from the darkness.

Stunned with fear, Elmo felt a hand grab at his collar and yank him backwards as though he weighed naught. The same hands spun him around so he was facing the owner of the voice.

'Mr Miller?'

'Be grateful I found you, boy,' Miller whispered harshly. 'At least you'll get to live.'

'That's a good thing, right?'

Miller looked at him suspiciously. 'You're under my feet, young'un,' he said simply. 'But I can't risk you blowin' this for me. You'll have to come along.'

'Where?'

'To hell,' Miller said. 'To hell here on Earth.'

Elmo watched as Miller pushed open one of the doors to the main hall and stepped inside, holding it ajar. As Elmo passed by, the old man held his index finger up to his lips.

The hall was deserted.

Elmo raised his eyebrows to show his confusion to Miller who answered him by pointing to the stage at the far end of the hall. The old man led him across the room slowly, checking the surroundings the way a wily rabbit checks for predators. At the stage he went to the lectern, probing its surface with his fingers. There was a sudden small click and, at the far end of the stage, a panel in the floor slid open.

The two of them went cautiously over to it. Concrete steps lead downwards.

'I didn't know this place had a basement,' he mouthed to Miller.

'It's got that and more,' Miller mouthed back, and stepped onto the stairway.

Elmo reluctantly followed when the old man was lost to view.

The stairs gave way to a long corridor with stark white, featureless walls. Every ten or so metres there were doors with plastic pull-handles that added to the clinical landscape.

'Building more than a scout hut, this lot were,' Miller breathed.

Elmo allowed fascination to babysit his fear for a

while and walked behind the massive shape of Miller. From ahead, the muted sounds of conversation could be heard. Miller led Elmo to a room one door from the end of the corridor.

Outside he muttered to Elmo. 'Whatever we see, say nothing.'

Elmo had no chance to entertain his growing anxieties, before Miller pushed open the door.

What Elmo saw inside robbed him of rational thought.

'Well if it isn't *Loser* Walker,' Edward Chorley sneered. He was leaning against the old battered shell of something that may have once been a car. 'What brings you here to Old Man Miller's place, I wonder?'

The boy straightened up, and Lucas noticed the cadet uniform. 'Keep wondering, Chorley,' Lucas said, his tone laced with ice. 'You've no place here.'

'That all depends, doesn't it?' Chorley mocked.

'On what?'

'The reason,' Chorley smirked. 'And I have a reason, Walker, believe me.'

'I guess you have permission, too?' Lucas asked defiantly.

'I don't need *permission*,' Chorley spat. 'I'm here executing a civic duty.'

'You've been watching too much CSI, moron.'

A smile on the face of Edward Chorley was never a good thing. And as his small, thin lips dragged upwards, Lucas felt the first vestiges of anxiety sweeping through him.

'Maybe I should cut you some slack, Walker,' he said. 'After what you did to *Coppertop* I should be shaking your hand.'

'You know nothing about nothing!'

'Oh, I know, alright,' Chorley laughed. 'I was *there*.'

'You weren't on *Seer's Rock*,' Lucas said.

'Not when it happened, you idiot,' Chorley hissed. 'I was there before, when you were being *prepared*.'

'Have you been sniffing boot polish again?' Lucas said. 'What are you talking about?'

'It is best that you don't answer that question, Edward,' said a voice from the shadows. 'He doesn't need to know how we play.'

The twins seemed to appear for nowhere, the dense shadow falling away from them like the folds of some ebony garment. They may have left the shadows behind, but they brought with them their impassive smiles.

'He doesn't *need* to know,' Chorley said to them sternly, 'but I *want* him to know. I want him to understand how he was manipulated to say stuff to *Coppertop*; that he's just a puppet and *we* pull the strings.'

'Well now he does know, Edward,' Gretel said calmly. 'I think you have told him everything.'

'You made me say those things to Beatrice?' Lucas said incredulously.

Chorley nodded, finding the other boy's pain

exquisite. 'Every word. They call it *mesmerising,* Walker.' Chorley jerked his head in the direction of the twins. 'And these two are masters at it. They were even able to erase the fact that you'd ever met them.'

'Did *you* ask them to do it?' Lucas said, barely able to keep his temper in check. He wanted to launch himself at Chorley so badly he felt giddy with the thought.

'I wish I could say "yes" to that, but alas not,' Chorley giggled. 'The architect to your demise was none other than *Marcus Macbeth.* Pretty ingenious; though his taste in girls sucks like a vampire from *Twilight.*'

At this Lucas gave out a cry of fury and threw himself at Chorley, catching the other boy unawares. Both went sprawling onto the harsh stone, rolling over and over as one twisted mass until Lucas found Edward's face underneath him and struck out with his fist. The punch caught Chorley in the face with a thick, dull sound that sent fire through Lucas' knuckles. It didn't stop him pulling his fist back again, ready to deliver another.

But Lucas never got the chance to land another blow. He was grabbed and dragged backwards by strong hands, having to watch the indignant image of Edward Chorley clamber to his feet.

He turned to look at who had hold of him, who had thwarted his attempts to pay Chorley back for his torment.

When he saw who it was, Lucas couldn't believe his eyes.

Unlike the corridor, the room into which Elmo and Miller stared was a deep red, the colour of blood and madness.

The twenty cadets sat bolt upright, each of them with a 15" TV monitor suspended directly in front of them.

And on the monitors was the *Blue Bolt* TV show, but accelerated so that the images were nothing more than a barrage of rapid, blinking frames.

The cadets didn't bat an eyelid, didn't move, didn't have any idea that they were being watched by those who had no place to be there. They were just consumed by the optical assault. Elmo shook his head, casting out the rapidly moving pictures on the screens but not just pictures. Single white words on a black screen, woven into the screen shots: *obey*, *trust*, *accept*. Adjectives with a sinister purpose—to control the viewer without their knowledge.

'Subliminal messages,' Miller said. 'It's as I feared. Come on.'

'We're going to report this, right?' Elmo said as they made their way back to the stage exit.

'I was too slow, too slow,' Miller babbled as he walked.

'Hold up,' Elmo said stopping completely so that Miller had no choice but to wait for him. 'We have to report what's happening here.'

'Haven't you been listening? *I was too slow.*'

'I'm getting that part,' Elmo snapped. 'But what does it mean?'

'It means we're already too late,' Miller said.

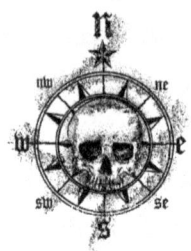

Beatrice couldn't see, couldn't think. Her whole world was consumed with *the scream.* It filled her head, vibrating, numbing the very bones in her skull, making her face contort with agony.

If Beatrice had been able to unscrew her eyelids for a second she would've seen Patience collapse against the sink unit of the Userkaf's kitchen with her hands clamped to the side of her head, ineffectually trying to shut out the terrible noise.

The sound had started when the lobster was coming to boiling point. Beatrice had placed the first creature into the steel pot when the water was tepid. As the water began to heat up, a small buzzing noise had both Beatrice and Patience looking around the kitchen for a wasp. Then the water bubbled and hissed and the buzzing noise seemed to morph into a single pitch, going from uncomfortable to agonising in mere seconds, immobilising both girls with its sonic scream.

The whole kitchen appeared to take on a vibrant green hue, as though every surface Beatrice looked upon was coated in a sickly slime. It ran in thick rivulets, bubbling out of the buckling saucepan, over the kitchen cupboards, pooled in purulent puddles on the kitchen floor.

Another wave of pain had her squeezing her eyes shut. Through the terrible noise, Beatrice imagined she heard a growling, mocking chuckle as though someone, something, was enjoying their torment. Then she was overcome with an undeniable feeling that the laughter belonged to the very thing that was also causing her pain.

'Stop it!' she cried out in her mind.

But her only reply was the laughter that rapidly became hysterical, its tone rising as though vocal cords had become stretched to ridiculous limits and mingled with the sonic blitz jarring her skull.

Through all of this, Beatrice heard another sound, the metallic pop of steel being pulled out of shape.

The pot was not only buckling, it was about to rip open!

Beatrice fought against the pain, managing to un-scrunch her eyes enough to crawl over to a writhing Patience.

'Have to get out—pot—explode—' she gasped through clenched teeth. She grabbed hold of Patience's dress and began dragging her friend who flailed blindly in an attempt to crawl across the slippery, ceramic flooring.

Overhead, a spot-light shattered, then another. Glass rained down upon them. Then the kitchen window erupted outwards—shoved into the street by the wall of sound. Wine goblets, bowls, in fact any piece of glass or crystal, shattered, causing the girls to shout soundlessly in terror and amazement.

Just as they got to the kitchen exit the pot finally gave in and ripped in two, spraying the devastated kitchen with a cascade of boiling, steaming water, the lobsters inside it now an obliterated mess that fell from the ceiling and rolled down the walls.

Patience cried out as water and lobster meat splashed on her bare legs and arms.

The pot, nothing more than a wrap of twisted steel, clattered to the floor, the sound harsh but insignificant compared to the now non-existent noise.

'Are you girls okay?' Mr Userkaf said stumbling up the hallway to their aid. Uncle Badru followed closely behind.

'Was that my surprise?' Uncle Badru smiled uneasily.

'No Uncle,' Patience said sourly. 'The surprise is that it's fish and chips for supper after all.'

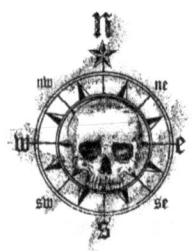

'Elmo?' Lucas said. 'What are you *doing*?'

His friend helped Lucas to his feet, just as Chorley made to run at them.

But Elmo didn't have time to respond.

'You lot are trespassin'!' Miller said from behind Elmo. 'Is that you, Chorley?'

Miller's question stopped Chorley's advance dead in its tracks. 'Who do you think it is, old man?' Chorley said. His left cheek sported a bruise as well as barely contained fury.

'Get out of here before I call the Constable,' Miller said coldly. 'Or maybe I should let young Lucas finish you off.'

Chorley appeared to mull this over, his eyes vehemently moving from Miller to Lucas. It was only when he sought out the twins and discovered they were nowhere to be seen that Chorley made his decision to leave.

'This isn't over, Walker,' he snapped on his way past.

'It never is with you.' Lucas chided.

Chorley disappeared into the night.

'Now then, lads,' Miller said. 'I believe we need to be sittin' down and chewing the fat, don't you?'

'I guess so,' Lucas said, and then caught Elmo's expression. 'What is it?'

'Let's get inside and I'll tell you,' he said quietly.

They walked away, all of them engrossed in the events at that time, but none of them more interested than the two children standing amongst the bric-a-brac, hidden by shadow.

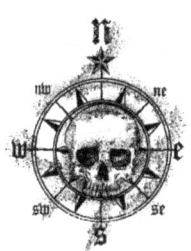

You hear the scream in the darkness. It is long and harsh and seems to go on forever. By the time the

bright waves of pain cause your hands to clamp against each side of your head you are aware that the scream is your own.

The thing that has been seeking you out is now trying a new approach. Its minion is now sent to bombard your psyche in order to wear down the defences you have put in place; spells and totems that provide a token reprieve since the day of the dream. The minion has a psychic connection that is somehow closer than the thing writhing in the ethereal landscape of Dorsal Finn and this proximity does give it greater, more potent influence.

It wants you badly. At first it pleads, telling you of a pact it had made long ago, a pact in which the world will change and you will be its instigator. Then it has tried temptation; whispered promises of wealth and power but you are not a purveyor of such things. Now it is angry and sends wave after wave of psychic energy from its place many, many miles away. It has help. Somehow you know that this thing is symbiotic with the events going on in the town. The totems would be no barrier had you been in Dorsal Finn and they waver even at this distance. The pain is great but you know it is nothing compared to what will come if the thing penetrates the spiritual shield.

Just as you fear that madness will become your new ally, the pain ceases. And the whispering starts again.

'Time,' it says. 'It is but a matter of time.'

CHAPTER FOURTEEN
WOLF AT THE DOOR

I**F MILLER'S GARDEN** was a tangled hotchpotch of junk, inside the shack was three times worse. There were spindly chairs blocking the narrow hallway, the boys having to navigate around them before finding themselves in a large living space littered with newspapers and magazines. Here and there buckets had been strategically placed to catch rainwater from the creaking, buckled roof. A table in the middle of the room appeared as though it would collapse if so much as a glass of milk were placed on it, and a small camping bed was under the large window, piled high with coarse, crumpled sheets and blankets.

To Lucas it felt as though he was in the belly of a pirate's galleon; one that had been peppered with Royal Navy cannon balls and was a hairsbreadth away from sinking below the waves. The wooden walls were warped and split, deep grooves in the grain giving the unsavoury impression of bloated veins.

Over in a corner, lying on a coarse, grey blanket, Wolfgang lay listless and moping.

'Is Wolfgang still sick?' Lucas said with concern.

'It's this town that's sick,' Miller said. 'Wolfgang is just able to sense it. Like any of God's good creatures.'

'This town?' Elmo asked.

'You know it isn't a normal place to live,' Miller said. 'Things happen here like nowhere else.'

'There's no denying that,' Elmo said. 'I mean, what other town would have Gideon Codd as Mayor?'

'Folk ain't always what they seem, that is true,' Miller nodded. 'But we ain't talkin' about folk now. We're talkin' about somethin' else. Somethin' old and bad. And it has a mighty will.'

'And Frobisher is part of it?' Lucas said.

'My story may not be as old as the evil in this place,' said Miller, 'but it began a long time ago. Long before Logan Frobisher.'

The two boys looked at each other.

'Have a seat, lads,' Miller said ushering Elmo and Lucas to a shapeless sofa keeping the precarious table company. 'I'm gonna have a drink. You want somethin'?'

The boys declined as Miller went to a rickety cupboard that surprised everyone by remaining attached to the wall after Miller had removed a glass tumbler.

'Think I'll be needin' this before we start talkin',' the man said pouring out a hefty measure of clear liquid from a green bottle. He didn't add anything to it. 'The past still has teeth.'

The boys watched him as he sat his bulk down upon a stool that didn't look up to the job.

'You got questions,' Miller said after taking a slug of his drink and exhaling noisily. 'I can see it in your eyes. But I'm goin' to ask you to just hold onto 'em for a little while, 'cause I got stuff that's been cooped up for far too long and now it wants out. You okay with that?'

Elmo and Lucas nodded.

'Can I ask one question?' Lucas said quietly.

'Sure,' Miller said, the tumbler disappearing into his beard again.

'Whose side are you on?'

Miller paused in thought before answering. 'I'll tell my tale and leave you decide that one,' he finally said. 'Deal?'

'Deal,' Lucas agreed reclining in the sofa as Miller began his story with a cautionary caveat.

'You might well ask: *Why am I telling you this?*' Miller said. 'It is a burden—that is the simple truth. And the young *should* be the ones to hear it for they will be the ones to remember and ensure it never happens again. The horror of it never fades, not with time, or with the tellin' of it.'

And with the creaks and pops of timber, and the distant, rhythmic sound of surf caressing shale, Miller began to speak.

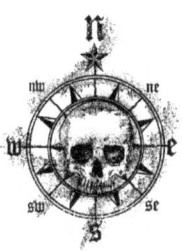

'I was born in Amsterdam in1932. My mother was a sales assistant and my father an engineer. We moved to Austria in 1937. I had one brother, Hada, and two sisters, Sabine and Maaje. My father would tell bad jokes, my mother would bake wonderful cakes and biscuits. Me and Hada would go fishin' and my sisters would often moan about us not lettin' them join in our games. We had our fights but we were happy in our world. Then, in 1938, under a dubious election, we became part of Germany and the problems began. War broke out a year later. The world turned sour.' Miller paused to take another drink of the clear liquid, the hand holding the glass was trembling badly. He continued, 'The war had been goin' on for eight months. We knew of it, but it seemed to be happenin' so far away. I know now that our parents protected us from the worst of it. At first nothin' seemed to change, there were soldiers on the streets and curfews but as kids there was little difference.

'Then the Nazi officials came and people began to disappear. Cars and trucks would come in the night and soldiers would get out. People would be told to pack a bag. It started with the elderly and the sick, but it soon changed. One day my father came home and spoke in hushed tones with my mother. We listened on the stairs as Father told Mother he had been visited by a Nazi official and commissioned to make somethin'. He didn't want to help the Nazis, but it meant his family would be kept together. A man visited him a week later, brought him some blueprints and food. The man had a kind face, but her looked tired and stressed out. And after that night Father locked himself away in his workshop at home, or went to his shop and made the things the Nazis wanted.

'It meant that we were safe; it meant Father could

keep his little shop.' Miller took a shaky breath. 'It took him months to complete, and on the day he finished the order, he was killed in an explosion at his shop. That night the trucks came for us. Soldiers told us that we were being taken to a camp for protection. They claimed Father's death wasn't an accident, that Jewish terrorists had found out about his collaboration with the Nazis. Confusion and fear robbed us of our grief for our father, but we were swept away with it, leavin' our home for those trucks, cryin' and scared and uncertain of our future. From our house we went to a holdin' camp filled with people equally scared and confused. Some whispered in corners of dark things happenin' elsewhere in Austria and Poland, tales of camps from which no one ever returned. Our mother tried to shield us from it all but the stories were everywhere. Then the trains came.

'The soldiers told us we were being relocated, and over a thousand of us were escorted to the station where a big, black locomotive waited. It had twenty or thirty cattle trucks attached to it, and I remember thinkin' it looked like a long, fat snake about to swallow us all. I wasn't too far off the mark. We were herded into a truck packed with so many people that you couldn't sit down, couldn't fall down. Three days we were on that train. No stops. No getting off, the car stank with the smell of fear and death. I recall thinkin' more than once I was going to die. Then, later, when the train finally stopped, and we fell out of the cattle trucks, I thought I *was* dead and I had been sent to Hell.'

Another shot of liquor and another swallow, Lucas and Elmo were held fast by Miller's story, neither of them wanting to hear any more but knowing they had to, that they needed to share Miller's burden in the name of truth and justice.

'So we arrived at Auschwitz-Birkenau concentration camp in Poland, and as soon as the door to the cattle trucks opened we heard the screamin'. It all happened so fast. Mother was dragged away from us, screamin' and kickin'. My sisters were beaten when they tried to hold onto her arms, and then beaten even when they had let go of her. Hada was sobbin' and I held onto him, tryin' to shield him from it all. I lost my sisters in the crowd. My mother's cries seemed to rise above all those about us. It was the last we boys saw of any of them.

'It was the sound of dogs barkin' that I remember most from that first few hours. Even over the screamin' of those around me. Isn't that odd? I think it's because the screams eventually died away, but the barkin' continued. It was relentless, savage and mindless like the events happenin' around me.

'Those first few hours were hard, watchin' life treated as though it meant nothin'; the old, the sick literally thrown into trucks and carted off, or left amongst discarded suitcases and broken crates. Babies ripped from their parent's arms. Terrible, terrible.

'Three days later, Hada got sick and they took him in the night to see the doctor. He never came back. I cried in the dark for what seemed like hours. I was alone and had thought I had seen the worst of it. Then I was chosen,' Miller's voice hitched with fear but he fought on. 'I was chosen for the *experiments*. A guard said if I helped then I could have some chocolate. A token thing, but it was as though he'd offered me the world. I went with him inside a huge shed, then I realised that a truck-load of chocolate wouldn't be enough to endure the terrible things the Nazi doctors were doin' to people. I saw awful things, things that would make an adult despair, let alone an eleven year old boy. But I was spared the fate of so many of those sent for *testin'*.

'In the place that I had come to call Hell, God sent an angel, an angel with a familiar face. It was the man who gave my father the blueprints at our home. He had come to fulfil his agreement. He had come to keep me safe.'

Miller finished off his drink and stood to get another.

'Who was this man?' Lucas said 'Was he a Nazi?'

Miller turned back. 'On the outside, yes he was. Inside? I know that he wasn't. He had a heart and a conscience. He had decency and civility, aspects that were barren in those vile monsters. He was a good man who did questionable things. The guilt claimed Klaus later.'

'What did you say his name was?' Elmo asked, his tongue tripping over his words.

'Klaus,' Miller said grabbing the green bottle by the scuff of the neck. 'Klaus Hessel.'

Beatrice approached the *News and Chocolate Emporium* picking stray bits of lobster meat from her hair.

She was still mildly irritated by how the evening had turned out. Her Lobster Stew having gone lobster *thermo-nuclear*, and Uncle Badru and the other dinner guests had to make do with a mountain of fish and chips from the Tasty Plaice. In truth, everyone had expressed their excitement around the whole affair, including the Userkafs. Beatrice had offered to clean up the lobster-splattered kitchen, but Patience's family wouldn't hear of it.

She had left Patience soaking the tiny scalds on her legs with *Sudocrem* as her mother fussed over a daughter who was far more upset with the way the ointment clashed with her new blouse.

Now, as Beatrice let herself into Crab Mill Terrace, her mind was focused upon why the lobsters had exploded in the first place. She had no theories, but the presence of vile green liquid and the disembodied laughter could never be considered a good thing. Both of these elements had disappeared as soon as they had arrived. They had, however, left Beatrice with the terrible thought that something unseen had been unleashed upon the world.

Beatrice closed the front door and made her way into the parlour, where she was surprised to see her father standing with a rather large policeman as Maureen and Thomas Beecham looked on. All of them wore their coats.

'Oh, hi there, Beatrice,' her father said happily. 'It would appear that you've come in at a bad time. We're just on the way out.'

'Where are you all going?' Beatrice said.

'Off to the police station,' Mrs Beecham said sedately. 'Your dad's under arrest.'

'What?' Beatrice said, agog. 'Why?'

'Well,' said George Beecham, appearing flushed with embarrassment. 'It seems that I forgot to report a recent indiscretion. It is a silly mistake that slipped my mind.'

'What indiscretion?'

'Clipped someone's wing mirror with my bicycle the other day. There wasn't anyone around and I intended to return to settle up with the car's owner. But with all the shop stuff it slipped my mind.'

'Mr Beecham is charged with leaving the scene of an accident,' the policeman said. His expression was dreamy, his voice vague. 'It was fortunate that young Thomas was able to alert us to such a misdemeanour.'

'What's Thomas got to do with this?' asked Beatrice.

'It's part of the *Blue Thunder* cadet's code to report all law breakers,' Thomas said matter of fact.

'*You* told on Dad?' Beatrice was incredulous. 'Are you insane?'

'I reported a crime,' Thomas said unabashed. 'It was my *duty*.'

'That's my boy,' Mr Beecham said with a smile. 'Duty is important in life.'

'Mum,' Beatrice pleaded as Mr Beecham followed the police officer. 'Can't you do anything to stop this?'

'I'm afraid not,' her mother said sadly. 'I'm under arrest too for aiding and abetting a known criminal.'

Beatrice looked from one face to another before settling on Thomas.

'You'd better hang around,' she muttered to the police officer.

'Why's that, Miss?' the officer asked.

Beatrice's stared coldly at her brother. 'There may well be another crime committed before the end of the night.'

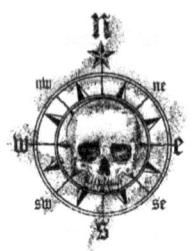

'Klaus Hessel wasn't a Luftwaffe pilot. He was a scientist, and he smuggled me out of Auschwitz in 1942.' Miller was back in his seat and he'd brought the green bottle for company.

'So what was he doing on a German bomber?' Lucas said.

'I'll get to that,' Miller said. 'There's a few gaps I need to plug before we get there.'

'Well that's gonna be a surprise for—' Elmo stopped himself from inadvertently betraying his friends. 'A few people,' he said instead.

'Maud and Agnes, you mean?' Miller suggested.

'You know?' Lucas gaped.

'Klaus spoke of 'em,' Miller said bluntly. 'He was grateful for their help. But they were kids, hell, we all were. He saw the future in us.'

'So what happened after the camp?' Lucas asked.

'He smuggled me out, had it all planned: forged papers, money to bribe officials; even gettin' me on board a plane.'

'A bomber,' Elmo reminded him.

'My ride to freedom,' Miller recalled. 'My ride to life. That's how we both saw it.'

'So why did Hessel come with you?' Lucas said. 'Was he trying to escape, too?'

Miller's response surprised them. 'No,' he said. 'Klaus carried a burden he never really disclosed. But he brought with him papers and diagrams. All he told me was that he'd been part of somethin' fantastic and terrible, and his savin' me was his attempt to atone for the awful things he'd seen. Awful things he'd *done* in the name of science. He needed to close it all down, make sure no one else got hold of what he'd been part of.'

'What *had* he been part of?' Lucas said from the sofa.

'He called it *Project Atlantis*,' Miller replied. 'Some kind of contingency plan should the Nazis fail. It was all he told me, this and his intention to make sure it never happened. He started by gettin' together all the information—all the evidence—on *Project Atlantis,* and either burnin' it or takin' it with him.'

'In the drop pod?' Lucas guessed.

'Yes.'

'Maud said that she saw three parachutes,' Elmo said. 'One was Klaus. The other two were you and the drop pod?'

'Aye,' Miller said. 'The pod landed in the sea. I got snarled up near *Bishop's Cragg*. Stayed there shiverin' and livin' on aircrew rations for a few nights.'

'What of the Cryptic Crypt?' Elmo asked. 'Was that Klaus' work, too?'

Miller appeared uncomfortable. He shuffled uneasily in his seat. 'No,' he said. 'That came later.'

'After Klaus died?' Lucas said.

'Yeah. The person who plucked me off *Bishop's Cragg* was responsible for hidin' the stuff in the crypt. Hid me from prying eyes, too. A distant saviour, set me up here, tended to me, and kept me safe and under the radar. This was the person who helped conceal Klaus' secrets in the crypt.'

'Someone from Dorsal Finn?' Elmo said incredulously. 'Who?'

'That's somethin' for no one's ears, not even in these current times,' Miller replied with determination. 'Someone risked it all to keep an orphaned Jewish boy safe. Took me in as their own for a while, and I owe them more than I can ever repay. I was told the crypt had always been there, from a time way before the church was built. I never asked the ins and outs. It wasn't my business.'

'And the transmitters?' Lucas said. 'No way they could survive a parachute drop, right?'

Miller nodded but his reply was cautious. 'They appeared several weeks after the war ended.'

'By boat I guess?' said Elmo.

'No,' he said. 'They *appeared* in the crypt. Without sound or warnin' they were there, tucked in the corner of the crypt like they'd always been there for us to find. The person who took me in just accepted it because they knew what oddities this town encouraged.'

The boys nodded as though this, at least, made some sense. Like most of those from the town, there was an acceptance of things; an innate understanding that Dorsal Finn was different, *magical*.

'So not even Klaus knew the transmitters were here in Dorsal Finn?' Lucas asked.

'If he did, he never mentioned it,' Miller said. 'And my ally from the village made sure that all the evidence was hidden away so those who sought it never found it again.'

'So why make a trail for others to find?' Lucas said.

'The trail was so others would find only the transmitters, so they could be moved should it become clear the Nazis were once more powerful and determined enough to search for Project Atlantis,' Miller said. 'Something must've snagged the tripwire and set off the alarm.'

'But—' Elmo began but Miller held up a hand.

'I don't have all the answers to this riddle, Elmo,' he said. 'If I did, Frobisher and his cronies would be comin' straight to me.'

Elmo nodded and the three of them listened to the slow, rhythmic pull of the ocean for a little while.

'Didn't you want to go back home, after the war?' Lucas asked.

'I had no home, I had no family,' Miller said, his words tinged with bitterness. 'The Nazis had seen to that. And my part in it was made clear by Klaus. The details of Project Atlantis were to be hidden. I was to stay here, keep an eye on things. The transmitters were sabotaged when I was not around. Parts were removed and put in a place I didn't know. This was done to protect me more than anything else.'

'Plausible deniability,' Lucas whispered. 'Just like those black ops movies.'

'Somethin' like that,' Miller said. 'If the Nazis came for it then the alarm would be raised, and people would come to my aid.'

'Maud and Agnes?' Lucas said.

'Perhaps,' Miller said. 'Though, again, that stuff was not made known to me.'

'Klaus said there was always a risk the architect of this vile plot would survive the war,' Miller confirmed. 'An SS commander by the name of Fleischer. The way I see things now, Klaus was right to be concerned. So, yes, they may know it is here in this town somewhere.'

'So Project Atlantis refers to an *actual* place?' Elmo said. 'Could the Nazis have actually found Atlantis?'

'These are strange days,' Miller said. 'Nothin' is beyond possibility. Whatever it is, it can't be opened without the Trident. That was its purpose. A special key to unlock a special place.'

'We found the transmitters,' Elmo said. 'They have trident markings inside them.'

'As they would,' Miller said.

'Maybe we should smash it all?' Elmo said.

'That time has passed,' Miller said. 'With what is goin' on in the hut we don't know if it will do more harm than good not havin' those things still workin'.'

'If Klaus felt this was always a risk why did he not destroy it all when he had the chance?' Elmo said.

'Klaus was a scientist,' Miller said. 'Even though he had contributed to creatin' somethin' terrible, I recall him sayin' he'd been duped as to the real purpose of Project Atlantis. Somethin' about the *greater good*. It may not have turned out to be the case, but in the months I was with Hessel I knew he didn't have a bad heart. I know his family were to be put under the gun if he didn't comply. But his work was meant to help people. Despite what it was used for, I think he still needed some good to come from his work. He hoped his science could still be made available to help mankind in the future.'

'That doesn't make sense,' Lucas said.

'Does any of it?' Miller asked. 'Guilt does strange things to people.'

'Tell me about it,' Lucas agreed. 'But for whatever reason, Klaus kept the keys to finding this place well hidden.'

'But where?' Miller asked. 'He never told me the location of all the pieces. Ignorance was to be my ultimate protection.'

'Right under your nose,' Lucas said standing up. 'I'll show you.'

But no sooner had Lucas climbed to his feet, the door to the shack was smashed inwards with the awful sound of splintering wood. Miller jumped up just as three large shapes, clad in *Blue Thunder* uniforms, filled the doorway to the lounge. Before he could cross the room, all aimed pistols at his chest.

'Now, now, gentlemen,' said a voice from the hallway. 'Let's not do anything hasty.'

The men in the doorway stepped aside, their faces grim and unfathomable. And as they parted, Logan Frobisher stepped into view, his smile as radiant as it was insincere.

'I knew you guys would be useful in the end,' Frobisher laughed. 'My little spies kept me notified throughout. People still doubted me, can you believe that? "Why are we waiting?" they said. "Why don't we just bring them in? Wash those dirty meddlesome minds once and for all?" But I told the doubters that if you wait long enough, kids *will* meddle. It's your nature if left to your own devices.'

Frobisher stared at Lucas, and the youth shuffled under his gaze. 'Now, boy,' he said softly. 'Let's see if what you found has been worth the wait.'

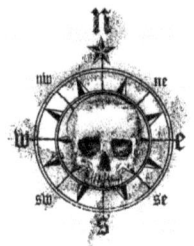

'Slow down, Beatrice,' Marcus said. 'You're not making sense.'

'That's because none of *this* makes sense,' Beatrice said into her cell phone. 'My parents have been arrested over something trivial, and my brother's responsible.'

'Oh, the younger kids can be a little *enthusiastic*. But I'm not sure what I can do,' Marcus said.

'You could come and talk some sense into my super-grass brother,' she said.

Marcus was about to respond when Beatrice heard another voice in the background. 'Hold on a second, Bea,' he said.

Moments passed as the distant buzz of a conversation elsewhere reverberated in her ear. Then Marcus was back on the line.

'That was my gran,' he said. 'She's suggesting that you bring Thomas here and we see if we can give him some perspective on the Cadet Handbook.'

'What good will that do?' Beatrice asked.

'At this minute Thomas is following the Blue Thunder cadet *Code of Duty* to the letter,' Marcus said.

'I've met kids like him before—keen and overzealous. My gran will work her magic on him.'

'If you're sure,' Beatrice said.

'My gran is very sure, Bea,' Marcus said. 'Don't worry, we'll get your mum and dad back home in a few hours.'

Beatrice relaxed a little. With Maud nowhere to be found and her parents at the station, she was feeling pretty isolated. Even *The Newshounds* were fragmented.

'I'll bring the snitch over right now,' Beatrice said.

'We'll be waiting,' Marcus said. And the phone went silent leaving Beatrice alone once more.

She found Thomas in the kitchen polishing the stainless steel sink unit.

'Go get your coat, super-grass,' Beatrice said bluntly.

'Are we going somewhere?'

'To see Marcus,' Beatrice replied.

'Cool!'

Without further questions Thomas left the kitchen in search of his coat. Somehow Beatrice feared that the rest of the evening wasn't going to be as easy.

Chapter Fifteen
The Last Supper

THE **MACBETH'S WERE** staying in a rented cottage not far away from Dorsal Finn's museum. The cottage was compact, yet consisted of many rooms that led away from a hallway made even smaller by wallpaper with deep purple flowers. There were many pictures dotted around the small wooden cupboards and dressers in the hall.

Beatrice noticed what she presumed to be images of the many stages of Alice Macbeth, one with raven hair and unblemished skin. Another had an image of a middle aged woman leaning on a cane with a moorland scene in the background.

'Welcome, my dear,' Macbeth said. 'It's good to see you again.'

'Thank you, Ms Macbeth,' Beatrice said politely despite her nervousness.

'Oh, call me Alice! Please go through to the lounge,' Alice said gesturing with her hand to a door a few metres away. 'Marcus is just putting together a little supper, seeing as we've brought our tea date forward a day or so'

'There really isn't any need,' Beatrice said, not feeling in the slightest bit hungry.

'Nonsense,' Alice said with a friendly-yet-firm tone. 'He'd already prepared most of it. We can still try to be civilised even if the hour isn't, eh?'

Beatrice nodded and walked into the living room, Thomas following meekly.

There were more photos on the cupboards in the lounge. Again images of Alice seemed to dominate proceedings. This time there were shots of a woman stooped on a stage, and beside the picture was a tub of face paint and a wad of prosthetic resin.

'Were you an actress?' Beatrice asked.

'One of many pursuits over the course of a long life,' Macbeth mused. 'I was not one to hang around. I tend to bore very easily, even now.'

'Did you star in many plays?'

'A few, but the world is a stage as they say,' she mused. 'Why pretend when you can live?'

'I *suppose* that makes sense.'

'Of course it doesn't make sense!' Alice chuckled. 'You're young.'

'Well what's been happening?' Marcus said as he came into the lounge.

Beatrice turned and as soon as she lay eyes on him, her heart seemed to lighten, discarding the despondency that had encamped there.

'Everything is wrong. I've got a bad feeling,' she whispered. 'Thing's are not what they seem.'

'You're right,' Marcus said suddenly. 'But we can try and sort things out. If anyone can put things into perspective then it's my gran.'

'I hope so,' Beatrice said.

'I have a question first,' Marcus said.

'Ask away?'

'Why have you got pieces of shell fish in your hair?'

Beatrice sighed. 'Another time, okay?'

'After supper I'll go and take young Thomas into the sitting room and have a chat about duty and honour and finding a happy medium.' Alice said, her wheelchair's motor purring as she navigated through the lounge to the table.

'That's really kind of you,' Beatrice said behind her blushes. 'You take notice of what Ms Macbeth has to say, Thomas Beecham.'

Thomas looked reverently at the old woman, and Beatrice realised coming here had been the right thing to do.

'But first,' Alice said, 'I have to eat. We oldies need our vitals.'

'I'll get the plates,' Marcus said and pointed at the chairs positioned around a small table which had been set for two.

'It really doesn't matter,' Beatrice began but Alice smiled.

'Food first, Miss Beecham. Host's orders.'

Beatrice acquiesced with a grin and sat down at the table; Thomas opposite her with a distant look on his face.

'Deep in thought as ever,' Marcus said placing plates on the table. 'Anyone ever tell you that you worry too much?'

'I only worry over the big stuff,' she replied, taking a plate from the pile. 'What's for supper?'

'Are you worried about that as well?' Marcus laughed.

'No,' she said. 'You know what I think of your cooking.'

He disappeared again and returned with trays laden with food. There was smoked salmon and scrambled eggs, a tureen of French onion soup complete with croutons, and a platter of meats ranging from honey roasted hams and mustard basted beef. He proceeded to lay all these things out on the brilliant white table cloth. Despite her angst, Beatrice was drawn into the culinary scene unfolding before her eyes. The presentation was intriguing and delicate, and her stomach rumbled.

'Are you going to try something?' Alice said as she adroitly positioned her chair in a vacant slot at the table.

'How could I refuse?' Beatrice chuckled.

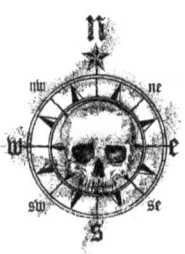

'I have to hand it to Hessel,' Frobisher said, his admiration genuine, 'he really has given us a merry dance.'

The men walked through the yard. Elmo and Lucas were with them. Ahead, Little Bertha was a skeletal silhouette on the horizon.

'He would turn in his grave if he knew scum like you still walked this Earth,' Miller spat.

'Well he's *in* the Earth, old man,' Frobisher said

coldly. 'And unless you wish to join him you will keep a civil tongue in that dirty mouth of yours.'

The group stopped once they'd reached the gun, and Frobisher looked at the two boys intently. 'Show me what you found, gentlemen.'

Lucas hesitated and Frobisher nodded to one of his henchman, who lifted his pistol and pressed the muzzle to the side of Miller's head.

'This isn't a schoolyard game, boy,' Frobisher hissed. 'Out here people get hurt for real.'

Lucas bustled forwards and activated the mechanism to release the secret panel in the foot plate. He reached into the gloom and pulled out the contents.

'Don't know about you guys,' Frobisher grinned malevolently, 'but I'm getting a pretty big Christmassy feeling here!'

Lucas reached out as though he was about to reluctantly place the wad of material in Frobisher's eagerly outstretched hands, but just as the *Blue Thunder* leader went to take hold of the material Lucas dropped the bundle onto the floor.

There was a sudden, low humming sound that sent a vibrating pulse through all who were present. Elmo felt his teeth chatter for a few seconds; Lucas began to shiver on the spot. Without warning, a huge screech blasted through the yard, almost knocking everyone over.

As he staggered backwards, Lucas could see that the wad of material he'd dropped was unfurling, and the valves were slowly but surely coming apart. They all disintegrated in a series of tiny explosions that no one had any chance of hearing. Then, as abruptly as it had come, the sonic wave ceased.

The guns were back on Miller before he had chance to take advantage. Frobisher grabbed at the valves but saw they were beyond repair.

'Oops!' Lucas said. His ears rang.

'You idiot!' Frobisher stooped to grab the swatch as though it were a fallen child. 'What have you done?'

'It was an accident,' Lucas said defensively.

'You have ruined the Trident!'

'It just isn't you day, is it?' Lucas said.

The blow came swift and heavy. Lucas fell sideways.

'You think that you're clever, boy?' Frobisher snarled. 'You have merely made sure that you are no longer any use to me.'

Frobisher turned to his henchman. 'Shoot them all,' he hissed.

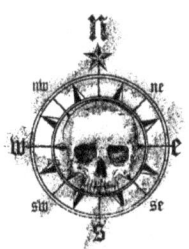

It is too late. You have succumbed to the onslaught. The thing is no longer behind the barrier, and you are no longer resistant to its whims. You do not know why you have been chosen as its vehicle, but you suspect it is to do with your skills. Contrary to the ways of literature, there are not many with your abilities. It is this that has proved to be your downfall. In some small way you felt pride that this vile thing had specifically sought you out, spending so much

time and energy to woo you. This vice allowed it to slip through your defences like a ghost and claim counsel.

You feel the world around you change. The bedsit fades; the walls rippling as the surface of still pond are disturbed by a skipping stone. Then there is the sound of the very air about you ripping open as blinding light and searing heat washes over you, causing cries of terror and pain to pump from your lungs. The room is gone and you are dumped unceremoniously upon cold, wet grass, yet it is a relief after the sizzling heat of moments ago. You lie in the grass for a while catching your breath and slowly become aware of what is around you. A lighthouse sends its beacon out into the night as the wind rifles through the grass. Then you realise: The thing has guided you back to the place where the dreams began, a small village by the sea. The minion is there. A twisted, gnarled thing with teeth and claws that embraces you; seeping into your skin the way a dank, dirty puddle is absorbed by the earth. The pain of this joining is bright and transcends agony. In that moment your will ceases to exist and you are but a skin suit for the being who wears you.

It still needs you more than ever. A plan to release a great power is in danger of being thwarted by those who are as righteous as they as meddlesome. Those who have vision are stalling in their duty and the plan in which your Master was principle is under threat. They are in need of a saviour, someone who can tap into the vile essence lurking in this town and in doing so bring darkness to the world.

You are given a name, and shown where to find

the architect of this new age of darkness. And it is there that you now go; the body of a man steered by the foulest of beings.

You have your destination but there is also murmur of a detour. This is not physical, it is a psychic diversion, your mind put on cerebral tracks that take you, at once, to another consciousness. Yet this mind is one in turmoil whilst the owner's physical form looks at peace in the world of the living. Your mind merges with your host, and through their eyes you can see the drip stand, the machine with its tubes and lines crawling into your nose and mouth, you hear the pulsing beep of the machine as it ticks away the moments of a life that is really on hold forever. Once you are courting this consciousness, the thing that guides you makes plain what it needs from the mind of the man once known as Tyrell. You seek out everything he knows about his time in Dorsal Finn, locate every piece of information that may be lurking there. You extract it, and in such an extraction your dark passenger knows, and you feel its excitement—its desire to be free.

When you have all that Tyrell has to give, you say one word to him:

'Die.'

The machine's beep now elongates and an alarm goes off in the distance. There are footfalls as nurses and medics plough into the room. By the time they begin working on Tyrell you have taken your leave, knowing their attempt to revive him will be fruitless.

After all, soon the last hours of the world will tick away, and you shall be its pendulum.

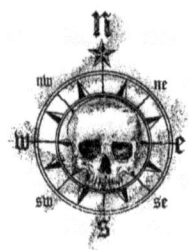

The meal was sumptuous, and accompanied by Macbeth's biting humour that had Beatrice guffawing mercilessly. Not since her evenings with Maud had she felt so totally at ease. Marcus' cooking rivalled her own, yet there was no hint of jealousy in her, only feelings for him becoming deeper. It should not have made sense, the speed with which she was falling for him, but everything felt right and all she wanted to do was go with it.

As Marcus observed her across the table, his eyes seemed to pull her in and she found herself feeling giddy with the sensation passing through her. It was a sensation usually reserved for her family, even Thomas on a good day, a deep yearning to always be with them. Time became syrup-thick.

'You okay?' Marcus said. His voice reverberated as though time had done exactly as she'd willed it, slowing to a point where his words stretched to infinity.

'I'm feeling sort of funky,' Beatrice said. 'That was some marinade.'

'Well I've got one last thing to serve up before you get too relaxed,' Marcus said standing and moving away from the table.

Beatrice watched him go through to the kitchen and Alice manoeuvred her wheelchair away from the table.

'And I'll be taking young Thomas here for a small chat while you two finish up,' the old woman said. 'Come along.'

Thomas stood as if under remote control, and followed Macbeth's chair out into the hallway just as Marcus returned carrying a silver platter covered with a large dome.

'What on Earth have you got there?' Beatrice laughed.

'One last thing for you to digest,' Marcus said. 'If you can that is.'

Beatrice tittered and put her fingers to her mouth to suppress it. The wooziness returned for a few seconds as Marcus placed the domed serving dish before her.

'Lift the lid and get the prize,' Marcus said. Beatrice watched his reflection in the dome and his wonderful smile appeared twisted and grotesque. The image unsettled Beatrice and she lifted the dome in an attempt to rid herself of the parody wavering upon the convex surface.

'Tada!' Marcus said.

'What's this?' Beatrice said as she stared at the platter, the dome held aloft in one hand. On the tray beneath lay a single slip of paper.

'Check it out,' Marcus said excitedly.

Beatrice put the domed lid to one side and picked up the slip of paper with fingers that felt thick and clumsy. She shook her head, trying to dislodge the sugar rush tingling in her temples.

She saw the logo on the top of the slip first, *Cornucopia Catering,* resting upon a wooden platter, and couldn't see the relevance of it immediately.

Through eyes almost squinted shut, Beatrice then saw the printed list and suddenly realised she was right, all was not as it seemed. And as the weight of the revelation brought tears to her eyes and a dull ache to her chest, she slipped from the seat and fell heavily upon the thick living room carpet.

Marcus stood and peered down at the drugged body of the girl he had duped with remarkable ease, the itemized receipt for the food he'd bought from Cornucopia Catering still clutched in her hands.

'See you in a few hours, darling,' he mocked and left the room.

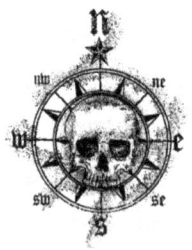

The wind whips at the sea and the fine droplets spray your flimsy clothing and leave the tang of salt on your lips.

You have made your way to the place from which you have hidden so long. It is the place that has been calling out to you. It wants something—needs something to happen. The beast that now owns your body is eager to please its Master. Promises have been made and the rewards are great.

But plans have gone awry. You are shown in an instant the roots and implications of the failure. It means the thing that is held captive will remain incarcerated for another eternity. The plan has to be fixed, made right. A pact has been made, after all.

How this can be achieved is made known to you. The process—the ingredients to create chaos—are planted into your head and you absorb them as if they are your own.

Contingency is the ethic. And you shall deliver it to the one person with the resilience to make it happen. It was not meant to be this way. The science of Man was to be ultimately responsible for its own demise. Yet there are too many things in Dorsal Finn that like to meddle in matters that do not concern them.

You cross the beach, the crunch of shale lost in the howling wind. As you near the broken building at the edge of the beach you sense a shift in your mind, a connection. It is as though someone remembers something important, something vital. You know that your presence is triggering this phenomenon. You feel uncertainty in the entity to which you are now entwined fall away and a powerful sense of relief returning.

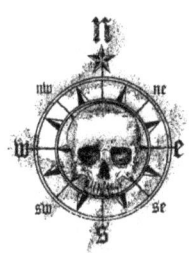

'Sir?'

'Don't question me,' Frobisher snarled at the henchman. 'Shoot them!'

'There's someone here, Sir,' the henchman replied. 'In the window of the shack?'

Frobisher turned to follow the man's gaze and saw a shape silhouetted against the glass.

'You!' Frobisher called. 'Come out here. Show yourself.'

'Would you have me discuss your salvation as your enemy looks on?'

Frobisher took a step backwards. The words had not been spoken aloud; they had appeared clear and unbridled in his mind. He shook his head as if to free his head of the thought.

'Do not deny it,' the voice said. 'Come. Talk with me.'

'Stay here,' Frobisher said to his men. 'If they move, shoot them.'

As Miller and the boys watched, Frobisher went into the shack.

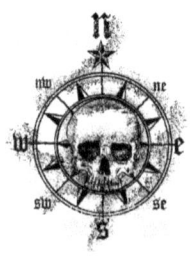

By the time Frobisher had walked into the small living area, the man at the window had sat down on Miller's misshapen sofa. The newcomer's head was shaved bare but he sported a bushy, brown moustache speckled with grey. His eyes were a deep brown and his lashes were so dark they appeared as though he wore mascara.

'Sit,' the man said. He played with the cuff of his tan suit that was mostly hidden by a silver/grey robe, edged with crimson.

Frobisher remained standing.

'Can it really be true?' he said quietly 'Are you really a servant of our ally?'

'Do you doubt it? Even with what you already know?' the man said.

'I have belief,' Frobisher said firmly. 'But we feared your vessel would not submit in time.'

'Your ally is still weak but remains powerful in the ways of persuasion,' the man said. 'It was difficult to ignore over time. As things became more desperate here, so I endured. And submission was inevitable.'

'Do you have a name?' Frobisher said quietly.

'Such things are beyond the tongues of men,' the man said. 'Call me "shaman" for that was the mark given to this vessel I now own.'

Frobisher moved over to one of the rickety chairs and sat down on it.

'Its existence still remains incredible to me,' he whispered.

'You are a sceptic?' the shaman said. 'You surprise me, given your roots.'

'What does that mean?'

'The Nazis spent a fortune seeking truth to the occult, did they not?' the man pressed. 'Their foundation was guided by astrological events and mystical symbolism. They sought out heritage, yet their goal was here all along.'

'Indeed,' Frobisher said. 'It is this that restores my faith in such things.'

'Faith is needed in order to succeed,' the man said.

'This shaman can help you achieve your ends but nothing is certain. The timeframe is not as it was foretold.'

'No,' Frobisher conceded. 'We had to accelerate the plan somewhat. Tyrell's discovery and his ability to report it was arrested by *local interference*, and has not come without cost. But we are nothing if not resolute. The pieces are in place, and with your timely arrival, shaman, I believe we are ready.'

'There are no such things as absolutes from this point on,' the shaman said. 'What lies beneath this village has vested interest in your success. But it will not come without sacrifice. Tyrell has already contributed to the cause.'

'You mean he's dead?' Frobisher asked.

'Indeed, he is. His knowledge of events, past and present, is now known to your ally,' the shaman said. 'As are *yours*.'

'Explain,' Frobisher said with suspicion.

'It knows, for instance, that Fleischer, the Nazi officer and architect of this whole affair, was your grandfather. That it is *his* grand design that you follow. It also knows that the old man known as Miller is, in fact, the son of the locksmith who sealed the chamber you seek.'

Frobisher considered this for a moment, and all during this time his fingers played with the sovereign ring. When he finally spoke his tone was casual,

'This is important because . . . .?'

'It shows that the fate of both Fleischer and the locksmith were ultimately entwined. Perhaps he was reckless in killing the Jew all those years ago. Such things remain to be seen. One thing is true, the old man and those boys still have a part to play in this business. They must be allowed to live, at least for now.'

Frobisher contemplated this for a short time. The shaman continued,

'Fret not, Frobisher. Your dark roots will sit well in the earth beneath this town. It embraces the questionable deeds of men like a long lost lover.'

'Your words suggest what I plan is not righteous,' Frobisher said with irritation. 'I don't appreciate it.'

'Be that as it may,' the shaman replied, 'it was the level of assurance that your ally needs to continue with its pact. Your grandfather pledged allegiance many years ago. It is good to know that, through you, his linage will honour his agreement.'

'Not much is known of this pact,' Frobisher said. 'My grandfather alluded to a dark heart that would serve our ends. And that it only existed here, in this place.'

'That is all there is to know,' the shaman concluded. 'Your ally is powerful. It will help you attain your goal.'

'I am a pragmatic man, well versed in the folklore of this place,' Frobisher said. 'Now our moment is at hand, I would like to see more than words.'

'Very well,' the man said.

The shaman brought his palms within inches of each other and muttered a few words. In the space between his hands a glowing green orb appeared and within its sickly, shimmering glow Frobisher could see an image of *Bishop's Cragg*.

'This is the place where the new world begins,' the shaman said. Frobisher now saw that the man's eyes were no longer brown, but glowing jade embers.

'Oh, my,' Frobisher muttered in awe. 'What wonderful times we live in.'

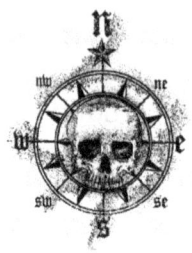

Frobisher walked towards Lucas, Elmo, and Miller. His steps were light and quick and he rubbed his hands together with fervour.

'Ah, the night has certainly taken a turn for the better,' Frobisher said. 'There's nothing that a good chat can't resolve.'

Lucas didn't like Frobisher's newfound optimism. It meant things were still on schedule. But how could that be?

Then the man from the shack stepped into the yard, his eyes now orbs of effervescent green, and Lucas realised that from this point on normality had no place.

'All is well once more,' Frobisher said confirming Lucas' worst thoughts. The man stepped up to his three prisoners. 'Now, then, gentlemen, seeing as you've all been *so* understanding, I think it's only right and proper that I invite you to come with us.'

'That's a loaded statement, right?' Elmo said.

'You're a fast learner, I guess,' Frobisher said, his eyes sparkling with malice. 'Now get in the truck before we shoot you.'

The truck was large and featureless, and had bulky

double doors at the back. One of Frobisher's henchmen, a big man with a shaven head, yanked open the doors with ease.

'Get in,' he ordered.

Lucas and company climbed reluctantly into the oppressive rectangular slab of blackness beyond the doorway.

No sooner had they disappeared inside the doors were slammed shut.

'Where are we headed?' Frobisher asked the shaman.

'To greatness,' he replied. .

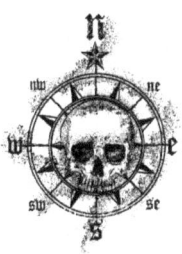

'I can't believe it,' Lucas sighed. 'Bundled into the back of a truck without so much as a harsh word. How did we allow this to happen?'

'I don't know,' Elmo said tightly. 'There's something about the guy that's quite persuasive.'

'That would be the gun, I suspect,' Miller said.

'Could be. I just wish we had held out a little longer.'

'Yeah,' Lucas said. 'But we did the best we could. The *three seconds* he gave us to decide were pretty tense.'

'Don't go beatin' yourselves up over it,' Miller said, his head bobbing in time with the bumps in the road beneath them. 'We'll have to bide our time. Use the opportunity to plan an escape when they're distracted.'

'Distracted?' Elmo said his face yellowed by the small torch they'd been allowed to keep. 'By what?'

'Can't you feel it?' Miller said. 'Somethin's comin'. It's in the air. Frobisher is gettin' close to completin' his mission, whatever that may be.'

'Finding Atlantis?' Elmo suggested.

'Happen so,' Miller said. 'And when he does, he's goin' to be so consumed by his own sense of worth he'll be forgettin' we even exist for a short time.'

'That's if he hasn't made sure we don't *exist at all* by that time, right?' Lucas said anxiously.

'Stay near me and keep a clear head,' Miller said. 'Do that and we might just get out of this in one piece.'

'But what if there *is* no escape?' Lucas said. 'Sure, we might get our escape, but where's the guarantee that we can outrun what's to come?'

'There ain't any guarantee,' Miller said. 'That's a luxury we ain't got enough pennies to buy.'

The truck rumbled on, its destination as uncertain as the fate of its cargo.

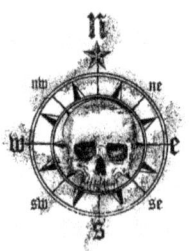

Beatrice woke with a start.

Her head was brimming with a dull ache.

She tried to get her bearings and was horrified to

discover her hands were shackled over her head, the chains clanking as she tried to yank at them. The pain in her head made her vision blur, yet she could see enough to realise she was in a small cave. There were flickering torches secured to the rough walls with gibbets, throwing sinister shadows against the rocks.

There was a sound in the cave, the rise and fall of the tide, and when she dragged her tongue across her lips Beatrice could taste the sharp tang of sea salt.

'Hello?' she cried. 'Can anyone hear me?'

The panic in her voice was amplified by her surroundings, its echo appearing to endlessly mock her. Beatrice tried to clear her head, tried to recall what had happened before she'd ended up here.

Then she remembered the supper with Marcus and Alice; the wonderful food that Marcus had prepared.

Or *not* as she'd found out.

The delivery receipt from the *Cornucopia Catering*; a list of the hors d'oeuvres that had been handmade, the menu of that very evening had been lavishly prepared by experts and served up by Marcus as his own. But this wasn't the only surprise. The food had been drugged and incapacitated her so that her alleged boyfriend could bring her here.

But why?

When she thought of how Marcus had duped her, Beatrice felt grief and anger taking bites from her, and the tears coursed down her cheeks in hot rivulets. She was scared and in pain and in desperate need to be free. But despite all of this, she remained intrigued.

Beatrice became aware of movement amongst the shadows and the shapes of Marcus and Alice came into view. Through her tears she scowled at them.

'Oh look, Marcus,' Alice said. 'I do believe that you've broken the poor girl's heart.'

Beatrice blinked her tears away, and her face went slack. Not because Alice's words were very nearly true, but because: Alice Macbeth may have uttered the words, but she sounded like someone else.

Someone *very* familiar.

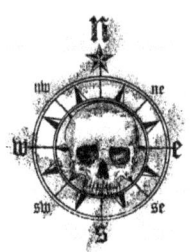

At the work station in her father's study, Emily shook her head. Not in disagreement, not in disbelief, but in an attempt to clear it of something that really should not have been there.

A sound. An indeterminate sound at first, but building until it became so clear it was impossible to ignore.

The sound of someone sobbing in total despair. And despite her attempts to rid herself of it, Emily became fascinated by it. She'd been two years old when she'd developed meningitis, the infection mercifully moving on before it could claim her life, but it took her hearing as a memento of its journey through her brain. She could feel vibrations in the air through her bones, the pulse of music shimmying her breast bone, cars and wagons buzzing against her temples. But she'd not heard a voice since before she knew what a voice really was.

Emily brought a hand to her brow and pinched the bridge of her small nose. In that instant, a potent image appeared before eyes that she'd squeezed shut.

A cave with a girl chained to the far wall as water surged in through a large fissure. The girl had bright red hair and her mouth was open as sea water poured into it.

Then the image, the improbable voice, disappeared but its memory did not. Emily gasped for air and felt a warm rivulet trickle from her left nostril. She wiped at it, her hand coming away crimson. She made for the downstairs bathroom where she balled toilet tissue into a wad and moped away her blood.

As she looked at her pale expression in the mirror above the sink, Emily recalled the girl in her vision and her heart thumped against her chest.

Most people would have questioned their own sanity, seeing things that weren't there, hearing distress when she simply couldn't. But for Emily such a thing seemed natural. Her father, after all, often talked about how other senses became strong to compensate for the loss of another.

Was it so much of a strain to go a stage further and suggest that sometimes senses didn't only become stronger sometimes they might be replaced by something quite different?

No, Emily embraced the idea, and with this unmitigated acceptance came the real cause for concern: Beatrice was in grave danger, and she had to do something about it.

The question was what?

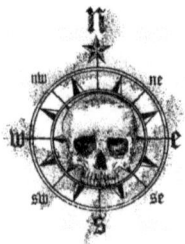

Patience waited on the corner of her block, uneasy at how deserted the streets were.

To combat her disquiet, she thought about recent events, especially a text message from Emily suggesting they meet to talk about "something terrible" that may be happening. A few text messages later, it had become clear that Emily wanted to discuss this face to face. She tried ringing Beatrice's mobile first and got the voicemail. She didn't fare any better when she tried to get hold of either Lucas or Elmo. Even Maud and Agnes seemed to have disappeared, adding to her frustration.

Now, she hopped from one training shoe to the other, trying desperately to calm her nerves.

There was movement ahead. A figure approached, steeped in shadows and edged by lamplight. Patience recognised Emily immediately and went to meet her, signing as soon as she was close enough.

'What's wrong?'

'I saw something,' Emily signed.

'I remember.'

Emily nodded. 'I saw Beatrice in chains and the tide rising.'

'Beatrice?' Patience spoke her friend's name as she signed. 'Where is she?'

Emily stared at Patience and began to sign but stopped, as though holding something back.

'Tell me,' Patience urged.

'You might think I'm mad,' Emily signed cautiously.

'Please, Emily!'

So Emily explained her vision. When she'd finished, Patience looked at her with wide eyes. She dipped into her small handbag and pulled out her phone.

'You thinking of calling the doctor?' Emily said.

'No,' Patience said. 'I'm calling someone else.'

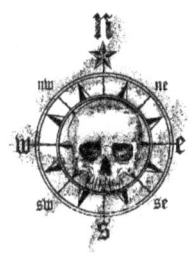

Beatrice blinked several times, but the tears just kept on coming. Her mind was a blur of thoughts and her emotions were a toxic mix of anger, confusion, and grief.

'What's going on?' she said.

'Now there's a question,' Alice mocked. And to Beatrice's surprise climbed out of her wheel chair, her back no longer buckled, but upright. She was very tall. 'What do you think is going on, dear girl?'

'I don't know,' Beatrice said honestly. The woman's voice was familiar but Beatrice had convinced herself her initial thoughts were just not possible. The person she thought she'd heard was not only considerably younger than Macbeth, but also considerably *dead*.

Beatrice peered at Marcus. The boy's handsome

features were impassive. She swallowed hard and tried to ignore the biting pain in her heart.

'Marcus, why?'

'I'll let Grandmother explain,' Marcus said coldly. His eyes were twin points of ice.

Alice laughed heartily and her gnarled hands went up to her grinning mouth. To Beatrice's shock, the woman began to claw at the face. The shrivelled skin came away in chunks, and fell to the ground. Beatrice watched in morbid fascination as Macbeth's withered features disappeared and a new face emerged.

'You!' Beatrice began fighting helplessly against her bonds.

'Too late the girl finds some perspective,' said the figure below.

'It can't be! You're dead!'

The figure chuckled and yanked twisted, latex fingers from each of its hands before discarding them to the rocky floor.

'Clearly not,' Xavier Pontefract said, wearing a cold, mocking grin.

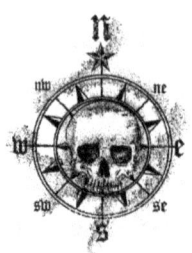

Albert Smythe pushed the accelerator pedal down and his beige, beaten-up *Mini Metro* picked up speed. Maud looked at the dials on the dashboard.

'Giddy goodness, Albert,' Maud said. 'How come

the only cars we're passin' are parked up for the night?'

'Very funny,' he said. 'I'd like to get to Bramwell Hall in one piece if that's all the same to you?'

'I ain't arguin' with that,' Maud conceded and patted his hand.

'The transmitters should be safe at the hall,' Albert said relaxing a little. 'The place is like a fortress once you get inside.'

'Aye, and just as soulless,' Maud said quietly.

'Don't go starting up about the Hall, Maud. You want the transmitters to disappear or not?' Albert griped.

'Yes, of course I do,' Maud said in a placating tone. She felt bad about testing Albert's loyalty to Bramwell Hall. It was a constant source of friction he could do without, especially now. 'I'm sorry, love,' she said gently. 'All this is gettin' a bit hard for ol' Maud to digest. An' it's makin' her as sour as a lemon this evenin'.'

'I know,' Albert said. 'Let's just get there and get it—'

Two figures stepped out into the road, the blaze of headlights so close their clothes and faces became featureless, save for the eyes—staring not in fear but in total amusement.

Albert swerved left. But the movement was too radical for the tired, old car to tolerate. The chassis groaned under the strain. The tyres zigzagged on the wet tarmac causing Albert to lose his grip of the steering wheel, sending the vehicle into a stomach churning spin.

As buildings swirled past through the car windows,

Maud's head hit the door with enough force to make her grunt before the world winked out for her. Albert fought to regain control of the car, grabbing the steering wheel and yanking it in an effort to straighten the tyres.

It was too late to prevent the inevitable.

The car made contact with a low wall that tipped the vehicle onto its side with the wrenching sound of metal, and the body slid ten metres along the wet street, a river of sparks marking its passage until it came to a creaking, clattering stop.

Steam hissed from its ruptured radiator, the front wheels continued spinning as though not realising the journey was finally over.

Dazed, Albert Smythe gazed through the shattered windscreen. The world was a crazy mix of spider web cracks and the two children coming towards the car showed no sense of urgency, no sense of drama. Instead their steps were casual. One of them—the girl— even skipped a few steps.

The children stooped to peer into the car, their expression gleeful.

'Adults are clumsy, aren't they?' the boy said.

'Yes,' the girl replied. 'But they are such fun to play with, don't you think?'

'Most certainly,' the boy agreed.

'H . . . help . . . ' Albert gasped his voice thick with pain and confusion.

'Oh look!' said the girl as she clapped her hands together with delight. 'It's trying to say something!'

From his skewed vantage point, Albert watched as another figure came into view. It was a youth, clad in the garb of a *Blue Thunder* cadet. But even in his befuddled state, Albert recognised the boy instantly.

'Well, look at this,' Edward Chorley said. 'Looks like we bagged ourselves two mischief makers in one hit.'

'Edward,' Albert muttered. 'Don't be a fool. Maud's hurt, call someone.'

'You must've hit your head pretty hard if you think I care about either of you,' Chorley sneered. 'Besides, no one would come. Frobisher's about to send them all to the land of the happy. There's no one to interfere in our affairs.'

'No mistakin' who yer father is,' Maud said suddenly. 'He must be proud at the way ye've turned out.'

At the mention of his disgraced, exiled father, Chorley chewed his bottom lip and his eyes were cold with anger. But he smiled as he watched Maud and Albert hanging precariously against their seat belts.

'Well now that you're out of the game, we really must leave you to it,' Edward Chorley gloated. 'Unlike you, I haven't got time to hang around.'

'Ye're about as funny as nettle rash,' Maud spat.

'There's more to come,' Chorley said. 'Over the next few hours the fun *really* starts.'

'Think about what you're doing, Edward,' Albert pleaded. 'No good can come from any of it.'

'I've tried "good",' Edward said as he moved away, the twins in tow. 'It's overrated.'

Desperately, Maud and Albert watched as the youths returned to the shadows.

'Now what?' Albert said helplessly.

For once, Maud said nothing.

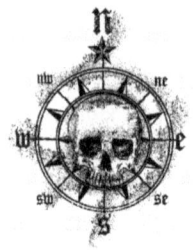

Beatrice fought to keep focused. The realisation that the man she'd thwarted from murdering and taking the place of Dominic Pontefract was still alive and was exacting his own cruel act of retribution was an incredible shock. But this paled compared to the fact that Marcus had duped her; ripping her into emotional pieces.

The tears continued to flow, and she hated herself for allowing them to pour down her face. Each strangled sob made Xavier shiver with delight; her pain was his gain, pure and simple.

Beatrice looked at Marcus and he held her stare, seemingly impervious to her misery.

'I thought you liked me,' she said. At that moment, even to her, the words sounded pathetic and desperate.

'You should've realised that all of this was too good to be true,' Pontefract answered for the youth standing beside him. 'I mean, you only have to look at Marcus to see the folly of it all. Is he not the perfect specimen of youth? Handsome, strong, brimming with nothing but potential. Now look at *you*. I shan't state the painfully obvious, but this is the real world, after all.'

Beatrice dug her nails into the palms of her hands to distract herself from the hurtful words. But her tears remained constant and bitter.

'Tears of realization, dear girl?' Pontefract leered. 'You are naïve at best. Only you could think cooking is something a girl should entertain. You've set the women's movement back over a century!'

'Maybe murder is a cooler way to spend your time?' Beatrice snapped.

'It is,' Pontefract said. His eyes told her that he meant it.

Beatrice yanked on her bonds, eager to be free of both the words and these two people who were enjoying her suffering the way one enjoys a football match or a particularly good episode of *Bones*. And as she squirmed against the manacles securing her to the wall, Beatrice thought she felt them give. She paused, afraid she'd gotten it wrong, that is was wishful thinking, but just in case her captors had noticed it too.

'Why are you doing this?' Beatrice said to keep the conversation fluid so she might try again.

'Because *I'm enjoying* it, dear child,' Pontefract smiled. 'Because: you deserve it. Not too long ago you watched me plunge from Monument Point and into the ocean. You and this infernal town left me for dead. In the spirit of fair play it seems only fitting that I should return the favour.'

Beatrice couldn't mask her despair—her face was an open book to her tormentor below.

'You are confused,' Pontefract said. 'Let me unfetter that simple mind of yours. This cave is a generous entity. It entertains every evening. But it is selective. It recognises that which has greater esteem. Soon its guest will arrive and you will be here to greet it.'

'You really have lost your mind,' Beatrice snapped.

'Perhaps you should consider doing the same—given your fate this evening,' Xavier replied. He turned to Marcus who appeared bored by the whole event. 'Come dear boy, I believe we are in danger of outstaying our welcome.'

Confused and frightened Beatrice watched as her captors exited the cave without looking back. In an instant she resumed her battle with her bonds, the chains rattling fiercely under her struggles.

Chapter Sixteen
Time nor Tide

MAUD STRUGGLED AGAINST her seatbelt.

'Trussed up like a kipper,' she groaned. 'Never saw that comin' when I woke up this mornin'.'

'Don't worry, Maud,' Albert said unclipping his belt. 'I'll have you out of there in a jiffy.'

'Me hero.' Maud grinned. 'Who said men are good fer nowt most of the time?'

'I think that was you, wasn't it?'

'Ye know somethin', ye might be spot on.'

'Yes,' Albert said positioning himself so he could assist Maud's escape from her confined and indignant position. 'Good job I ignore such rubbish.'

'Aye, ye're a good un, no doubt about it,' Maud conceded, patting him on the arm.

'Don't you be going soft on me now, Maud,' Albert said working on the seatbelt mechanism which appeared stuck.

'Me? Nah,' Maud said. 'It's this blood rushin' to me noggin.'

'Well, I'm working on it,' Albert grimaced as he yanked on the seatbelt clip.

'Hold up, Albert,' Maud said, her nose wrinkling suddenly. 'Ye smellin' that?'

Albert sniffed the air, his eyes widening in fear. 'Oh my, Maud,' he said frantically resuming his attempts to free her. 'We've got to get you out of there.'

Maud breathed through her mouth, yet the acrid taste of petrol on the air made her cough and gag. 'Do it quick, Albert,' she said between gasps. 'Or it's lookin' like this kipper's gettin' smoked this evenin'.'

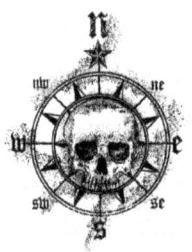

'There's no answer from anyone,' Patience said testily to her mobile. In the half light, Emily looked at her bemused. Patience signed an apology and reiterated her frustration, prompting her friend to nod her head sympathetically.

'We should go to the police,' Patience signed.

'And say what?' Emily replied. 'That I had a vision? It's bad enough living life as a deaf person, without being branded insane.'

Patience chewed her lip thoughtfully. 'We could always try Agnes,' she said finally. 'The library is not far.'

'There's no time.'

'Then we'll have to split up,' Patience said, though in truth it wasn't a premise she favoured.

'I'll go to *Cooper's Cove*,' Emily said. 'You go get help.'

'From where? A seventy year old, hard of hearing librarian isn't exactly The Avengers is it?'

'We have to do what we can. Our friends are depending on us,' Emily said, her eyes searching Patience's face, hoping, praying that the troubled expression she saw there would slip away.

'Okay,' Patience finally said. 'I'm on it. Go to *Cooper's Cove,* but please don't do anything that'll get me in trouble with your parents.'

'See you soon,' Emily smiled coyly before heading off in the direction of the shoreline.

With a sigh, Patience Userkaf went in search of Agnes Clutterbuck and any sort of help. She was unaware that over the next few moments even this door was about to be closed upon The Newshounds.

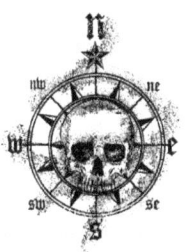

An air of expectation pervaded the homes of Dorsal Finn. In every lounge, sitting room and bedroom, people were watching the TV. Giant plasma screens or small flat screens, young and old, everyone held their breath as the emblem of the *Blue Thunder Foundation* wavered, before Frobisher faded in—immaculate and commanding. It had been a long time coming, a long time to wait. But now anticipation would be sated, patience rewarded.

As a pre-recorded Frobisher stood before his audience, the big man leaned forward and in the living rooms, sitting rooms and lounges of Dorsal Finn, everyone leaned towards him.

With a gleam in his eye and a smile on his lips, Logan Frobisher said one word, and at his command all who heard it obeyed without question.

'Sleep.'

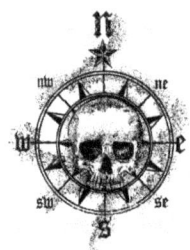

In another part of town, beneath the *Blue Thunder* HQ, thirty cadets awoke from an enforced sleep. It was no coincidence that life sparkled in their eyes at the very moment most of Dorsal Finn's population were falling under Frobisher's cyber-induced slumber.

As the cadets removed the wires from their foreheads and temples and stood as one, it was not those who had succumbed to Frobisher's order who were the focus of this youthful, brainwashed army.

It was those who had not.

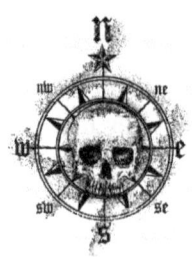

The truck pulled up at White Wharf, a broken and buckled structure jutting out into the ocean like a gnarled and knotted finger. The wharf had once been painted white but time and tide had worked a number on it, peeling back the layers of paint and finally corrupting the wood.

Tied to the decrepit structure, a motorboat bobbed in time with the surf, crewed by two men, one of them carrying a rifle.

Frobisher gave the crew a wave from the cab of the truck.

'All is well,' he said after consulting his wrist watch.

'You can never be certain with this place,' the shaman cautioned beside him. 'It's allegiance is unknown.'

'And that is why I have you here with me, dear fellow,' Frobisher said, placing a hand upon the smaller man's shoulder. 'One cannot presume loyalty. This is a fact I have learned over the years. It is true of men, so I dare say it shall be true of nature.'

'What lies at the heart of this village transcends both,' the shaman whispered.

'I'm sure,' Frobisher said.

The beast inside the shaman calmed its thoughts. It had been in the service of the thing at the heart of this town for a timeless age. No one outside of its accursed magic could ever understand the demands the entity placed upon its minions. Or the punishments it levied for failure.

'You are here to bring balance to our cause, shaman,' Frobisher said.

'For our goal to succeed, both the innocent and the

malleable must succumb to our will,' the shaman said. 'In these early stages, it is vital.'

'Indeed,' Frobisher said carefully before calling to one of his henchmen. A mountain of muscle clad in a blue suit ambled over.

'Sir?'

'Go get our guests,' Frobisher said. 'And don't let Miller out of your sight.'

The henchman nodded and went to the truck.

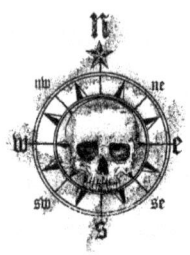

Beatrice sobbed, her heart was broken, her spirit decimated in ways she'd never known. As the tide-waters began to surge into the cave, she didn't seem to acknowledge them, such was her angst.

Pontefract was her nemesis, she knew this now. His scheming knew no bounds, his lust for vengeance impervious to time. And then there was Marcus, a boy who had manipulated her heart and then squashed it in his hands. This thought sent another wave of pain through her chest and she gasped for breath, her vision fogged with fresh tears that due to her shackles she couldn't even wipe away.

But despite her trauma, the insistent ocean finally demanded her attention. The churning, foaming water pulsed through the cavern, smashing into the shelf and sending an intermittent curtain of spray in front of her.

Panic pushed the pain from her heart, panic and the will to survive. She fought against her bonds, hoping to have some impact upon the manacles about her wrists. She pulled and squirmed, her teeth clenching with the strain of it, until her metal bonds raked into her wrists and she cried out with pain and frustration.

But her cries were lost amid the thunder of the rising waters.

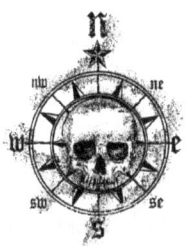

Emily ran, breathing in time with the vibration of her feet hitting the cobblestones. The promenade passed by her, giving way to an incline leading down to a cluster of rocks. Nestled within was *Cooper's Cove*, a place with a past as mysterious and sinister as events unfolding at that moment. There were old stories of strange goings on, and recent tales to match.

But to Emily there was no such thing as "strange". There was only what was. And both she and her new friends were all in danger. There was no shaking off the feeling that the mysterious gears of a monstrous machine were now turning for the first time in quite a while.

Clambering over the rocks, Emily relished the spray on her face as it cooled her cheeks. It caused her to pause.

This is what stopped her walking into Xavier

Pontefract and Marcus Macbeth as they emerged from the cove.

In the shadows, Emily clung to the rocks as the two figures passed within a few metres of her. She looked upon their malevolent smiles. She knew such countenances well for she'd seen them many times before on the faces of those who teased and taunted her because she was deaf, because she was different.

And she knew in that moment, beyond all doubt, Beatrice Beecham was in real trouble.

Lucas, Elmo, and Miller were bundled out of the truck and frog-marched to the motor launch.

As they neared the craft, the boys noticed that the shaman was still with Frobisher. The shorter man was pale and sickly, but his jade eyes seemed to shine like emeralds in the beams of the searchlight on the motor launch.

'Where'd you dig him up?' Miller said to Frobisher.

'It was not I who brought this fellow into this,' Frobisher said. 'He was *chosen*.'

'By whom?' said Elmo.

'For what?' said Lucas.

The motor launch pulled away from White Wharf, arching left before heading out to sea. Frobisher watched the shoreline recede before giving his reply.

'He was chosen by the only thing capable of making such a decision,' he said. 'This town.'

'You talk as if it's alive,' Elmo said.

The shaman butted in, 'It's best not to dwell on it, youngster. The Dark Heart knows fear and will seek it out in those who live here. But be of token cheer, it cannot influence the innocent. Not yet. Not yet.'

'No,' Frobisher said pulling a pistol from his waistband. 'But we have *other things* that are just as affective.'

'Ye're a real hero,' Miller growled.

'Some would support that,' Frobisher came back. 'Those who matter.'

Lucas scanned the shoreline, now several hundred metres away, and saw several boats heading towards their position. For a moment his spirits span skywards as he suspected the flotilla heralded imminent rescue, but then he saw the smile of Frobisher's face as a walky-talky crackled into life in his pocket.

'Eagle, this is Hawk, come in. Over.'

Frobisher pulled it free and spoke into it, 'Hawk, this is Eagle, go ahead. Over.'

'Enough of this Hawk and Eagle rubbish,' a bright yet irritated voice rattled in the receiver.

Lucas and Elmo recognised it immediately. It was a ghost, had to be. It was Xavier Pontefract.

'Most of the villagers are all sleeping like babies,' Pontefract said. 'And those who didn't see the broadcast are being interned in the school hall by our eager, if somewhat robotic, cadets.'

'Good,' Frobisher said. 'And what of your little venture? Has it reached a satisfactory conclusion?'

'The Beecham girl has a broken will and is about to

be put out of her misery at *Cooper's Cove*,' Pontefract said happily.

At Beatrice's name, Lucas' heart tried to climb up his gullet. He acted without thought and dove off the launch, hitting the ocean with a small splash.

The henchman took aim and fired three shots into the surf, before Elmo knocked his arm into the air so two more bullets intended for the water were sent skywards. Elmo was clubbed to the ground, and Miller took a step forward. Frobisher aimed his pistol at Elmo's chest but his cold eyes were fixed on Miller.

'Take one more step and another child's blood is on your hands,' he said. Miller froze.

'What the blue blazes is going on, Frobisher?' Pontefract said through the handset.

'Nothing that isn't now resolved,' Frobisher said. 'Rendezvous at *Bishop's Cragg*. Out.' He switched off the radio and slipped it back into his pocket, though the gun remained fixed upon Miller.

'What about the boy overboard, sir?' the henchman said.

'Let the ocean have him,' Frobisher said.

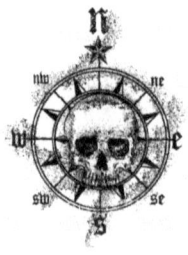

At Dorsal Finn library, Patience immediately saw there was something wrong. To begin with, the library doors were open, not ajar but thrown wide.

'Where's someone who's brave and gullible when you need them?' she whispered as she stepped into the library foyer. Patience called out into the huge room beyond.

'Agnes, are you here?'

Nothing.

Her feet were almost obstinate. Patience moved into the library and saw the second thing that told her all was not well.

Lying on the crimson, mottled carpet were the torn and tattered remnants of many, many books. They were piled high, pages screwed into balls or shredded, the bindings and covers buckled and broken. It was a sorry sight, a scene of literary carnage. As Patience moved forwards her foot caught something and she glanced down.

There, glistening in the lights overhead, were Agnes Clutterbuck's reading glasses. Patience picked them up and her eyes went back to the heaped mountain of books in the centre of the room.

'Where are you, Agnes?' she asked the room. 'Where have they taken you?'

If the room had been witness to the events leading up to that moment, the resonating silence demonstrated its eagerness to keep its secrets.

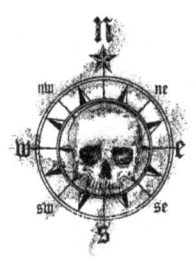

Beatrice watched as the tide powered into the rock chamber. Her whole world had collapsed and now it was about to be submerged beneath the roaring, churning waters of the Atlantic.

Salt spray created an intermittent curtain of fine mist that drifted from the ledge beneath her training shoes, and through this shimmering vista she saw something move. There was a shadow, an indistinct shape standing on a shelf of rock opposite, and separated by a churning chasm of water. The sight of it had her calling out in desperation.

'Hello! Help! Is there someone there?'

'Yes, Beatrice,' a voice called back above the cacophony below.

Beatrice almost cried out for joy. 'Thomas? Oh, thank God. Please, go and get help! I'm chained to the wall!'

But to her dismay, Thomas merely smiled; his face was serene and enchanted.

'I can't help you, Beatrice,' he said. 'You are an enemy of the *Blue Thunder Foundation*. You must be punished.'

'It's all phoney, Thomas,' Beatrice pleaded. '*The Blue Thunder Foundation*, Marcus—all of it. Something is wrong!'

'There's only *you* that's wrong,' Thomas said bluntly. 'But you will soon be *corrected*.'

And with that Thomas Beecham turned and left his sister to her fate, his mind focused on a world where nothing but loyalty and order mattered, irrespective of all else.

Beatrice called his name over and over, the cavern mocking her pleas by handing them back to her until they were ultimately swallowed by the din of the ocean.

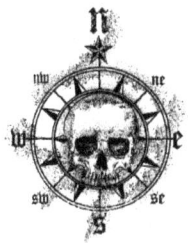

'The damn thing's stuck!' Albert groaned as he wrestled with the seatbelt imprisoning Maud. 'I think the mechanism's broken.'

'Then ye go an' get somethin' to persuade the thing to be lettin' ol' Maud go before she ends up havin' to be buried in this infernal machine like one of Thomas' ol' *Transformers*!'

Albert slapped his head in realisation. 'Of course, my toolbox in the boot. Hold on, Maud, I'll be back in a few seconds.'

'Well, ye can be sure I ain't goin' anywhere in the meantime,' Maud chirped, though Albert saw anxiety in her eyes.

Albert carefully placed his feet so that he didn't trample on Maud, and used his back, then his shoulders, to force the driver's door open, pinning it open with his arms. He hauled himself out of the car with a groan and slid down the roof to the ground. His feet landed in fuel, the wet cloying fluid splashing his shoes, spurring him on.

Panicked, he dashed to the car boot and rummaged through the shattered carcasses of the three receivers, until he found a small metallic toolkit, which he yanked open and dragged free. It may have been the sudden movement, it may have been the sweat coating his palms, but somehow he lost purchase for a moment and the toolbox upended, spilling its contents onto the street. He saw a cold-chisel spinning in almost slow motion, its sharp, bevelled edge carving a shimmering arc in the air before hitting the hard, petrol-soaked cobblestones.

The spark ignited the fuel with a roar, and the heat was immediate, driving Albert backwards. He shouted in anger and fear, grabbing at the chisel, ignoring the blistering heat in his hand, motivated only by the need to free Maud from the infernal seat belt.

As he made his way back to the car, he lost his footing, and went sprawling, the chisel spinning from his hands, and his head struck a lamp post. He grunted with surprise and pain, his vision clouding with dizziness and smoke.

Albert tried to stand, but his legs failed him. His left knee sent a wave of searing agony through his thigh. He called out in frustration and despair, collapsing in a hopeless heap, his head bowed, afraid to look at the flames as they licked against the upturned car.

Instead he whispered Maud's name as his tears splashed the cobblestones.

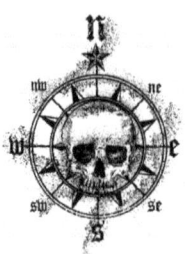

There comes a time when things become so crazy,

instinct takes over. The primordial instinct innate to the human psyche finds itself at the helm and steers us on a pre-ordained course, a course that is based not on duty or friendship but the pull of safety and emotional comfort and family.

Home.

And when Patience Userkaf found Dorsal Finn library rifled and ruined, and its owner missing, she instinctively sought solace in her family. She ran down the library steps, lost yet resolute that home held all the answers. The thought of her kind and beautiful mother, her proud and hardworking father, even her gregarious and often irritating uncle, spurred her on as she hurtled through the eerily, desolate streets, silent save for the pounding of feet on pavement and cobblestone.

Patience heard something amid her footfalls and slowed her pace so she could listen. It was a crackling sound, the kind that reminded her of sitting around a campfire many years ago in a hideous mud-brown fleece with *Brownies* etched across the chest in happy yellow letters. Then the sharp tang of smoke caught her delicate nostrils, just to confirm what she'd already decided.

Something was on fire; something *significant*, and yet there were no sirens. But she did hear a small voice on the air, its tone harsh and desperate.

'Help! Help! Won't somebody help us?'

Part of her wanted to press on, ignore the voice and go find her family. She peeled right, in the direction of the cries for help, picking up pace with renewed vigour, yet her fear remaining constant.

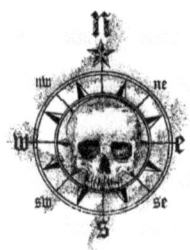

The world was a dizzying mix of freezing cold, turbulent darkness, and the disorientating rush of water in the ears.

Despite his fear of the icy depths, Lucas Walker had a greater fear of being shot. He stayed under the ocean for as long as his lungs would allow, his ears having heard the loud pops of the rifle, his eyes watching the bullets zip past him, the sea water marking their passing as tiny, tubular streaks.

When he surfaced, he drew in a breath and then scanned the area, ever anxious that the gunfire would resume. He needn't have worried—the motor launch and the flotilla were heading away from him, towards *Bishop's Cragg*. Multiple 'V' shapes sliced through the surf.

Lucas kicked his way towards the shore, the incoming tide helping him on his way. He knew his actions had been reckless, he knew it may even have jeopardised the safety of both Elmo and Miller, but the thought of Beatrice left alone in *Cooper's Cove* at high tide managed to override rational thought.

The shoreline came up fast, his limbs thankful, given that the side current had taken him past White Wharf and to the left of *Cooper's Cove*. Lucas gauged that given his present course he'd wash up on the shale near *Seer's Rock,* over a quarter of a mile away from Beatrice's watery prison.

Sure enough, several minutes later, Lucas emerged, gasping and spluttering, from the sea. His clothes were leaden with water causing him to cast off his jacket and leave it in a sodden heap on the shale. No sooner had he fought his way to dry land he was running, his lungs were steel in his chest, his determination just as firm.

He mounted the steps leading up to the promenade and then charged towards *Cooper's Cove*, hoping, praying that time would cut him some slack.

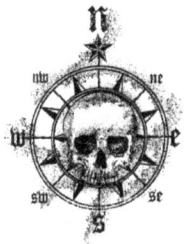

The waves lapped against the ledge, and Beatrice was distraught with fear and frustration.

The manacles were slick with blood, *her* blood—the result of struggling against her bonds. Her shoulders ached, her cries for help went ignored. All seemed hopeless.

'Hello, *Coppertop*,' said a voice to her left.

Beatrice yanked her head towards it, jarring her neck. Edward Chorley peered at her through a small opening only a few feet away. From her position flat against the wall, it appeared as if Chorley's head was emerging through solid rock. Then he stepped out into view, his face a mask of total and utter delight, despite the huge bruise on his cheek.

'Well, look at *you*,' he giggled.

'Edward, please,' Beatrice begged. 'Help me. You can't do this, it's murder.'

'This isn't murder; it's justice,' Chorley said, conviction filled his voice. 'Soon *they* will rise, and the Chorley's will have their power restored, power that you and your loser friends stole from us.'

'Edward, listen to me—'

'No, you listen!' Chorley yelled, the force of it making her wince. 'You're finished, Beecham. I came here to see you broken and alone.' He paused and gave her a cold, cold smile. 'And it feels *good*.'

Beatrice's blue eyes leaked fresh tears, her lips moved but no words came out, just the word 'please' mouthed over and over again.

'Goodbye, *Beatrice*,' he said. And then he was gone.

Beatrice sobbed silently, her head hanging down, chin upon chest, and the water slopped around her training shoes into her socks, ignorant of the terror its presence instilled.

She struggled with the notion that her time left on earth could be measured in moments. All the things she wanted to do, wanted to see, wanted to be, were soon to be stolen by the thief called Death. And in that moment of hopelessness her mind sought sanctuary, retreating to a place where confusion and trepidation found a champion.

Jamie's Kitchen.

At *Bishop's Cragg*, the small armada of commandeered boats alighted and its very human cargo disembarked. Frobisher stepped from the launch first, instructing Miller and Elmo to stay where they were if they did not want to incur a bullet.

Xavier Pontefract came next, Marcus with him, followed by the twins.

'You've done well my dear children,' Frobisher said proudly. 'You epitomise the new order.'

'Then God help us all,' Miller said coldly.

'You are beyond help, old man,' Frobisher snapped. 'You're still alive only the bear witness. Now, shaman, fulfil your destiny and set the wheels in motion.'

The shaman stepped forward and lifted his arms out before him. He turned his hands so his palms hovered over the rickety landscape and whispered a few words.

Elmo gasped as the shaman's fingers began to shimmer and sudden, green tendrils of light danced on the air.

'Amazed, boy?' Frobisher said. 'Then take a breath, we're only just getting started.'

Chapter Seventeen
Chamber of Horrors

PATIENCE COULDN'T BELIEVE what was going on, despite the evidence playing out before her very eyes. Albert's car was on its side and on fire. Its owner was on his knees, hands clasped behind his head, an unearthly howl playing on his lips and reverberating around the street. But amid the howl was one word that had Patience moving towards him, fast.

Maud.

'Albert, what's the matter?' Patience crouched beside him.

Albert looked up suddenly, his confusion matching that of the olive skinned girl squatting next to him.

'Patience?' he said. 'Maud, the car . . . '

'Are you saying Maud's in the car?' Patience clarified. 'The *burning* car?'

Albert nodded, the lump on his head glistening in the lamp light. 'Seatbelt's jammed.'

Patience looked around and espied the cold chisel. She grabbed it and sped to the car, the heat almost making her hesitate. She fought on. She got to the open door and peered in, thick smoke hampering her vision as she made out the struggling figure of Maud, weakly pulling at the seatbelt.

'Patience!' Maud gasped. 'Get out of here!'

Ignoring her pleas, Patience leaned into the car and wedged the chisel into the plastic locking mechanism, and yanked it harshly. There was a sharp cracking sound as the plastic shattered under the torque and Maud was free to clamber from the cab, assisted by Patience.

She near enough dragged the coughing and spluttering old woman away from the vehicle, until both of them landed unceremoniously on their backsides as the fuel tank exploded.

The explosion was thick and spectacular, and sent fiery debris rocketing skywards. As pieces of burning material rained down about them, Maud and Patience held on to each other as a groggy Albert Smythe crawled over to them; his arms embracing his aged beau and her youthful saviour, whispering words of comfort and thanks.

There were several loud pops and cracks as the wreckage burned brightly. Maud wiped her smoke smeared brow and looked Patience up and down.

'Well, I'm guessin' I'm owin' ye big time once we've stopped this town goin' to ruin,' she said grimly.

'I'll settle for a hair brush,' Patience muttered.

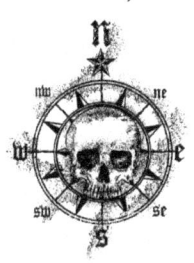

The slurping sounds of the ocean teasing the rocks created a rhythmic backdrop to the events unfolding at *Bishop's Cragg*.

Elmo watched, silent and sullen, as the shaman chanted. His words were as cadenced as they were unintelligible. The man's lower arms had become gauntlets of green light. A strange yet wonderful sight then occurred as the course ground at the centre of the islet began to shiver. A brilliant shaft of light streaked skywards, painting the bloated clouds above with a sickly yellow sheen. The column stayed in the air for a few moments before drifting away like smoke on the breeze.

At the centre of the islet, the light had pooled and then seeped into the ground. Then Elmo could see that rock and stone had given way to a rectangular opening.

'Another bloody tunnel?' Elmo groaned. 'How *predictable*.'

Frobisher laughed. 'Maybe so, boy, but finding this entrance has been a significant headache.'

'That would be Hessel's plan,' Miller said.

'He was meant to *seal* this place until we were ready to use it,' Frobisher said. 'Instead he became weak. He locked it up all right, and then threw away the keys, it seemed.' Frobisher nodded to the shaman, who stood with his head bowed and eyes closed. 'So after the wild goose chase of the past few days, we had to just accept that we needed to get someone to pick the lock.'

'What have you got down there, Frobisher?' Miller said.

'Do you really want to know?' Frobisher chuckled.

Miller's voice was suddenly in his ear. 'Whatever happens, stay by me. You got that?'

'With both hands,' Elmo said.

Frobisher walked over to the entrance and clicked on a pen torch. He followed its beam of light as he aimed it at the opening. After a cursory nod, he turned to address those standing about him.

'Ladies and gentlemen, despite the best efforts of Klaus Hessel, we are now able to enter *Atlantis*.'

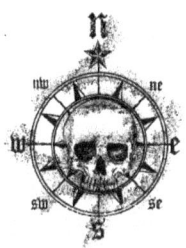

The Culinary Council was now in session, Jamie Oliver presiding. The cheeky chef was resting against a supermarket display picturing several, fat ripe oranges. At the checkout, Gary Rhodes, Mario Batali, and Raymond Blanc watched with embarrassment as Gordon Ramsay tried to take a laden shopping trolley through the *Ten Items or Less* aisle.

'Time's running out for me, Jamie,' Beatrice said.

'Nothing worse than waiting on a delivery that doesn't arrive, don't y' think?' Jamie replied.

'Being chained to a wall at high tide might come close.'

'But when you've hungry punters to feed, y' just have to make do,' Jamie said with no sense of urgency.

'I'm not sure where you're going with this,' Beatrice sulked.

'To the pantry, of course!' Jamie said with effervescence. 'Throw open those big old doors and see what's there, what can be created, right there on the spot. Sometimes magical things can happen when a chef is forced to—'

'Use only what's available?' Beatrice said.

'Lovely!' replied Jamie.

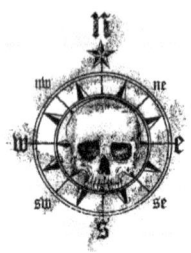

Beatrice battled her fear. She understood it was as much a threat to her survival as the incoming tide. The ocean was around her waist now, its chill embrace numbing her legs, its pulsating power lifting and dropping on a whim.

She looked up at her bonds, slim chains secured to an L-shaped bracket. They were new, glistening stainless steel things that she knew had been placed here solely to entrap her. She forced herself to remain focused.

Beatrice thought of what she had available to her, what could she use to break free. She saw that the shiny bracket was not quite flush to the cavern wall, the undulating rock didn't allow for it. There was a gap, a gap behind which something could be used to lever the bracket away from the wall!

But what could be used as a lever?

The chain itself? Could she hook it behind and try to yank it free?

Deep down a small spiteful voice started up.

'You're not strong enough to do such a thing,' it said. 'It would take the power of ten people to yank the bracket free from solid rock.'

But this thought did not give rise to dark despair, instead hope sparkled bright and welcoming in her heart.

'I haven't the power of ten people,' she admitted to the spiteful voice of doubt. 'I have something far greater. I have the power of the *ocean*.'

As if to confirm it, the tide surged in again, lifting her into the air as though she were nothing at all. When it fell again Beatrice lashed the chain around the bracket, her exhilaration an anaesthetic to the pain as salt water soaked her skinned wrists.

She left enough slack in the chain to be able to turn herself and plant a foot against the wall of the cave. She held her breath as she timed bracing off on her foot and pulling on the chain with the tidal surge. Water foamed around her shoulders, its tang finding her tongue as she cried out with the effort it took.

The bracket didn't budge.

Beatrice stamped on her anxieties and remained resolute to the task. Again the ocean lifted her; again she pulled against the bracket.

This time she felt it move.

The water was up to her chin now. She prepared for a final effort, knowing this was her last chance. As the waves rose, covering her with water, the bracket slid away from the wall with a burst of bubbles.

But it was not enough to set her free.

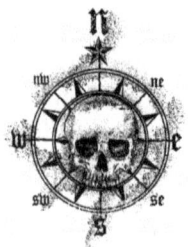

Agnes Clutterbuck looked at the quiet despair going on all around her.

She sat on the floor of the school hall, her back resting against Victorian brickwork, dabbing a tissue on a small scratch over her right eye brow.

Around her, clusters of people were huddled together, some staring, others spouting quiet tears of fear and anguish. Patience's parents and uncle were in the hall, too. Mrs Userkaf was crying against her husband, and Uncle Badru was staring grimly at the boys barring the doors. Both men had been badly beaten and nursed several cuts and bruises around their faces. They were all still in their party clothes.

Agnes had counted twenty other people in total, twenty who had not succumbed to Frobisher's televised command. It wasn't long before the cadets came for them—silent and sinister they had forced entry into their homes and subsequently marched these unfortunate souls to the school, locking them in the hall, and guarding every entrance and exit. Those who had resisted were beaten, the children of Dorsal Finn now brutal task masters for their ruthless cause.

They had grabbed Agnes from the library, but not before destroying all the literature on The Third Reich as they screamed 'lies, lies, lies!' in high pitched, frenzied voices. When Agnes tried to intervene, they had turned on her, knocking her to the ground and threatening her with more violence if she continued to interfere.

Cadets had dragged her through the streets, she was buffeted by several bigger boys, all wearing full cadet regalia. She noticed others being herded towards the school. It was difficult not to think that the most heinous of events was happening; that in an insidious manner The Third Reich had returned.

Initially, Agnes had thought the cadets were marching their prisoners to the hut. They were approaching it when her hearing aids began acting up, an intermittent beeping sound that had started earlier in the evening began getting louder as they neared the stark white building. But then the line veered left and began its journey to the school hall. At one point, Agnes feared what might happen to those who were under guard.

'Ms Clutterbuck?'

The librarian turned to the voice disturbing her reverie. She was thankful of it, even when she realised its owner.

'Mayor Codd,' Agnes said, noting immediately the fatigue etched into Gideon Codd's face. 'Are you a prisoner or the jailer?'

'I assure you, Ms Clutterbuck,' Codd said, 'I have been as duped as anyone by the antics of Logan Frobisher.'

'One wonders how that could possibly happen to someone dedicated to serving the best interests of this town,' Agnes sniped.

'And that was the intention,' Codd said uncomfortably. 'If Frobisher had made good on his promise.'

'A sugar-coated pill is still a pill, Mayor,' Agnes said, looking at the forlorn folk in the hall.

'Yet a pill is still good in its purpose,' Codd said defensively. 'Full responsibility cannot be laid at my door. I am still a servant of the electorate."

'After tonight that may change,' Agnes said, and Gideon Codd visibly shivered at the thought of losing his title. His facial muscles did a small jig and his head sought solace between chubby fingers.

'What have I done?' he said, voice muffled by his palms.

'The important question is, how do we sort it out?' said Agnes.

Codd came out from behind his hands. 'First we have to get out of here,' he said. 'Get a message to the outside.'

'No phones are working,' Agnes said. 'I suspect we are being gagged.'

'Then we need to make ourselves heard,' Codd said.

'And then what?' Agnes said.

'Then I go get my town back.'

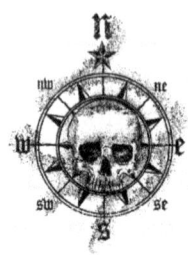

Lucas almost staggered into *Cooper's Cove*. He had lights flickering before his eyes, and his brain felt as though he'd been eating ice cream by the bucketful.

His vision fogged with exhaustion. Lucas fought his

way blindly towards the rocks where he knew a small blow hole lay. He knew this from his many childhood trips roaming the beaches of Dorsal Finn. The covert entrance was at the highest point of the cavern beneath, and the nearest means of access.

As he navigated the rocks, fuelled by his desperate need to help Beatrice, a shadow stood before him, barring his way. Lucas found himself staring into the mocking face of Edward Chorley.

'My, my, Walker,' Chorley laughed, 'You look like you'll be dead before that Beecham bitch.'

'You've seen her?' Lucas gasped. 'Is she okay?'

'Well on the way to becoming fish food,' Chorley mocked. He appeared pleased by this as a concept. 'I've already said my goodbyes. Man, she's such a mess. She was pleading with me in the end. Can you believe that?'

'You're a bastard, Chorley,' Lucas spat.

'And you're out of time, Walker.'

Chorley threw himself at the unsteady and unsuspecting Lucas Walker. The force of the assault caught Lucas off guard, and Chorley was able to land several punches as the other boy fell backwards. Lucas cried out as sharp rocks raked the flesh of his hands, Chorley silencing him with a blow to the temple that jarred Lucas' head sideways.

'Not so sharp now, are you, Walker?'

'I'd say go to hell but I think you'd like it there,' Lucas rambled woozily.

'Always the smart arse,' Chorley said bitterly. 'But I'll leave you with a thought that'll smart more: our little spat has made sure the ocean has its first *minging mermaid*!'

'No!' Lucas tried to stand but Chorley knocked him down again.

'You're too late, Walker. Blub, blub, Beatrice!'

And there, before his sworn enemy, Lucas Walker sobbed at the loss of his dearest friend.

Chorley revelled in his foe's misery.

'Hey Walker,' he whispered. 'Here's an interesting fact for you. The fish eat the eyes first. Think about that before you die you, too.'

The lights were going out, all the air in Beatrice's lungs now stale and almost spent. In the rushing, gushing vortex that was the ocean, she felt life slowly slipping away. She kept pulling and yanking on the chain, though.

The bracket hung out of the wall, held by a reluctant bolt that glittered even in the gloom. As the world began to fog, Beatrice became aware of a creamy radiance around her. It seeped through the murky waters and her body suddenly felt cocooned by its warmth. The chill in her bones faded to nothing, the ragged air in her lungs suddenly fresh as a spring breeze. The din of the mighty ocean also fell away to nothing and Beatrice thought this must be what it was like to die, for she now knew nothing of fear, or regret, pain or anger. There was only the light and its warmth, and an overwhelming sense of peace.

'You are the *Bringer of Joy*, Beatrice Beecham,' a soft, serene voice said. 'If you so choose.'

'Am I alive or dead?' Beatrice replied.

'You are in a place where those words have no meaning,' said the voice.

'But how else is this possible?'

'Because someone *wills* it so,' the voice whispered. 'We are on the cusp. A great evil is due to be set loose upon the Earth. Bad magic has weakened the walls of its prison.'

'You mean the Nazis?'

'They are pawns, minions to what is desperate to crawl from the heart of this town. The unearthly are drawn to this place, they sense the shift in that which is natural and that which is not. They come to bear witness.'

'Bear witness to what?'

'The Resurrection.'

'But who is it? What is it?' said Beatrice.

'The corrupted heart beats in many forms,' the voice said. 'Will you choose to be its adversary, *Bringer of Joy*? Or shall this moment play on and we will see the ocean claim you for its own?'

'Death now or death later,' Beatrice whispered. 'Not much of a choice.'

'A choice all the same,' the voice said. 'And there is hope that you will bring light to the approaching darkness. Only an act of clemency will avail you in such an hour. Remember this.'

'How do I know you're not working for this thing in the town?' Beatrice said. 'How do I know I can trust you?'

'You have always sought our counsel,' the voice said. 'And we have always answered.'

'I don't understand.' But no sooner had Beatrice

thought these words she found that she did understand. She understood perfectly. 'The Culinary Council,' she said.

'Yes,' the light said. 'A complex and frightening concept made simple for a young mind. But now you are beyond such things, *Bringer of Joy*. Now you are part of the light. You must see us for who we really are.'

In her mind she saw Jamie, Gary, Gordon, Raymond, and Mario. They were all looking at her, their smiles bright yet there was a hint of melancholy in their eyes. The edges of their faces began to shimmer, an effervescent dazzling light consumed them and Beatrice was confronted by five golden orbs that now danced in front of the pervading light about her, each with a corona of undulating flame. One orb moved forwards and oscillated in the air before Beatrice.

'Jamie?' she said.

'You may call me that if you wish,' the orb said. 'But time has given me many names. Now, what is your choice? Will you become the champion of your kind, or will you slip into eternal sleep?'

'Get me out of these goddamned chains,' she said. And suddenly, rather than slip into darkness, Beatrice's world turned to brilliant white.

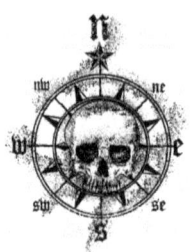

A portentous flicker of lightning danced across the undulating horizon, a storm making its presence felt to all on *Bishop's Cragg*. Whilst most glanced at the jagged light show, Frobisher and the shaman kept their focus on the recently unearthed doorway. Inside, there were steps leading down into darkness beyond the reach of Frobisher's torch.

'This is a moment, is it not?' Frobisher said, his voice smooth yet tight with excitement. '*The* moment of the 21st Century. We must enter now, and begin that which was planned so many years ago.'

Frobisher took a step, but the shaman held up a hand, stopping him. 'A moment. I fear something is not right.'

'How can you fear anything, shaman?' Frobisher said in frustration.

'There is a presence here, one not foreseen.'

'I will not hear of it,' Frobisher snapped, knocking the shaman's hand away from him. 'You will deal with the unforeseen—that is your purpose, is it not?'

'My purpose remains to be seen to all, including me,' the shaman muttered, but he stepped aside regardless.

Before Frobisher moved he turned to his henchmen, 'I want the old man and the boy to go in first,' Frobisher said. 'If they refuse, shoot them both.'

Two men came forward, both holding pistols. They motioned for Elmo and Miller to move towards the doorway and they did so without protest.

'What's down there?' Elmo said as a torch was thrust into his hands.

'Where's your sense of adventure, boy?' said Frobisher. 'Wait and see!'

331

'Great,' Elmo said and began walking down the steps, the torch beam revealing dry cement walls. His nose wrinkled with the heavy aroma of age and something faint, an odd smell that made Elmo think of science lessons.

Miller stayed just in front of Elmo, giving words of caution as they made their way down the steep stairway, until it ended as a square platform of concrete, their passage barred by a heavy, iron door. And on this door was a stencilled black eagle clutching a wreath-enclosed Swastika.

Frobisher and his henchmen shoved past Miller and Elmo in their haste to get to the door.

Frobisher placed his palm against the metal, his grin broad; a crocodile smiling at something that has fallen, struggling and helpless, into its watery domain.

'Opening this door will release the past,' he said. 'It will make things right'

And with that he pushed down the handle, dragging open the door that screamed on its hinges as though in protest of the travesty about to be imposed upon the world.

Elmo grimaced, fingers in his ears, as the screech reverberated for several seconds, as though a flock of gulls had been disturbed by some errant school kids combing the beach for sea shells.

Lucas would love this, he thought. A stab of fear pierced his chest as he recalled his friend leaping from the boat.

Then there was Beatrice and Patience, Maud and Agnes. Here in the murky underworld of Dorsal Finn, Elmo didn't know if his friends were safe or not, all thanks to the very people around him. Xavier

Pontefract turning up was bad news enough. That he was in cahoots with Beatrice's so-called boyfriend meant that it was bad news for Beatrice, too.

There was a sudden, dull sound, far off in the distance, a cough and splutter, and an eventual incessant drone of a generator kicking into life. Then, flickering overhead for several seconds, lights—their bulbs, milk-bottle thick and caged behind grills—wavered and then poured creamy light on those below.

'Seems Nazi engineering was as efficient as their insanity,' Miller sniped at Frobisher.

'Come, come, Miller,' the Blue Thunder leader said from the door way. 'Sour grapes don't suit a man of your reputation.'

The group walked through the door, beyond which was a huge, arched tunnel made from sculptured cement. At regular intervals more caged lights were secured high into the ceiling, and the walls of the tunnel were nondescript, save for a single yellow strip of paint halfway up the walls, horizontal and streaking off into the distance. The chemical smell was there too, strong enough to leave a slight metallic taste at the back of Elmo's throat.

Elmo noted dark green mounds scattered about the tunnel, he counted twenty before his nerves took over.

'Help me,' Frobisher said to the henchmen, three of which came to his aid. Between them, they dragged a swatch of grey, camouflage netting to the floor to expose a mountain of stacked crates, each with a Nazi eagle seared into the wood.

A henchman broke open one the crates, the splintering of wood harsh as it echoed about the tunnel. He reached in and pulled something black and angular from the wreckage, handing it to Frobisher.

'This is a tool to restore order,' Frobisher said holding the object for them all to see.

'MP40,' Miller whispered.

'Isn't that a motorway northwest of Bromsgrove?' Elmo asked.

'That's the M40. This is a machine pistol,' Miller muttered. 'The weapon of the Nazi trooper.' He looked at the multiple mounds in the tunnel. 'It's a weapon cache of some size. This is not good'.

'I decided after the shooting-at-Lucas gig,' Elmo said. 'Why all this stuff?'

It was Frobisher who answered him. 'Because we are going to *war*, boy—isn't that obvious?'

He leaned forward, the smile slipping from his face as though it had been stuck there with cheap glue. 'This place has *secrets*, my boy. Shall we go find 'em out?'

'Shall we not?' Elmo said uneasily.

'Let's not be coy,' Pontefract said retrieving his own MP40 from the crate. 'Isn't meddling in other people's affairs what kids like you do?'

'Oh,' said Elmo. 'You noticed that, I guess?'

'Then let's not break with tradition,' Frobisher said walking off down the tunnel.

Frobisher instructed one of the crates be transported to Dorsal Finn. Marcus and one of the henchmen went to oversee the task.

'Our proud youth shall be armed worthy of the cause,' he said proudly.

'He's giving guns to children?' Miller said in disgust. 'Madness.'

'I dunno,' Elmo whispered. 'Right now I'd be pretty pleased to have one.'

'Weapons are the tools of the ignorant, Elmo,' Miller said.

'I can do ignorant,' he complained. 'Especially when I'm scared shi—erm—*witless*.'

Frobisher continued into the tunnel. They all followed. Some eager, some reticent, others bound by duty, but if all were honest, not one amongst them could say that were not in the slightest bit intrigued.

Chapter Eighteen
March of the Cadets

Dennis Hodges woke with a start, his head pounding fiercely.

'Dear Lord, stop yer drummin' in me noggin',' he said to the ceiling. A cool breeze whipped across his face, and he relished the moment. Then he heard the rumble of thunder.

'Couldn't 'ave shut me bedroom window,' he said, opening an eye. Then he saw the black, nebulous clouds overhead. 'Couldn't 'ave made it home, either.'

After helping Albert and Maud load the transmitters into the back of the Metro, Dennis had decided to treat himself to a Cinder's Cider or two. Problem was, when Hodges talked about two, he usually meant jugs. In a way, he felt it was a minor celebration given that the immediate danger had passed with the transmitters now safely in their possession.

He risked sitting up, his hands grasping the surface supporting his large frame. He felt wooden slats against his palms; recognising where he was immediately since he often found his way to this place when out on a night with his best friend, *Cinder's Cider*.

A park bench facing the ocean.

The sky grumbled again, and a flicker-flash of lightning splashed the clouds.

'Best get off home before I get mesself an early shower,' he said getting carefully to his feet. He felt the world wobble beneath him as though the paving stones had turned to jelly while he'd been asleep.

'C'mon Dennis ye ol'soldier,' he cursed.

He made his way unsteadily from the promenade and into town where his cottage lay waiting for its prodigal owner. The streets were silent, devoid of revellers, and those who often came to the promenade to watch the tide reclaim the beach. Neither were there any vehicles on the road, not one car; not one bicycle. A terrible feeling started up in his guts, keeping his excess company.

Just when Dennis thought he'd slept through a quiet Armageddon, he suddenly heard shouting in the distance, his feet instinctively heading towards the din. At a street corner he saw long shadows thrown against shop fronts, preceded by the rhythmic thud of marching feet.

'Get a move on, scum!' a voice yelled. 'To the hut with you all. Then we shall decide your fate!'

'Belay that!' came another voice. 'New instructions from Commander Frobisher. He doesn't want this rabble spoiling the plan. They are to stay away from the hut. Take them to the school hall.'

'Very well! Move, move!'

Dennis almost gasped when the procession came

into view. It was a line of brow beaten townsfolk, bound together with thick ropes about their wrists and marched through the street by teenagers in *Blue Thunder* uniforms, some younger kids following on behind carrying standards and banners.

The faces of the townsfolk were bemused and weary and frightened. In contrast, their captors bore hallmarks of sinister enjoyment their newfound power brought to them.

Instinct told Hodges to step forward and help free his friends, but something held him back. And not only the hangover.

If the kids were told not to go to the cadet hut then something was bound to be going on there, and if he could stop that then he figured it would be a better way of helping the poor souls being marched up to the school.

Dennis stepped back into the shadows, sobered by the task ahead, and made his way to the *Blue Thunder Foundation* HQ. It was as he emerged from a side street opposite the cadet hut that he walked straight into a group of people, and his hands came up, big fists clenched and ready for a fight.

'Pickin' on old'uns an' young'uns these days, Dennis Hodges?' said a rasping voice. 'Ye've become a real hero.'

'Maud?' Dennis said dropping his hands. 'What the hell happened t' ye? Ye're lookin' like ye've been sleepin' in the coal bunker at Bramwell Hall.'

'Ye silver tongued Devil,' Maud grinned. 'I got semi baked in Hell's Kitchen an' was saved by me two angels, that's what.'

'The town's gone crazy,' Dennis said before telling them about what he'd just seen.

'Was Agnes with them? My parents?' Patience said anxiously. 'They took Agnes from the library, and then wrecked the place.'

'I didn't see any of 'em but I'm thinkin' it's likely they all were. These young'uns ain't messin', they got orders to keep folk under control.'

'So we have to go and get Agnes,' Maud said. 'An' the others.'

'Won't that be dangerous?' Patience asked.

'It'll be a picnic after what ye did just now,' said Maud.

'I'm not sure how much more of this picnic my hair's going to tolerate,' Patience grumbled. 'I'm going to be conditioning for a week as it is.'

'Hold up, Maud,' Dennis said. 'We're in danger of attendin' the wrong party.'

'How so?' said Albert, his hand firmly in Maud's.

Dennis explained the cadet's reluctance to take the imprisoned villagers to the hut.

'If there's a weakness, it's there, as sure as God made little apples,' he concluded. 'All we have to do is find it.'

'Whatever it is, it'll be guarded,' Albert said. 'We'd best be prepared. That means me and Dennis going alone.'

'That sounds fair,' Patience said.

'Aye,' said Maud, 'for a couple of cave men who ain't ever heard of Emmeline Pankehurst!'

'Maud?' Albert said.

'Don't *Maud* me, fella. I can't speak for our young'un here, but ol' Maud's gettin' on this train, 'cause she's earned her ticket. Besides, ye've got a battered knee, Albert. Who else is goin' t' be yer crutch from here t' the hut?'

Albert's shoulders sagged in resignation. 'Okay, Maud,' he said. 'You win.'

'What about ye, Patience?' Dennis asked. 'Ye goin' to duck and dive an' hope ye don't get caught, or are ye comin' with us?'

'Is that meant to be a balanced choice?' Patience said.

'There're others, but they all end up with less sugar 'n' spice,' said Dennis as they turned to leave for the hut.

'Adults,' Patience muttered following them.

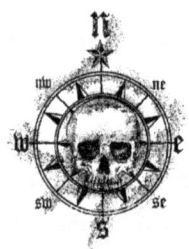

The white light faded to a dull glow in the writhing surf. The orbs winked out. Even though her lungs were crazy for air and Beatrice's mind was fogging with the need for oxygen, she knew within seconds that she wasn't alone.

Then she saw a sight so welcome, the last of the precious air in her lungs was almost lost in a submerged cry of joy. Emily was with her, the girl's flaxen hair flowing around her like a wonderful mane of gold, a determined look on her face.

Emily swam to the bracket and clutched it in her small hands, and within moments Beatrice was finally free of her prison, the bracket trailing behind her as she followed Emily's torchlight through the tide and into the space through which Chorley had disappeared. It was a short tunnel, a blow hole eroded into the rock, and Beatrice saw the light around her change, spurring her on, the world becoming sluggish as the lack of oxygen finally took its toll.

Emily came up to her knees, her head and shoulders breaking the surface, and within moments Beatrice felt tiny hands grab roughly at her clothing, hauling her free of the water.

Had Beatrice any breath left in her lungs, it would have been dragged away by the mighty wind slapping into her face as she surfaced. But she had never experienced joy like it, the euphoria at being able to suck in huge mouthfuls of cold, buffeting air. She devoured it, consumed it with the zeal the starving would a royal banquet.

Emily held onto her as Beatrice fought to regain her strength, the comfort as welcome as the wonderful, wonderful air.

'Thank you,' Beatrice mouthed. Emily merely nodded, her face concerned, her demeanour perplexed.

'What is it, Emily?' Beatrice gasped. .

'Does this mean you won't be seeing Marcus anymore?'

Despite her ordeal, Beatrice laughed until she almost lost consciousness for a second time.

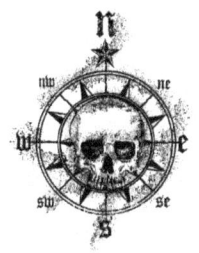

Lucas Walker struggled to get to his feet, but Chorley kicked him in his side, winding him and sending him rolling across the rocks.

'You got some spirit, Walker,' Chorley smirked standing over him, 'I'll give you that much.'

'Beatrice,' Lucas moaned clutching his side. 'You've got to save her.'

'What is it with you and that girl, Walker?' Chorley asked. 'The whole world's about to change and she's all you've got to think about? Do you *love* her or something?'

Lucas looked up, one of his eyes was swollen, but he made no attempt to hide his feelings. He tried to get to his feet again.

'Oh, you *do* love her!' Chorley laughed harshly. He walked over to Lucas and kicked him back down again. 'It's a gross thought but it does make this all the sweeter, that's for sure. Think I'd have a special celebration once all this is over. '

'Then I've got a little present for you, Chorley,' a voice said behind him causing him to spin around. He recognised Beatrice shortly before he saw the rather large piece of driftwood in her hands, a piece of driftwood that filled his vision before taking him into darkness for a while.

Chorley crashed backwards in an untidy heap, but Beatrice didn't watch him fall. Instead, she went to Lucas and scooped him into her arms.

'Oh, Lucas,' she cried, 'Are you okay? Are you hurt?'

'I've been better,' Lucas said, his arms wrapping around her and hugging her tightly. 'You've done wonders for my ego. I came to save you, and you ended up saving me.' He pulled away from her so that he could seek out her eyes. 'I need you to know it wasn't me who said those horrible things to you at *Seer's Rock*. I mean, it *was* me but the words weren't mine. I would never say those things. Not to you. *Never* to you.'

'I know,' Beatrice said. He smiled weakly when he saw understanding in her eyes.

'I never knew there was so much hate in the world,' she said tearfully.

'Not just hate, Bea,' Lucas said softly, his hand stroking her cheek. She noticed his fingers were trembling. 'There's love too.'

'The Newshounds have shown me that,' she sniffed. 'You're all special.'

'*You're* special, Bea,' Lucas said, he sounded groggy for the beating. 'Don't ever forget that.'

'Thank you,' she said, her hand holding his tightly.

'Thanks yourself. I guess the Marcus thing went the way of the pear?'

Beatrice nodded, her cheeks flushing a little. 'Yes, trying to murder your girlfriend tends to put a downer on a relationship.'

'Well, there's other things you should know about the guy. And *The Blue Thunder Organisation*.'

And with quiet urgency he explained all that had happened.

'You guys could've told me,' Beatrice said.

'Would you have listened?' said Lucas.

'Maybe not,' she admitted.

Emily was suddenly with them. She pointed to the horizon, towards *Bishop's Cragg*, where a streak of brilliant light cavorted; its intensity producing a ragged silhouette.

'Elmo's out there,' Lucas said trying to stand. 'God knows where the others are. It's all gone to hell.'

Another crack of thunder rolled across the sky, powerful and ominous. Beatrice held onto Lucas as he steadied himself.

'Where do we go from here?' Beatrice asked.

'The whole thing revolves around what's going on right now at *Bishop's Cragg*,' Lucas said. 'We need to get out there and stop it.'

Emily watched Lucas' lips intently, and then turned to the ocean where the waves were bubbling under the rising wind.

'How do we get to *Bishop's Cragg* in this?' she said.

'Boat,' Lucas gestured. 'But I don't know if there's anyone who'd take us out in this. Even if they weren't under Frobisher's control.'

'Oh, I can think of someone,' Beatrice said suddenly. 'Let's get to the docks!'

The two girls hauled Lucas to his feet and he stood between them, an arm around each of their shoulders as they took his weight. He felt a small nudge to his right and found himself looking into the face of the pretty girl with wet, blonde hair slapped close to her scalp and face.

'I'm Emily,' she said with a big grin. 'And you've got a great black eye.'

Despite his bruises, Lucas nodded and smiled.

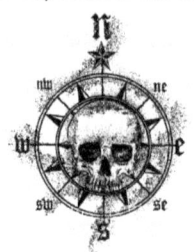

As if the tunnel beneath *Bishop's Cragg* wasn't impressive enough, the chamber it led into was something that Elmo thought could only happen in *James Bond* movies. The tunnel ended as a set of huge metal doors, secured to a horizontal mechanism with gears and teeth, designed to drag the gates apart. Frobisher scanned a panel embedded into the door frame, and struck a large red button with the heel of his hand.

The ground trembled as the gears engaged and the iron sheets slid away from each other, and all who witnessed the sight beyond gasped in wonder.

To call it a chamber undermined reality. It was a vast space, spanning half a kilometre, and the same in height. High in the ceiling, several bulky nets hung like bloated hammocks, their mesh securing many blue-grey boxes packed tightly together. From these nets long cords snaked down to several red oil drums on the floor of the chamber.

But the space also housed other countless objects Elmo recognised from the Klaus Hessel's blueprints: cylinders of grey-green metal, topped with glass. They stood upright, stacked no differently to the crates housing the MP40s, yet each had a galley, a walkway made of metal and mesh, built into a frame with a ladder leading to ground level.

Elmo looked back at the canisters, recognising shapes standing behind the glass panels.

People.

Silhouettes of people, shadows on a field of milky white light.

'How?' Miller said in muted awe. 'How in a time of war could this be done here?'

'It could only *be* done here,' Frobisher said. 'This place is special, because *this town* is like no other. Everyone who lives here knows it exists, but never dwells on it for too long. It's like the elephant in the room. My subliminal technology has nothing on the collective denial on show in this village.'

Miller appeared unsure. Frobisher continued. 'Hessel did well to cover his tracks, but the path was already well worn. Once you know where you need to be, then planning how to get there is pretty damn easy.'

'But at a time of war?' Miller said.

'The infrastructure was built before the war, idiot,' Frobisher scoffed. 'As the British turned their eyes to an unsettled 1930s Europe, we built this *Trojan Horse* under their very noses. War just made it easier to make this area taboo. The sighting of a rogue submarine in these waters feigned Nazi interest in the area. The submarine was a ruse of course. With stretched resources, all the British navy could do was to lay sea mines. The mines were disarmed by Nazi secret agents working here as soon as the war began, clearing the way for the final phase of the project: Laying these masterful souls to a temporary rest. The results of which can be seen here, now.'

'How could something like this be kept secret?' Elmo said. 'And why not use this to win the war?'

'Good questions, boy,' Frobisher conceded. 'I shall answer the latter first. The man who planned this eventuality did so because he knew losing the war was inevitable. In Hitler, the Nazis had a blinkered dictator who refused to concede to the advice of his military advisors. So it was decided to prepare for the future, and, as you can see, prepare we have. Hessel was meant to come over here and secure the site. Clearly he had other plans when he got here.'

'You mean you knew about Klaus and his plan to escape?' Miller said.

'He didn't escape,' Frobisher laughed. 'Do you think he could have just strolled out of Nazi Germany at the height of the war? He was allowed to leave. His last job on the project was to close the lid on his work, literally. Trust the naïve fool to suddenly decide to question the end game. Very frustrating. Especially for my grandfather. It set us back so many decades. What we didn't know about, however, was you, Miller. You were the fly in the pie that's for sure.'

'This still doesn't add up,' Elmo said. 'You knew this place was here. You knew where the entrance was. Why not just break in?'

'Because this was all a *contingency*, boy,' Frobisher said. 'Built by those who always had foresight to plan for every eventuality. For example, what if this place was found by the allies? What if they came down here and saw what was being planned? They would never trust the Nazis again—and keep them under close scrutiny forever more.'

'Yet they would still find it,' Miller said.

'They would find the entrance, perhaps,' Frobisher said. 'But without the dedicated keys a Jewish locksmith created, Miller, this place would be wiped off of the face of the Earth. Look above you,' Frobisher said, indicating the netting and the boxes overhead. 'It is rigged with over a thousand pounds of high explosive. No theory on outcome here, just a big bang!'

But Miller was distracted by Frobisher's previous comments.

'Locksmith? What locksmith?' Miller said.

'The locksmith commissioned to secure this site,' Frobisher said.

'What happened to the locksmith?' Miller said, his voice becoming tight with anger.

'He was put down like the Jewish dog he was,' Frobisher sneered. 'My grandfather pulled the trigger himself.'

Miller's face scrunched up with anguish, and his hands came up to cover it.

'That was my father!' he wept into his palms.

'Well it is a small world,' Frobisher laughed. 'I'm not sure what is more astounding, that my grandfather killed your father or that any of the locksmith's family managed to survive *The Camps*.'

'You animal,' Miller said coldly, his hands now at his sides and balled into fists. 'Your poisonous kin killed us all.'

'You are all entwined,' the shaman said. 'Your fates steered towards this moment. Each of us are pawns in a game beyond your understanding.'

'This can't be happening' Miller whispered.

'It is happening,' Frobisher snapped. 'And it is happening now. Your father built the transmitters and they were designed to lock away the work that was done here. But thanks to interference,' he looked sharply at Elmo, 'we needed to pick the lock. And that's where the shaman came to our aid.'

'Sounds like coincidence,' Miller said as he stared coldly at Frobisher. His grief had turned to quiet fury, and Elmo could see that the old man appeared very red in his cheeks and neck.

'As I said, only in *this* place could such a thing happen,' Frobisher said.

In amazement, Elmo looked at the cylinders. The shapes behind the glass were becoming clearer. Faces were evident, grim with mouths fixed into grimaces, eyes wide and staring, yet each iris was as opaque as the glass in their metal coffins.

'They look—' he began but couldn't finish it.

Frobisher helped him out. 'Dead? Yes, science and engineering could only take *Project Atlantis* so far. The plan is nothing without a heart. And my grandfather's men scoured the Earth looking for the *darkest heart* to bring life to those who gave theirs to the greater good. Three divisions of Hitler's *Waffen S.S.* lie here, waiting for resurrection.'

'Nazi zombies? You guys have been exposed to way too much *Netflix*, dude.'

'*Zombies?*' Frobisher spat. 'An insult to what is happening here. Cryonics preserved these fine men, but its science is crude even today. In 1941, even more so. They represent the last phase of *Project Atlantis*, placed and hidden here; awaiting the day they would be called upon to fulfil their duty, *this* day!'

'Madness,' Miller said.

'If you see madness here, then I look at you and see only stupidity and gullibility,' Frobisher snapped. 'A young boy left with such a burden of keeping such secrets, *hiding* such secrets. You had help, I'm certain of it; help from this town, their resources—natural or unnatural—to continue with the deception. Who they *are*, or who they *were* for that matter, I have no interest. Not now.'

'I knew nothing of its *purpose*,' Miller snarled.

'If this is a thing of evil then you are equally culpable!' Frobisher said. 'You, old man, plead ignorance, but I only see hypocrisy. A better man would've not kept that which is claimed to be evil. A better man would have destroyed it all at any cost.'

'Hessel knew his work would eventually help mankind, not destroy it,' Miller said but Elmo could see how flustered he was by Frobisher's accusation. 'This process could save people's lives.'

'Naïve fool,' Frobisher scoffed. 'Look at the world we live in. You would have all of this knowledge handed over to mankind? Man who still kills man for his land, his wealth, his power? I am bringing Hessel's work back to the purer cause. His science is being used to bring order to the chaos of man, bring method to the madness. I respect such work. And I shall use it to make the world better.'

'You are no saviour, Frobisher,' Miller growled. 'You are a monster holding the leash of evil.'

Miller stepped forward and one of the henchmen aimed an MP40 at Elmo.

'Behave, Miller or your young investigator will suffer the consequences,' Frobisher said.

Miller stopped and glowered at their captor.

'Sensible,' Frobisher said. 'All of this is irrelevant now. Questions have been answered, and that which was lost has been found in this incredible, terrible town.'

'What did you find?' Elmo asked.

'A powerful ally,' Frobisher hissed. 'Shaman?'

The man in the robes came forward.

'It is true,' the shaman said. 'Dorsal Finn is alive, but its life force is fuelled by corruption, it will be able to give life to this soulless army.'

'Careful with your tone, shaman,' Frobisher

warned. 'There is no evil here, only redemption. You best remember that once you have conducted the ritual.'

'I fear nothing from you,' the shaman said coolly. 'You are not my master. My fate is not yours to decide. This event will happen because this town *wants* it to happen. Do not renege on the bargain, or you may find your ally unforgiving.'

'Very well. Conduct the ritual,' Frobisher replied through lips white with anger. 'Give life to my army.'

'This is a bad move,' Elmo muttered to Miller. 'How do we stop it?'

'That chance has passed,' the shaman said as though Elmo had shouted his concerned through the chamber. 'The only one capable of stopping this has been dealt with.'

Elmo almost keeled over with the realisation of the shaman's words.

He was talking about Beatrice.

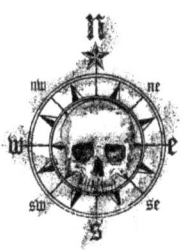

'What have those young tykes been up to this time, Agnes Clutterbuck?' Edna Duffy said sourly. 'Arrested in my own home by a bunch of *scouts*? This has Newshound mischief stamped all over it.'

To say Edna Duffy was constantly trying to blame others for the ills of her world was a little like saying the sun was a bit bright or giving birth smarts a bit. In the school hall, Edna's head frantically bobbed up and down to highlight her escalating irritation.

'I have to agree with you, Edna,' said a reed-thin woman called Dorothy Arnold who carried with her a big bag of bon-bons. Dorothy often agreed with Edna because not agreeing was often not worth the trouble.

'Well, I *certainly don't*,' said Agnes sharply. 'What's happening here can only be attributed to one man.'

Gideon Codd shuffled at Agnes' side.

'Logan Frobisher,' Agnes concluded as Mayor Codd let out a sigh of relief.

'Yes, ladies,' Codd said. 'I must concur with Ms Clutterbuck. We have, all of us, been duped.'

'Well that's a first,' Edna said immediately suspicious. She glared at Codd. 'But what I want to know is what *you* plan to do about it?'

'As an elected representative, I feel that Mayoral authority needs to be reasserted,' Dorothy Arnold said, reaching into the bag for one of her favourite fruit bon-bons. 'These young *whipper-snappers* need to be shown who's in charge. A little respect for their elders is called for. I would also suggest a smacked bottom or two for good measure.'

'Some of those children are over six feet tall, Dorothy,' Agnes said. 'Good luck with that.'

'Well we have to do something,' Dorothy said as her jaws began working on the bon-bon. There was a lot of sucking and slurping as she battled with the sweet.

'Mayor Codd,' Edna said expectantly.

'Very well,' said Codd, though not without

uncertainty. As he stood, he adjusted his suit jacket and pulled himself up to his full height, which in reality still wasn't very tall, and marched over to a youth barring one of the exits. He was considerably bigger than Codd; broad and in his late teens. The youth's face was grim-set and handsome, and the Mayor didn't recognise him from the town.

As Codd neared, the youth gave him a contemptuous look, his hand resting on a long stave hanging from his belt.

'Young man,' Codd said in his best presentation voice, loud and commanding. 'I demand to speak with your superior.'

'Sit down or I will hit you on the head with this baton,' the youth said as he casually tapped the handle of the stave.

Codd shuffled on the spot before nodding. 'I shall go and sit down.'

Back with Agnes, Edna and Dorothy, Codd resorted to sitting on a bench grumbling to himself.

'Maybe we should've sent Dorothy with her bon-bons,' Edna said bitterly.

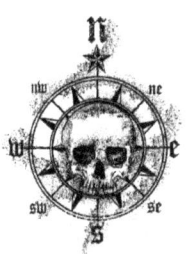

Dennis Hodges scanned the scene ahead. The hut appeared quiet, a stark contrast to the fantastic events happening throughout the town.

'Coast looks clear,' Dennis said.

'I beg to differ,' said Patience as the storm winds whipped and knotted her hair.

The rain swept in from the sea, the torrents illuminated and turned into a solid swirling mass by the arc lights. The flag pole rattled fiercely under the onslaught. Blasts of thunder and streaks of lightning added their thoughts to the evening as the group made the decision to approach the building.

They moved as one, a single sodden mass of people closing down the distance quickly, despite reticence, age, and inclement weather. At the doorway, Dennis placed an ear against the wood, but a huge blast of thunder rattled the door in its frame.

'Ah, to hell with this,' Dennis cursed stepping back. 'If we can't hear them then they sure as hell ain't gonna hear us.'

And before anyone could protest, he aimed several kicks at the doors, forcing them open with relative ease. Without caution, Dennis entered the hut, and was confronted by two Blue Thunder cadets, both easily in their late teens, thick set and determined to prevent him getting any further. In their hands, wooden staves were raised and ready. He met them head on, and one of the youths swiped at him, the stave just missing Dennis' ribs, the air whistling at its passing. The big man took hold of the youth's arm and swung him into the wall, where he crumpled, unconscious.

The ease at which Dennis had dispatched his colleague caused the remaining *Blue Thunder* cadet to hesitate. Dennis used these vital moments to close down the space between them and knocked him flat with one punch. The youth flew through the air and landed on his back, the polished wooden flooring allowing him to continue on his travels until he struck the stage twenty metres away.

'I ain't seein' any scouts' honour in this joint,' Dennis said as he beckoned the others into the main meeting hall. 'What we lookin' for?'

'Anythin' capable of influencin' young minds,' Maud suggested.

Albert hobbled to the stage and stopped as he climbed the steps. 'I got a trap door here!'

'How convenient,' Patience said. 'Don't suppose it leads to a passageway that's not covered in dust and *stuff*, does it?'

Albert peered into the trapdoor before grinning grimly at Patience. 'You know, this just might be your lucky day, young lady.'

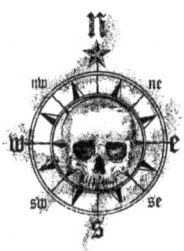

At Dorsal Finn High School, Marcus Macbeth arrived with his special delivery of a crate crammed with MP40s.

He dismounted from the truck which had served as transport from White Wharf, accompanied by one of Frobisher's henchmen. Between them they had carried the crate to the corridor feeding into the main hall.

Over twenty Blue Thunder Cadets formed an orderly line, and each was given a gleaming weapon, glistening with gun grease, and several clips of ammunition in pouches, secured to a webbed body belt. For some of the cadets the weapon was almost as big as they were. Yet they all knew how to operate it, they had all been told via the relentless bombardment of corrupt information delivered by electrodes and *Blue Bolt* multi-media. And no one was more excited at receiving a weapon than Thomas Beecham. He slammed in the ammunition clip, pulled back the firing pin and clicked off the safety catch like a military veteran.

Once everyone had been armed, Marcus faced the under aged platoon standing before him.

'Behind those doors, in the school hall, are the enemies of the New Reich,' he said. 'They are Psychophants feeding on the decent and righteous. Their blood will be the symbol of a new dawn. A dawn made red with the blood of the weak. They have no place in the New Order. Open the doors and put them down like the sick dogs they have become!'

The troop activated the firing mechanisms on their weapons, the corridor alive with pops and clicks, faces blanched with rapture and ignorance. Marcus smiled as the kids stood outside the hall doors, waiting for their comrades inside to let them in so they may fulfil their devout, yet despicable, duty.

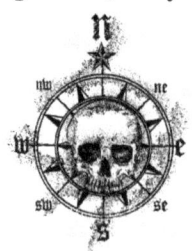

The Albatross was tousled upon the raging ocean, its prow lifting high into the air and then slamming down into the water, a fan of spray rising before being whipped away by the gale.

In the wheel house, Beatrice watched as Colin Cresswell fought with the helm, his eyes never once leaving the writhing water ahead.

They had found him at the docks, sitting on his boat fixing his nets even as the rain lashed down on him, his yellow rubber trench coat making him appear like a big, animated banana. Much to Beatrice's relief, Colin didn't need much persuasion once he'd heard their swiftly told tale. Nor did he need proof. He'd already heard strange stories of screaming, and exploding CD players, from a very nervous Cochran over a few beers at the Salty Sea Dog that evening.

Now *Bishop's Cragg* approached, a small land mass in a vast, wavering seascape. Lucas and Emily were with her of course, neither of her companions prepared to leave her to go on without them. Lucas was hunched over a bucket as his stomach bucked and rolled in time with the ocean.

'The day can only get better, right?' he groaned.

'Hang in there, Lucas,' Beatrice said offering comfort by rubbing his shoulders. 'We're about to get off.'

'I'll pull alongside, but I ain't gonna be able to get too close 'case I hit the hard stuff,' Colin said.

Beatrice noted the other boats moored at the islet. Some had been dashed against the rocks and were buckled and broken in the shallows.

'Can you get close to those boats?' she said. 'We can use them as a bridge.'

'Aye, I can do that. Hold onto yer life vests, I'm goin' in,' Colin said.

It was perilous, but Colin and *The Albatross* were experienced, and he was able to hold steady as Beatrice, Emily, and Lucas alighted, the motor launches bumping into the hull of *The Albatross* with dull thuds. With careful timing, the children navigated the boats, until they scrabbled over the rocks, clothes sodden, and their life vests gleaming in the search beam sweeping in from *The Albatross*.

'I'll stay here as long as I can!' Colin assured them.

Beatrice waved her thanks.

'Look!' Lucas pointed to the entrance in the ground.

'Better get down there,' Beatrice said. 'But let's be careful. We've been caught out too many times, right?'

Lucas nodded, his nausea, his beaten body now shelved for a while. Emily wiped her wet hair from her brow and unclipped the torch before discarding her life vest, the others swiftly following suit.

They tentatively descended the concrete steps, intrigued not only by their environment but the eerie sounds coming from ahead. It was a fusion of mechanics and distorted voices.

And a lilting hum that made Lucas falter on the steps.

A sinister rendition of *Edelweiss*. It drifted up to them from the landing below, an aural nightmare piercing his heart with fear, and bringing anger to his belly. His mind poured forth images that had been locked away from him: the twins stepping out from an alley as he walked away from his meeting with Marcus Macbeth, the words on their lips, the look in their eyes, all designed to put thoughts in his head—their thoughts. As the memories came he was somehow purged of them and he was left breathless for a moment.

'You okay?' Beatrice asked putting a hand on his arm.

'Yeah. Let's hold up a minute,' he whispered. 'It's Hansel and Gretel. Their words are poison. They can get inside your head, make you do stuff.' He paused, sheepish. 'Say stuff.'

'Want to let me in on things?' Emily interjected.

Lucas apologised and told her. To his surprise, Emily merely smiled. Then, without warning, ran down the steps.

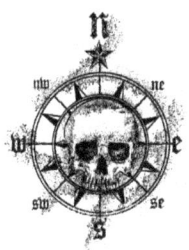

Emily was feeling different. Something inside her was changing. She didn't know how, but she was beginning to understand that her visions were only a small part of who she was. The way an iceberg breaking the surface of a calm, cold ocean is part of something much, much bigger.

And this was growing, even as she padded down the steps. It was as though being here, in this place, had switched on something fantastic, something incredible, and it was pumping through her like water through a tributary.

She found the twins standing in front of the door leading to the tunnel. And, as she approached them and saw their beaming fixed smiles, she was able to see what lay beyond, what miseries they had endured to make them who they were, the pain, the suffering, a childhood lost to the world of device and artifice. She felt at once sorry for them. Their hidden misery brought tears to her eyes.

'Hello,' the twins said.

'You really shouldn't be down here,' added Hansel.

Emily smiled back, but her eyes were sad.

'No,' said Gretel. 'It would be better for you to go back up the stairs and play in the sea.'

'Yes,' said Hansel. 'Go and paddle in the waves. It will be fun, we promise.'

But Emily stayed put, and for the first time the twins appeared bemused, uncertain.

'How about you hold your breath for five minutes?' Hansel tried again. 'Try and beat the world record.'

Emily just smiled back at him. Then she said five words and the twins were suddenly shivering with confusion.

'*I know who you are*,' Emily said.

And in that instant she showed Hansel and Gretel exactly who they were, planted the images of a lost life back into their minds so that they found it again, and the twins held onto each other sharing not only the pain of the memories but the joy of it too. They collapsed in each other's arms, weeping, consoling each other, suddenly disillusioned and oblivious to what was going on about them, brother and sister now reunited.

A misplaced childhood, found.

In the chamber ahead, Frobisher gestured to the three empty cylinders.

'These are yours,' he said to Elmo and Miller. 'Let's not say I'm nothing if not generous.'

'And the point of this is what exactly?' Elmo said.

'They intend to use us to kick-start this monstrosity,' Miller said.

'Very good,' said Frobisher. 'I admire those who catch on quick. Saves having to explain it.'

'Explaining it is good,' Elmo said quickly. 'I'm happy to hear the long version.'

'You will be sacrificed, and the electrical activity in your brains will be used to harness the power to unlock the army of the New Reich,' Frobisher said.

'Maybe not in so much detail?' Elmo said.

'Nothing can be left to chance,' Frobisher said. 'The sacrifice will satisfy the entity enmeshed in this town, and under its influence the army of the New Reich shall be invincible!'

'You've three chambers,' Miller noted. 'You're a sacrifice short, Frobisher. So much for planning.'

'Yeah,' said Elmo, 'It's the same when you need to change batteries in your TV remote. Don't ya just hate it when that happens?'

But Frobisher laughed. 'You think that there isn't

one cadet here who wouldn't willingly give their life for the greater cause? But as it happens, it shall not come to that since we have someone to step up to the mark.'

He nodded to his henchmen and three stepped forwards and clubbed an unsuspecting Xavier Pontefract to the ground before he realized what was happening.

'No hard feelings, Xavier,' Frobisher said. 'But you were quite the maverick insisting on dealing with that Beecham girl. Besides, business is business.'

'That was quite devious,' Pontefract said spitting blood onto the floor. 'You've gone up in my estimation, though I'm not as confident of your chances of getting me into that contraption alive.'

'And I wouldn't expect anything less, dear man,' Frobisher said, promptly spraying Elmo, Miller, and the defiant Xavier Pontefract with a small canister he had secreted from the pocket of his bright blue jacket, the fine mist hanging about them made their faces slack and all three slumped to the floor.

Frobisher watched the mist dissipate before breathing in again. Standing over the incapacitated shapes, Frobisher nodded with contentment.

'As I said, *nothing* has been left to chance.'

The white corridor underneath the stage was deserted.

Dennis and Albert went first. Maud and Patience followed on behind.

'Busy little blighters, I'm thinkin',' Maud said.

'I'm thinking why is this place so deserted when it's so important to them?' said Albert cautiously.

'Smacks of arrogance, t' me,' Dennis said. 'They think they've already won.'

As they neared the last door, the entrance to the room housing the equipment designed for the sole purpose of subduing and influencing the youth of Dorsal Finn, the group stopped. Dennis peered into the room to see if the coast was clear. A huge hand shot through the gap and grabbed him by the throat before dragging him into the door frame as though he were a rag doll. His head connected with solid wood and Dennis crumpled to the floor.

The ungainly bulk of a *Blue Thunder* henchman came out into the corridor, his shaven head gleaming under the fluorescent lights.

He regarded the others with eyes glistening with amusement. 'Now then,' he hissed. 'Who's next?'

CHAPTER NINETEEN
BATTLE BENEATH THE EARTH

THE DOORS TO the school hall clicked open, those guarding the interior moving to one side to allow their comrades access.

The captives inside the hall groaned with fear and dismay as they watched twenty children file into the hall and line up facing them.

Agnes couldn't believe when she saw Thomas Beecham among them, and even Edna Duffy was officially lost for words as twenty MP40s trained on the crowd in the middle of the hall.

Marcus Macbeth walked into the hall and addressed those cowering before the guns.

'You are the first to bear witness to the New Reich! Weep if you must, kneel to your God, but today is for the *young*. Today is for the *Reich*!'

Marcus turned to his comrades and lifted his arm. 'On my command, open fire!'

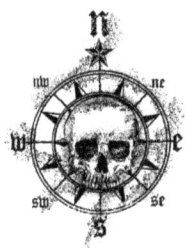

'Oh, this is starting to annoy me,' Patience said sternly to the big man barring their way. 'Haven't you people got anything better to do than take over the world and make a general nuisance of yourselves?'

The henchman appeared confused. 'Do you realize how screwed you are, girl?' he barked.

'And do you realise how many outfits I've ruined this week? And shoes? Well I've had enough! So I suggest that you move out of the way because this *girl* is coming through.'

The henchman's face did a jig, the corners of his mouth flickering as he tried to keep his lips from curling into a smile, then he began to chuckle, building into a guffaw that shook his shoulders and had him leaning against the wall in total hysterics.

'I'm not sure you're taking me seriously,' Patience pouted, and this made the man laugh even louder.

'Stop it! Stop it!' he gasped, 'You're killing me.'

And that was when Patience moved. She ran at the man, head down, and made contact with his stomach at full pelt, knocking the wind out of his lungs. More importantly, she knocked him backwards where his legs became tangled with the slumped body of Dennis Hodges. The man fell backwards; his head striking the back wall with such force it left a crescent shaped dent in its surface, exposing the plasterboard beneath.

Patience watched the henchman slide down the wall, face slack and eyes closed. When she turned, she found Maud and Albert staring at her, totally dumbfounded.

'Well, enough's enough, isn't it?' Patience said in a huff.

'I ain't about to argue with that,' Maud said with a grin.

'Oh, me bloody head,' Dennis said sitting up. 'An' I only just got shut of me hangover, an' all.'

Albert helped him to his feet as Maud and Patience entered the room, astonished by the equipment they found there.

'Look at the consoles,' Patience whispered.

The banks of TV screens stated three words, written in black on a stark white background. And the words blinked rhythmically, chilling all who looked upon them.

The words read: 'Kill them all.'

Across town Marcus held his hand in the air. He relished the bliss in the faces of his brothers in arms, almost as much as the fear seeping from the crowds in the school hall.

This was power. This was the sensation he craved above all else. The destruction of Beatrice Beecham was but a taster. This was the main course. This was the banquet.

And he savoured each second that passed. Slowly, deliberately, he lowered his arm.

'Fire!'

'Where do we start?' Patience asked.

Anywhere,' Albert said upending terminals and keyboards which exploded in loud pops and showers of sparks as they hit the floor.

Dennis Hodges joined in, despite a lump the size of a goose egg now standing proud on his forehead.

Maud, on the other hand, went over to a bank of electrical sockets and flipped them off. The remaining screens all died and the incessant hum faded from the room.

'There,' she said. 'That'll save on the tidyin' up later.'

'Aye,' agreed Dennis going over the sockets and ripping the plugs from the cables. 'Just to be sure,' he said.

'Okay,' said Patience, 'Now what?'

'We should be able to get word out,' Albert said. 'Get hold of the coast guard and tell them to head out to Bishop's Cragg. And fast!'

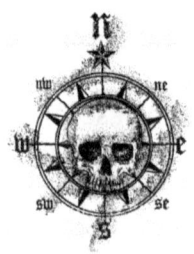

'I said *fire!*' Marcus shouted. But in the school hall the guns remained silent. Instead, many of the children were dropping their weapons as though they were contaminated.

'What's the matter with you? Pick up your weapons! Fight for the Reich, you idiots!'

At this most of the younger children began to cry out for their parents.

All but one.

As Marcus began to reach for a discarded MP40, the muzzle of another was placed against his chest.

'Thomas?' he said shocked. 'What are you doing?'

'*Blue Thunder Foundation* is a lie. You're a lie. You left my sister to die in *Cooper's Cove*.' There were tears in Thomas' eyes, but his expression was that of confusion and hatred. 'You are a *bad* person.'

'Thomas,' another voice, soft yet urgent. It was Agnes. 'Let me have the gun, son.'

Gideon Codd was with her, he held an MP40 like a man who was more than comfortable with it. He held it on the youth who had threatened him earlier, a *Blue Thunder* regular who wasn't influenced by transmissions in the ether, but because he was fundamentally evil.

'He left Bea chained up in *Cooper's Cove*,' Thomas protested. 'She might've drowned for all I know.'

Agnes could see that Thomas' finger was dangerously close to the trigger and his hands shook with a quiet rage.

'This isn't over yet,' Agnes said gently. 'And we won't know who is safe and who isn't until it's finished. This isn't our way, Thomas. It is theirs, and we're better than that, aren't we?'

Thomas thought for a moment and nodded.

'You people are so weak,' Marcus spat as Thomas lowered his weapon.

Thomas struck him in the stomach with the butt of the MP40 so that the youth doubled over, and then Thomas knocked him out with another blow to the back of his head.

'And you're *so* going to have a headache tomorrow,' he said.

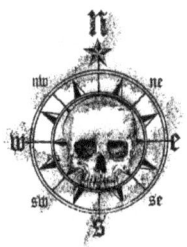

Beatrice and Emily raced through the tunnel, spurred on by the din coming from a chamber in the distance. It was the sound of chanting, and the cries of people in agony.

Lucas stopped briefly to examine one of the many crates, whistling as he lifted one of the MP40s from the open box. He pulled free a magazine and slammed it into the chamber, released the firing pin.

'Who said playing *Call of Duty* is for geeks?' he

said, limping after the girls, who were by this time over a hundred metres ahead.

Beatrice entered the chamber, and had trouble comprehending the confusing events inside. She could see three cylinders nearby containing people she recognised. Elmo's expression was one of agony as he writhed behind the glass, hands restrained by leather straps and his head bristling with electrodes. Miller was next to him, his mouth wide in one long scream.

Then there was Xavier Pontefract, eyes wide, a quivering grimace pulled taut across his face. Beatrice recoiled from the shock of it all. But as she moved forwards, the shaman spotted her.

'No!' he cried. 'The *incorruptible heart* is amongst us! She must be cast out!'

Frobisher yelled for the several henchmen to open fire, and they did without hesitation. Multiple muzzle flashes and staccato bursts of machine gun fire resulted in the entrance to the chamber becoming a mass of tiny explosions as bullets riddled the walls and hanger doors. Beatrice dived to her left; bullets singing in the air all around her. Emily went right, behind the chamber holding Elmo, and several bullets struck the metallic surface in an array of bright sparks.

'Hold them back whilst the shaman finishes the ritual,' Frobisher ordered.

The MP40s continued their barrage, the shaman continuing his chant though most was lost in the cacophony bouncing around the chamber.

Beside her cylinder, Emily crouched, watching bullets ricochet off the casing. Her hands reached for a panel bolted to the container and emblazoned with an array of buttons and switches, her delicate fingers pressing these at random. Though she didn't hear it, there was a sudden hiss and the lid sprang open, its ascent bringing it into contact with a wall of bullets that peppered its surface and shattered the glass.

The shaman raised his hands high, screaming, 'It comes! My master gives power to the cause!'

The whole chamber was suddenly illuminated with a fierce green light that swamped the cylinders, leaving a viscous green fluid that trickled over their surfaces as though the very metal was sweating.

'Live, soldiers of the Reich,' Frobisher yelled with delight. 'Fulfil the will of the Furher!'

Then, one by one, the lids throughout the chamber creaked open and, to her horror, Beatrice watched as slowly, stiffly, the Nazi army began to rise.

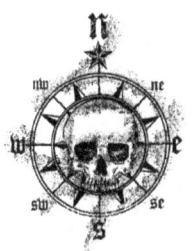

On the storm ravaged ocean, the boats came. There were ten of them, each containing men with knowledge that they were to avert a terrible rebirth, by any means possible. They sat in their respective holds not quite believing what they had been told, but clear of their mission.

War had come to a sleepy coastal town. And, in keeping with their instructions, this was a war that was to be waged quietly.

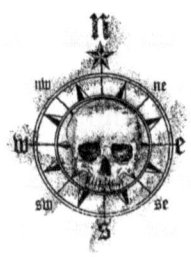

From his place by the hanger doors, Lucas could see the lumbering shapes climbing from their metallic caskets. But this paled compared to the sight of his best friend in pain. He could see Elmo, electrodes clamped to his forehead, the discomfort creasing his brow in countless lines.

The blasts of machine gun fire held him at bay for a while, but when he saw Emily open Elmo's casket, and his friend struggling to be free of it—despite the bullets ripping the air about him—Lucas knew he had to act.

He aimed at a group of henchmen standing dead ahead, getting ready to open fire on the emerging Elmo, who was already ripping the electrodes from his scalp, and pulled the trigger on the machine gun. The weapon jerked left, cutting a bright arc in the air in front of him.

Surprised, the henchmen dove for cover, though one of them fell to the ground clutching an arm that was bloody and twisted out of shape.

Another barrage of bullets came from the chamber, and Lucas hunkered down, his heart pounding in fear.

Beatrice scrambled across the floor, keeping low, her intention to rescue Miller, who continued to endure great agony inside his prison of glass and steel. Bullets kept her at bay for a while, but despite her terror, she pressed forwards, reaching out to the control panel.

A hand clamped about her wrist like a vice. She gasped, and tried to wrench it back, but the grip was strong, unnatural. The shaman's face came from the shadows, his eyes no longer marred by fear—they had distance to them, and glowed like green fire.

'It is good to see you again, Bringer of Joy,' the shaman hissed, though Beatrice somehow knew the words came from the thing that haunted Dorsal Finn. 'The world is about to change. And you cannot stop it. Darkness will sweep across this Earth, and your light will diminish. All hope will die.'

'Who are you?' she said, wincing as the hand around her wrist seemed to burn her skin.

'I am the darkness. I am the light. I am everything,' the shaman's dark passenger said. 'But that is no longer your concern. You are too late."

'For what?'

'To stop us.'

'That's not what the light said,' Beatrice said.

The shaman appeared uncertain. 'There is no light here. Only darkness.'

'There is light, it spoke to me. It saved me, so that I can destroy you.'

'That is not possible,' the shaman screamed, releasing her wrist. 'It has no place here!'

Beatrice used his confusion to kick out, her foot connecting with the shaman's chin, jarring his head backwards. One of his teeth arched through the air and bounced into the corridor.

She rolled away from him, almost into another volley of bullets, but just when she thought the explosive gunfire would catch up with her, the shooting stopped.

What replaced it were the slow, shuffling steps of many, many boots.

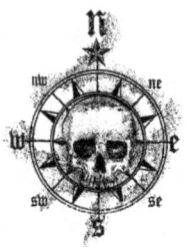

Colin Creswell did as he was told. He moved away from *Bishop's Cragg*, back into the storm, leaving behind a flotilla of assault boats that discharged its cargo efficiently and effortlessly. The mini army loaded its weapons and entered the underworld, their mission: to stop hell coming to Earth.

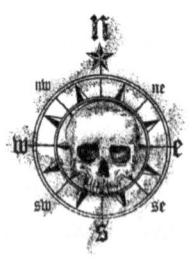

The Nazi soldiers were tall, clad in uniforms that were once black, but time had rendered them gun metal grey. Their gait was more reminiscent of machines rather than men, and their eyes were no longer silver, they were red, like dying embers in a grate.

Frobisher stood before them, and held up his hand.

'You are the army of the New Reich. The world will tremble under your boots! Heil Hitler!'

The soldiers saluted and five hundred voices shouted 'Heil Hitler' in unison. Their voices were thick and several disgorged thick, green fluid as they gave their salutation.

Beatrice and Emily used the distraction to release Elmo and Miller, both of which were exhausted from their ordeal and needed support to clear the caskets. Lucas came to them and hugged Elmo, Beatrice watching them both, realising how much these boys meant to her. She wiped away a tear, forcing herself to focus on the job at hand. It wasn't too difficult, given that the chamber was filling with Nazis.

'We have to get out of here while we can,' Lucas said. 'You guys okay to move?'

'I'm feeling better now the bone crunching agony has kinda moved on,' Elmo said. 'You know you've got a black eye?'

Lucas gripped his friend's shoulder and smiled sadly. 'As days go, this one might have me writing a new song.'

'Promise me that won't happen,' Elmo said.

'Come on, guys,' Beatrice urged.

'What about him?' Lucas said indicating Xavier Pontefract, who remained in his casket, face undulating in silent agony.

'What *about* him?' Beatrice said coolly, her eyes unblinking.

No one had an answer for her.

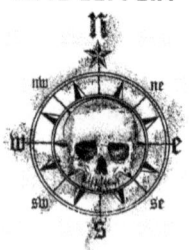

They made their way back into the tunnel, limping, bruised and battered, the intention to place as much distance between themselves and Frobisher's sinister army before their absence was noticed.

But Beatrice hadn't gone more than several meters into the passageway before she heard the shaman's high pitched cry alerting Frobisher that all was not well.

They moved as fast as they could along the tunnel, the sounds of dragging boots behind them, and the harsh tone of Frobisher barking orders. A third of the way to their exit Beatrice spotted a welcome, if not incredible sight. Marines, too many to count, were coming to meet them; torches strapped to the barrels of rifles and machine guns ricocheting light off of the tunnel walls.

But before Beatrice and the others could call to them, the tunnel was suddenly alive with gunfire. Beneath the Earth, the war had begun.

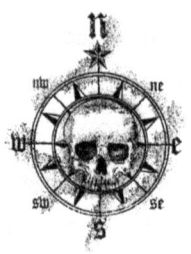

Miller bundled them all behind a stack of crates. His strength was slowly returning, as were his wits.

Bullets zipped through the air from both sides of the tunnel, tearing chucks of concrete from the walls and floors, smashing into the camouflaged crates.

Several hundred metres away one of the arms caches exploded, sending fiery debris through the confined space, the roar bringing with it cries of pain from stricken marines caught in the blast. The level of gunfire appeared to increase, and Miller quickly kicked open a crate and helped himself to an MP40, loaded it and pointed it towards the chamber.

They came as one, a wall of uniforms, soldiers from another era, MP40s blazing, a myriad of fiery lights, spitting bullets towards the enemy. In response, the marines sent a seemingly relentless volley of fire back down the tunnel, the tracer rounds streaking like a thousand horizontal fireworks. The noise was deafening.

Miller joined the firefight. He aimed and fired, the target so big it was impossible to miss, yet his bullets were ineffectual, they struck the oncoming figures, chewing through clothing, and beyond, but each impact brought with it tendrils of green light that immediately sealed the wounds.

'Bullets have no affect!' Miller said in dismay.

'They really are zombies,' said Elmo, incredulously.

'No they aren't,' Beatrice said through gritted teeth. 'The shaman did this, his ritual has awoken something powerful.'

'How do we stop them?' Lucas said as he unleashed another salvo of machine gun fire towards the relentless army. 'Our soldiers don't stand a chance.'

And this question took Beatrice away for a while.

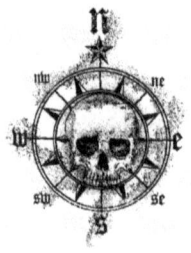

Jamie Oliver leaned against his favourite stainless steel work surface, a fresh mug of tea in his cupped hands.

'Things are pretty hopeless,' Beatrice said. 'I can't see any way out of this one.'

'Not every chef knows everythin',' Jamie said. 'Not even at the beginnin'.'

'How could they?' Beatrice nodded.

'Even with hundreds of hours of kitchen time under y' belt, sometimes it's better to go back to basics, just to remind yourself of the important things. The things that matter.'

Jamie's face shimmered, and beneath the skin Beatrice felt as though she could see a golden orb of flame pulsating rhythmically.

'I've done that with some recipes,' Beatrice admitted.

'We can take herbs and spices for granted; we forget the humble spud or the innocuous impact of salt and pepper. They're always there, but we use 'em so often it's like they cease to exist in our memory. We forget their importance until it really matters.'

'Oh,' Beatrice whispered as realization dawned on her.

The image of Jamie wavered and the orb emerged,

gilding her skin in its potent and brilliant light. When its radiance touched her, she knew in an instant that her world would never be the same again if she failed to do something that was integral to any decent human being.

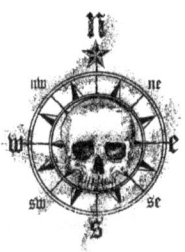

'I have to go back,' Beatrice said.

'Are you *insane?*' Lucas said. 'That's suicide.'

'It's Pontefract,' Beatrice said. 'He's the link between the shaman's ritual and the magic that's making the Nazi army invincible. I have to disconnect him.'

But it's more than that, isn't it? Beatrice thought. *It's about going back to basics, it was about considering the things that really matter, the things that we take for granted as we go through life.*

Like *life*, for example.

Life and humanity; forgiveness and tolerance. The important things—integral things— the very things making mankind different from animals.

Different from the Nazis.

'Ye have to get past a reanimated Nazi army!' Miller said. 'Ye'll never make it.'

'Then help me,' Beatrice pleaded. 'This isn't going to stop unless I free Pontefract. And I need to do it *now.*'

'That's not a good idea no matter how ye sell it?' Miller said firmly.

Suddenly, Beatrice noticed someone was missing.

'Where's Emily?' she cried, scanning around her frantically.

No one had anything for her. In fact, most people couldn't remember seeing her for some time.

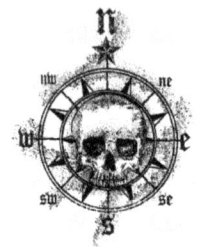

Emily was in silent agony. But the pain was not hers. It belonged to Xavier Pontefract. It had struck her down as she'd tried to leave the hanger. An overwhelming sense of loss, of wrongness, washed over her, and she felt the need to remain. Until now, she didn't know why.

But something had happened. In the past few moments certainty had arrived, bright and conclusive, she had to set Xavier Pontefract free of his torment. She didn't question it for she somehow knew this revelation didn't belong to her any more than Pontefract's agony, it was a borrowed thing borne from her growing relationship with those around her.

Emily went to Pontefract's casket, and began pressing buttons. The glass lid popped open bringing with it the reek of sweat and a faint smell of burning. She reached in, clawing at the electrodes as she did so, and then went to work on the straps holding Pontefract in place.

It was then that someone grabbed her by the shoulders and hauled her backwards. She landed heavily on her back, the air knocked from her lungs. She tried to sit up but a heavy foot came down, planting itself on her chest, pinning her small frame to the floor. She looked up into the grey-green face of a Nazi soldier; its eyes reverted back to glass grey. It was yelling something, but Emily couldn't hear it, just felt the vibration of gunshots and explosions coming to her through the chamber floor.

The foot began to squeeze against her, and she tried to scream, but all the air in her lungs was spent.

Slowly the world began turning grey.

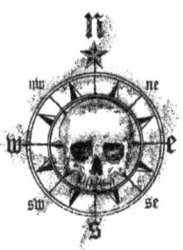

Beatrice bolted towards the chamber, driven by the need to help her friend.

She found passage by weaving in and out of the stacked boxes, a precarious journey, but better than being caught out in the open. Beatrice kept hunched down, dodging in between crates, rolling to avoid stray bullets, clasping her ears when one of the many explosions erupted in the tunnel.

By the time she got to the chamber, the vast space had been purged of Nazis. She peered around the edge of one of the hanger doors and her breath hitched in her throat. Emily was clawing frantically at the trousers of a Nazi soldier who was slowly crushing her with his boot.

Beatrice looked about her for any kind of weapon, spotting a heavy wrench lying atop one of the arms crates. She hefted it and charged; her cry louder than she intended, exaggerated by the high ceiling. The trooper looked up and Beatrice swung the wrench, though she assumed it would be token, ineffective given the supernatural immunity it had been given. The wrench connected with the Nazi's chest with a sickening crunch of shattering bones, the impact jarring Beatrice's arms.

To her amazement, the Nazi cried out in pain, clutching his breast and falling over where he rolled around pitifully.

Beatrice went to her friend who lay unmoving, but she was impeded by a blow to her temple. It sent her reeling, and she almost fell upon Emily.

Dazed she peered at her assailant, and found herself confronted by the shaman who hurled abuse at her through clenched, broken teeth.

'What have you done? You interfering heathens,' he yelled, but he was staring at the felled Nazi. 'You have severed the sacrifice. You have undone a promise made to a great power.'

'Not our promise,' Beatrice said groggily. 'Yours. And since you broke it, I guess you'll be paying the bill.'

The shaman came at her again, this time he intended to use words as a weapon, some kind of incantation that played upon his lips.

And as he spoke the world about them changed,

the very air rippled as though made of water and far from welcoming it, the shaman was screaming with fear.

A shape moved within the writhing folds of the world now bubbling up to the surface, and with the words came a voice Beatrice had heard before, the voice of the thing that professed to be Dorsal Finn itself.

'You have failed me, minion,' it said. 'I revoke my power in return. And those who have betrayed my trust shall now be forfeit.'

The very air appeared to fold in on itself, great waves that clutched the shaman who carried on screaming until his mouth was full of the substance bubbling around him. His eyes rolled into the back of his head and his neck snapped with an audible crack that rose above even the gun battle from the tunnel.

Shocked, Beatrice watched the life disappear from his eyes, and his screaming finally stopped.

The shaman sank into the air, swallowed by it until there was nothing left to mark its passing save for a small shiver in a space a few metres off of the ground.

Whilst the shaman had gone, the voice had not.

'*Bringer of Joy* they call you,' it sneered. 'And the incorruptible heart decrees the rescue of her nemesis. How noble you are Bringer. As noble as your sister is brave. Your kind reeks of humanity. It has no place here. But you are two when there must be three. Only then can you influence that which you cannot see, and only then can the light touch those in darkness. And in the darkness, Bringer, *I will be waiting for you all.*'

There was a huge clap of thunder, the blast of it knocking Beatrice backwards, and onto Emily. And when she opened her eyes she saw the deaf girl staring at her, a playful smile on her lips.

'We have to stop saving each other,' Emily said. 'Lucas will get jealous.'

Before Beatrice could respond Logan Frobisher was running into the chamber, and letting loose an MP40 on those who were chasing after him.

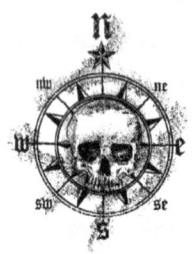

Frobisher had realised quickly things had gone awry. He noticed as soon as his reanimated army began to clutch at their wounds when bullets struck them, toppling like nine pins under the onslaught brought by the marines.

Screaming in anger and frustration, self-preservation kicked in, and the *Blue Thunder* leader ran back into the hanger, turning occasionally to deliver short bursts from his machine gun, but most of the shots were erratic and ineffectual.

This was good news to Miller, Elmo, and Lucas who made their way through the crates, using the chaos of battle as cover for their advance.

'Can you see Bea?' Lucas said urgently as they neared the hanger doors.

'No,' Miller said. 'She has to be in there with Frobisher.'

Lucas clutched his MP40, and dove headlong into

the chamber. Frobisher was blasting away as Lucas rolled behind a casket, the bullets denting the metal.

Miller used the opportunity to open up, trying to catch Frobisher off guard, and sent him for cover behind his own casket.

Elmo stayed by the doorway, he'd purloined a fallen weapon, and was keeping watch on the tunnel behind them. He could still hear gunfire but whilst loud it was sporadic. The battle was almost over, and he could no longer make out the rhythmic stomping of boots, but instead the patter of running feet as their rescuers headed towards them.

'Give it up Frobisher,' Miller yelled. 'It's over!'

'Not while I have breath in my body,' Frobisher screamed back from his hiding place. 'All this work, all this planning, you think I'm going to give it up? This is a place of order! There's no room for weakness.'

And with that Frobisher pulled a grenade from his belt and unscrewed the pin.

'For the Furhrer! For the Reich!'

With that, Logan Frobisher detonated the grenade and the explosion rocked the chamber to its very foundations.

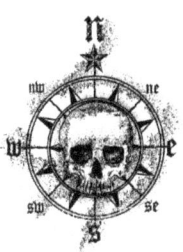

The structure was ancient. The explosive booby traps strapped to the ceiling equally so.

When the grenade exploded, igniting the unknown chemicals in the barrels nearby, the conflagration lifted high into the air, igniting the explosives hanging in their netted baskets. The ceiling was tolerant of the pressure of the ocean, but it was a token tolerance, begrudging. The detonation was too much for its fragile resilience.

Rocks crumbled, creating undulating fissures that gave way under the pressure of the ocean high above. The walls simply crumpled, allowing thousands of gallons of sea water to force its way into the chamber.

Beatrice observed the water pouring through the rocks like countless waterfalls.

'Not more bloody water,' she muttered.

'Up!' Miller said dragging Emily to her feet. 'We have to move. Now!'

'Wait!' said Beatrice as the first wave of water washed against her ankles. She ran to the casket containing Xavier Pontefract who was struggling against his bonds. Her hands clasped the restraints, popping the buckles easily.

When he saw her, his eyes blazed with a mixture of amazement and confusion.

'Either I'm in Hell or we have both embarked on a most fortuitous day, Miss Beecham.'

'Just get out of the casket,' Beatrice said coldly as bigger waves coursed though the chamber. 'From here you're on your own.'

Pontefract nodded his understanding and climbed from his metal prison.

Beatrice went back to her friends and they fought their way through the water, now knee-high, and out of the chamber. They met marines in the tunnel who grabbed at them, scooping them up into their arms, and ran with them through the raging tide. Beatrice felt herself being passed from one man to another until she recognised the stairway, and a big marine with a beard planted her on the steps, and shouted for her to climb, fast.

Beatrice ran up several steps before looking back. The others were behind her, Lucas with his black eye, Elmo supporting Emily who clutched at her chest, and Miller who looked pale and grey even in the half light.

They were all there, battered and bruised but able to make their way to the surface before the ocean could claim them.

Outside now, the storm was moving on. The ocean was still rough yet it had lost its ferocity. Beatrice could see rows of assault craft beached on the rocks. As the rain lashed her face and the remaining marines poured from below ground, *Bishop's Cragg* began to tremble.

'Get to the boats!' one of the marines yelled, and Beatrice and her friends were dragged bodily to the landing craft. With engines screaming, the boats reversed and arced into open water, leaving the islet tremulous in the ocean.

'Would you look at that?' the marine with the beard standing next to Beatrice said in disbelief.

They all watched as *Bishop's Cragg* was illuminated by a brilliant green flame that wrapped itself about the rocky landscape before the whole islet sank below the surface.

Beatrice looked at the others, mouth agog, yet it was only Emily who nodded an acknowledgement when the flames had consumed *Bishop's Cragg*. It really had appeared as though a huge fiery hand had clutched the land and dragged it beneath the ocean.

EPILOGUE
THE VAGUE HORIZON

BEATRICE STARED AT the ocean, the gulls and a few mottled clouds the only things marring an otherwise azure sky.

It was three weeks later and, on the surface, life in Dorsal Finn had returned to some semblance of normalcy. This was not much of a surprise given the town was never that far away from the unusual in the first place.

Investigations followed, and allegations were made. Fingers pointed, but those in Dorsal Finn shrugged them off. *The Blue Thunder Foundation* collapsed and Mayor Codd was absolved given the national scale of duplicity that the organisation had managed to orchestrate.

Xavier Pontefract had disappeared on the night that the Nazi army had been brought back to life and reacquainted with death. It was an issue for Beatrice knowing her arch nemesis remained at large, yet she knew that he would neither be caught or resurface for some time. But she had more pressing matters to occupy her time.

Once the *Blue Thunder Foundation* had relinquished it subliminal grip on the town, Beatrice's parents had been released from jail with a staunch apology, and Thomas had spent a great deal of time using pocket money to buy small treats for his family, platitudes for his behaviour whilst a *Blue Thunder* cadet. No one blamed him, of course, but they all accepted his gifts, especially Beatrice who learned of her brother's response to Marcus in the school hall. It upset Beatrice to see her brother so repentant on the behalf of those who really should have been more accountable. She'd quickly learned that cowardliness and ignorance were the bedrock of fascism.

As for Marcus Macbeth (Beatrice still didn't know if this was his real name) he was arrested and taken into custody. Beatrice had witnessed the police bringing him into the station when she went with Maud and Albert to collect her parents.

Macbeth had offered little by way of apology, and in truth Beatrice didn't want such a thing from him. Having justice served was enough for her. Besides, Macbeth may have just done her a huge favour by bringing her closer to Lucas.

Edward Chorley was as slippery as ever, blaming his actions on the subliminal messages in *Blue Thunder* products. He offered written apologies to both Beatrice and Lucas, though made sure he was unavailable for a face to face meeting, presumably because the driftwood Beatrice had hit him with had left a knotted indent in his forehead destined to stay for the rest of his days.

Maud and Agnes still held their annual remembrance ceremony for Klaus Hessel, but the flavour of it was somewhat tainted by his scientific contributions to the whole affair. It didn't stop their feelings for him and the good things he'd attempted to do, as misguided as it appeared to those who knew of it.

Having heard of her involvement in Dorsal Finn's insurrection against the *Blue Thunder Foundation*, Emily's parents had also changed their views on what was best for their daughter. Emily's bravery had, after all, resulted in saving Beatrice's life, as well as many others in the town. Mr and Mrs Hannigan could not help but agree that far from being a victim, their daughter was in fact a hero. A hero made stronger by her newfound friends. As such, Emily was now a fully fledged member of The Newshounds, and all her friends were learning sign language to show just how much they valued her.

The Newshounds were unaware who in the village had collaborated to hide the transmitters in the Cryptic Crypt. Whether this help was natural or supernatural was beyond anyone's knowledge, but it became clear to all that the crypt itself was not designed as part of Frobisher's plot and, perhaps, still had a part to play in a very uncertain future. The Newshounds were also unable to decipher the strange, unfathomable writing that Patience and Elmo had found in the crypt; much to the continued annoyance of Patience. However, Beatrice sensed such things had a habit of surfacing in the future. That was how Dorsal Finn preferred to exist, a town of surprises.

Yes, life was getting back to normal, but for The Newshounds, and for Beatrice, things had most certainly changed. While there was much that could be explained by scientific means, there was plenty that couldn't, and Beatrice didn't try. She accepted there was something supernatural and maligned in the town, and it had designs on all their futures.

Such notions should have raised anxieties, and of course they did on occasion, but Beatrice knew enough things from which to take comfort.

First of all there was "the light". Hard to deny since it had physical presence, as seen in the cave where its luminescence had visited Beatrice at her most desperate hour. It was also sentient; it had spoken to her, advised her on ways to act. It did, after all, suggest that an act of clemency—in this case rescuing Xavier Pontefract from certain death—would be needed to undo the terrible magic seen beneath *Bishop's Cragg*.

Then there was what Beatrice now referred to as *The Darkness*. As with The Light it had both physical and intellectual presence. And great power, the way it had claimed the shaman was evidence enough. But Beatrice felt that The Darkness was somehow unable to use such power against her at this point in time. It had appeared not only frustrated but thwarted by her actions in the chamber. Emily had also been named by it.

It was an intriguing statement that The Darkness had referred to Beatrice and Emily as "sisters". She had no idea what it meant, nor the suggestion that there was another who was to join them.

Above all these mysteries, all these uncertainties, it was clear to Beatrice that The Darkness feared both her and Emily. And this satisfied her to some degree.

'You going to eat that?'

'Eh?' Beatrice said, falling away from her thoughts.

'That ciabatta,' Lucas said beside her, 'you going to eat that or wait 'til the gulls start getting brave?'

'Be my guest,' she said handing the sandwich to him. 'Who am I to deny the invalid?'

'You're a funny girl, Bea Beecham,' he winked before taking a large bite.

On *Seer's Rock* the waves crashed against the huge, eroded rocks, and spray created a fine mist in the air. It was Beatrice's favourite place on Earth. It was her favourite place because it was where Lucas loved to be. And Beatrice loved to be with him.

'Things are different now,' he said, putting down the sandwich and taking her hand in his.

'For the better?' she said resting her head on his shoulder. He turned to kiss her crown, relishing the smell of her hair, the warmth of it against his cheek.

'Most definitely,' he replied. 'I wish we could stay here forever.'

'What happens when the tide comes in?'

'There is that,' he conceded. 'But here it's easy to think that it's all over, isn't it?'

'It is *for now*,' Beatrice said. 'And that's all that matters.'

'But what happens next?' Lucas said. 'And are we ready for it?'

Beatrice stared out to sea, and the waves filled in the seconds as they passed by. When it was clear that no answer was forthcoming, Lucas joined her, searching for his answer on the simmering horizon, but neither of them expecting to find it there.

THE END?

Not quite . . .

Dive into more Tales from the Darkest Depths:

The Final Reconciliation by Todd Keisling—Thirty years ago, a progressive rock band called The Yellow Kings began recording what would become their first and final album. Titled "The Final Reconciliation," the album was expected to usher in a new renaissance of heavy metal, but it was shelved following a tragic concert that left all but one dead. It's the survivor shares the shocking truth.

Where the Dead Go to Die by Mark Allan Gunnells and Aaron Dries—Post-infection Chicago. Christmas. There are monsters in this world. And they used to be us. Now it's time to euthanize to survive in a hospice where Emily, a woman haunted by her past, only wants to do her job and be the best mother possible. But it won't be long before that snow-speckled ground will be salted by blood.

Tales from The Lake Vol.3—Dive into the deep end of the lake with 19 tales of terror, selected by Monique Snyman. Including short stories by Mark Allan Gunnells, Kate Jonez, Kenneth W. Cain, and many more.

Sarah Killian: Serial Killer (For Hire!) by Mark Sheldon—Follow foul-mouthed and mean-spirited Sarah Killian on an assignment from T.H.E.M. (Trusted Hierarchy of Everyday Murderers), a secret organization using serial killers to do the dirty work for their clients. Sarah's twisted sense of humor alone makes this Crime Fiction/Horror/Thriller a worthy read.

Gutted: Beautiful Horror Stories—an anthology of dark fiction that explores the beauty at the very heart of darkness. Featuring horror's most celebrated voices: Clive Barker, Neil Gaiman, Ramsey Campbell, Paul Tremblay, John F.D. Taff, Lisa Mannetti, Damien Angelica Walters, Josh Malerman, Christopher Coake, Mercedes M. Yardley, Brian Kirk, Stephanie M. Wytovich, Amanda Gowin, Richard Thomas, Maria Alexander, and Kevin Lucia.

Run to Ground by Jasper Bark—Jim Mcleod is running from his responsibilities as a father, hiding out from his pregnant girlfriend and working as a groundskeeper in a rural graveyard. Throw in some ancient monsters and folklore, and you'll have Jim running for live through this folk horror graveyard.

The Final Cut by Jasper Bark—Follow the misfortunes of two indie filmmakers in their quest to fund their breakthrough movie by borrowing money from one dangerous underground figure in order to buy a large quantity of cocaine from a different but equally dangerous underground figure. They will learn that while some stories capture the imagination, others will be the death of you.

Blackwater Val by William Gorman—a Supernatural Suspense Thriller/Horror/Coming of age novel: A widower, traveling with his dead wife's ashes and his six-year-old psychic daughter Katie in tow, returns to his haunted birthplace to execute his dead wife's final wish. But something isn't quite right in the Val.

Tribulations by Richard Thomas—In the third short story collection by Richard Thomas, *Tribulations*, these stories cover a wide range of dark fiction—from fantasy, science fiction and horror, to magical realism, neo-noir, and transgressive fiction. The common thread that weaves these tragic tales together is suffering and sorrow, and the ways we emerge from such heartbreak stronger, more appreciative of what we have left—a spark of hope enough to guide us though the valley of death.

Devourer of Souls by Kevin Lucia—In Kevin Lucia's latest installment of his growing Clifton Heights mythos, Sheriff Chris Baker and Father Ward meet for a Saturday morning breakfast at The Skylark Dinner to once again commiserate over the weird and terrifying secrets surrounding their town.

Apocalyptic Montessa and Nuclear Lulu: A Tale of Atomic Love by Mercedes M. Yardley—Montessa Tovar is walking home alone when she is abducted by Lu, a serial killer with unusual talents and a grudge against the world. But in time, the victim becomes the executioner as 'Aplocalyptic' Montessa and her doomed 'Nuclear' Lulu crisscross the country in a bloody firestorm of revenge. HER MAMA ALWAYS SAID SHE WAS SPECIAL. HIS DADDY CALLED HIM A DEMON. BUT EVEN MONSTERS CAN FALL IN LOVE.

Wind Chill by Patrick Rutigliano—What if you were held captive by your own family? Emma Rawlins has spent the last year a prisoner. The months following her mother's death dragged her father into a paranoid spiral of conspiracy theories and doomsday premonitions. But there is a force far colder than the freezing drifts. Ancient, ravenous, it knows no mercy. And it's already had a taste . . .

Flowers in a Dumpster by Mark Allan Gunnells—The world is full of beauty and mystery. In these 17 tales, Gunnells will take you on a journey through landscapes of light and darkness, rapture and agony, hope and fear. Let Gunnells guide you through these landscapes where magnificence and decay co-exist side by side. Come pick a bouquet from these Flowers in a Dumpster.

The Dark at the End of the Tunnel by Taylor Grant—Offered for the first time in a collected format, this selection features ten gripping and darkly imaginative stories by Taylor Grant, a Bram Stoker Award® nominated author and rising star in the suspense and horror genres. Grant exposes the terrors that hide beneath the surface of our ordinary world, behind people's masks of normalcy, and lurking in the shadows at the farthest reaches of the universe.

Little Dead Red by Mercedes M. Yardley—The Wolf is roaming the city, and he must be stopped. In this modern day retelling of Little Red Riding Hood, the wolf takes to the city streets to capture his prey, but the hunter is close behind him. With Grim Marie on the prowl, the hunter becomes the hunted.

The Outsiders Lovecraftian shared-world anthology—They'll do anything to protect their way of life. Anything. Welcome to Priory, a small gated community in the UK, where the only thing worse than an ancient monster is the group worshipping it. Is that which slithers below true evil, or does evil reside in the people of Priory? Includes stories by Stephen Bacon, James Everington, Rosanne Rabinowitz, V.H. Leslie, and Gary Fry.

If you ever thought of becoming an author, I'd also like to recommend these non-fiction titles:

Horror 101: The Way Forward—a comprehensive overview of the Horror fiction genre and career opportunities available to established and aspiring authors, including Jack Ketchum, Graham Masterton, Edward Lee, Lisa Morton, Ellen Datlow, Ramsey Campbell, and many more.

Horror 201: The Silver Scream Vol.1 and *Vol.2*—A must read for anyone interested in the horror film industry. Includes interviews and essays by Wes Craven, John Carpenter, George A. Romero, Mick Garris, and dozens more. Now available in a special paperback edition.

Modern Mythmakers: 35 interviews with Horror and Science Fiction Writers and Filmmakers by Michael McCarty—Ever wanted to hang out with legends like Ray Bradbury, Richard Matheson, and Dean Koontz? *Modern Mythmakers* is your chance to hear fun anecdotes and career advice from authors and filmmakers like Forrest J. Ackerman, Ray

Bradbury, Ramsey Campbell, John Carpenter, Dan Curtis, Elvira, Neil Gaiman, Mick Garris, Laurell K. Hamilton, Jack Ketchum, Dean Koontz, Graham Masterton, Richard Matheson, John Russo, William F. Nolan, John Saul, Peter Straub, and many more.

Writers On Writing: An Author's Guide—Your favorite authors share their secrets in the ultimate guide to becoming and being and author. *Writers On Writing* is an eBook series with original 'On Writing' essays by writing professionals.

Or check out other Crystal Lake Publishing books for more Tales from the Darkest Depths.

Acknowledgements

In this small space I have to thank those who made a big contribution in moving this novel through to publication. First of all my thanks goes to Joe Mynhardt at Crystal Lake Publishing for embracing the madcap concepts contained within what is, the Beatrice Beecham universe. Thanks also to Monique Snyman, editor extraordinaire, who helped me to see how to get the best out of the story I needed to tell. Both are true team players and, from this day forward, honorary Newshounds!

Thanks also goes to Dean M. Drinkel for going over earlier manuscript drafts (you are a star, sir), and Mark West for the incredible support, balanced critiques, and encouragement to continue doing what it is I do.

No acknowledgement would be complete without mentioning my wife, Justine, who has given me the gifts of time, patience and encouragement to progress my writing career—such as it is. Since Beatrice was created twelve years ago, Justine has always had faith that our second daughter would find a good home.

About the Author

Dave Jeffery is perhaps best known for his UK #1 bestselling Necropolis Rising series of zombie books released through Severed Press. His Young Adult work includes the critically acclaimed Beatrice Beecham Series (Crystal Lake Publishing), BBC: Headroom endorsed Finding Jericho, and the 2012 Edge Hill Prize Long-listed Campfire Chillers short story collection. His short story, Masquerade was nominated for The Horror Society's IGOR Award.

He has published over 14 novels and collections with a variety of publishers. His short stories and essays have featured alongside many horror impresarios including: George A. Romero (Night of the Living Dead, Dawn of the Dead), Wes Craven (A Nightmare on Elm Street, Scream), John Carpenter (Halloween, The Thing, The Fog), Tom Holland (Child's Play, Fright Night), John Russo (Night of the Living Dead, Return of the Living Dead) and Tony Burgess (Pontypool, Ejecta).

Jeffery is also screenwriter and producer at multi award-winning VLM Productions whose short films have featured at major horror festivals worldwide. He has adapted two of his most successful novels (Finding Jericho and Necropolis Rising) into feature length screenplays ready for option. Finding Jericho is currently being adapted for the stage.

He lives in rural Worcestershire with his wife and two children; where he is considered to be quite odd.

CONNECT WITH THE AUTHOR

FACE BOOK AUTHOR PAGE
(https://www.facebook.com/DaveJefferyAuthor)

WEBSITE
http://www.davejeffery.webs.com/

Hi, readers. It makes our day to know you reached the end of our book. Thank you so much. This is why we do what we do every single day.

Whether you found the book good or great, we'd love to hear what you thought. Please take a moment to leave a review on Amazon, Goodreads, or anywhere else readers visit. Reviews go a long way to helping a book sell, and will help us to continue publishing quality books.

Thank you again for taking the time to journey with Crystal Lake Publishing.

We are also on . . .

Website
http://www.crystallakepub.com/

Books
http://www.crystallakepub.com/book-table/

Blog
http://www.crystallakepub.com/blog-2/

Newsletter
http://eepurl.com/xfuKP

Instagram
https://www.instagram.com/crystal_lake_publishing/

Patreon
https://www.patreon.com/CLP

YouTube
https://www.youtube.com/c/CrystalLakePublishing

Twitter
https://twitter.com/crystallakepub

Facebook page
https://www.facebook.com/Crystallakepublishing/

Tales from The Lake Anthologies Facebook page
https://www.facebook.com/Talesfromthelake/

Writers on Writing Facebook page
https://www.facebook.com/WritersOnWritingSeries/

Beneath the Lake Videocast Facebook page
https://www.facebook.com/BeneathTheLake/

Google+
https://plus.google.com/u/1/107478350897139952572

Pinterest
https://za.pinterest.com/crystallakepub/

Tumblr
https://www.tumblr.com/blog/crystal-lake-publishing

We'd love to hear from you.

With unmatched success since 2012, Crystal Lake Publishing has quickly become one of the world's leading indie publishers of Mystery, Thriller, and Suspense books with a Dark Fiction edge.

Crystal Lake Publishing puts integrity, honor and respect at the forefront of our operations.

We strive for each book and outreach program that's launched to not only entertain and touch or comment on issues that affect our readers, but also to strengthen and support the Dark Fiction field and its authors.

Not only do we publish authors who are legends in the field and as hardworking as us, but we look for men and women who care about their readers and fellow human beings. We only publish the very best Dark Fiction, and look forward to launching many new careers.

We strive to know each and every one of our readers, while building personal relationships with our authors, reviewers, bloggers, pod-casters, bookstores and libraries.

Crystal Lake Publishing is and will always be a beacon of what passion and dedication, combined with overwhelming teamwork and respect, can accomplish: Unique fiction you can't find anywhere else.

We do not just publish books, we present you worlds within your world, doors within your mind, from talented authors who sacrifice so much for a moment of your time.

This is what we believe in. What we stand for. This will be our legacy.

Welcome to Crystal Lake Publishing.

We hope you enjoyed this title. If so, we'd be grateful if you could leave a review on your blog or any of the other websites and outlets open to book reviews. Reviews are like gold to writers and publishers, since word-of-mouth is and will always be the best way to market a great book. And remember to keep an eye out for more of our books.

THANK YOU FOR PURCHASING THIS BOOK

Lightning Source UK Ltd.
Milton Keynes UK
UKHW02f0827290818
327976UK00009B/328/P